Also available from Bloom Books

WILLOW CREEK

Spur of the Moment

Spur of the Moment

Juliana
SMITH

Bloom books

Published by Bloom Books, an imprint of Sourcebooks
1935 Brookdale RD, Naperville, IL 60563-2773
(630) 961-3900
sourcebooks.com

Cataloging-in-Publication data is on file with the Library of Congress.

Printed and bound in the United States of America.
WOZ 10 9 8 7 6 5 4 3 2 1

To Wil Renfroe. An excellent brother
but an even better friend.

CHAPTER ONE
Lottie

I love picking weeds.

Specifically ones that have sprouted through concrete, popped up from the sun-dried cracks littered everywhere. Little green leaves poking their heads out like curious meerkats.

The satisfaction of wrapping my fingers around them, giving a quick tug, and feeling every root being ripped out of its place.

My mom used to have a rule when we got in trouble that we had to go out and pick weeds until she said we could come back in. With over six hundred acres of land to roam, weeds were bountiful, but pickers and sprayers were not. "I want this driveway clean as a whistle," she'd say and point out to the curved U-shaped pavement that led to the gravel road from one guest cottage to the next. She always thought it was a more efficient punishment than forcing my brother and I to our rooms. We loved our rooms.

What she didn't know was I loved picking weeds even more.

Some early June sunrises, when she was at the stove watching smoke rise in the house while cooking, I'd tiptoe in and back-talk my way out of Sunday breakfast. Just enough for her to let me slip out and get the weeds all to myself. I'd hop from rock to rock, bending down to every lime-green sprout, every little dandelion, even the dried-up clovers from the sun's beating heat, and rip them right out before tossing them in the grass. I think for my mom, it was less a need for her driveway to be aesthetically pleasing and more of a "there are too many noises, my roux is burning, and the dogs won't stop licking things, so get out before someone gets knocked out" need.

Funny and ironic—I can't even remember the last time she asked me to leave the house. And the incessant back-talking has not toned down whatsoever, so that certainly can't be attributed to my suddenly being an angel of a daughter.

My breath pants frantically in and out, a pearl of sweat forming at the base of my neck and trickling down my spine. The gravel beneath my feet crunches with each running step I take. My shoes dig into the rocks as the sun rises in the distance, the mountains forming a kaleidoscope of light blue, peach, and rose. My body craves rest, but my mind craves permission for more.

Just a little longer. Push further. Go harder and see just how far you can make it.

I don't have a habit of running this early, but I slept horribly last night—a real problem considering my health relies on sleep and low-stress environments. Knowing I desperately needed rest—knowing my body was thirsty for it—I still tossed and turned all night. My stomach churns at the thoughts that come racing back up, the nightmare of what's to come. I only have one last carefree summer before I'm chucked right back to crowded school hallways and watchful stares.

Did you hear what happened? Is that why she doesn't ride anymore?

I can feel it settling in my bones. I can hear them all over again. I see what's meant to be a perfect, fun, and successful senior year playing out before me as a mockery. Empty promises and whispered secrets and spread rumors.

Shepherd, one of the stray ranch dogs, skips right alongside me. He pretends to nip at my ankle like I'm one of his goats to herd, and I let him steer me right back to the house.

Even the dogs don't want me going far.

Fifty feet from the wooden front doors, my chin dips as my attention draws to a single tiny weed poking out. I can't remember the last time I stopped to pick one. We have a whole crowd of people now that spray the gravel we don't want to weed eat or mow down.

My steady speed halts to a stop as I eye the dandelion poking out in the middle of the road, tire tracks on either side in a narrow miss. Thin, warm-yellow petals facing directly up at me. In every way, shape, and form, this weed shouldn't be here. It's on the busiest road by the front end of the property, right in front of the big house where countless tractors, trucks, and trailers are running back and forth daily. But there it sits, bright and yellow and smiling in a taunting manner.

See, even I *can fight against my odds.*

Blood rushing through me, anger pulsing, I reach down and wrap my fingers around the flowery weed and *rip* it from its roots in the ground. Satisfaction works its way through my fingertips, up my forearms, settling in my chest, hefty and fulfilling. So I find my way to the grass, where weeds are bountiful and pick another one. And another. I pick each weed until my mind and body feel satisfied enough.

And even then, I pick some more.

"You know." Flick tugs at her tight curly hair and it bounces right back up. "I was thinking maybe we could skip tonight?"

I turn on my heels to my best friend so fast there should be a burn mark in my carpet.

"We could *what*?"

"It's one night," she reasons. "And you know how I feel about leaving the ducks alone with Knox for too long."

She knows my brother will take their little herd—or whatever you call a group of baby ducks—load them up in his truck, and head straight to the first drive-through he finds.

"Just tell him to not get them pup cups."

"I've tried; he won't stop spoiling them. I found french fries in their stool the other day."

"This should be common sense, but I'm going to say it anyway—I don't need to know anything about your animal's stool."

Flick leans to the edge of my bed while I curl the last tendril of blond hair around my iron. "Stool aside, we've already been to two others this week. Why does this *one* party matter?"

This party matters because every party matters. I am extremely limited on my days of existential freedom. I will not allow myself to waste it on duck sitting and watching reruns of *Charlie's Angels*.

"Flick." I turn off my iron, set it down, and climb on my bed with her. "Do you know how many days are left until we go back to school?"

Her deep brown eyes squint. "Mmm, fifty-something?"

"Forty-three."

Her hand pops out, palm up, as if to say, *See?* "That means we have at least ten more chances to go out."

"It means I have a tight deadline on my last summer of fun before I am tied down for life."

While everyone is going off to college, jump-starting their careers, or moving off to big cities, I will be exactly where I am now. Picking weeds in the driveway and cursing at the wind for fate's unwavering, torturous hand.

Flick opens her mouth to argue but closes it right back up. She knows what senior year means for me as well as I do. If it's anything close to what the last two years of school have been like, sideways glances, pity A's, and questionable amounts of days missed, then my reasoning for stretching summer out as long as possible is more than valid.

"Okay." She nods. "Okay, we'll go tonight."

If there's one good thing to come from these last two years, it's this: Flick never says no to me. And believe me, if there was ever a time for her to say no, *this* would be it.

The packed cars in Ledger's parents' long driveway should've been an indicator of what we're walking into tonight. The two-story cottage-style house has peeling white paint and a sagging porch swing that hosts four recent graduates testing how long they can go before it falls. My bet is on four more minutes. Cicadas chirp endlessly as the Southern night presses in, thick and warm.

Inside is no better; it's basically a sauna with all the heat and none of the health benefits. There's one sad ceiling fan spinning like it gave up in 2013 and a faint smell of microwaved hot dogs. Someone apparently brought a fog machine, for reasons I can't even understand, so it's like walking in a haunted house, but instead of ghosts it's just juniors making out in corners and Ping-Pong tables with red Solo cups formed into triangles.

"Lottie!" a familiar voice calls, and I turn to see Ledger at his coffee table, a deck of cards in hand and a wide grin on his face. He's holding exactly what I came here for.

I tug Flick's wrist, and we find our way past the bouts of chaos to the corner. We squeeze through the kitchen where someone's trying to microwave leftovers from the tavern but forgot to take the foil off. There's smoke and yelling and the sound of a fire alarm chirping. But I have tunnel vision on the one thing I can use as an escape while the summer's still here.

Knuckles popping and neck straining, I take a seat at one of the two empty spots at the table.

"I thought you were going to chicken out." Ledger, a dear friend since second grade and the very gullible bane of my existence, shuffles the cards poorly.

"I never chicken out." I hold a hand out and he sets the deck in it, the weight of the cards familiar as I square them against my palm. The paper corners are a little worn, but they feel like silk when I give them a quick shuffle. I barely look down as my fingers move on instinct—thumbs flicking just enough pressure to lift the top cards, index fingers guiding them back into place. Click. Click. Click. The rhythmic sound is almost as satisfying as the perfect arch they form in my hands.

I remember the first time I saw this trick. *Magic*, I thought. Maybe I still do think that, but I'm the one making it, and for some reason that dulls the incandescent glow in my chest that this upscale shuffling used to bring me.

"You stress me out," Flick mutters. "I couldn't contort my thumbs like that no matter how hard I tried." She lifts her tiny hands to the golden light for proof.

"Less about the thumbs and more about flexibility of the cards."

This illusion wouldn't be half as satisfying if we had a brand-new stack here.

I smile, already moving into a separate riffle shuffle—splitting the deck evenly, arching the two halves just right so they meet in a satisfying *fffffi* sound before I bridge them together with an echoing snap.

"Cut?" I offer the cards to Ledger, and he squints.

"You'll be fair this time?"

My eyes roll to the seventies popcorn ceiling and back down. "I always play fair."

The skepticism in his look never dulls, but still, he slowly reaches over the cherrywood table, picks up a small stack, and cuts the deck for me.

"Perfect." I turn my head to the side, eyes closed. "Pick your card off the top."

I hear the card slipping off the deck and the sounds of friends and acquaintances humming their acknowledgments before Ledger clears his throat. I turn back with a full deck, minus his card.

"Alright, place it wherever you want."

He sticks it close to halfway, and the magic begins. Fancy shuffles, mostly for effect, a few flips of cards, some face up, some face down. I flip the deck, flick the top of it, blow for the dramatics, and hand the deck his way. All the while, I keep my eyes locked on the wall behind my friends. Mostly because it is a counting game, and if I lose track of exactly where my numbers are, I will ruin the entire trick. And if I see the look on Ledger's face, I know I am going to burst out laughing.

"Check the card."

"You're bluffing," he accuses. "It's not there."

"*Bluffing* is a funny word, isn't it?" I let my lips squish together, long and exaggerated as I draw the word out.

"*Blllluuffffing.* Doesn't even sound like a real word if you say it enough."

"Fine, you're lying," he alleges.

I shrug. "We don't know, do we? What card's on top, Ledge?"

His blue eyes squint at my hand like there's something hiding behind it and if he focuses enough, he'll find it.

"I saw you pick up the two of hearts earlier."

"So you think I'm holding that?"

"That's not what I said."

I click my tongue and hum the *Jeopardy* theme song, relishing in my friend's brows pinching together. It's always fun to pull this trick on strangers, but I have never seen someone get as mad as Ledger. Mostly because he's been trying to figure it out for over a year straight and gets angrier every time he loses his bet. Also he bets more money than anyone else, so that's a plus.

"Last chance. Ten…nine…"

Ledger looks like he's going to combust as he shouts, "Three of clubs!"

I falter and Flick snorts beside me. "Ledge…that's not even your card."

"I panicked."

I flip over the top card, and sure enough, it's the four of spades. It technically doesn't matter what suit or number it is—all that matters is I know for a fact this is the one he picked.

"Witchcraft." He whispers it like a promise to the wind, and I relish Flick's giggles beside me.

"I never get sick of this."

Ledger puts a twenty on the table, and I happily slip it into my denim shorts pocket.

"Ledge giving me money? Me neither."

"It's just..." She snorts. "He falls for it every time."

Our friend's face gets more red as he crosses his arms over his chest. "Fine, do it with a blindfold on."

I...don't know about that. Everyone says they can do at least one thing in their life with a blindfold on, but when the threat is actually there, can you really do it? My whole "magic trick" has everything to do with me counting my cards and nothing to do with seeing them, so maybe...

"I'll bet a hundred."

Well, I could do just about anything blindfolded for that.

"Alright." I reach a hand out and we shake as Flick pulls out a crocheted bandanna and ties it around my face. I can see the same as before, if not more. It's like the holes make my eyes focus in on every little movement around me.

"Flick...the holes."

"Wait, I have more!"

She winds up layering a grand total of four homemade pastel bandannas around my head before my view is fully blocked. There's a pressure building in my temples from the darkness, but I brush it off.

"Okay, same move."

I grab the deck and close my eyes, as if I have a choice, and get to shuffling. The sound of movement is all around me, the low thrum of a bass from the speaker in the corner and the tapping of Ledger's date's heels on the hardwood. A shuffle of people moving nearby in tandem with the shuffle in my hand. The arguing over whether I can get this right.

"Mind if I get in on it?"

This voice is...new. Foreign. Deep and odd and not belonging to someone I've ever done this with before, that's for sure.

"You can certainly try." Ledger lowers his voice to a whisper. "I think she's a witch."

A throaty laugh comes from directly across from me. "I'd like to see it."

For some reason, this pushes me back into focus, this voice. I continue my shuffle and pull the same trick, the head turn, the split deck. The oohs and ahhs of this mystery guy on the other side of me as I pull out his chosen card and put it right back in the deck. I can feel the heat of a stare through all the bandanna layers, and my cheeks glow, all warm and fuzzy.

"Placing a bet?" I ask the stranger.

"A pretty big one, I think."

Well, I will be the judge of that.

I stretch it out, adding a flare of magic as the shuffles I have practiced alone in hospital waiting rooms and during prescribed bed rests come to me easily even with the blindfold. When the time feels right, I flip the deck, take the top card, and hold it up for everyone to see.

Gasps and laughter and questions arise—if money wasn't involved here, *that* would be my favorite part. The sense that I did that. I caused that joy, that spark. And for someone who feels like she can't do much right now, that's one thing I can happily do right.

Flick helps me untie the array of crochet bandannas around my face and I smile.

"Ah-ha, pay up, good sir. I accept cash, check or Ze—"

By the time the last bandanna slips off my face, my words are gone and a metal gate locks the emptiness in place. My eyes land on who is across from me and everything else in the room, maybe on this entire planet, fades away.

I know it can't be, but I swear he's right there. In the same city. The same house. The same room. He is *inches* away from me.

"Hi, Trouble."

No. No, no, *no*.

Walker Lane.

Walker, who picked me strawberries in the mornings and left notes in my mailbox to meet me late at night. Walker, who went to Fourth of July barbecues and summer festivals, running with me in the field under cotton candy skies with laughter seeping into my bones. Walker, who convinced me that I was brave enough to ride my first bull. Who saw me get my first trophy for it too.

Walker, who I have spent the last two years trying to forget. Who left me wondering all this time what was so wrong with me that I couldn't keep him around.

He never even got to see the worst of me, and he still ran off.

Walker's light-brown eyes dance across my face, down my hair and neck. My everywhere. I wonder if he's processing the same way I am. Wonder if he's cataloging every way a person can change in the span of twenty-four months. Doesn't sound that long when you think about it that way. Feels like an eternity to me, though.

Chaotic dark strands barely peek out from beneath a well-worn cowboy hat. His hair's shorter now; he always left it on the long side. I remember joking that if he kept growing it out, I would be able to toss it into a man bun, and he said, and I quote, "The day I allow you to put my hair in a man bun is the day I go bald."

There's a tick in his jaw when he looks back up at my face, at whatever I must look like right now. What face does someone make when a ghost walks in the room?

I glance over my shoulder and see over a third of the people here staring at us. Well, not us. Walker. Anyone new in this town is a sight to be seen by every member of the population, but someone like Walker—young and tall, all soft eyes and strong hands—he doesn't stand a chance at not being assessed.

"You—" My throat catches. What am I even trying to spit out right now?

You're here. You're standing so close. You're staring at me. You're a lying jerk.

You're here. Why, oh why, are you here?

He's smiling at me, soft and familiar, and yet a stranger. The devastation of seeing him with no braces, no snaggletooth poking out, no "What color bands should I get this summer, Trouble?"—it all hits me like a rock to the stomach.

This might be Walker standing in front of me, the boy I loved more than anyone else in my life, but he's just as unfamiliar as a stranger.

Words fail me. In the end, however long we've been sitting here—feels like an hour, maybe two?—I say nothing. Not one syllable escapes these lips.

After I stand up, I press my boot heel into Ledger's parents' questionable carpet, turn a complete one-eighty, and all but sprint out of the house. The sound of Walker calling out for me to wait and the distant chatter and laughter all filter out behind me. I bump into someone standing in the doorway, and their bright red drink sloshes over and lands on my shoulder. It smells like apple cider vinegar and it makes me want to gag.

"Sorry, Lot, are you—"

I don't answer, don't look to see who is talking. My legs are taking off before my brain can catch up, racing down the front steps, across the driveway to where a field of cars are lined up. I'm mere feet from Flick's small blue sedan when I hear boots hitting the gravel behind me. It's Walker. I always know it's Walker.

"Lottie!" His shouts are muffled, but they're his all the same. "I'm sorry, please, just one minute."

It's his fault. He has to know it's his fault. If he had just stayed, if he had just told me everything, I wouldn't be like this. I wouldn't be *broken*.

My phone lights up in my hands with a text from Flick.

Everything okay? Need me to take you home?

I only respond with the word Please and know she'll be here soon.

Walker calls out again, closer now, and I turn, keeping my eyes just past his shoulder, watching for Flick to come out any second now.

"Wait." His voice is so much deeper than it used to be. It's got a cut to it, like he's swallowed sea glass. I think I hate it. "Please, just two minutes. That's all I need."

I look again and see the front door of Ledger's home swing wide open. Flick's eyes wander from me to Walker, and I'm sure she doesn't recognize him. At least, not like I do. Either way, she is sprinting over here, and two minutes is a far cry from possible.

I relent just enough. "You've got twenty seconds."

"You have always loved putting me on a deadline."

The joke misses me, landing somewhere in the grass behind me with a splat.

"Sorry—I don't know how to do this. I didn't think—"

"Ten seconds." Flick is *really* picking up speed behind him.

"Shit. Can I see you? Maybe tomorrow? I didn't even know you were going to be here. I had this whole plan when I first saw you." I can catalog the moment he must've heard Flick's sneakers hitting the gravel behind him because he rushes like an audiobook put on two-times speed. "Everett James asked if I wanted to come with him here tonight, and I swear I didn't know you were here, but then you were right there, and I will never *not* say hi to you, and you looked—" He keeps rambling as Flick's car unlocks and she wordlessly slips into the driver's seat. I've never seen Flick ignore someone. I think it's as far as her anger can go, if you could even call it that.

"Lottie, I'm sorry."

"Wait." I pause just outside the passenger side, fingers curling the handle. "When did you see Everett?"

I know for a fact all he did today was work the back fields. Dad has had him and Knox both working overtime the last two weeks, trying to figure out something with the irrigation systems. Everett's barely been able to breathe, much less go off gallivanting with random strangers. And unless Walker has Everett's number—a real shock considering he didn't even have *mine*—then how would he…

"I'll see you tomorrow and explain." He nods like it's a sure thing. And I know it has to be.

Walker never breaks his promises. Even if it means breaking your heart.

CHAPTER TWO
Lottie

Despite the few chances of freedom I'm allowed, my parents do one thing very right. Every summer, at least for the last two summers, I get to stay at my aunt's cottage until the school year returns.

Technically, I suppose it's less of a cottage and more like a duplex that she splits with seasonal members of the ranch's team. But her side always felt like a cottage to me. Maybe it's the worn grooves of the old hardwood floors or the front porch swing that faces each morning's red-and-gold sunrise. Maybe it's all of her vintage pink Pyrex on the open wood shelves in the kitchen or the quilted blankets her mom made when she was just a little girl. Or the old ballerina music boxes and stained glass artwork hanging in the windows. Or the ceramic teapot in the shape of a flower with a fairy sitting on top.

With three bedrooms, two bathrooms, and the best wraparound porch I have ever seen, it's the perfect family house.

But Aunt Dot's family started and stopped with my own family. She never married, never had kids. She lived every moment of her life for herself. In passing, I've heard whispered rumors through town of an old love she had back in her twenties. The belief is that he left her with big plans for the future and never came back. Once, in the Common Ground coffee shop, I overheard a gaggle of old ladies call her Oak Ridge's very own "Delta Dawn" as if it was an insult.

As if my mother's sister who could do anything she dreamed of was put out by her life's turn of events. Anyone who thinks Dot's day-to-day life is disappointing must not know her the way I do. Just two weeks ago, when I packed up a few suitcases and skipped my way over here, she left a note on the counter for me saying, "Went skydiving in Georgia, will be home by lunch. Don't drink the wine on the counter. I'm saving it for something special. Toodle-oo!"

She has a flip phone unironically and only watches TV if it's Tuesday night reruns of *Murder, She Wrote*. She has needlepoint pillows with curse words on them, for crying out loud.

She is my first, and possibly only, role model. Everything I strive to be.

Confident, beautiful, kind, independent, never lonely, always moving.

That being said, due to her always moving, she is rarely home the same time I am, and spending my summer here feels like spending my summer in my first apartment. If the apartment had 1950s curtains and floral wallpaper and a back porch view of mountains that stretch for miles.

It probably shouldn't be as comforting as it is, but this is much more of a home than my childhood house ever was. A part of that is due to the fact that my parents don't have keys to the place. But that means when I wake up at nine a.m., half dead to the world and half cognizant, I get to receive texts from my mom threatening to barge in here.

Mom: Miller said he saw you running this morning. Is everything okay?

Mom: The new ranch hand is here and he needs to get a key to the other half of the duplex, do you still have it?

Mom: You're not answering.

Mom: Please answer.

Mom: I will get Knox to break down that door, Lottie Jane Turner, I swear.

Mom: Where is my sister??

A spike of adrenaline rushes through me and I shoot up from my strawberry-patterned sheets. Dear God, *please* do not let her be outside right now. I instantly press call on her contact, her answering in only two sharp rings.

"Ugh, she's fine, Jason." Mom spoke in the distance before the phone was lifted closer to her ear. "Lottie Jane, you nearly gave me a heart attack."

My eyes roll as I stretch my free hand out above me, pulling the tight tendons in my back. "I don't know why you automatically go to the worst possible outcome. And please don't ever send Knox to kick down my bedroom door. What if I was naked?"

"That's a sacrifice I'm willing to make." I hear her shuffle around in the background, an easy picture of her rifling through the main house kitchen cabinets coming to mind. "Did you see what I said about the key? I need your spare for next door. The last tenant claims he lost it down the drain."

"I think Tom just locked himself out and decided to leave it at that."

Dot's old neighbor, Tom, actually told me it fell out of his pocket in the hayfield and he spent three hours looking for it until the clouds turned gray and rain sputtered around him in heavy drops. It's pretty common—people losing their keys in the fields. Once it falls in the grass, it might as well be on another planet.

So I unlocked the door for Tom once, and he said he'd left it unlocked ever since. Dot and I swore to cover for him when the time came, which just so happens to be now.

I stand from the bed, taking a brief moment to let my heart rate settle to a standard beat before going down the hall toward the kitchen.

We only allow ranch hands who go through extensive background checks—courtesy of Travis, our favorite sheriff—to stay on the joint side of the property beside Dot. The rule also meant we needed to allow the ranch hand a key to her side of the property in case of emergency. Luckily, every seasonal worker we've had up to this point has been either a sweet older gentleman who checks on me every other day and offers to bring us freshly picked peaches, or married men whose wives occasionally drop in but never linger for long.

"Well, double-check for the key. I don't want to get on the 'What's Happening in Oak Ridge' Facebook group to ask who's the best locksmith and have Emily Greer come back to me about it not being Marketing Monday."

I step into the kitchen, standing in front of the light-blue cabinets with wooden countertops, and pull on the golden handle of Dot's junk drawer. Fabric scissors, triple A batteries, an old bra that she swears she's going to take to the thrift store eventually, a tiny grocery notepad that we never use, and—

Ah, there it is.

"Found it." My fingers twiddle the key around. "Want me to bring it to the house?"

"Actually, we're going down by the blooms, if you can make it."

"Give me twenty minutes."

I quickly change out of my sweaty running clothes that I accidentally passed out in and slip on my white tank top, Levi's, and red Hunter boots. I skip wearing a bra entirely, mostly because I am lucky enough to pull that off, and who knows when these girls are gonna go south, but also because our ranch hands never so much as glance at me in an unscrupulous way. It was one of the reasons I never felt uncomfortable knowing they could access mine or Dot's houses.

With my hair tossed in a high bun and my entire face lacking anything beyond a little leftover drool, I walk straight out of my front door and head down to the Bloom Barn.

The Bloom Barn is an addition we added about six years ago, but it's my personal favorite. There are rows and rows of wildflowers in a variety of colors, all in full bloom, from vibrant red poppies and sunny-yellow daisies to deep-blue cornflowers and soft-pink cosmos. The barn itself is behind the flower field, surrounded by a grassy area that Knox always keeps neatly trimmed. The barn's white siding is covered in climbing vines of honeysuckle or clematis, depending on the season, delicate flowers with fresh pops of color against the vertical walls.

It's my favorite year-round.

Pumpkin patches come and go, crops grow and are harvested, visitors leave, but every season there is always *something* here in these fields. Even pink camelias in the winter season pop their heads out to wink at us. There's always a vision to be seen here. And if I *were* allowed to have any job at the ranch beyond working with the bulls or horses, it would be right here.

I take my time walking down the dirt-and-rock path all the way to where the white barn sits in the distance. It's still early enough that the sun isn't beating down on my shoulders and the smell of freshly cut grass fills my nose with each step I take.

Before I can see her, I hear my mother's laugh. It's a filthy kind of laugh. The kind that bubbles up and hits low in your belly. It's raspy and strong despite the cracks in her own life. It's my favorite laugh, one that I never get to hear enough of from her.

I round the corner of the barn to see my mom, mostly brunette hair with streaks of silver peeking through, and a tall man facing the opposite direction, staring out into the tall fields expanding before them. Overwhelmed, I'm sure. I can't even imagine what a first visit here would be like. Flower fields, the Bloom Barn, fruit fields, offseason pumpkin patches, a hayfield in the back, cattle to the side, a main house, five guest cottages, a bakehouse, an event venue, a string of apartments for the workers. The list went on and on.

Strong and mighty, and a tad too immense, is our Willow Creek Ranch. And I adore every single bit of it.

"Hi, I'm Lottie. Nice to mee—"

My sentence instantly cuts off when I catch a view of that tattered cowboy hat closer up. The same stupid hat from last night. The broad chest expanding out in pure delight. And the same shy, dimpled smile from the last fourteen years staring back at me. There's a redness rising on his cheeks, and I know it has nothing to do with the early summer heat and everything to do with the fact that I'm staring at him. He always used to blush when I stared at him. Though back then it was in admiration, and now my face contorts like someone poured an entire glass of lemon juice in my mouth and told me to rinse and repeat.

It is *not* nice to meet him. It is not nice to see him even a little bit. I knew I would somehow be thrown into seeing him at some point today, but *now*? And like *this*?

"No." I cross my arms, suddenly entirely aware that I am not wearing a bra, and although my...*facilities* are on the smaller side, I feel like Walker has X-ray vision directly through my clothes.

Because Walker, *WALKER*, is right in front of me. This time I know exactly who he is without a sliver of doubt. Walker Lane. On my family ranch, in my flowers, wearing *my* family's Willow Creek–designed T-shirt. The only thing I should have of his is the cash in his wallet directly deposited into mine. But I stormed out before he could pay up and that is far less satisfying with him standing in front of me, looking like I may have won the battle but he'd won the entire war.

"No, what?" My mom peeps around Walker.

"No, he is not working here."

And he is *certainly* not staying next door to me and my Dot for the entire summer. A house reserved for kind old men, off-market husbands who carry their kids on their shoulders, and an occasional cousin popping into town. The sister house was never meant for a seducing, lying, betraying, dimple-having, town-leaving cowboy. A house surrounded by fresh flowers only a frolicking skip from strawberry patches could not hold this, this...*heathen*.

"Wha—what do you mean?" Mom stares between Walker and me.

He looks me dead in the eyes, that wolfish grin not missing a beat. "Hi, neighbor."

CHAPTER THREE
Walker

There are a lot of things I know to expect from life. No matter what's going on around me, there are a handful of consistent guarantees.

Older women always love me—chalk it up to my Southern manners if you'd like. I always order fajitas at Mexican restaurants—something about it coming out steaming hot gets my blood really going. I always love an Adam Sandler movie. And the Fourth of July is always my favorite holiday.

But the one thing, the last thing, I expected in following a dirt road to a random house party with a guy I just met was running into Lottie Jane Turner.

I knew I was going to see her soon—today, in fact. I had plans and an idea of reintroducing myself. Instead, I embraced the universe's offering, which happened to be a blindfold and the smile of a girl I once knew.

Truthfully, I'm not much of a party guy. Even less of a gambling man. But I knew if I went to Willow Creek Ranch,

I'd run into her. And going to town felt risky. Staying in my hotel alone for one night felt weird. So when I met Everett in passing while fueling up my truck and he mentioned a party…I don't know. Something about it pulled me in. Where else would I go?

And then, there was Lottie. She sat at the coffee table surrounded by people, this new version of the girl I once knew. I didn't have to see her eyes to know it was her.

The girl I picked weeds with. The girl who snuck away with me to eat late-night snacks by the pond. The same girl who gave me my first kiss and made me promise her another summer every year. The same short blond who rode bulls like she owned them, even from the day I met her.

She was no longer short, and the kind, shy smiles she gave me once were now replaced by confident, full ones. She sat across that wooden table thinking the whole time that I was in the palm of her hand, and maybe, in a sense, I was. But meanwhile, with each card she shuffled, I kept thinking she had *no* clue who she was playing with.

I had plans beforehand. Applying as an overqualified ranch hand at Willow Creek was a last-minute idea, but I knew it was the best one. I needed somewhere to lie low this summer, somewhere that didn't feel so fast-paced and gave me time to think about what's coming next. The last place that felt like that was right here. In this field, with this girl. Originally, I was thinking I'd come for a quick visit. Take a week and stay in one of the guest cottages they had listed on their website and pray to God I would get five minutes of her time in passing. But then I saw it in a bold blue button on their website: *Work with us.*

The only position hiring was a seasonal ranch hand, one of many, I assumed. I adjusted my resume, toned it down a bit to take away any suspicions, and when the call came from Lottie's Uncle Miller, I accepted instantly.

The pay was terrible, of course. But you could stay here for free, which was kind of the whole point. I started packing my bags when I got another call from the same number. It was Miller, telling me the living spaces for ranch hands were all filled for the season. The remaining housing? One half of a duplex, which he shared with his niece and sister-in-law. My grin grew wide, praying the only niece he had was a certain blond who loved to pick weeds.

Now, standing here in front of that scowl—like that of a kitten who had been pet too many times—I knew I made the right choice.

"Hi, neighbor." I smile at her. My face is so warm, from her, from the sun, from this entire interaction, and I know she can't miss it. I've never been very good at hiding how I feel around Lottie.

"You are *not* staying there," she grumbles in the back of her throat, far different from the girl I heard the night before.

"I think I am."

"Do you two know each other?" Mrs. Turner glances between us.

"He wishes."

I smile even harder. It's so nice to see her. To just be *near* her. "Maybe I do."

Maybe all I needed from this break was to see her for a single moment. It certainly is taking my mind off the things waiting for me back home.

"Don't say it like that." Her mouth twists in disgust.

"Like what?"

She squints. "Like you're welcome here."

"I...*feel* welcome here." I point at the green shirt I'm

sporting—the Willow Creek tagline printed on the front in bold white text: *All Are Welcome.*

"*All* minus backstabbing little traitors," Lottie huffs with an accusatory finger directed right at me. "You tricked me."

I point a finger back toward her and watch her eyes trail it, just like she did last night when my hands would have willingly given her all my cash had she not run off. "*You* actually tricked *me*, if we're being technical."

She definitely slid a card under the table when I wasn't looking.

"I played fair and square."

We're inching closer to one another, and I can feel the fire in her eyes blazing over me. Her chest is rapidly panting up and down, the knuckles of her fingers whitening as she pulls her arms closer together.

"Oh, Lottie, were you out placing bets again?" her mother asks beside us with a disappointed sigh. "We've been over this; it's not good for your stress—"

"It actually relaxes me very much."

Mrs. Turner faces me and whispers low, "Matthew, dear, did my daughter unfairly *borrow* some money?"

At the use of my full name, Lottie cackles—loud enough to cause a cicada on the white barn behind to go flying across the field. "Matthew," she mocks. "Oh, precious *Matthew*."

"It's my legal name, *Charlotte*."

If I find a button, I push it.

"You can say all you want about me being unfair, but you didn't even say who you were, *Walker*."

"At least I'm not a tricking thief."

"Get over yourself. I didn't *steal* anything; you could have just watched."

Mrs. Turner sighs again, lifting a hand to her brows,

pulling and stretching the skin there. "I think I need to sit down." She gives a pointed look to her daughter. "No more betting. It's a problem, Lottie."

Lottie kicks a spare rock at her feet as she mumbles, "Only a problem if you're losing."

Mrs. Turner murmurs a curse to the ground in response. Her phone buzzes in the back pocket of her overalls, and when she pulls it out, her eyes roll up to the sun-filled sky and back down. "I have to take care of…something." She glances at her daughter wearily. "Give him the key; show him his half of the duplex. And no. More. Betting."

"I'm almost eighteen now. A legal adult. You can't exactly boss me around."

"Try me." Lottie's mom hops into the ATV she drove me here in and cranks the engine. "Be nice." She points to her daughter before widening her eyes at me. "We are *very* glad you are here, Matthew. I apologize in advance for Lottie's behavior."

She turns down the road before I can form a response, kicking up dust behind her. As it settles around us, Lottie and I turn back to one another, a foot closer this time. The freckles scattered around her cheeks and nose come into full view, not a thing hiding them from my gaze.

My lips press together to keep from smiling. "I want another round."

"That's what they all say."

"Yeah, well, I mean it."

The sparkle in her eyes slips down to her smile, unzipping in one corner. "Funny, they all say *that* too."

"Look." I sigh. "I'm sorry I didn't say it was me as soon as I sat down. I didn't want the first time we saw each other again to be at a random party. You…threw me off. The main reason I even knew for sure it was you was the birthmark."

She glances down at her bare arms, at the white splotch right off her shoulder, like she forgot it was there. We joked once that God missed a spot when he painted her. Though I knew even then that nothing on Lottie Jane could ever be a mistake.

When she looks back my way, the message in her furrowed brows stands clear: My apology means entirely *nothing*. "You shouldn't have done that. You really messed with my head."

She means more than just the day before, I know. And I can't stop the rushing guilt that washes over me. For running out with no explanation. For never answering her emails, never coming back here. For leaving a really, *really* great opportunity behind me. How did I think I could make up for two years' worth of apologies in one conversation?

"Sorry." I cough, and my cheeks heat even more. "Are you gonna show me the duplex?"

"You know where it is."

"Well, can you give me the key?"

She looks down at her hand and spins the pink cow keychain holding the silver key around her finger. "This key?"

"I'm assuming that's the one, yes."

"The *only* one."

"Okay?"

With a hum escaping her lips, Lottie considers me, then the key in her hands. In an act of rage, she lifts her arm, pulls her arm back, and chucks the key far into the flower fields. The key to my new home sails through the air, a silver flash against the kaleidoscope of bright flowers, and lands gently in the field.

"You wanna act like a dog? Be a good boy and *go fetch*."

My eyes watch in delight as Lottie turns on her heel, her bright red boots flinging dried dirt as she stomps off.

A hypnotizing pendulum swaying, her hips pulling my full attention.

"Woof!" I bark at her, and I laugh in pure delight when she lifts a middle finger in the air right back at me.

This might just be my favorite summer yet at Willow Creek. Lottie doesn't know it, but I'm determined to make it her favorite too.

CHAPTER FOUR
Lottie

A tray of deep-fried cheese and burnt burgers wrapped in red checkered paper rushes past my head.

"Corner!" is shouted in my ear as one of the new waitresses rushes from the back. Nineties country music plays over the radio to my left and the thrum of various conversations dances all around me. A couple I go to school with is making out in the far corner booth. It smells like bacon grease and cheap beer and *home*.

The clock above the bar ticks forward, and right on time, "Check Yes or No" plays again, which means another hour has gone. Another shift spent doodling on my whiteboard while all the waitresses rush past, dropping off plates and collecting tips. Someone else walks in, but they don't glance my way—I'm just another fixture of this place, like the scuffed-up barstools and the broken jukebox that only plays the same country songs in the same loop every hour.

At the bar, Beau, our favorite bartender, listens to Agnes Whitmore complain that the youths are getting into her year-round Christmas lights again. She claims they're supposed to be for "Christmas spirit every day," but we all think it's because she's too cheap and stubborn to hire someone to take them off her roof for her.

Ada, fellow senior and my favorite seasonal waitress, along with a regular member of my book club, winks at me from her table of balding old men who meet here every Monday at lunch to have their town meetings. They're not a part of any committees or politics; they just have a lot of opinions.

I look down at the podium I'm at, doodling on my little whiteboard that Riley insisted I should be using to seat people as they walk in. As if everyone in this town doesn't already know exactly where they like to sit when they come in here.

But still, pity hostess job and all, everything feels *right.*

It feels like this is still *my* town. *My* territory. Not a place that had me turned upside down. Unlike this morning with a tattered cowboy hat pointed my way and a six-foot-five man standing over me. Ridiculous dimples and that familiar eyebrow scar that shoots both nostalgia and pain through my veins in the most confusing IV treatment ever.

My fingers wrap around the pink Expo marker. I draw tiny hearts and sunshine smiles in the corners of my board. My job at Riley's Tavern is a simple one: stand here, doodle, pretend I am actually needed, get free food and drinks, and… yup, that's about it.

I initially joined Riley's team as a much-needed waitress last spring. She claimed she was desperate for someone immediately and was willing to hire me on the spot, no interview required. I was handed a cutoff shirt, a black waist apron, two colored pens, and a notepad. One of the girls taught me to always wear my hair in pigtails for extra tips, and I carried a jar full of cash home after a single shift.

I remember busting into the dining room at home, twirling on my toes, and flashing three crisp hundred-dollar bills. "I made this in one night!"

Mom's fork clinked against her plate. Dad, cleaning his tools, dipped his head just enough to reveal the furrow between his brows. Knox shot me a wary glance over the rim of his sweet tea, already bracing for the inevitable argument. No one shared my excitement. Their reactions all mirrored each other: worried, overwhelmed, confused, and worried again. Which is how they reacted to most things involving my life; I was just still new to it back then.

The next shift I showed up at, Riley asked me to have a "talk." We sat down in the back room, two untouched Diet Cokes on the table, as she explained I wasn't *qualified* for waitressing yet, and that I should be a hostess. She promised pay would stay the same, minus tips, and swore it would be a very *relaxing* work environment.

As soon as she mentioned "relaxing," I had a very clear idea of who had put this sudden change into action. Knox swears he never said a word to Riley, but his left eye twitches when he lies—and whenever I bring it up, that little sliver of skin bucks around like a bronco.

I trace over the same heart on my whiteboard for the third time, watching as my coworkers weave effortlessly between tables, pocketing tips with satisfied smirks. I'm just here, waiting for time to pass.

"Hi, girlie," a familiar voice pops over my shoulder. Beside me is Ada, hands on hips where her apron is pulled tight, the strings acting as a makeshift corset. Her long blond curls are everywhere, a colorful array of pens lined up in the right pocket of her apron, a notepad in her left.

"Hi." I smile at her and flash my whiteboard her way,

displaying my Picasso-level cartoon hearts and a little sunshine with watery eyes and a very large nose.

"Beautiful, as always."

"*Useless*, as always."

"You're not useless." She bumps my hip with hers. "You did a really good job cleaning the windows earlier."

I glance over her shoulders to the sparkling windows that I used a toothbrush to scrub until my arms were sore. "Mmm. True."

"You seem down. I can talk to Riley. See if you could pick up some of my slack? I feel like I'm drowning out there."

"No." I smile, so convincingly sincere that it feels like a lie all on its own. "That's fine."

Riley would say no. She would come up with some kind of excuse for me to sit my butt on this uncomfortable stool all day with an occasional break to clean windows or count inventory in the back.

Complaining about getting paid to do a job where you do nothing seems ridiculous in retrospect. But the days, months, and years have gone by with all of these emptied hours adding up to nothing. No special experience for a resume—unless you considered "listening to citizens of Oak Ridge complain about the groundhog outbreak" a special skill worthy of Times New Roman font.

It's the same as everything else I've done in life: making it day by day with the same monotonous regimen, and for what? So I could one day live in my old-lady house, with a hundred families coming and going and watching everyone around me grow into beautiful fields of flowers? Meanwhile I was still just the stupid weed in the driveway.

Even Agnes Whitmore, with her year-round Christmas lights, has *something* she's dedicated to.

"How about this Saturday I go with you and Flick to that bonfire at Odelia's?" Ada offers. "We can make it a girls' night. I can bring a new deck of cards and watch boys drool over you while Flick reads by the fire. When we're done, we can stop by a twenty-four-hour drive-through and eat our weight in cheese fries."

My lips curl. "Really? 'Cause last time, you said you were never coming back."

"Well, last time I also lost four hundred dollars to a hillbilly *named* Billy in thirty minutes, and it's taken a few months to leave the trauma behind."

"You could go see Mike with me; he's a great teacher."

He's the one who taught me everything I know about cards, really. And although the time he spent teaching me tricks in the hospital were some of the worst, most traumatic moments in my life…they were also some of the most useful.

"I already tried. He said I didn't have 'an eye' for it." Ada shrugs her shoulders and checks her lipstick with the silver tray previously propped on her hip. "Whatever that means."

I think it means that a lonely old nurse saw a reflection of his younger self in me: someone with too much time on their hands and too little excitement in their life.

Someone that is tied to the realm of nothing.

I try to convince myself excitement is overrated. Adventures don't matter if you're just going to die one day anyway. But then I see others and wonder what it would be like. To do anything you wanted. There are people out there like Dot that skydive, jump off bridges, swim with dolphins, climb Mount Everest. There are people who are underwater welders. I mean, they *weld underwater*, for goodness' sake. I can't even drive a car to any of those places, much less physically do them.

And when I allow myself to piece it together, it is truly astonishing how small this world feels. When there is not a single person in your life to relate to the deepest part of yourself, what do you really have going for you if not a desperate desire for excitement? For adventure even in the smallest of doses?

And if going to a small-town party and placing bets with unsuspecting members of society is how I get my serotonin levels fixed, then so be it.

My mind rushes with a fury back to the last bet I placed at a party.

"Hi, Trouble." Walker's voice, all smoke and slow-poured honey.

My jaw clenches at the memory, molars grinding together like a faulty slot machine. That stupid, ridiculous hat. That shy look, like he actually cared. If there's any justice in the world, he's still out in that field, tearing up dirt for keys he's never gonna find.

I hope the one locksmith in this town is booked for the next month and won't be able to take Walker's call, forcing him to go to the only motel in Oak Ridge. It's filled with rats and poor decisions, and a perfect place to send a young, rugged cowboy to think about his bad behavior.

"You look like you're doing long division in your head," Ada whispers in my ear, and I realize my face is scrunched into a tight ball, eyebrows furrowed and lips scrunched together. "And don't look now, but there is a super-cute out-of-towner walking in right now. So fix your face before he comes over here."

We never get super-cute out-of-towners. Which means I already know exactly who's standing behind me.

CHAPTER FIVE
Walker

I think my favorite part of Willow Creek is the air.

It's just different here. Always smelling like fresh-cut grass. And warm, like the sun baking over your skin. It's nostalgic in a way that nothing else could be. It has a way of sliding itself inside of your mind and your chest, looping around in circles until everything around you feels lighter.

I've spent the last hour and a half in the fresh air, back hunched over as I waded through rows of wildflowers. I've searched for anything that the blaring sun might reflect against. I have, so far, collected three quarters, two bottle caps, and a Miss Piggy Statue of Liberty keychain.

"Did you lose a shoe?" a voice calls out behind me. I crane my neck, my fingers still in the dirt, to see Knox, Lottie's brother and one of the few people I knew I would have to run into at some point.

My hands wipe the dirt off my work pants. "Why would I lose a shoe?"

"Happened to me once out here." Knox uses the toothpick sticking out of his mouth to clean his teeth before shrugging. He looks around my feet at the soil. "What are we looking for?"

"A key to the duplex. I'm staying there and I…" *Pissed your sister off enough to have her chuck it right into an acre of flowers, never to be seen again.* "…lost it."

"Wait a sec. I've got a metal detector in my truck."

Knox turns on his boot's heel to walk down to where a beat-up F-150 is parked. I keep my head down, still searching, and a few moments later he pops back up with a black device in his hands.

"Come on." He hands me a handheld shovel. "I'll search, you poke around and see if it's hiding under some of the flowers."

We make our way down the row, listening to the steady beeps of his metal detector in hopes it would speed up sooner rather than later.

"You already had the tour, then? You see my babies?"

I glance around like maybe he isn't talking to me, but he is staring directly at my face.

"Your…babies?"

He's super young to have kids. If I remember correctly, Knox is a year older than Lottie—the same as me. I mean, it's not impossible. The last two years, I've been so busy with life that I haven't had much time to do anything beyond have my head stuck in a laptop. The few times I looked up the ranch, it was out of curiosity for Lottie, not any of her relatives.

"Yeah, the fields?" He gestures back where the rows of strawberries line up. His sunglasses dip low enough to flash green eyes identical to his sister's. "My pride and joys. Grew 'em myself."

"Oh." Well, that makes more sense. "Uh, yeah, I passed them. It's not my first time here, though, so I didn't—"

"I knew you looked familiar. *Damn*, I am good." He's shouting as he slaps a single hand to his thigh, causing his machine to make a loud *clink*. "Where do I know you from? Is your family a vendor? Nah, I know most of them."

"I actu—"

"No. I have to guess. You sourced our tomatoes last year? When Trantham couldn't, right?"

"Nope."

"You brought us those fancy mushroom crops? The rayshee or something? The hippie-dippie ones."

"Uh, no." I push farther down the row. "I could just tell you?"

"NO! Gah, give me two seconds, would you? You came to the peach fest two years ago? The guy with the"—he points to his blond hair with a winced face—"you know."

Dear God.

"I was friends with Lo—"

"*FRIENDS WITH LOTTIE.* Yes. I was getting around to it. I thought I recognized you. How long has it been? Were you one of the college guys in town earlier this year?"

Desperate to move on from any *college guys* that Lottie was *friends* with, I spill it all. "I used to come every summer for the Rancher in Training camp. Lot and I were friends for a while. We hung out with you and another girl a few times at the creek—"

"SLIM JIM!" Knox throws the metal detector into the soil, its plastic giving a groan. Before I could react, two long arms wrap around my shoulders, yanking me into a crushing, tight hug. "Why didn't you just start there? Geez, that made me seem ridiculous. Man, you got big." He steps back to size me up. "You used to be all elbows and knees, like me."

"Yeah, well"—I shrug—"metabolism's a crazy thing."

Just like working out nonstop for a distraction is a crazy thing.

"What are the chances you'd end up back here? I guess the chances are pretty good since you're here. You still know how to dig a killer trench? That was you, right? We might need to do that again soon. So, you've seen Lottie, then?"

All of his questions come out rapid-fire, squishing together in one breath.

I choose to only answer the last one. "Yeah, we kind of ran into each other in passing last night."

"Good, at least you know your neighbor." Knox picks up his detector and we search down the next row. "Have you met anyone else yet?"

My eyes stay glued to the dirt, tracking for any semblance of a key. "Just your mom and Miller." I clear my throat. "Haven't ran into your dad yet."

I am hoping I don't have to, not today at least. It's an event I'll push back as long as possible.

A hint of vulnerability flashes across his face, but it's gone as quickly as it arrived. "Oh yeah, he's kind of hard to run into. He's still the head guy, taking after my grandfather, so you'd have to run in circles to track him down."

"Noted." Ready to move on, I point to the beeping machine. "You sure that thing's working?"

"Yeah, for sure. Suzie has never steered me wrong bef—"

BEEP. BEEP. BEEP.

Knox and I both stop. "Attagirl, Suze."

Using the small shovel, I gently push the flowers around until a small sliver of something shiny pops out. I toss the shovel to the side and use my fingers to pull up the key caught in a root in success.

"Thank God, I've been out here forever." I hand the shovel back to Knox.

"You need a ride to the duplex? It's kind of a long walk."

"That would be great, thanks."

I follow behind him to his truck.

"Scuse the mess." Knox throws a mound of various trash, including duck food and empty fast-food cups to his back seat. "The kids always make it so dirty in here."

"Your *crops*?"

"My ducks. I've got joint custody. She hates when I take them through the drive-through, but they love a good pup cup. I'm about to be a grandpa, so I spoil them a little."

I nodded along as if anything he said made sense and buckled my seatbelt. "Gotcha."

We eventually pull up to the far back left of the property, turning off a dirt road to face a one-story house with white siding that stretches wider than the main house. Wooden shutters, boxed flowers hanging from the large windows, only a break between porches splitting the two main entrances, and a shared pitched roof. There's a front porch swing on the right side and some rocking chairs on the left. Outside the split house sits an old off-white Ford Bronco in the shared driveway, untouched judging by the thick layer of pollen on top. Is this Lottie's?

I spot a decal on the back that says "Locally Made" in the outline of a strawberry. So, yes, it's Lottie's.

"Your sister has a Bronco?"

"Huh?" Knox lifts his head from his phone blowing up with notifications. "Oh, yeah. Can't drive it, though."

I nod. That makes sense. Most people can't drive stick now. The only reason I can is because my last boss had a six cylinder that he taught me to drive around his property. The transmission was tricky, and it was easy to slip out of gear, but she was a gorgeous truck.

"Alright, well, I'll leave you to it. You got a truck back at the main entrance or…?"

"Nope." I was determined to leave everything behind, and that meant my personal truck too. "I'm getting mine out of the shop sometime later this week. I was supposed to just borrow a company truck until then?" Another upside to this position that Miller presented me with.

"Oh, right. Here, let me text you, and I can pick you up tomorrow to take you to the shop we keep them at." We exchange numbers and I circle the key with the squishy cow keychain dangling from my fingers.

"Cool, thanks, I—"

"Oh, and everyone's going to Riley's tonight. I'll ask Felicity if we can get you on the way."

"Who's everyone?"

"Everyone." Knox shrugs and keeps typing away on his phone. "I'll come back in a couple hours."

He came back within thirty minutes with a girl I recognized in the passenger seat who was waving my way. Felicity, or Flick, I think. Light-brown skin and tight coils of black hair bounce around as she basically vibrates in his truck. The same girl who drove Lottie home yesterday.

The second I open the back door, she turns to me. "Walker! I'm Lottie's best friend. Do you remember me?"

Her accent is thicker than Lottie's or Knox's. The words seem to string together in one long breath, like she's speaking in cursive.

"Yes, ma'am, I do." I nod and give a tight smile. My long

legs squish between crumpled receipts, empty bags of duck food, and mud-covered boots.

During the ten-minute drive to Riley's, Knox and Felicity chat away, their voices filling the car. They bounce from topic to topic, like cattle dogs herding sheep. One minute, they were bickering about dishes, and the next, they were gazing at each other as if I were the only obstacle to their kiss.

We pull into a packed gravel parking lot, cars and trucks lined up in unmarked spots and a steady thrum of Johnny Cash thumping against the sides of the truck.

Felicity is telling Knox to "make sure he knows it's her turn for movie night" because he did something wrong with their "babies" yesterday. I'm still unsure if it's the berries or the ducks, but it seems to always go back to one of those.

I lean closer to the truck door, waiting for Knox to take the hint that my door doesn't open on its own without one of them letting me out.

My throat clears and Felicity turns toward me, curly hair bouncing with her. "Sorry, sometimes Mommy and Daddy have disagreements."

Knox scoffs and rips his keys from the ignition. Felicity turns back to him with fire in her eyes. "Case in point: Sometimes Mommy doesn't like when Daddy forgets to give the babies the right kind of food."

Knox points to the empty bag of duck food by my feet. "And sometimes the babies clearly don't want the prescribed stuff your little vet thinks they should get, so Daddy does what he must."

I tap my knuckles to the window. "Can I have a safe word or something to get me out of this conversation? Or do I need to just throw myself into moving traffic next time?"

"Funny." Flick snorts. "I don't think this town knows what traffic means."

"Throw myself under a moving tractor, then," I correct.

Felicity turns her head to look at Knox. "Ooohh, our safe word can be *tractor*."

"Great idea, babe." Knox smiles at his passenger. "Quick wit as always."

There's the look again.

"Alright, well, it's getting a little tight for me, so if we could just—"

"Oops! Sorry, Walker." Felicity opens her door and jumps out of the passenger seat before opening mine. "So rude, Knox."

Felicity walks off into the tavern, Knox staring at her swaying hips until I clear my throat beside him.

He turns to me with a crooked smile. "Lottie's gonna lose her mind when she sees you."

"In one way or another," I mumble, and walk to the door, but just before we get there, Knox clears his throat and gives me a signal to wait back.

One hand shifts in his pockets, while the other rubs the back of his neck. "She…uh… By the way, there's something you should know before you go in there." The shift in his voice makes my stomach twist.

"What is it?"

"Lottie has epilepsy."

Everything in me freezes.

I hear him and understand the words, but my brain struggles to stitch them together into something that makes sense. I blink a few times, like maybe if I do it enough, my mind will reset and I'll hear something different.

"What?"

Knox exhales, all previous ease gone. "Yeah, they diagnosed her a while ago. It's managed, but you know…things are different now. Than they were back then. She can't do what she could before."

Managed. Different. Can't.

My limited knowledge of epilepsy is mostly from overhearing random stories from TV or podcasts. But now that I know Lottie has it, my mind is trying to do a deep dive on everything I have ever heard in passing about the illness.

What does it look like for her?

Seizures? Shakes? Passing out? Is it permanent? And what signifies "a long time ago?"

Memories flicker in and out—all the times I saw Lottie running around the farm that last summer I saw her at fifteen, all fire and energy, never slowing down for anything. The idea of her having to stop, to think twice before running headfirst into life like she always has? It doesn't fit. Doesn't feel right.

The pieces start to click together. Why there's been talk that she's no longer riding. Why she didn't drive over to give me the key.

"Does she…" I swallow and try to focus on one question at a time but it's all running through my head at once. "Is she okay?"

Knox's jaw flexes, like he's weighing how much to tell me. I resist the urge to shake him for answers.

"She handles it," he finally answers. "But…yeah. It's bad enough. She can't drive or do much beyond her day-to-day routines without a doctor's approval."

Handles it.

"When… How—?"

Knox gave me a look. "I'm not going to be the one to give away all of her business. I don't go running around telling everyone her story. I only want her to be safe. She wouldn't have ever told you. But I thought maybe you needed to know since you're staying next door to her and Dot for the summer, so you can keep an eye on her."

I *did* need to know, and yet I have no clue what to do with it.

Inside Riley's, with my hands in my pockets, I make my way past the table and over to Lottie, standing there with a dry-erase board hanging on her hip and a bored expression on her face.

"Hi." I lean forward to land in her eyesight.

Her green eyes dart to mine, glancing down at my Willow Creek shirt and back up. "Hmm, found your key yet?"

My tentative smile pulls into a full one, bright and big. *See, nothing is different. This changes nothing. She's still the same sassy blond girl you knew you were going to see.*

"I did. In fact, a very helpful squirrel found it for me."

"You mean a helpful squirrel with a trucker hat and a big mouth?"

I look back to Knox, who is now shaking his shoulders out to gear up for some kind of karaoke machine. Flick is beside him, popping her knuckles.

"Exactly."

"Well, you can go back to your table now." Lottie waves a dismissive hand at me.

"Why?"

"Why what?"

"Why would I go?"

A couple brushes past us and I have to take a step closer so they can squeeze through. Lottie leans a few inches back. "So…you *won't* be here."

"Maybe I'm here for a reason."

"And maybe I would prefer it if you weren't."

Lottie looks up at me, and I see it there for a split second: the girl I once knew.

The words slip out before I catch them. "I'm sorry, Lottie."

I worry she'll mistake it as I'm sorry *for* her and not just sorry. For everything I did. For what I apparently missed while I was gone. For the way I left and the way I came back and everything in between.

"For?" Her brow arches. Does she know I know?

"Leaving."

She huffs. "And?"

"Not telling you I was coming back. Or who I was last night."

"*And?*"

I look down. "And...for wearing this shirt?"

Lottie hums, her fingers tapping on the whiteboard. "Okay."

"Okay, you forgive me, or okay, okay?"

"Okay."

"Come on, Trouble." I lean closer to the podium. "What is it going to take?"

"For what?"

"I want to earn your trust again. To be us again."

Lottie, still staring up at me, has a freckle near the edge of her mouth that stretches as her frown dips. "I don't do relationships in any way, shape, or form."

"I, uh, didn't necessarily mean in *that* way." My arms cross my chest, warmth spreading across my neck to my ears. Am I *blushing*? Again? "We could just be friends."

"You're working here seasonally." Lottie busies herself with cleaning the glasses of melted ice and watered-down Coke at a nearby table. "For the summer, and that's it."

"And if I get hired on full-time?"

She scoffs. "Don't plan on it."

I lean down on the table she's working on; I see at least two other tables of people staring at us, but they're the least of my concerns right now. Right now, all I want to focus on is this girl and a way to get to know her like I used to.

My forearm rests inches from her moving hands as she ignores my presence. "Come on, Trouble, don't make me beg for it."

"Beg for what?" Her head jerks on a swivel. "And don't call me that."

"You. Just…you."

It's true. I don't need anything more. Maybe it's a lie to myself, but that's fine; I'd rather lie to myself than lie to her. If I can just find a way to get us somewhat back to normal, I know the rest of my life will fall into place after.

"I don't…" Her sigh is exasperated. "Walker, you can't just randomly come skipping down my driveway and beg for friendship with your big, stupid hat."

My grin spreads, head shaking from side to side. "What *is* it with you and my hat?"

The ratty, worn-out straw hat looks like a dog chewed on the edge. It's huge and old, but somehow it works. And it wasn't my hat originally, but an old friend's.

"You can fit probably fifteen of me in it."

"I thought everything was bigger in Alabama?" I offer.

"I—that's not—" She scowls. "Stop that. It's Texas."

"Here, let's do this." I grab her dry-erase board and look at her. "I'm sure you don't mind me erasing your… Is that a sloth?"

"I was going for a panda."

"Right." I use the end of the marker to erase her

questionable creation. "Let's make a pros and cons list of being my friend. Here we go. Pro—I am an excellent listener."

"Con." She takes the board and marker and makes her own column in black. "Listens, but doesn't obey."

"Pro." I pull it back my way. "I am *determined*."

"Con, your voice is getting on my nerves."

"Pro, I make a mean batch of everything cookies."

"Con—" She pauses mid-grab on the board. "What are everything cookies?"

My grin stretches wide. "Be my friend and I'll show you."

There's a small flicker in her eyes for a moment, but it's gone in a flash. "Do you have any references?"

My smile holds, but there's a crack in it, barely there. A hairline fracture waiting to split. "Well, my best friend died six months ago, so probably not. Though, I think your brother is getting fond of me, as long as I don't look Felicity in the eyes for more than five seconds."

"I'm…sorry."

"Don't be, we can't pick who we're related to—"

"No, about your best friend."

"Ahh." I shrug. "He was eighty-seven. And had cancer in his spinal cord. Not much of a shocker there. Though, I still think his hat fits me pretty well."

Lottie drops her hands and the dry-erase board to her sides with a smack. "I made fun of your dead best friend's hat?"

"You can make it up to me if you want to"—I bend low, whispering deep in her ear as my fingers tap on the board. She smells like vanilla and honey—"form an alliance?"

"What are we allying against?"

Um… "Pollution? I don't know."

"Pollution *is* a bitch." She nods.

"It really is." I nod back like the desperate man I am.

We're still whispering when I grab the board out of her hands and bring it out of her view to write again. I turn it back around, and she squints to read my tragic handwriting.

Lottie x Walker friendship contract:

I hereby agree that I, Lottie Jane, will hencforth be friends with Walker Lane.

"You spelled henceforth wrong," she notes.

I correct it with the tip of the marker. "Forgive me, I don't read Shakespeare enough."

Consideration crosses her face, eyebrows dipping low and green irises scanning me up and down. Her chin dips once. "Okay, I'll sign." My chest sinks in relief just before she adds on, "If you ride Goliath."

"What is *Goliath*?"

She points to the old bucking bull ride in the corner that couldn't have been used in at least twelve years, and I mean at the *very* least. There are dust bunnies that are procreating like…well, bunnies over there.

"You're not serious, are you? That thing hasn't moved in a decade."

"Ride Goliath, stay on for"—she glances my body up and down, and I'm overcome with the need to flex—"ten seconds, and I'll sign."

"Ten seconds?"

"The longer we sit here, the longer I'm requiring…fifteen, sixteen…"

I laugh, hearty and full. A cup overflowing. "Alright, that's how this is going to be?"

"Listen, if you can't take it, we can just erase the contract." She lifts the back of the marker and begins to wipe the edges of my writing.

"I didn't say I couldn't take it."

Maybe she doesn't remember how well we rode together, but I certainly do.

Her smile is tight. "Then I'll tell Beau to hook it up."

"Good."

"Fine."

"Great."

The dust in the corner flies up in giant chunks as the bartender pulls the leather covers from the monster beneath. He yanks the last piece of covered fabric away, revealing a brown-and-black mechanical bull with red eyes pointed directly at me. The seat is worn, paint and leather chipped where previous riders must have saddled, the sides rubbed down to shiny metal where my legs are going to sit. Two long horns peek out from the beast's skull, which maybe would be less terrifying if they didn't also have dust bunnies resting on the points of them.

The bull creaks as I slip onto the saddle, the small handle on the base of the bull's neck chipped and unstable.

A small crowd gathers around me, but my focus stays on Lottie. She's talking to a short waitress, who glances between us, her smile shifting into something like concern.

The same bartender from before, Beau, his nametag shows, steps to my right. "You sure, man? It hasn't run since I started working here in high school."

In the back, Lottie Turner is joined by her best friend and her brother. Pure pride is filling her face, those pouty pink lips tipping up at the edges with a smile that says she's sure my capabilities will not allow me to do this. Knox and Felicity both talk in Lottie's ear, the sound of country music and locals chattering overpowering their words, but the evidence is clear as she keeps her locked gaze on me.

My pretty new neighbor knows exactly what I am getting into and is smiling proudly at her idea.

I've never sat on a mechanical bull. But then again, I never needed to.

After I left Willow Creek, I worked on a ranch that wasn't nearly as nice as here but gave me the best mentorship I could've dreamed of. A mentorship that meant learning to ride wild horses and roping in cattle daily. That being said: I have no experience with mechanical bulls, but *plenty* with real ones.

Which of course, Lottie doesn't know.

Lottie raises one eyebrow at me, the challenge clear through her mock sympathy. *It's not too late to give up*, she mouths.

I answer the man to my right but keep my eyes zoned in on hers. "Yeah, I'm sure."

Beau steps behind the operating panel, turning it on and blowing the dust off the handles.

"Alright, you ready?"

I nod, my oversized hat sliding down over my eyes. I lift one hand and raise it above my head, the messy strands of my brown hair falling disastrously around my face, blocking most of my view. All except Lottie's blond hair at a bar top table across the room. She has a look on her face that screams success. It's the same look she gave me at the poker table. A look that says, *Go home now, I've already won.*

Maybe some guys would. But maybe Lottie doesn't remember just how stubborn I can be.

With my hand in the air, the robot beneath me begins to rattle, vibrations settling in over my thighs and up my groin. My hand tightens around the small chipped handle that's meant for me to cling to. Fifteen seconds. That's all I need. Or is it sixteen?

My thoughts dart away as the bull swings to the left, no easy start-up on this thing. It jerks right, trying to hurl me off. My fingers clench around the handle, muscles straining as I grunt through each brutal twist.

Hips grinding down as my hands keep their steady lock, I hang on as the turning and yanking from left to right transitions into the front base moving up and down. My head stays clear, locked on the horns below me as a target to prevent the dizziness that threatens to overtake my body.

The bull speeds up. It bucks harder, like a live animal desperate to send me flying. My thighs burn, my grip slipping as the machine jerks from side to side. I grind my teeth and lock my core. The cheers and music blur into background noise as my pulse hammers in my ears.

I feel like I'm in the mouth of a magnificent beast, swishing me side to side like a morning shot of mouthwash.

I have no idea how much time has passed, but it's at least eight seconds. Maybe ten. The small crowd around me is chanting and cheering, nosy eyes waiting for their turn to watch me fumble.

If the stakes weren't so high, I might have by now. But the fact of the matter is, I have a bet that I have no plan on losing. And the reward is priceless.

I hear someone shout "TEN" beside me, and my hand clutches on even stronger. *Almost there.*

My surroundings rush by in a blur, but I keep my eyes right on the head of the bull, following its every movement. Up and down, angle to angle, side to side, I toss around with my thighs pressing as hard as they can down on the saddle below me. I won't lose this. Not now. Not when the opposite results are detrimental. I will not be going back to where I was before. And if sitting down on this saddle for sixteen seconds is what it takes to have Lottie Jane Turner in my life again, then consider the job done.

When I am one hundred percent sure the agreed-upon time is up, I let my hand go from the handle and swing one leg off to the side, jumping off the old robot with my pride somewhat intact. Warmth spreads in my cheeks as I realize just how many people are staring at me, but I brush right past them with a single look over my back at the ticking clock.

Twenty seconds.

My slow grin turns into a megawatt smile as Lottie's dropped jaw comes into my view. With one hand, I pull off my old hat as I approach her, plopping it down on her long blond hair. It swallows her, dropping to cover her eyes so she can't look up at me when I dip low enough, just for her to hear, and whisper in a hushed tone.

"See you around, *friend.*"

CHAPTER SIX
Lottie

It's been nearly twenty-four hours since I watched Walker Lane take on Goliath like it was nothing but a field mouse, and my brain has thought of little else.

When did he even learn how to do that?

Last I saw him, Walker was more of a watcher than a rider. When I decided to join the circuit, he would practice with me for fun. Sometimes we'd saddle up on our horses and go down different trails and chase each other. But he was never *that* good.

And now he's this big show-off? What a… I mean, who does he think he is? Coming into town like he never left, like we're still kids who can pick up right where we left off. Us being "just friends" ended in a dumpster fire last time, and it's like he's completely forgotten about it. Maybe he has. Maybe I'm the only one clinging to a broken friendship.

But I turn eighteen in just a couple months. My days of fun and adventure and friendship are over. Eighteen is the cutoff and the sign of moving on to bigger, more important things. Like filing taxes. Or trying to actually enjoy matcha.

Walker Lane doesn't belong in this life anymore. The one with doctor visits and uncertain futures. I know how this goes—people like him show up, shake everything up, and then leave. Again. I'll be a pebble he kicked down the street: passed by and long forgotten.

After graduation, my schedule will be filled with hanging curtains, organizing junk drawers, and switching to nontoxic kitchenware. *That's* the kind of future that awaits me after senior year. Not spending my spare time watching an objectively attractive man ride mechanical bulls with half the town cheering him on.

Yet, my mind recalls the scene over and over: his hands gripping tight to the knob between his legs. How his wild, dark hair swished from side to side with every turn. How he locked eyes on me every chance he got. The proud smile he wore on his way straight to me, ignoring all the gawking eyes of our town that would be sure to discuss this over the phone later. And how I blushed the entire ride home with this ridiculous hat on my head while Knox and Flick argued in the front seats about who hit Mariah Carey's high note better. Apparently they drove Walker there but have no clue how he got back home since I claimed the two of them and ran.

I don't know why I didn't take the hat off the second he set it on me. A mere moment of delusion. Instead of throwing the thing away, I mumbled something along the lines of "I think I left the stove on at home," and shuffled out the back door to the employee parking lot. Behind me, Flick said, "She doesn't even know how to turn the stove on."

Dot's working tonight, another overnight shift at the hospital, and Mom has no clue she's not here, so I'm completely alone as my fingers pick at the fraying strings of my pink pajama pants with tiny strawberries on them. I thought it might be a little lonely, but now that I'm cuddled up with my warm mug and a patched-up quilt, the hum of the AC low and crickets chirping outside, it's nice. Much nicer than being in the main house with my parents, anyway.

I keep my eyes locked on the TV in front of me while my favorite scene in my favorite movie replays again and again.

It's a secret. One that only my best friend knows, but I am a closeted romantic. *Strictly* for fictional characters. I love to watch these people—raw and real and yet somehow fictional—find their happy endings in the most dramatic and unrealistic ways possible.

Which is why I have a monthly—*cough*, *weekly*—rewatch of *Romeo & Juliet*. Flick and I argue on a regular basis about which is better: the 2013 or 1996 version. She believes that the 1996 version is better overall, and I believe she is wrong overall.

The way Douglas Booth stares into Hailee Steinfeld's eyes...there is no way someone is *that* good of an actor. It's impossible. The palpable heat would be enough to warm my entire house in the dead of winter.

See, I want it to work out for them—because *they're* fictional. Because Romeo wouldn't leave Juliet behind on purpose. Because she'll never wake up to find he's left her, no explanation, no goodbye. And in my maladaptive daydreams, the two lived together until they were old and gray with grandkids running around, and they simultaneously died in each other's arms. The end.

It's easy to fall into the trap of picturing the happily ever after for them because it's not *mine*.

I rewatch the scene again. And again. And then one more time, rewinding to the exact moment he spots her out on the balcony. My mouth trails the words as Romeo speaks them.

"With love's light wings did I o'er perch these walls, for stony limits cannot hold love out, and what love can do, that dares love attempt."

I sigh, watching his eyes track her every movement.

Something *good* to cling to there. To know that even if it doesn't exist in this world...in some universe out there, a love like this is *real.* And it's unwavering, and it's faithful, and it just shows up at your front door when you least—

A familiar chime sounds over my doorbell alarm. I reach behind me, pull the thin curtains back, and see Walker Lane standing on the front porch.

No doubt wanting his stupid hat back. Good. I hope he takes it with him.

I stand and open the door just a crack, to where he can see me but not the movie on my screen or the pile of Rolo wrappers beside his hat on the coffee table.

"Can I help you?"

Walker's eyes bounce back and forth between mine. "I just wanted to check in on you."

"Why?"

"I don't know if you're aware how thin the wall is between our living rooms, but I heard you playing the same scene over and over again, and it was getting a little concerning."

I close the door to block any view of Douglas Booth's mouth paused mid-confession.

"It's been lagging," I counter.

Walker glances down at my face and back behind the door, and I know there is no way he can't see the square jawline displayed behind me. Aliens on Mars could see it. Still, I hold my arms across my chest, unwavering.

"And the thumping?"

"*Thumping*?" Was I bouncing my knees that hard?

"Thumping. Every half hour or so. It knocked a few books off the shelves."

Ohhh, *that* thumping.

"Henry."

His nose scrunches. "Henry?"

"Yes. Dot has a very bored ghost here. Henry. He doesn't have much to do, and he's not quite committed to the whole 'vengeful spirit' thing, so he just knocks a book off the shelf and uses the walls as a back scratcher."

Dot thinks it's an old lover from the 1800s looking for his forever bride, but then I remind her this house was built only ten years ago, and she claims I am no fun.

"He's not going to make cereal at three a.m. or walk around in sheets with the eyes cut out, is he?"

"No, but I think I heard him practicing a monologue for a George Strait movie production."

Hope builds in Walker's voice. "Really?"

"No, he usually just does the book thing. Although, the last guy that lived next door swore his socks went missing regularly, so I assume he has a foot fetish."

Walker curves his mouth down in a frown that's also a smile. "A foot fetish ghost is the least of my worries right now. Honestly, not even cracking my top five."

"Yeah, well, he's been here for a while, so get used to him."

There's a teasing lilt to the curve of Walker's lips, but he packs it in. "Right." He turns sideways to face his front door, only feet from my own. "Well, I'll just—"

"Why are you here?"

I don't know why I ask. Something between his smirk and the way he's looking at me like I'm a puzzle he can't wait to solve has my common sense deciding to pack up and leave.

"I just told you—"

"No. Why are you in Willow Creek?" Of all places, here? He has to be *here*? He has to pop up on my front porch, in my solace, in my hometown to...what? Reconnect? Find someone he knew two years ago? She's not here anymore.

"It was the first place I thought of." He shrugs and the white T-shirt spread across his chest puckers with it.

"For?"

"Running away."

He graduated this spring with a million opportunities to move forward. What could he possibly have to run from?

"From?"

His eyes glint. "Why don't I remember you asking this many questions?"

"Why don't I remember it being so difficult to get you to answer them?"

The dimples on each of his cheeks form miniature canyons as his smile picks up higher. "You haven't looked me up?"

The air between us shifts, thick and buzzing, and suddenly my strawberry pajamas feel like they're suffocating me. "Why would I do that?"

He shrugs, and it's innocent and cute and far too much like the fourteen-year-old who ran to tell me he had a crush on me. No questions, no skirting around the topic. Just a shout across the front yard: "I think I like you more than a friend!" As if the moment he figured out, he had to tell me too.

I push my mind back to the topic at hand.

"Did *you* google *me*?"

"Of course I did."

Of course he did? What would he... Why would he? Who just goes around googling random people from their past? I certainly don't. Well, typically I don't. But now I wonder what could possibly pop up in Walker's history. Or even more, what could show up for mine?

A picture of eight-year-old me crying tears of joy over meeting Darth Vader on my mom's *very* public Facebook flashes in my mind. I quickly decide it's best if I don't know what happens when you type *Charlotte Turner* in a search engine.

But Walker…what could his results show?

"Why—Why would you…" I stammer over the many questions relaying in my head, wondering which one to pull out first.

Why would you come back?

Why would you leave me in the first place?

Where did you go?

Before I basically recite the lyrics of "Cotton Eye Joe," Walker is turning on his heel and responding in only two sentences.

"I came for an escape, Trouble. And I think I've found it."

So, with him tossing the ball right in my court, I let it fall in silence. Walker cuts through the gravel sidewalk to his side of the sister house, opens the door, winks at me, and closes it behind him.

By the time I close my own door, I notice I never even brought him his hat.

The next morning at around seven a.m., the doorbell chimes, a steady hum bouncing through my thin walls as I lie in bed. I let a moment pass to see if Dot's going to grab it, but when the ringing starts again, followed by a knock, I'm thrown into a maddening urge to tell whoever is on the front porch to go away.

It's not like it's that early in the morning, but it's enough to make me wonder how the toss in my schedule is going to make the rest of the day go. If that dull ache in my temples will creep its way in.

Out of the guest room, I grab a nearby pink checkered throw blanket and toss it around my shoulders to shuffle down the hall. I knock on the main bedroom of the house and wait for Dot to respond. When she doesn't, I crack the door and see her spread out like a starfish on her bed. The neon blue of the TV lights up her willowy frame, along with the drool across her pillow.

So, that's that.

With Dot's bunny slippers on and my hair in one giant matted knot laying over my neck, I stumble my way through the house and briefly wonder if it is Walker again on the other side of the door this morning.

Does he want a rematch? The chance to beg me to tell him just how I got so good at cards? To fall at my feet and beg for…I don't know, something?

But when I squint through the glass of the front door and see a scrawny figure, I know exactly who it is. The doorbell rings once more, and I finally move to open it, feeling far more optimistic about my appearance around a young Kit than my neighbor.

His smile is slightly crooked and his eyes are wide and innocent, always shining. Like a little ball of sunlight bouncing around this farm. He's only been working for my family for about a year—he lives in town with his family—but he carries his weight just as much, if not more, than the rest of us, especially for someone so young.

"Hey, Kit, what's up?"

Kit is probably my favorite guy at Willow Creek beyond

my direct family. He minds his own business, but I know if I need help, he's going to have my back. I also like that he will never let you open your own door; he has to do it for you every time.

"Hi, Miss Lottie." His smile is as bright as a lightbulb, his thick drawl settling into the morning summer air. "How are you today?"

I also love that he always calls me Miss. Like I'm actually an adult to him.

"I'm good, it's early." I glance at the clock on the far wall of my kitchen; it's not even seven yet. "Can I help with something?"

His cheeks are flushed and his mouth shakes with a stutter, like he's working on building up courage for what is to come. I am going to feel *so* uncomfortable if this little baby is about to ask me out. "I was wondering, I mean maybe, like, if you're not busy, could you possibly…"

Oh, dear Lord, where is this going?

"Teach me to ride?"

"Ride what?" My eyes bulge out. "*Bulls*?"

His chin ducks. "Yeah."

"I'm…sorry, Kit, I can't ride anymore."

"No. I know, I just thought maybe if you *taught* me, you wouldn't have to actually get on one. I didn't really know who else to ask about it."

My mouth waters at the thought of being near the reins again, near the saddles—the dust kicking up, the crowds hollering for just one more second. I haven't been near an arena in about two years. About as long as I've gone without seeing Walker.

Maybe it would be nice. A trip down memory lane. Or maybe a trip down what-could-have-been lane. Unless…

"Did my family put you up to this?"

"What?" Kit shakes his head. "No. I didn't tell them, because I thought they'd get mad at me."

I consider it for a moment. Imagining my brother's ears turning red, steam pouring out of them at just the thought of me being near a bull. My mom's frantic stuttering, begging for me to "just stay home and relax." Then I consider the other outcome. Watching outside the ring, prepping the riders.

"They *would* get mad."

"It's okay, I understand. Anyway, just thought I'd ask. I'll leave you to it—"

"Tonight!" I practically shout, and thank God Walker isn't next door to hear. "Tonight at six, when everyone is at family dinner, I'll see what I can pull together."

"Really?" His young eyes sparkle, twin pops of color rising on his cheeks.

"Yeah. Don't tell anyone, though."

His fists are clenched and that boyish smile is spread wide. "Cool, okay. Bye, Miss Lottie."

"Bye, Kit."

I close the door and sink onto my couch. Coaching someone to ride. Changing up the routine. Walker living next door. Every single bit of it floating around makes my head feel like it's spinning. I've gone from absolutely nothing exciting happening in my life to all of *this*.

CHAPTER SEVEN
Walker

My phone won't shut up.

For the past thirty minutes, I've been debating chucking it into the spring behind me, but I have no idea how long it'd take to replace it out here. Or if I'd even want to.

My parents' missed calls stack up every day. Some days, just once. Most days, three to five each.

"Uh, Walker, right?"

I turn around from digging postholes for a new fence line to see a skinny blond kid holding up a posthole digger like the one I have. We're wearing the same shirt, but his is swallowing him whole. Fourteen or so. He's probably here for the same reason I was all those summers ago. Willow Creek had a Young Ranchers in Training summer camp where you could learn, live here, and leave with a hefty reference to put on future resumes for job opportunities. It's the only reason I ever got to meet Lottie. My parents were looking for an excuse to drop me off somewhere for half the summer, and this was the longest summer camp they could find.

I suppose if I had to be grateful for one thing from them, it would be that.

"Yeah?" I answer the kid.

He takes his gloves off, covered in what seems to be horse shit, and sticks a hand out to me. I do the same, knowing my gloves are worse than his, and shake his hand. "I'm Kit. Mr. Turner sent me over here to help you with the fence."

I jerk my head to where my fingers hold the tool, and he joins me.

The kid lifts the tool surprisingly well and tosses it into the marked posthole a few feet to the left of mine. He pushes his body into it, and I wince. He's definitely new to this. Posthole diggers don't take kindly to brute force. They'll wreck your back for weeks if you let them.

Kit catches me wincing at his technique, and I turn back to my own tool, lifting and guiding it into the hole I started before he came up.

"Knox said you're friends with Miss Lottie." He says it as if he's asking more than telling, and if he is anything like the rest of this town, I know he is digging for more than just fence postholes.

My lips curve up. *Miss Lottie.* Like she's that much older than him.

"We were, yeah." I consider the other night and correct myself. "Are."

"Cool." The kid nods and lifts his tool again, putting his back into the act in hopes of pulling out more dirt, and I just can't take it anymore.

"Can I give you a tip?"

He shrugs and I jerk my chin for him to watch what I'm doing.

"It's all about gravity. And velocity. Don't just throw your whole body into the movement; you're going to kill your back after a day of that." I would know. I did a fifty-acre fence line with Knox and two other guys my last summer here, and my back was wrecked. I was addicted to Icy Hot for weeks. Or maybe addicted to the excuse of having Lottie baby me for weeks.

Kit tries again, but he is throwing his whole body into the movement without realizing. And as small as he is, he's going to feel it way worse than I did.

"Look." I lift the posthole digger and just toss it in there upright without using anything beyond the muscles in my arms. "See how I am not pushing it, I'm just guiding it in?"

Kit nods. "Right."

"When you hit the hole, they slide down." My hands adjust and twist the tool around again, repeating over and over. "Pick it up, rotate. Pick it up, rotate. If you still can't do it, rock it a little to break it loose. Don't fight it."

My phone vibrates again in the back pocket of my muddy pants, and I know there is no way I can keep avoiding this. I reach in and pull it out, cursing at the ground when I see the name.

"Here." I hand the tool over to the kid. "Use mine, the grips are broken in. Might help."

Kit nods and attempts the hole again, this time using more arms and less back. He's got a ways to go, but it's way better than it would've been if I hadn't stepped in.

I take a few paces back and accept the call. "What?"

The moment I hear his voice, my spine locks up. "You know, if you actually answered, this would be a lot easier."

"Right, well, if I answered, then you would assume I actually want to speak to you and just keep calling."

"See? Why are you like that, Matthew?"

Matthew. I hate that name. I feel like my skin is turning inside out every time I hear it.

"Why am I like *what*?"

His tone doesn't rise. It never has. It's cold and meticulous and thought out. If he raises his voice, he doesn't have the upper hand. And he always needs the upper hand.

"You have a great opportunity here. A rare one that I worked hard to put in place, and you're just leaving it behind to do whatever you're sneaking off to do."

As if I owe him a thing. As if this was just such an *amazing* opportunity that I should forgive everything they forced me through as a kid and go straight to thanking him for the job I could only ever get because of him.

"No one asked you for that."

I look back at Kit to see him glancing up for my approval of his technique. It's still off, but it's miles above when I left. I toss a thumbs-up, and he moves to the next marked post.

"It's called a favor."

"Well, it's unwanted."

Any job where my father is involved is one I refuse attachment to. No matter how badly I would have once begged for an opportunity like this, if it was coming at me this way, then it wasn't happening.

I can all but see him pinching the bridge of his nose, weathered eye bags and gray hair strung about. "You only have until August to decide before they'll give it up."

"I don't need until August. You can tell them now that I don't want it."

"You don't understand what you're giving up. A jump start with an incredible internship that has free schooling. In five years' time, you could have the best salary, the best retirement, the best health care. You have no clue—"

I let him ramble on, dropping the phone to mouth to Kit, *Try to rock it*. I move my hands in an example motion. He looks down at the digger and notices the ends are tightening up before nodding and fixing it.

By the time I lift my phone back to my ear, my father is still rambling on about benefits and sign-on bonuses and growing real estate costs of the area.

Here's the thing he never learned, even though he's in his sixties: Excess anything never leads to good in your life. I've seen what too much of anything does to a family. It hollows you out. Money, cars, houses, alcohol. All of it piles and piles into something distant and unfamiliar to where you don't even recognize the life around you. He searches for more opportunities and money to bring him something resembling joy, but he has no idea he'll never find it. I would know; no amount of money ever made me feel the comfort that this ranch did.

"I don't care."

"You *should* care; you don't know this now, but your future 401k is the livelihood of your—"

"No." My voice is thunderous and loud, and I remember all those conversations where he told me that raising your voice never makes you right. My voice lowers back to a normal volume. "About any of it. The school, the internship, the money, the benefits. I'm done."

"You don't understand what you're giving up. A future with NASA that could lead to endless—"

I move my thumb to the red button and hang up, making my way back to Kit.

"Alright, you ready to keep moving?" I ask, and he nods back.

We pick up our diggers and go to the next post.

"They don't have any augers here?" I ask, more out of need to fill the deafening silence than to know the answer.

"I think Miller had to use it for something a while ago and broke the attachment, or maybe Knox is watching us and laughing at how long it takes."

I sniff a laugh. "Maybe."

"So, about earlier, with Miss Lottie…" Every time he says *Miss Lottie*, like she is his favorite first-grade teacher, my lips pick up at the edges. "You were friends with her…back then? When she used to ride?"

I nod. I still see her clear as day—reins tight in her hands, barrel racing under the golden haze of a summer evening. We used to sneak into her dad's office and use his laptop, researching female bull riders. We came to learn that women have been competing in the Men's PBR Championship for over twenty years. The smile that leaped up her face when she looked at me, the screen from her dad's computer lighting up her silhouette…

"If they can do it, why can't I?"

So she did. She trained like she was preparing for war. Running, weight training, protein-packed diets. The last summer we had together was both of us deciding to get in the best shape possible. She did it for riding bulls. I did it just in hopes of catching her eye.

And in all those times I got to see her on an actual bull, not a simulator or a training post, it was like the heavens shined down on her.

I could feel the sun radiating off that smile, the golden glow in her hair as one hand stayed loose in the air, her hips and legs tight around the saddle. The quick nod she gave me just before they launched the chute open, the angry bull under her trying its hardest to knock her off. The stubborn grip she kept on that rope until all eight seconds were up.

"Yeah." My throat clears. "We were friends."

"And? Was she as good as everyone says?"

I consider for a moment and pause mid-dig. "Better."

CHAPTER EIGHT
Lottie

"Say 'I looveeee you.' 'I love youuu.'"

Squawk. "Eat shit."

"Flick," I groan. "That bird is a menace."

My feet perch on my best friend's ottoman, while she drinks strawberry lemonade with the world's loudest parrot sitting on her shoulder, tangling himself into her kinky curls.

"He just needs a loving environment for maybe three more months. Once he's lived with me, he will be full of pleasantries and can go to a family. He's so good with kids—"

Squawk. "Bodies in the basement."

The bird happily hops down her arm onto the couch and over to me, staring with curious eyes and jerky head cocks. My fingers open for him to climb up, and he accepts, resting his claws on the edge of my hand. "Where did this thing even come from?"

"An assisted-living home. The old lady swore like a sailor and binged *NCIS*. He picked up a few things."

"Bodies in the basement."

My nose flares. "Can he *unlearn* that one? It's freaking me out."

"Unfortunately, no. They can't unlearn something. But I can teach him enough nice phrases that he shouldn't slip up with those bad ones except every so often. Right, Nigel? Huh, pretty bird?" She lifts a hand to scratch under the small green bird's chin. "Say 'I *love* you.'"

I give her a pointed look, and Nigel tops it off with another "Eat shit."

"Alright, that's enough of that." Flick delicately lifts him from me and walks over to Nigel's cage and sets him inside with his food. He immediately starts dancing in the mirror, bobbing his head up and down with excitement at his reflection.

"I can't believe Riley let you bring him in."

"I didn't give her much of a choice; it was one of those 'ask for forgiveness, not permission' kind of things."

Unlike my situation, where I'm signing up for a practically empty house all summer, Flick's decision to move in with Riley was less of a decision and more of a dire need.

"Okay, sorry." She sticks a snack in for Nigel before running back over to me. "Now, back to what you were saying."

I catch her up on everything with Walker from the night before, my words tumbling over one another.

After considering the interaction, Flick hums. "To be fair, after that last married couple, I feel like you should've remembered those walls are super thin."

"Oh yeah." I shiver at the memory. "We kept having to go on late-night walks when they would play Salt-N-Pepa."

"Well, first things first." She sets down her glass on the table beside her. "We have to google him."

"Right?"

We pull her laptop to the ottoman in front of us, searching Walker's full name.

"Okay, Walker Lane, let's see here."

The very first result to pop up is "Revolutionizing Agricultural Engineer, Young Walker Lane Has Now—"

The article name is cut off. "Oh, try that one." I tap the screen, but Flick is already selecting it.

"Here we go. 'Walker Lane is a new high school graduate piecing his knowledge of agricultural welfare together with his passion for aerospace as he gears his focus toward,' blah blah blah, go down to the highlighted part."

Flick scrolls the screen to the juicy stuff.

"'Revolutionary engineer in training, Walker Lane is the youngest man to complete a finished model of the LJ CropGuardian, a drone that is fit to test thermal temperatures of crops at extremely high speeds so as to catch diseases such as bacterial soft rots, leaf spots, blights, wilts, and many more before they die off at alarming speeds. With this simple discovery, Mr. Lane has the potential to save farmers hundreds of thousands of dollars. Though shockingly, Mr. Lane decided to decline the sale of the patent to John Deere for—'" I groan as my eyes catch on the rest of the article being entirely blurred out. "It's cut off, why is it cut off?"

Flick sucks in a breath and sighs. "You have to pay to see the whole article."

"What? I'm not paying for that."

"Then I guess you'll never know."

Do I need to know how this ends? Not exactly. But do I *have* to know? Yes, of course.

"How much is it?"

"Let's see..." She scrolls down to the subscriber area and

clicks on it. "Thirty a month. Ooh, and you get a free keychain on your first payment."

"*Thirty a month?*" Is that really worth me knowing just a pinch more about this guy who is, essentially, a stranger?

"Well, media platforms like this are beginning to die out. Supporting them wouldn't be the worst—"

"Alright, alright. Give me the thing."

I take the device in my hands, type my numbers in one by one, and click Submit Payment to let the rest of the article load. If I experience credit card fraud, then it was at the expense of education.

"Two hundred thousand dollars."

He turned down two hundred thousand at eighteen years old? My stomach twists. I glance at the half-melted ice in my lemonade and back to the article. Walker easily could have sold a patent for something he made for two *hundred* thousand, and yet he's working at my family's ranch for twelve dollars an hour?

"*What*?" Flick's back shoots up, and we are both sitting, literally, on the edge of our seats.

"That's what this says." I would know; I've reread it ten times over to make sure I'm not hallucinating.

"No way. Walker, *your* Walker—"

"Well, he's not *mine*."

"—made something that he could have sold for two hundred thousand?"

My fingers stretch and pop. This doesn't add up. "He said he was looking for an escape. What kind of escape do you need when you could've had that kind of money?"

Flick flexes her jaw and twists her mouth. "Hmm. Maybe it's like when people win the lottery and they don't want anyone to know, but then they buy an exotic tiger and twelve marble statues of Danny Devito."

I shake my head. "This is insane."

"Ask him about it."

"Ew no, I don't want to."

"Well, he openly said he googled you. You could just say you returned the action and noticed he, I don't know, declined a ridiculous offer."

"Exactly—who works a job like this with the opportunity to have money like that?"

"Yeah, what's that about?" Flick asks.

"What do you mean?"

"Clearly he doesn't need to work since he could have taken the money." I gesture to the laptop in front of me. "So what is he doing working here specifically?"

Flick hums, her curiosity seeping in as much as mine is. By the time we have settled on theories that he is either running from possible tax fraud, escaping an ex-wife, or going undercover for the USDA to take us down, my brain is tired along with the rest of me.

Exhaustion seeps down into my bones. Every inch of me begs for sleep, for rest. My body's been begging me for days. Even if I get a full nine or ten hours of sleep, it doesn't matter. I wake up and it's like my body is, at max, 30 percent energy. And as the days roll one into another, it never gets above that. I feel like a towel that's been wrung out and left to dry. My arms are limp and my brain is sleepy and I am begging for rest, but when the time comes, no amount of rest does me any good.

"You're okay, right?"

I look up and see Flick staring at me with cautious eyes. She's scanning my pupils, checking the dilation. She's waiting to see if I'm about to have a seizure. She knows what to look for by now. She's seen enough of them to know the symptoms.

They never come at a consistency that's enough to predict.

But they do have the same symptoms. A wave of something like déjà vu but heavier, like my brain has a little chip in it warning me. It gets all confused. Like it can't place the people around me. The world blurs. My speech becomes slow and languid. And then…I don't know. Because I never remember. I've been told it looks like someone staring off into space or daydreaming, but deeper. They can try to get me out of it, but it's not up to them. It's not up to me.

It's only when Flick stares at my hands "resetting" my arms that I catch my actions. A trick from my doctor that's been told to ease nerves. A firm press on the top of my arms, then just above my elbow, then my wrist. Repeat.

"Oh, fine. Sorry, I'm just tired."

Her smile is cautious. "Let's walk you home."

"No, I said I'm fine."

"Lottie…" Flick's sigh is as tired as I feel. It's drawn out and fluid and holding so much more than just my name.

The worst part of epilepsy is never what people think it is.

It's not the headaches or the blinding pain when you come to. Not the embarrassment of having no clue what happened. Not the exhaustion that seems to never leave my body.

The worst part of epilepsy isn't what it does to *me*, but what it does to everyone around me. It's the way people look afterward—like I'm fragile, like I might break apart right in front of them. Like I already have. They all live in fear, and I can't *not* see it. I'm a fish in the world's smallest aquarium, crowds surrounding me and waiting.

"Felicity." My eyes are heavy, but I keep them locked on hers.

Her gasp is playful, trying to defuse the tension. She can't let us argue; she worries what it would do to me. And for one tiny moment, I wish she would, just once. Just to see I'm not as fragile as she and my brother and this whole town seem to think I am.

"You full-named me."

"Well, you deserve it. 'Let's walk you home.'" I mock her accent, only a smidge thicker than mine. "Like I'm a nursing home patient."

"Sorry, sorry." She sucks in a breath through her teeth. "I just love you."

"Yeah. I love you too." The softest, gooiest part of my heart belongs to her. The rest is hardened and cracked, but my best friend owns the center, and she knows it.

Flick clasps her hands together. "Speaking of parties—"

"We weren't speaking of parties."

"We need to find something to do to celebrate senior year. We could throw an end of summer party with all the girls and take Knox as our bodyguard? Oh, and you can invite Walker and convince him to drop some of his gazillion dollars."

I chuckle, and even I can't convince myself that it's genuine. "Hmm, maybe."

This summer is my last grand one, and I have to make every second of it count.

"Yeah, we can figure something out for it later."

"I'll be thinking of all the fun things we can do. Two words: ducks and crocheting."

I stand up, stretching my arms and making sure my head doesn't get a rush from the sudden movement. When I feel steady enough, I let Flick walk me to the door.

I poke my head around her and wave to the bird swinging from a bar in his cage. "Bye, Nigel!"

Squawk. "Eat shit."

"You have got to get rid of that bird."

Flick whines. "He's got a good soul."

By the time I leave Flick's house and I'm heading back to Dot's, I see that her car is gone before recognizing the beat-up truck parked on the other side of the driveway to be Walker's. I do a full-body shudder. Something about knowing what he gave up and not knowing why makes being around him feel…weird. So, even though I should find my comfortable seat on the back porch and watch the sun set, I just keep on walking. Past the house, past the Bloom Barn around the guest cottage, and all the way back to the main house.

As I'm walking down the gravel road, I see two large trucks in front of the main house. They're unloading a new bathroom vanity off the back, a heavy wooden one with a marble countertop. Four men, three of which work here, are doing all the heavy lifting while my mom, in her red Lucchese boots, bosses them around with the energy of a cruise director.

"What's going on here?"

Mom spins around, her hand flying to her chest as though she's just been caught in a lie. Her eyes widen, and she takes a breath—like she's been holding something in for too long. "Oh, Lottie Jane, quit jumping me out of my bones. Gonna be the death of me."

"Are you and Dad renovating again?" My tone is cautious.

I see the hesitation in her eyes as she refuses to meet my gaze. Because we both know what renovations mean. Not just in the house, but in anything. Anytime Mom gets a new horse or shows up to family dinner with diamond earrings we haven't seen before or the kitchen cabinets have new upgrades means it's a payment. One my father gives her periodically as a shitty apology for his past. A payment to thank her for turning a blind eye on his traitorous infidelity from years ago.

"Oh, you know me. I always love to switch it up."

The noncommittal hand wave she does only makes my blood boil hotter.

I cross my arms tightly, narrowing my eyes. "So it's the same old game? Buy more things, distract yourself, pretend everything's fine while nothing's fixed?"

The glare she gives me has her warm brown eyes cut into slits, like she can't possibly believe I would dare speak the truth aloud.

"Mom, why do you stay?" I whisper to avoid the ears of our nosy workers. The men on this ranch love to pretend like they couldn't care less about drama, but I know for a fact when they get home to their wives, their jaws are yapping about anything and everything they've picked up.

"Not now," my mother whispers out of the corner of her forced smile.

"Okay, fine. Not now. Not two years ago, not the next year, or the next. Not when I'm thirty or when I'm on the brink of death and I beg for answers with my last living breath."

"Lottie Jane, you're being so dramatic."

"And you're being too casual."

"It's been so long. Let the man do what he wants to do; it's sweet."

My arms cross tighter, a surge of heat rising in my chest as I watch the workers wrestle the vanity inside. "You guys have to *talk* about this. I'm not a marriage counselor but *this*." I point to the men struggling to lift the expensive vanity up my childhood home's front porch. "This is insane."

"My love for your father outweighs our past."

Our past. I scoff. I cross my arms tightly, the muscles in my jaw clenching as my mind races. She can't possibly believe this is okay.

I love my dad as a dad. He's a great one. He cares for us, protects us, makes sure we're clothed and fed and overall a happy bunch. He checks on me daily, even if it's without meeting my eye. And he sacrifices his entire day just to pursue our happiness. As far as fathers go, he's up there with the best.

But he's done wrong by his wife. And I love my mom enough to say it. The thought of being where she is and no one stepping up to defend me is saddening. She's settling. Pretending everything's okay when nothing is. It makes me sick.

"I don't want to end up like that… So wrapped up in someone you can't see what they've done to you."

The offhanded comment hits harder than I planned for it to. I see it in the way her chin jerks back from me. In how her eyes disassociate from the conversation entirely. She's lost now. And I can't get her back.

My voice softens. "You don't have to pretend everything's fine."

"Everything *is* fine, Lottie. Leave it all alone."

So I do. Just like always, I leave the house with my fingers itching for a deck of cards and a bet to be placed.

CHAPTER NINE
Walker

My fingers tighten around the wooden handle of my Damascus knife, the other hand steadying the base of a stick. I plant my feet on the front porch, only shifting when the rocker beneath me sways in the evening breeze.

Lottie shuffles around loudly next door. She wasn't kidding about the walls being thin; everything she does is abundantly clear on our connected back porches. The distant sound of her humming from one Dolly Parton song to the next and doing whatever she does on a Friday evening. Another party? My ears perk up for each noise beyond the distant sound of cattle and the summer breeze blowing over the mountaintops around us.

I ran into the house's owner, Dot Hannick, this morning. She brought over biscuits in her scrubs and told me I was "welcome over anytime, but more welcome when Lottie is alone." I haven't gotten to see her niece—not since two nights ago. And even still, the curious part of my brain won't shut up. It wants more. Just one more interaction. One more conversation.

A thud from next door snaps me out of it, followed by a

muttered "dang it." My lips curve as I picture her stumbling around, probably trying to slip on her boots and knocking into a dresser. Or maybe it's those heels again. Maybe she's going out to the same house I first saw her last Saturday. Maybe she's going to sit across from a table of boys who will all leer at her. And maybe I don't want her to.

My grip tightens around the handle of the knife, *Gerald* written in chicken scratch just above my thumb. My eyes trail each sharp line in the letters and my fingers relax slightly.

Maybe I shouldn't have taken the thing after I ran away. Maybe it was supposed to go to the family. But when I lost my best friend and the closest thing I had to a father all at once, I felt like being a little selfish. So I took the two things I saw him with the most: his hat and his knife.

This knife has seen some things. Building fences, cutting wires, used as a last-resource screwdriver when Gerald was too lazy to go back to his truck for his toolset. It's rusted and the tip is slightly curved—not the most practical knife. But he never cared.

I've witnessed the man cut a rusty bolt in two and wipe the blade clean on his pants leg, just to cut a peach and eat the slice off it right after. It's a wonder he didn't leave us sooner, really.

Lottie's door creaks open, then shuts with finality. And there she is—same sun-kissed skin catching the last light of the evening. Same long blond hair trailing down her exposed back. Chill bumps line her spine through the cutout shirt and I push down the urge to cover her in a jacket. For a second, the world presses pause. No cattle, no wind, no porch beneath me. Just her.

I keep my eyes on Lottie's, resisting the pull to look anywhere else. But I wonder—does she still have my hat inside?

I don't need it back. Not if she's gonna wear it.

"Big plans tonight?" I ask her, staring at the knife steady in my hands.

She shrugs, fiddling with her keys in the lock. "The usual." She fixes her pink lipstick in a compact mirror and my grip tightens around the pocket knife, slicing another chip off the stick.

"Someone wise once told me that when you're sittin' at the table, there'll be time enough for counting when the dealing's done."

"Very nice, Kenny Rogers."

I snort a breath, and she takes a seat at the table in front of her door, only a section of mulch separating us.

"Got a ride?"

"Uber."

"Ahh."

The air is thick, and I feel the need to fill every silence. "Where's your aunt?"

She squints across at me.

"The one you're living with for the summer," I press further. "Is she here?"

There's a pause of hesitation before she answers. "She works nights. She's kind of a night owl in general. Hard to catch her on time in her schedule."

I nod, and again, with each passing minute, there's this calling over my shoulder: *Don't let her go.* Do not let her get in some stranger's car to go to a random party and come home in a different stranger's car again.

"You know...I'm sure you've got a deck inside. You could save a whole lot of time and money if you let me do a rematch from last week."

"Yeah, you wish. The only reason you want a rematch is

because the money you owe me, that I rightfully earned last time, was basically spare change to you."

"You looked me up?"

"You basically told me to."

Hmm. Time is ticking and I want nothing more than to convince her to stay right here. "Give me just one game, really fast. I know you've got a pack of cards in there somewhere. Consider it a warm-up."

Her movements pause halfway down the porch steps, hands completely still. "Just one?"

"It's all I need."

Lottie opens her phone, and after a brief pause, she turns to me and mumbles, "Uber will be here in ten minutes, that's all you get."

All I need.

Ten minutes, two rounds of no limits, and a canceled Uber later, Lottie Jane Turner is still sitting across from me at the small table. Dressed to kill, with $200 of mine sitting proudly next to her.

We play round after round, and I keep praying she doesn't notice the time moving on. She said five minutes ago she would reorder the Uber after the last round. But now we've started up a new one, and she still hasn't mentioned a word about stopping.

I clear my throat and ask, "So, what got you into cards?"

"No."

"No?"

"No, we're not doing backstories, catching up, and all of that."

My brow lifts. "We're not?"

"No."

"What if we…upped the stakes?"

She gives me a questionable look, and I know I have her attention now.

"If you win, I'll put in an extra fifty and I'll answer anything you want to know."

"Anything?"

Her interest only makes my smirk grow. "Anything. But only if you do the same for me."

It's hard, considering her face stays stone still the whole time, but I manage to win by sheer luck in the first round.

"Why did you start placing these bets?" I ask.

"I'm not fragile when I do them."

I'm not given anything else, and the next round is all hers.

"Why did you never come back?" Her voice is sheepish. Shy and low. "Or answer my emails?"

"Is that two questions or one?"

"It's two in one."

My eyes squint. "Is that allowed?"

"Only for me, yes."

Her rules, not mine. "Fine. It's pretty much the same answer. When I went back home, they told me my grandmother had died while I was here."

"Your grand… Wait—*Nonna* died?"

"Yep." My chest still aches, remembering how I missed the last chance to say goodbye. They could have gotten me sooner so I could see her one more time. And they didn't. They waited to tell me one day before the funeral.

"I—I'm so sorry."

"It's okay." I shrug and grab the deck to shuffle.

"I mean that makes sense why you didn't come back, but what about the emails?"

I look up, wondering just how much to release here.

"I found some stuff out. And in a nutshell, I thought if I blocked you out, it would be easier on you."

That I would save her if I didn't contact her.

She takes so long to answer that I shuffle the deck twice before she responds with "That's such a vague answer that it's not even an answer."

"Well, that's what you get for putting two in one."

The next round is mine. I think she gave it to me, but I take it all the same.

"When did you get diagnosed with epilepsy?"

If there's any shock at my knowledge of her diagnosis, she keeps it to herself. "Post-traumatic epilepsy," she corrects me, like it's any less scary. "And a month after you left."

My entire body goes rigid. Knox said it was a long time ago but… "A *month*?"

She nods.

"And you've been having seizures since?"

"I mean, not all the time, no. But I've yet to go six months without one. I'm on month two right now, so who knows?"

"Wow. You must've fallen off pretty hard for it to do permanent damage."

"Fell off what?"

"The… Did it not happen while you were on a bull?"

She snorts. "I was too good for this to happen while I was on a bull." She pulls her hair back, and there's the remnant of a scar on her scalp. "I got locked out of the house and was worried my parents would get pissed, so I climbed the old oak tree by the office window, got distracted, and the limb broke." I remember warning her strictly about that tree. I recall the kudzu vine crawling up the trunk that showed its life coming to an end. My stomach lurches. "It fell at just the right angle. Cracked my head open. My dad ran out to save me; it was a whole thing." She sounds so bored with it all.

"He ran *out* to save you?" I say, confused. "Like out of the house?"

"I didn't know he was in there—long story."

"Lottie, that's…"

"Shitty."

"Really, *really* shitty."

"Yeah. It's not as bad as some others have it. I'm in a good amount of online forums and support groups for young people with epilepsy. Some have it far worse than me. My seizures aren't full-on grand mal—well, except for the first one. They're called focal impaired awareness seizures. It's a lot to explain, but they don't always look like what you assume they do."

"What-what do they look like?"

"Before I got diagnosed…" She swallows and I almost regret asking it at all. But I want to know. I feel stupid that I don't already know. "I always thought seizures were like what you saw on TV. The…theatrical side, I think. That it was either the really big, scary ones or it was nothing at all. And then I got my diagnosis and ended up in some forums and different groups where everyone shares their experiences, and I realized it was nothing like that. Knox has videos of mine, for the sake of showing them to the neurologists, but I haven't seen them, so I can't say what mine look like exactly. But I think it's like my brain…restarts itself. Like I'm here but I'm not. My eyes stay open, and if I'm standing, I stay standing, but things in my hands fall, and I never have any memory of what happens during them."

I try to keep my face neutral. I think it's a lost cause.

"What is grand mail?"

"Grand mal," she corrects. "That's a seizure that affects the whole brain. Mine is just the frontal lobe." Lottie taps above her brow. "Mine are nowhere near as bad as the people I've talked to that have those."

"That doesn't make it not shitty, Lottie."

She shrugs.

"And there's no…cure?" I ask. "No, I don't know, surgery or medicine? Have you researched to see if there's any diet changes or—"

"You think I haven't tried it all? Think me and my entire family and everyone who loves me hasn't already done enough research for a lifetime?"

Shit. "I'm sorry, I didn't mean to make it sound like that. I just thought… I don't know."

I am a fixer. I've always been this way, and my brain naturally goes to the side of "there is a problem and therefore I must find the solution." But if there's no solution in this scenario, how am I supposed to be there for her or help at all?

Lottie twists her long blond hair, and I would love nothing more than to just keep my big mouth shut.

"I'm on medicine. I've tried lots of them. They help, they slow things down and can control around 70 percent of them. Without the meds, I'd be…a lot worse."

My mind trails off to Knox's warning and his mention of her not driving, and it snaps like a puzzle piece in place.

"I can see why your brother and everyone else is so cautious."

She shrugs. "Yep. So cautious that I don't even get a social life without sneaking around."

"*This* is social." I gesture to my cards.

She scoffs. "Okay."

Lottie wins another round. I don't think I let her win it either.

"Where did you learn to ride a bull like that?" she asks. "I don't remember you being that good when we practiced together."

My smile is impossible to contain. I wondered when she would mention that.

"I wasn't that good back then. Or good at all, really. The ranch I worked on right after graduation had a lot of cattle and Gerald"—I look up from my cards—"the guy with the hat; he taught me everything. I worked a lot with their horses, and eventually I got to ride a few steers. Nothing too crazy, just daily to-dos, but it helped me learn everything I know about riding now."

We play another round. She wins, *again*.

She goes for the gut. "What are you escaping?"

I wonder how much of this she found on her own without me having to tell her, but even if she knows bits and pieces, I'd rather give her full honesty in hopes I'll get the same back.

"A job opportunity. And school, too, I guess. I, um, worked hard on something and someone found it worthy of an offer, and after my parents found out about me declining it, my father had this whole thing where he used it as negotiation for his work. So he got a higher-up to send me an even higher offer."

That's vague enough, but not too vague, right?

"He still works at NASA?"

I suck in a breath. "Yup."

"And the offer is…"

I wince. "A similar one to the first. An upfront payment plus a part-time job as a product engineer intern while I go to school. Then full-time after I graduate."

"Oh my gosh." She sits up straight. "A product engineer at NASA? That's like…your dream job. I mean, it *was*. Back then. It may not be now."

"Yep." My fingers shuffle the cards in my hands. "But I don't want it if it means working with him and..." *Becoming him.* "I just don't want to waste all of my time working a job that's going to leave me with nothing left."

I don't have to explain further. She knows. She remembers my parents dropping me off here every summer without so much as a goodbye. Dropping me off at another camp the second I had a day off school. After-school care. Babysitters. You name it. Any chance to not see me, to avoid being a parent, they took.

"So, you came here for a *legit* escape? Like he has no idea where you live?"

"Nope."

For now. It's only a matter of time before he catches on. And I dread it when he does.

The last round she gives to me again. I have a million and one questions sitting on my tongue. But she's yawning, the cool sway of the night air making her shiver, and I know it's not the time.

I stand up from the table and she hesitantly follows.

"Have a good night, Trouble."

"You aren't going to ask a question?"

I smile to myself and turn to my door. "I've got all summer."

CHAPTER TEN
Lottie

Something else I never expected to be met with at seventeen: boredom.

And I have been through my fair share of hobbies to combat it, believe me.

Knitting, sourdough, painting ceramics, adult coloring books, watching old *Wheel of Fortune* reruns to see if I can guess the phrase faster than the contestants, watercolors, and cross-stitching. I have done everything that someone might classify as a hobby within the parameters of my health guidelines, and not one has satisfied me.

The only two things to ever fill that cavity were a good deck of cards and daydreaming of getting that buckle one day. Imagining being near the action, near the reins again. The wind chopping my hair, the power of the beast beneath me. Sharp bucks, my grip slipping, the rope loosening from my palm. The bull twists one final time, and my grip falters. I'm thrown forward, the air rushing by me before the dirt hits like a ton of bricks. My back lands hard, wind knocked out of me, but the crowd's roar fills my ears before the pain catches up. I can still hear Knox cheering me on. Flick too. I hear every single person I love shouting for me to get up and do it all over again. And I long for one more ride.

Eight more seconds of pure torture and beauty mixed into one.

Time goes on, things change, but I'm still there. And when it all washes away, there sits anger. Strong and tight in my belly. Rage at the loss of my future. How dare a single slipup, one moment in time, cause the entire downfall of my life. I used to dwell in that kind of rage. I let it fester and build until there was nothing but red around me.

Now, I know better. Now, I know anger for what it truly is. It goes by another name: grief.

My phone vibrating shakes me from the visual of a belt on my waist. I dig it out and see a text resting at the top of a screen full of notifications.

Knox: HONK AND DRINK. NOW AT ADA'S.
Knox: BRING THE NEW GUY.

A week ago, I would have said I wasn't up to it and just stayed home. But now...I've hit the maximum content of boredom allowed. I swap my pajama shorts for denim, tiptoe through the living room so as not to wake Dot one room over after another late shift, and march myself over to Walker's door.

I knock on the heavy front door and wait for a couple minutes. When Walker doesn't answer, I glance back at his beat-up truck sitting in our shared parking space, right next to my Bronco. He has to be inside.

I pound my fist on the door a little harder.

There's some shuffling around, the sound of a closet slamming, a one-footed hop to the door, and a deep "one sec" shouted back at me.

What can he possibly be so occupied with right now? It's his day off.

Then, like the gates of heaven pulling open a crack, Walker opens the door. And the sight is pure devastation.

With a medium-sized—at best—white towel around his waist, Walker is standing in front of me shirtless, water dripping from his messy hair down his bronzed chest. My eyes stay locked on the most gut-wrenching bare chest I have ever seen. Not that I've seen many.

He's…*softer* than expected. I don't know what I was fully picturing before now, but considering he lifts hay bales and cattle rather than weights, I thought everything would be so tight. That it would look like his skin was heat sealed across his muscles. I mean, don't get me wrong, he's large for an eighteen-year-old. He's got all these muscles and ridges, but when I make face-to-face contact with his chest and belly button, they're…abnormally *normal*? I think I expected abs—a six-pack and tight chest muscles. He's fit, that's still clear. But you can't get this kind of fit in the gym. This is the abdomen of a boy whose work *is* his gym.

My face contorts in some way. I don't know what I look like, but I do know my entire body is very hot and the tendons surrounding my cheek bones seem to just go all…mushy.

"What's wrong?" Walker checks me for hints of anything off, but I'm not the problem. It's him taking up this entire doorway smelling like leather and pine and *man*—that's the problem.

"Get dressed," I mutter, forcing my eyes to lock on the bookshelf directly behind him. There's a single book sitting on the otherwise spotless floor, and I know that Henry has left evidence of his presence.

"What's wrong?" he asks again, and my patience is practically flinging itself out the window.

Where does he get the gall, answering the door *shirtless*? What if I was anyone else? This is…inappropriate of him. It takes two seconds to get dressed. He couldn't do it before answering the door?

A low rumble sounds in the back of my throat before I clear it. "Put a shirt on and let's go." I, for the sake of pushing the timing, glance at his chest again. A bead of water from his hair is now trailing dangerously close to the white towel wrapped around his waist. "You're gonna cause an accident looking like that."

Once he's dressed and ready, Walker and I make our way to Ada's parents' house. It sits off the main street—as "downtown" as Oak Ridge can get. The whole area feels like someone pressed pause on time, with the crooked, pastel-colored cottages lined up in rows. There are cracked cobblestone streets, and her house is less than a block down from the Bake House, so I can smell the sugary scent of cinnamon rolls wafting through the air.

Everyone—and by everyone, I mean *my* everyone—is in lawn chairs with different cans and red Solo cups and whatnot set up with cornhole behind them and a sign that says You Honk, We Drink.

It's the same sign we've used since Ledger first made us start coming over here. It's torn at the edges and it flies out of its holder at least every hour, but it accomplishes its purpose.

All of my friends, and some family, sit in their chairs waiting for cars to start honking.

“Wow.” Walker takes in the sight of Ada’s lawn stretched out like a tailgate. “You literally meant honk and drink day?”

“It happens like twice a month in the summer. We did it once near Christmas time but only lasted a couple hours before we all went inside to thaw.”

“No one’s parents care about underage drinking?”

“Oh.” I shake my head. “It’s not alcohol. They’re mocktails. Ledger once tried to get us to do honk and drink with real drinks, and everyone was sick for two days straight, plus our parents all found out and we weren’t allowed to hang out for a couple weeks. That’s why Ada’s dad is monitoring.” I gesture to the tall bald man halfway chaperoning all of us through his screened porch while he watches the most recent Braves game again. *Monitoring* is used very lightly here.

Just then, a yellow Bug zooms past us, honking three times in quick succession. Mr. and Mrs. Patterson wave from inside their car, grinning wide and raising Common Ground paper cups in a toast, as is tradition.

Walker and I step closer, and I can already see the two rickety and rusted lawn chairs they’ve set up for us. They’re older than me and definitely look like they could give you tetanus if you scratched yourself on them, but again, tradition.

Knox waves us down. “You made it! And you brought this guy.” He pats Walker on the back, his hand wrapping around his shoulder.

Walker tilts his head and attempts to pull back, but the grip isn’t budging. “How long have y’all been doing this?”

I shrug. Knox is still holding my neighbor rather tightly. “Since last summer, it was…” I turn to the woman in the lawn chair beside us and ask, “Who’s idea was it again?”

“Ledger, remember?” Ada answers from her pink seat. “He

used to flirt with the girl at the counter when she mentioned the rest of us drinking by the road."

"Ohhh, yeah. So, technically, Ledge started it."

Walker slowly creeps back from Knox as he gets distracted by a cornhole bag flying into the wind. Our eyes lock for a brief second, and I see the glimpse of panic wash across his face as he watches the entire conversation. I realize the confusion in his eyes is because he has hardly met any of these people.

When Knox grabs us drinks, I give Walker beside me a brief summary of who everyone is. Which, unfortunately, requires him to bend his spine so that he is low enough for my hushed voice to reach his ears. The warmth of his body engulfs mine, so I make my rundown short.

Ada's in the pink chair, her blond curls framed by a crocheted pink bandanna wrapped around her head. Odelia is the one with dark-brown waves fixing the speakers. Flick's sitting in her chair with Knox standing above her, deep in conversation. Odelia's brother, Lawson, is waiting on Knox to come back to the cornhole board. Ledger's off to the side looking at Ada's parents' cars with curiosity.

My brother hands Walker a water bottle before he reaches into a cooler and grabs a Ziploc bag filled with liquid, dumping its contents into a plastic cup. He thrusts the cup toward me, and I think I see a strawberry stem with its leaves floating in the bottom.

"Whatever that is, I'm not drinking it." I give my brother a pointed look as he tries different positions to hand me the glass, like if he raises it any higher or lower, I might consider it.

"But I made this one specifically for you—from my strawberries."

I grab the cup from my brother, take a sip, and Flick's

right—it's perfect. Bursts with fruitiness, blending tangy citrus and a hint of wildflower honey.

"Not bad," I grumble, before walking over to my chair and plopping down next to Flick. My eyes land anywhere but where Walker is. It's like when you're twelve, ordering a nonalcoholic margarita at the pool bar, hoping the cute lifeguard will forgive your awkward front dive in your tankini and see you as the *real* woman you are.

I take the cup and settle into the open seat left just for me between Ada, Odelia, and Flick in the half circle they've made to watch Knox and Lawson toss bean bags into holes in the boards that are about twenty feet apart.

Walker shifts uncomfortably for a second behind us before eventually sliding over to where the other men are counting up scattered bags for points.

"You didn't tell me you have a new friend, Lottie." Ada leans back further in her chair, and without a hint of shame, she stares at my neighbor.

"I wouldn't call him a friend." I don't know what to call him at all.

"He seems nice." Odelia smiles, her voice like a soft whisper.

"He's..." I search for anything to fill the gap and land on "something."

"I have a good feeling—" Flick starts to say, but then a black Equinox passes by with three quick honks, and we all tilt our cups back.

"He's just here in passing; here for the summer and then leaving."

"He doesn't look like he's just passing through." Ada lifts her sunglasses up, like that will get her a better view of his broad shoulders.

Meanwhile, Walker, setting down his water in the grass, looks back at me with a shaky smile. He lifts his hand like he's about to wave, shakes it in a quick rush, and then drops it as if he changed his mind.

Flick snickers. "Aww, he's nervous."

"This is so cute," Odelia coos.

"It's like an elephant that's terrified of a mouse," Ada jokes.

I turn to her. "I'm the mouse?"

We both look back at Walker as he tosses the bag in his hand out to the board, instantly nailing the hole.

"You're certainly not the elephant."

At least fifteen cars have honked since I sat down, and if this bag-drink did have any alcohol in it, I would be three sheets to the wind. The steady blaring of the heat warms my back, and the makeshift fan I have made out of a paper plate is doing very little to combat it.

"There is no reason for it to be this hot out," Flick says just before her jaw goes slack when my brother's shirt is tossed into her lap as he decides to do a victory lap.

"Seriously." Ada picks another clover. "It's so hot I think I saw a bird blowing on a worm before he ate it."

Knox stops his victorious run right in front of Flick beside me, falling dramatically to the grass and letting his head fall in her lap. My best friend tangles her fingers in his hair to pick out the clovers that Ada's been throwing in it.

"What are we talking about?" he mumbles against her shorts.

"Lottie's love life."

I laugh. "No, we were not."

"We were working our way to it," Ada counters.

"Lottie can't have a love life." Knox laughs loud enough for literally everyone to turn to us.

On the defense, I force out a "why not?"

Knox sits up from Flick's lap and looks at the people around us like he expects someone to support him in this. Everyone stays quiet rather than taking either side.

"I didn't mean it like you *can't*. Not like can*not*."

"That's what *can't* means, Knox."

"I know, but I didn't mean it that way. I just meant you probably don't—I mean you can't—and I don't know what I'm saying, but can I just sit here for a second? I just ran in a circle for probably two miles, and the sky is kind of blurring together?"

All eyes turn to me like I'm this ticking time bomb ready to explode. I feel like I'm in *The Truman Show*, except instead of being oblivious to the cameras, I am well aware, which makes it somehow worse.

"Walker," I call out and his head shoots up to me like I've hit his honing beacon. I ignore the rush of heat in my ears and jerk my head back to the area where his truck is parked. "I need a ride."

Without a moment of hesitation, my neighbor, and possibly one of my few friends, tosses the bag in his hand to the dirt and heads toward me with long strides, not bothering to say goodbye to the guys he was laughing with mere minutes ago.

The walk to his truck is mostly just my legs frantically keeping pace like one of those sandpiper birds running along the beach. I stumble on a rock at one point and feel Walker's hand reach out for me, but before it can come into contact with my skin, I catch myself.

I can feel the smile he's sporting behind me, hear the joke resting on his lips. And maybe if things were different, I would be smiling at the slipup too.

We both climb into his truck, the engine roaring to life beneath us.

Knox is staring. Maybe the others are too. It's hard to tell from my peripherals, and I am not about to look back right now. Thankfully, through it all, Walker stays silent before he finally breaks the silence. "Your brother is calling you, I think." He points to the screen like I can't see it. Like I don't feel the anger boiling in my gut from the restraints pulling tighter at my leash with each vibration.

I know what's going to happen if I answer. My brother will apologize. I accept it every time. We both give it a week, and we're right back at it.

I don't know why I tell him. I guess I have such little skin in the game that it really doesn't matter either way.

"What do I have to do to make them see I'm not…" I search for a word that fits better than the ones running through my head. Fragile? Broken? Needing to be coddled? "Do I need a tattoo on my forehead that says *ADULT* with an arrow pointing down?"

He lifts one shoulder beside me and takes a right-hand turn. "Well, that is certainly what most adults would do."

I toss my head back onto the headrest. "I'd like to go home. Or just…somewhere else."

To his credit, he doesn't push.

"Just tell me where."

My nose scrunches. "Why are you being so agreeable?"

"I'm always agreeable." He flashes those straight white teeth and looks away from me to take another turn. "And you seem to be having a bad day."

"They're all bad days."

"Nah. They're not."

No. They aren't. There is technically a sun behind the

clouds each day. But does it matter if the clouds are too stubborn to move?

I think the microplastics from the bag holding my drink are seeping into my brain and things are just fuzzier. Still, I rest my head against the window of the truck and lie there. "Take me home, please."

"Yes, ma'am."

When we pull into the familiar gravel drive, I pull out my phone from my back pocket, ignoring the screen lighting up, and slide it in my back pocket.

Walker turns the truck off, pulls the keys out of the ignition, and leans back into his seat. He makes no move to pull at his door handle. And neither do I. If either of us makes the first move for the door, it would feel like being the first to hang up the phone.

Then again, when has guilt ever stopped me? My hands reach for the metal handle, but before I can give it a tug, he says my name.

"Lottie."

"Yeah?" My answer is so fast I might as well have thrown my caution to the wind with it.

"Can I ask you something?"

"I guess." I'm already here. I'm already dreading going back inside and facing another night of nothingness. Might as well keep this moving.

"What's it like? For you? I mean—"

He doesn't have to specify it; maybe he should. But he's never had to with me before.

"It's different for everyone. Depending on your diagnosis, the cause, the treatment you take. Surgery, no surgery. Therapy, no therapy. Medication. Just…depends."

"But for *you*?"

"For me." I suck in a breath and try to find the words. The seizures themselves are one thing. The life that revolves around them is another. "You know when it's the dead of winter and you get all depressed because you keep thinking of all the things you got to do last summer? But now it's freezing outside and you can't go jumping in a lake or frolicking in a field? It's like that. It's like looking outside and seeing all of the things that you *could* be doing on your horizon, and yet, there's nothing you can do about it. You're chained."

It takes him so long to answer that I begin to wonder if he's going to say anything at all. Then, quietly, like he's saying it to himself, he hums. "I always hated January."

"Me too."

After a brief moment of silence, Walker lowers his head so I have no choice but to look at him, face-to-face, eye to eye. Those pupils flicker from one of my eyes to the other, like he can't decide which is the safest one to land on. His body leans a little closer, the smell of leather and a small hint of the soap from his shower earlier lingering in his presence. "You're not fragile." He shakes his head, and it causes the mess that is his hair to flop in his eyes. "Not in the way they act like you are."

"I know." I *should* know that. I've spent years telling myself.

It must sound believable, too, because he hits back with a confident "Good."

Walker dips his chin back at me and leaves the car, taking long steps toward his porch that sits beside mine. Our twin doors side by side, mine a pastel blue, his a dark navy. My porch swing with its embroidered pillows and throw blanket across the arm. A clay pot of zinnias growing beside it. His porch rockers, wooden and bare. A small table beside the rockers with a deck of cards resting on it, the box wide open.

Without looking over his shoulder, Walker reaches for his door, and I watch as he almost slips inside.

"Walker," I whisper. Quiet enough to where he probably wouldn't hear it. Outward enough to say I did it. That I tried.

But he turns on a dime. Those big shoulders jerk back and those whiskey eyes hit me like a sucker punch.

I know, looking in those eyes, I have no choice but to say exactly what's on my mind.

"I'm glad you know it too."

Because if anyone could see that I'm not fragile, it should be the one who never had to watch me break.

The corner of his mouth lifts. "Yeah?"

"Yeah." I keep my feet grounded on the rocks below me. Unwavering. "Since we're legally bound as friends."

The small quirk of his smile spreads into a real one. Into the one that I fell in love with so long ago. "Very true." He opens his mouth, shuts it. Opens it again. And settles on, "Have a good night, Trouble."

So I settle too. "You too, Walker."

CHAPTER ELEVEN
Walker

There's a spot at Willow Creek I like to call my own. Tucked past the strawberry fields, by the last guest cottage where the dirt path narrows and the air smells faintly of wildflowers and earth. Beyond a line of hay bales, there's a single oak tree in the middle of a clearing, right where the hill rolls to the top and grass settles around it in clear patches.

I curve the corner past the last hay bale, my boots crunching on the dry dirt path, and there she is. Lottie is leaning against the base of the tree, head swaying side to side, waves of light blond hair covering the tanned exposed areas of her neck and chest. Her birthmark, a tiny pink splotch, stretches as she moves. With a floral notebook in her lap, knees propped up, red Lucchese's dug into the ground, and a pen in hand, she's feverishly writing. Then scratching through. Then writing again.

I stand there for a moment too long, watching the early-morning breeze sway the free tendrils of her hair. It's been a couple nights since I've seen her last, with no opportunity for us to cross paths between now and then.

"Writing an autobiography?" My voice comes out scratchy, like I haven't spoken in hours, and I clear my throat, unsure if it's the right thing to say.

Lottie's eyes meet mine. For just a moment, I see something flicker—relief, maybe? She quickly masks it with a smile, but it lingers in her gaze before she turns her attention back to her notebook.

"Actually, my last will and testament."

"Never too early. Tell me: Who are you leaving your old man hat collection with?"

"You know, I was thinking Flick, but it would certainly traumatize my parents, so maybe them instead."

I nod, biting down on a smile. "Wise choice."

"Indubitably."

I take a few hesitant steps and wait for the calm on her face to expand to something territorial, like a trainer entering a tiger's cage. But it never comes. She simply folds her notebook over and scoots to one side of a large root.

My eyes move to the empty spot beside her, and she nods in invitation. I take a couple steps and sit beside her, my legs stretched out past hers.

"You're up early," I remark.

I don't typically make it a habit to know my neighbors' routines, but when we share walls, it's impossible not to.

"Couldn't sleep."

"Too excited?"

"In a way."

"The kid mentioned that you're teaching him some stuff." I dig my fingers into the crook of my elbows as my arms cross. "Kit. He said something about wanting to ride."

Lottie's eyes shoot up to mine, pink fading into her cheek bones. "He told you?"

I nod. "He asked if we were friends."

"And?"

"And what?"

"What did you say back?"

"Well, there *is* a contract."

She snorts a laugh. The wind blows her hair toward me, blond strands falling on my shoulder. The smell of her shampoo takes me back to the last time we leaned against this tree. Our hands wrapped around each other. Heat pulsing through my veins. The biggest problem in my life back then was just trying to figure out how I could kiss her.

I guess not much has changed. I'm still chasing after the farmer's daughter, trying anything to get her attention.

"He just asked me a few things," I rephrase. "I think he'll be good at it. I think *you'll* be a good coach for him."

Her eyes widen a bit. "You do?"

"Well, yeah."

Even at her younger ages, Lottie had more talent in one pinky than most female riders had with ten years of training.

"Did you tell anyone else?"

"Nope." I shook my head. "Have you coached before?"

"No. I never considered it, really. I'm too young and inexperienced for that—most trainers are at least five years retired. But when Kit asked, I couldn't say no."

"I think it's good for you. Gets you out there. Away from"—I jerk my thumb back to the big house—"all of that."

"Yeah." She nods excessively. "I think so too."

"Do you plan on doing that, you know, for others?"

"Is this your way of asking me for lessons?"

I laugh, head tossing back against the bark of the old oak tree. "You want to teach me?"

"Not really." Her nose scrunches like a small bunny. "You seem like a horrible student."

"You're probably right."

"I usually am."

"So, you've got riding lessons coming up. What else are your plans for this summer?"

"Plans?"

"Yeah, you know. Fourth of July parties, county fairs, all the usual Lottie Jane summer stuff."

"Well…" Her hands ring around the notebook in her lap, the pen in the spirals making little circles.

"Whatcha got in there?" I try to tap the notebook, but she yanks it just out of my reach before I can touch it. I lift my hands up innocently. "I wasn't going to take it."

"It's personal."

There was once a time that there was nothing too personal between us. Now all that seems to be between us are boundaries, lines, and rules. I don't know where they start, and I don't know where they end. But I know I want to push them out as far as I can with her.

"I just… I turn eighteen in August," she says quietly, like the number itself weighs more than it should.

"The twenty-eighth."

Her lips quirk up for a second, a fragile smile that dulls after a moment. "Yeah. It's…harder than I thought it would be"

I hum, hoping she'll keep going. And just my luck, she does.

"I thought it all would be different by now. My senior year—riding, awards, family, friends—I just had this picture in my mind of how it all would be. And I look around, and it's not even close."

She glances up at me, maybe to see if I'm listening, or

maybe to make sure I won't stop her. I don't move. I keep my eyes locked on her, hanging on every word she mumbles out.

"So." She opens the notebook halfway, exposing the page she was previously working on. "I was thinking of some things...to do this summer..."

"Before you go back for your senior year?"

Lottie brings the notebook back to her chest. "It's so stupid."

I grab the top of her notebook, pulling it away from her chest so she can't block her writing. "I think it's incredible."

She gives enough leeway for my eyes to trail the list.

One after another, these little check boxes appear below in a bucket-list type style. Some items are underlined—maybe they're more important to her? I take note of every single one. Some are crossed out and rewritten beside the original list. About fifteen items total on the list.

"Lottie these are—"

"It's so silly." She laughs like, *Isn't that funny? Aren't I so juvenile?* And it breaks me. "I was thinking like eighteen things before eighteen. Like a bucket list or something. But it's—"

"Incredible," I reaffirm and keep my eyes locked on the notebook, checking each line one by one. I feel Lottie's gaze on me, but I am in a different world as I think of her accomplishing each item.

Take a yoga class
Learn to cook an actual meal
Go line dancing
Fall in love with something new
Have a picnic
Go to an estate sale with Ada
Get a pet (??)

~~Find a new hobby~~ Go camping for one night—in a real tent!
Try pottery painting
Go to the Fourth of July fest this year (don't be a chicken)
Have a girls' night
Get Kit into a junior competition this fall
Finish a book for the book club
Take on one of the long trails
Collect more physical media (CDs, DVDs, VHS, other three-letter words)
Go night swimming
Have a bonfire (s'mores are mandatory)
TP someone's house (apologies in advance, Flick)

"Seriously." I look back at her. "I think this is great. I think you should do it. All of it."

"You do?"

"Every single one. I think you should teach something and learn something. And find new things that you love. I think it's all amazing."

"I don't know where to even start."

I look back down. "Get a pet. That seems pretty easy?"

She hums, and her response is quiet between us. "I want one. But if I tell Flick, she's going to saddle me up with rambunctious ducks and cussing birds and ferrets and groundhogs. I mean, I was thinking maybe a dog would be nice? But even that feels"—she blows out a harsh breath—"overwhelming to do. Plus, I would have to talk to Dot about it. Even if our living arrangements are temporary, it feels rude to just pop in with a stray animal."

"Maybe I…could help. With some of these."

I watch her consider it, eyes darting around us and back to the notebook. "Would you tell anyone?"

The thought of a secret that's just ours, something small for just us, lights my body up like a Christmas tree.

"*Never.*"

"Then...I might take you up on that."

I smile. "You should."

"I *might.*"

She stands, dusting off her denim shorts, and then extends her hand to me. It's the same gesture I've always made, the one I've always relied on. Me lifting her back up. Today, it feels heavier—her hand extending toward mine.

Regardless, I wrap my hand in hers and accept her help.

"Maybe we do have an alliance." She smiles, big and bright.

"Add it to my pros list." Our hands are still clasped as we shake them up and down. Warmth spreads across my palm and up my forearm.

"Will do."

Lottie drops her hand from mine and clutches it around her notebook, lifting it to her chest. "I'll see you around."

"Bye, Trouble." I smile and watch her walk away toward her home, right next to mine.

"Hey!" I call out when she is almost out of reach. "I still haven't gotten my hat back."

"What's that?" She keeps walking away from me and points to her head. "I can't hear you."

I hope I never get that hat back. Not as long as she has it.

CHAPTER TWELVE
Lottie

Random number: Hey :)

Me: Hello?

Random number: This is Walker

Me: Wow. Are we there already? At the texting part of this "friendship?"

Walker: It would seem so. I grabbed your number from the contact list on the fridge magnets.

Me: Right, of course.

Walker: I actually texted to ask if that old waterfall by Chimney Peak is still closed off?

Me: Think so, why?

Walker: Working on your first assignment.

Me: Assignment sounds too FBI-y.

Walker: We can't have that.

Me: It does deserve a name, though.

Walker: "You're getting old, get over it" list?

Me: Offensive.

Walker: Guess we could keep "18 before 18?"

Me: We could, but unfortunately, there's not even eighteen things to do in this town beyond breathing and basic photosynthesis.

Walker: I think we can find some together.

"Your cheeks are going to be sore from all that smiling."

I look up from my phone resting on the hostess podium to see Ada, forehead drenched in sweat, with a sly grin on her face. "I know it's not Flick causing that."

I consider spilling it all to Ada. She's the second-closest friend I have. Looking at her face, lit up and expecting something really juicy, I know I should. But she's the same as everyone else is with my health, even if she hides it better than the rest.

"Inside joke," I say with a playful eye roll for added believability. "Long story."

Just then, the side door opens so hard that it smacks against the cash-covered wall. If there wasn't already a hole where the doorknob fits in the sheetrock before, there is now.

Flick comes rushing, no, *dancing* in with a large stack of pink flyers in hand. She is practically shimmying on the tips of her toes over to me.

"What are these?" I grab a handful of forms and smile down at them.

"Knox had this amazing idea of doing a charity event to help get some of the extra little guys get adopted at the shelter." She points to the poorly designed flyer. "He made them for me."

I look from the clip art of a dog with its tongue out to the extremely uncomfortable smiley face sitting beside it with a gloved thumbs-up poking out.

"Wow."

"I know," she squeals.

I realize that love is probably something that makes you just a little stupid. Or maybe blind. Possibly both. But looking at this poster and back up to Flick, I can tell my best friend is so blinded by infatuation that she has no idea that this is a travesty.

And because I am on what appears to be a spree of volunteering my time to everyone around me this summer, I instantly offer, "What can I do to help?"

She considers it for a minute, then says, "Okay. I would like some help maybe setting up snack tables. Or decorating?"

I clasp my hands. "Snacks and decorating, done and done."

She smiles, and every cynical piece of me just burns away watching her beam. "I can't wait."

Watching my best friend glow over a dog event and knowing my coaching lessons for Kit are this afternoon, and I've made the whole list of what I plan on doing with the rest of my time on Earth as a seventeen-year-old, for once, I feel like my life is…glimmering. Like a shiny new toy tossed in with all the rest of my daily functions. A flicker of hope. And I am going to cling to it as hard as I possibly can and ride it till sunset.

An hour later, I am staring, very confused, at Kit's feet in the dirt.

"First things first, we've got to change your shoes."

At my words, Kit glances down to his weathered work boots held together by silver duct tape. "What's wrong with these?"

"The heel," I point out. "It's not gonna work well for

balancing yourself. Knox has a million cowboy boots, ask him for some in your size next time."

"Okay, but, now what?"

We're at the same practice pen I'd spent my preteen years working at. Thankfully, the same old man, Otis, works with the cattle outside that helped me sneak in when I was twelve. So, when Kit and I slipped past the main entrance where someone would surely see us and notify the authorities—any of my relatives—Otis simply tipped his head in a nod and smiled for us to go in.

Kit's eyes immediately clung to the open arena, the dirt in the middle settled from lack of movement in the late afternoon. I showed him the area, taking time to let him see each part before settling on the bucking chute with wide, excited eyes.

Which has led us to where we are now, with Kit attempting to balance on a heavy weighted ball, rolling it under his feet back and forth.

"I still don't see how any part of this is supposed to help me. When can I get on a bull?"

"You can't even *look* at a bull right now." I squint at him. "I need you to be able to stand still on this ball for five minutes, then we can move you on to the next step."

Kit nods. "Got it."

He climbs back on the ball, and I time him, over and over. He trips up many times, but eventually, he stands for five minutes. Once I am fully convinced that I can trust his balance, I guide him to the next training area where the bull simulator sits. It's less of a simulator, like Goliath, and more like a very rickety seesaw. But it's the best tool we can possibly use right now.

The sun is starting to set and the lighting in here is basically nothing but a streetlamp thirty feet from the open building. We have maybe an hour, but if the kid is anything like I was, he will soak in each one.

"Okay." I tighten my grip around the rope attached to the see saw. "Here's your bull."

"That"—Kit points to the rust bucket behind me—"is not a bull."

"Well, it's the closest thing to a bull that you're getting." I reach up and pat a hand on the square metal seat. "Hop on, cowboy."

Kit climbs up to the seat and I let go of the rope attached, letting him shoot up to the air.

"Geez," he coughs out when his legs start to slip, but he catches himself before he can fall the four feet back down to the dirt. "A warning would be nice."

"Bulls don't give warnings."

"I'm starting to think I'm safer with them than I am with you."

"Hush." I wave a hand and show him the strap in front of him. A replica close enough to what you would typically grip when riding something smaller, like a steer. "Adjust your hold."

What's the saying? Those who can't, teach. I think that's me. I can't do half of what Kit can on this raggedy setup, or at least I couldn't tell anyone if I did. But watching him up there lights a fire in me that's been smothered for so long.

"Don't just hang on tight." I pull on my end of the seesaw, letting him fly up and down in the air. "It's not about being strong. You have to dance with him and go *with* his movements. You can be the strongest man in the world, but you'll still never beat a two-ton bull."

My eyes clock his free hand in the air. It's kind of just dangling there, not really serving its real purpose.

I raise my hand up and let it fall back down in a familiar move. "Try raising your hand with the bull's thrashing; it will help balance."

Kit nods and copies my movement. It takes him a few rounds, but he is slowly straightening his back, like the height of it isn't as threatening to him. I don't say it out loud, but he's going to have to get used to the height, because the next manual simulator is way higher.

"How long are we going to do this before I get a real bull?" he groans after thirty minutes, riding up and down nonstop. He's going to be dizzy if I don't give him a cooldown by the time we're done, but the longer he can stand this, the better he'll be.

"You've got a while to go. I need you to nail this first. Oh, and the ball. The balance is by far the most important part. It's got to be so natural that it just moves over to the side of your brain that makes something a habit. It's like—"

"Driving a car?"

I wouldn't exactly know about that, but sure.

"Yes. Do it over and over. Do it in your sleep if you have to. The day when it comes down to the ride, the less you think, the better. That's why this has to be second nature."

"What's it like when you're riding?" He grunts when I throw a left swerve in there before slowly letting him back down to earth.

I try to find the words for it and come up short. I don't know if there's anything out there that can fully explain it. If there's something that can compare.

Skydiving. Or maybe parasailing. But with the adrenaline of knowing there is a two-thousand-pound beast under your legs trying his best to knock you off. To kill you. The beauty of the lights flashing around you, distant shouts cheering you on. It's a high—one that's more addictive than any drug out there.

Once you get a single ride in, you'll never stop. Not until they force you to.

"It's like you're flying."

His eyes widen in excitement, and I pray he can hold on to it a little longer. I'm going to stretch him as long as I can before letting him hop on. Whether he wants to acknowledge it or not, Kit is tiny. He's got some height on him, but his lean frame isn't built up enough to carry his weight properly. That, on its own, would be fine, but he also has poor balance.

I'll give in on one of those things, and it's not going to be balance.

My phone buzzes in my back pocket. I yank it out while Kit tries to find his balance from bouncing around in the air for the last half hour. My eyes land on my new (old), friend's contact.

Walker: Have you got plans tonight?

I smile.

Me: I'm actually helping Kit with something right now
Walker: And...are you free after?
Me: Depends
Walker: On?
Me: Whatever you've got going on in that space cowboy head
Walker: Come to my side of the house as soon as you're done. I've got something we can cross off the list.

CHAPTER THIRTEEN
Walker

A single hour after I text Lottie, I have her in my passenger seat.

She's fiddling with the radio in a poor attempt at getting it to connect to anything local, and there is a pile of towels in the backseat.

When we texted ideas back and forth, finally coming up with the final list, I initially asked which item she wanted to check off first and she told me she wanted me to surprise her.

Deciding the first thing to cross off Lottie's list felt daunting. I didn't know what was more appropriate or what would be her preferred choice for the very first thing—something not too big but not too small either—then, after some thought, it was all too simple. She needs a sense of adventure. I need a sense of freedom. So, going on an illegal hike to the backside of a waterfall is the perfect version of both.

I drive down the makeshift road, gravel kicking up behind my truck as we slow to a stop on dry dirt.

Lottie took me here when we were sixteen—my last summer here.

She said she had somewhere "super cool" to take me after I'd spent hours that morning trying to get a hold of someone in my household. I'd forgotten to pack my favorite boots and had hopes of someone turning the car back around to bring them.

Over ten missed calls on their end, not a single one on mine.

Lottie sat by my side the whole time. "You can wear Knox's boots. I'll steal 'em if you want me to?"

But it was about more than the boots. It was about abandonment. No, I wasn't some baby being dropped off in a box at a fire station, but it felt close to it. A spare kid they didn't know what to do with, so take it to the longest summer camp you can find, throw a handful of cash their way, and don't look back.

"What if I was hurt?" I asked Lottie. "What if I broke my wrist?"

"Did you?" She grabbed my wrist, turning it to her.

"No. But it's the thought of it. It wouldn't matter if I did."

Then she sighed, wrapped her fingers around my wrist, and gave it a quick tug, taking me with her.

We took one of the off-roaders when her family wasn't looking and popped down the road until she pulled into the same spot I'm in now.

We hiked the whole way through until we reached the back side of the waterfall.

The harsh, rushing water was so loud we both covered our ears until she reached over to pull my hands down. The piercing noise slowly dulled until we both settled into it. Then she lifted her chin and yelled out into the wind and water.

I looked around, waiting for someone on the trails to hear and come running after us. But they never did. Because only Lottie and I could hear her shouts of frustration and anger and then laughter. Loud, bright, big laughter that was so strong it started up my own.

Then I yelled too. We held each other's hand and screamed out into the midmorning air. And maybe it was childish looking back—we *were* children—but I can't remember a time when I'd felt lighter.

So, we did that every couple days after. When one of us was pissed off, or if we were just bored, we would slip down this abandoned road and scream behind the waterfall and watch the harsh gushing flows of water cover the sound.

I glance over at Lottie, and her eyes are caught on the DO NOT ENTER signs with a blank, unreadable expression. Is she picturing it too? How our hands used to tingle, palms pulsing, when I would lift her over the rocky hillside? How we'd spend hours away, as just the two of us in our swimsuits chased each other around slippery rocks and splashing freezing water?

It feels like it's all I can think about some days.

Who we used to be. Who we are now. And trying to find the tie between the two.

For a second, I feel this pull between freedom and responsibility. I have a flash of worry in my mind. *Is* this the right thing for Lottie? I want her to have fun and feel adventure and excitement, but never at the cost of her own health.

I turn toward the passenger seat. "You're good with this, right?"

The smile she gives me is megawatt. Like being out here with me, hiking down a mountain on a Saturday night, isn't the worst thing in the world.

"I'm *great.*"

We make our way down the dirt path, each curve of the old hike bringing a new wave of nostalgia, each bend taking weight off my chest. The manmade road cuts off to another Do Not Enter sign by a small rusted gate.

I climb over the gate, turn, and hold a hand out for Lottie to take.

She eyes it for a moment, then reaches her own hand around the gate, hopping it herself.

CHAPTER FOURTEEN
Lottie

I'm climbing fences. I am. *Me.*

If Knox knew where I was, he'd pass out. My parents? I'd pay to see their faces. Even I wouldn't have believed this a week ago.

The trail disappears into the dark; the Closed sign we stepped over a few minutes ago is already lost behind us, swallowed by ferns and shadows in the night. The Southern air smells like wet earth and pine sap, and way downhill, I can already hear the rush of water echoing through the trees.

My white sneakers squelch in the red clay. Every few steps, I nearly lose my footing on a slick root or a rock pretending to be solid ground.

"Hold up." Walker leans toward the steep drop-off and memories flood my brain.

The smell of wet rock and honeysuckle, Walker standing on this rock—it all takes me back to our last summer together.

Fifteen again. Sitting on this same rock, dangling my feet off the edge as I waited for Walker to work his way down so he could help me. *Help* being a bit exaggerated. I could've gotten down on my own—I've always had long legs. But then I wouldn't have gotten to feel Walker's hands curl around my waist, digging into my shorts as he yanked me down. I wouldn't get his arms tight around me, our chests pressed together with nothing but my shirt in between. I wouldn't have gotten to climb down his body, hands clinging as I begged him not to drop me. And I wouldn't have gotten to hear his rough rumble, "You know I've got you," combined with that deadly wink.

Safe, warm, and a dim light growing brighter, bigger, and stronger between us. A bond I only knew with him. And an attraction that took my breath away.

The memories make my throat hum. My thighs slam shut as I watch Walker inch his way down around the drop-off. His height difference in the last two years is a clear indicator of how much has changed.

There's a storm in those hefty gray eyes of his. I can't say what they're thinking, but there is a definite question settling into them.

"Need help?" His chin dips down, and we both know exactly what he's asking.

I want to say no. I *should* say no.

Every logical sense in me says this is a bad idea. It's one thing to sign up for this cute bucket list agenda, but to actually feel Walker's hands on me? Knowing that by the end of this summer, chances are Walker won't be here? It's not a good idea. No, I don't need help. And judging by how Walker is looking up at me with a playful smirk and the glint in his eyes, he knows it too.

Still, I take advantage of the offer and lift two hands out for him.

His lips reach up in a faint smile, tugging slightly at the

corners of his mouth. His eyes are a touch brighter, too, a crinkle near the corners.

We are both liars in a dance of pretending we're not.

Walker takes two steps forward, shoulders at my legs. He curls his hands around my waist, squeezes once, and lifts me down to him.

Thank God for the dark evening sky, otherwise the blush I'm sporting would be far more visible.

"I've gotcha." He slowly carries me down with my hands on his shoulders.

I settle onto the dry ground with my feet steady, and still, Walker's hands stay right there. "Good?" I hear his smile more than I can see it.

"Good," I confirm, and I let my hands take a slow tumble from his shoulders to his chest and finally down to my own sides.

Walker's eyes tear from mine and he clears his throat. "Come on, Trouble," he says, jerking his head toward the sound of rushing water. "About half a mile left."

There's a part of me poking the back of my mind. *You're already tired. Leave it all right here, you've gone farther than you thought possible.* But if we don't go all the way, then was it even worth it? And if I all of a sudden whine to Walker about the exhaustion pulling behind my eyes, will he turn on a dime like everyone else?

"When's the last time you were here?" Walker asks, offering a hand as we slide down another muddy slope. I wrap my cold fingers around his warm ones and delight in the chance to stop thinking about how tired I am.

"When did we last go?" I ask.

"Two years ago, the last week of August."

"Then that's the last time."

There's a pause in his step, a hesitation in his speech, too, before eventually he mumbles low, "I'm glad we're going now, then."

When we curve the corner closer to the end of the hike, he guides me down the hill to the rocky edge. The water rushing beside us is loud enough to cover the noise of our joint laughter as our shoes get muddy from the red clay mixing with sprayed water.

I follow Walker behind the water, standing on the rocky platform we once were at years before.

"Now what?" I yell, loud enough for him to hear.

"You know what." His smirk is easy and warm, and I repeat the action back at him. Yeah, I know exactly what we do now.

Like only a blink of time has passed, we lean our heads back, cup our hands around our mouths, and shout out into the rushing flow of water. I think of all of the things that have added up in the last couple months. Couple years, really. I add up the doctors' visits, the continuous surveillance, the feeling of so many people around you, yet being so entirely alone. I let it sink in my chest, build in my lungs. I lean back to spill it all out in our joint shouts. The sound of the rushing water covers us as our yells transition into fits of laughter.

It's a sight that I will only allow Walker Lane to witness. And simply because he's seen it so many times before.

In a life surrounded by people who want me safe and quiet, Walker pushes me to climb and yell.

Maybe it's because, to him, I'm still little old Lottie. Maybe he sees me as the girl I once was—full of fire and passion. Maybe he doesn't know how burnt-out I am yet.

I know he'll see this new, dull version of me one day, but I don't want it to be today.

When our screams are nothing but sporadic gasps of air

and us laughing at each other—Walker pointing at my face, asking if I just snorted, and me actively snorting through my hysterics—we settle onto the cold rock below us. I roll up the towel he gave me and use it as a pillow beneath my head.

"So." Walker lays down a few feet away on his own towel, hands behind his head and arms flexing. "I probably should have asked this sooner, but you don't have a boyfriend or someone that's going to threaten to shoot me for being here alone with you, right?"

My breath hitches. "If I said yes, would you still be here?"

"Yes." A long pause. "But I would've practiced running up a mountain beforehand."

I open my mouth to reply, when a branch snaps and there's a distant high-pitched crying noise.

"Shh, do you hear that?" I lift a hand to pause so I can listen to whatever it is.

It sounds like distant footsteps splashing against water. The waterfall is big enough to give us privacy but not big enough where you wouldn't be able to notice someone, or something, new walking in.

"Shit." Walker shoots up, grabbing his towel off the wet rock.

The footsteps of whatever is near us are gaining traction, and I'm not willing to find out if it's Bigfoot or just Scott from the police department.

Walker cusses under his breath. "You can run, right?"

I save the effort of being offended for later and nod.

"Great, 'cause we're about to do it up the side of a mountain. Guess I really should have practiced, huh?" He grabs the towel in my hands and tosses it over his shoulder with a wink at me. "Not like you haven't done this before, though, right?"

I shake my head with a tilted smile and follow his movements guiding us out from behind the waterfall. We stay silent and steady in hopes of getting an idea of what's nearby. With both of our flashlights off, the moon is our only guide, and she's shy tonight, hanging behind a cluster of clouds.

Walker reaches back, patting against the rocky edge until I come into his range. His hand grazes my shoulder, sliding its way down until he intertwines our fingers. "Stick close to me. We're gonna go toward the truck," he whispers, turning out to be far closer than I expected. The warmth of his body is a magnet, directing me closer to him. Our shoulders brush and the chill of the night air meets with the heat of his skin against mine.

"Right," I whisper back, and I do my best to ignore the way my chest is thumping sporadically. "Because going anywhere other than the truck would be ideal."

"Can you *not* be a smart-ass? Or is it biologically engineered into you?"

"No, I think it's like a chemical imbalance that can't be fixed."

He squeezes our hands together once and gives a gentle tug, telling me to follow. I do.

Thankfully, the path going up is always easier than going down. It's a killer workout on your legs, lots of deep lunges and pulling yourself out of red clay. Still, it's quicker than trying to figure out which step is going to have you sliding down the hill, or free-falling entirely. I cling to Walker as my eyes adjust to the pitch-black night, only able to make out a few trees and rocky edges.

This man must have some kind of secret night vision, because he knows every single step to take to get us out of here as quickly as possible. Well, until—

"Shit," Walker chokes out as his leg slips out from

underneath him, chin falling directly to the ground. And since our hands are joined, and my grip on him is that of a vise, I tumble with him.

The sting of tiny gravel scrapes my knee, and if I weren't running on pure adrenaline, it might've actually hurt. I can't see it, but I feel the clay spread across my legs, muddy water running down my shins. These shoes are going to be a nightmare to clean.

"Are you okay?" Walker asks, *way* too loud.

My eyes adjust enough that I can make out the smear of mud across his jaw and cheeks. My laugh cracks down like thunder, and then, as if he finally realized how loud his voice is, Walker lowers it and whispers, "Sorry, are you okay?"

"Shut up," I wheeze out. My knee has its own pulse and my eyes are straining from the dark, but I can't remember the last time I smiled like this.

"You're the one laughing so loud. They're going to hear your snorts and assume Wilbur snuck out."

"Shut"—I snort—"up."

There goes Walker's laugh. A diesel truck turning over—deep, strong, and hardy. And *far* too loud.

He bends at the waist, wraps those big arms around my muddy thighs, and lifts me straight into the air like I am nothing but a pillowcase. He tosses me over his shoulders, the dirt from his hands making their way up my hips as he sets me in place over him. My thighs squeeze together when his fingers slide into the small sliver of exposed skin between my shorts and my shirt.

"Good Lord," I choke out as the base of my abdomen curls over my old friend's shoulder.

"Sorry," he whispers, in contrast with his unapologetic tone.

Walker runs us up the mountain way faster than we were going earlier, and before I can register how much longer we have to go, I can see the fence where the truck is parked in the near distance.

"How close is he?" Walker asks in a grunt.

"I can't tell. You're shaking me like a chihuahua."

"That is *not* a saying."

I squint, trying to see the very out-of-shape silhouette of our local sheriff, and boy, he is really struggling. I almost wish we gave him a head start.

"Two, wait, no, he's about three hundred yards away."

"Translate that to feet."

"Oh, he's like nine hundred feet away. But really, really out of breath. Poor guy. You know, Scott probably hasn't had to chase anyone since Glazed and Confused took that cookie dough donut off their menu and everyone rioted at the town square in protest."

"I'm going to throw you over the fence."

"Wait, wha—"

I have zero reaction time because as the words leave my mouth, Walker has me straight up in the air, hands on my butt, tossing me over like I'm a dog hopping the gate to the kitchen.

Miraculously, my feet land first and I don't break an ankle. I try to imagine anyone in my family or friend group willingly tossing me around, and it makes me want to laugh. Even Dot, the least strict of them all, wouldn't attempt to pick me up out of fear.

But Walker doesn't even hesitate. Doesn't think twice about it. I like that a whole lot more than I should.

Walker jumps the fence the same way he did when we first got here, but this time the towel on his shoulder is snagged and left there as evidence of a transgression.

"Come on," he hisses as I stare at him in shock. The man hopped over a six-foot fence like it was nothing but an average Tuesday, and he expects me to casually go about my business?

"How do you do that so well? Have you been in prison the last two years?"

"Do I need to carry you again to move this along?"

I open my mouth to answer, but a sudden flash of light shines at the top of the hill behind the fence line, and Scott is moving faster than I have ever seen him.

I turn, and Walker is already in the truck, engine turning over and windows down. I throw the passenger door open and slide in. Despite the depravity of our situation—Walker racing down the beaten road with Scott bent over behind us, hands on his knees and chest heaving—the corners of my lips are permanently glued to my cheeks.

I feel like a pageant girl wearing Vaseline on her teeth so she never stops smiling.

Walker does a three-point turn where the road splits and drives us straight out of there without so much as a backward glance.

It's only when the truck's AC begins to finally cool me off and settle my heart rate that I realize how filthy I am. My fingers lift to turn on an overhead light, and I track the clay spread between us both. My T-shirt is covered and my chest and shoes are a mess, but the only thing I can keep my focus on is my legs. I have Walker's muddy handprints outlining the sides of my thighs where he lifted me over his shoulder, his thumb a clear indent against my skin. Something about it makes me shift in my seat, which spreads the mess below me even more.

"I think I'm getting mud on your seats." I wince.

"Don't worry about it."

"Are you sure? I don't want to—"

"Lottie." I look up from the dirty seats, and Walker is *beaming* at me. He's out of breath, and there is a clear indication on his white shirt where my muddy abdomen was, but there is this gorgeous, incandescent smile on his scruffy face. I sit still so I can soak it in, like the slightest movement might make it fall.

"Don't worry about it," he reassures me.

So I don't.

We settle into our spots for the quiet drive back, thankful that no red or blue lights pop up behind us. Walker's speakers hum the low baseline of a George Strait song, and though I don't know the words, Walker is humming right alongside it.

I try to conjure up a recent memory that is comparable to this one and fall entirely short. The closest thing would maybe be when Flick and I snuck out of the house after my last ER trip.

It's rare that I need to go, but this one was bad enough that it called for it. The seizure wasn't grand mal, where your whole body gets all stiff right before it starts to jerk uncontrollably, but it was enough to cause me to lose balance and fall. I hit my head on the edge of the porch steps and knocked myself out.

Flick called 911, an ambulance came, and it was an entire ordeal.

Knox and my parents both quarantined me, studying my heart rate and overall activity for the following week after. But I was getting cabin fever. So at one in the morning, I woke Flick up and begged her to take me for a watermelon slushy at the nearest 24/7 gas station. She offered to get it and bring it back to me instead, but that wasn't the point. The point was for me to get out of the house, and for me to finally feel like myself again by doing something somewhat normal. And to us, one a.m. slushy runs were normal. Plus, my slushy would be nothing but red dye-filled syrup by the time she got back, and that was not the vibe I was going for. So, with lots of pleading and promising of future rest, I convinced her.

That feeling, that rush of doing something freeing and wild, is nothing but a pebble compared to how it feels in this truck right now. I feel entirely free, without a deck of cards in my hand or a bet to be placed.

This might be my favorite summer of ours yet.

CHAPTER FIFTEEN
Lottie

My fingers dance along the rusted edge of the old practice chute, feeling the cool metal bite against my skin. The arena is almost silent, nothing but the echo of wind whistling through the beams, kicking up dust from the dirt floor. It feels like it's been a lifetime since I last climbed over these gates and I sat in that chute with nothing but raw nerves and adrenaline holding me together.

Funny how life does that to you. One day you can be riding the high of your future, and in the next moment, you're surrounded by people saying you'll never get what you wanted.

No one said it outright, but I could see it in their faces. My mom wringing her hands, my dad pacing the hospital floor. The neurologist flipping through his clipboard, casually deciding my future like he wasn't about to shatter everything I'd built my life around. "It's too dangerous, one seizure at the wrong moment and…" He never finished the sentence. He didn't have to. We all understood.

I exhale slowly, pushing off the gate. There's no use

standing here, drowning in what-ifs. The past is simply that—the past. It's done and over, but maybe what's ahead of me is still worth holding on to. Even if I have to learn how to love this sport from the other side of the fence.

"Umph." Kit's feet slip off the balance ball for the third time. "How do you honestly expect me to stay on here for ten minutes?"

Wait until he finds out I am working him up to standing on it for an hour straight.

I point to the setup. "Again."

The past few training sessions, I've still had Kit working on his balance. His reflexes are sharpening, his core is learning to stabilize, and—slowly but surely—he's starting to move *with* the momentum instead of fighting against it.

I grab my laptop and pull up the highlighted clips of world champion bull riders. I set the screen so it's tilted toward him and jerk my chin back. "Here, try to walk the ball closer."

"I feel like a bear in the circus."

"Don't be ridiculous. A bear would handle this way better."

When he gets close enough, I make the video go full screen but keep it paused.

"You need a visual. Something to go off more than just me teaching you without being on an actual bull."

Kit exhales through his nose, rubbing his palms over his face before begrudgingly finding his balance on the ball. "Yeah, I've watched a lot of local matches."

"Ah." I wave my hand. "Those guys are good, but you're going to be better. Plus, they're nothing like you."

"What does that mean?"

"Take..." I think of the better riders in the area, and only one comes to mind. "Lawson."

We're not super close, but he's Odelia's brother, and if

I were going to watch anyone's match in the local tournaments—it would be his.

"He's tall and lean, but the guy is *jacked.* His forearms alone are massive, and when you watch how well his reaction time is, it's not just luck that's on his side. He's worked out a lot for that kind of strength." That's probably why I catch Ada constantly staring at him when he eats at Riley's. "Now, you on the other hand—"

Kit's cheeks flush and his brows sink. "I *know* I'm skinny."

"I'm not saying it's a bad thing. I'm not gonna tell you to bulk up and destroy this version of yourself if you don't want to. But, if you don't want to hit the gym and count macros and all that junk, then we need to give you a visual of someone extremely successful that has a similar body type as you."

He nods, a little less on the defensive side. I click play on the video, occasionally pausing to point out certain moves and hand motions for him to practice, and Kit studies like he's about to take the ACT.

Watching how the grooves in his eyebrows deepen, how his focus is so entirely pulled in on what plays in front of him, all feels like I'm looking into a piece of the past. Into this small sliver of the kid I once was too. The determination I felt to stay on that bull just a few seconds longer, to push myself a little longer.

Kit nods, his jaw tightening in focus as he shifts his weight, adjusting to the ball's subtle tilt. He's getting there. And maybe I'm getting somewhere too.

"She pushing you too hard?"

We both turn to the voice, and there's Walker, leaning against the entrance behind us with his arms crossed. Hair tousled, jeans all dirty, and heather-gray Willow Creek T-shirt stretching across his chest, he sucks all my attention from coaching directly to him. I feel like a balloon is blowing up bigger and bigger in my chest, ready to pop at just seeing him leaning against the door, smiling at me.

"Not pushing enough, actually." Kit crosses his arms to his chest, then almost slips off the ball and makes a poor attempt at recovering himself. "Shut up," he mumbles without looking back at us.

Kit grumbles something else under his breath, and I move closer to Walker with an uncontained smile.

"What's up with him?" He dips his chin to our young friend.

"Preteen angst."

"Ahh."

"I am *not* angsty," Kit hisses behind me, and I squint at Walker. *Sure.*

"What are you doing here?" I really do try to keep my voice from sounding like a puppy excited for its owner to pull into the driveway, but the usual edge in my tone has been slowly sanded down the last few days.

"Just finished up helping Knox round up the cattle; thought I'd stop by."

I hum a squeak-like "Mm!" and Kit snorts behind me somewhere.

Walker lowers his voice and steps a little closer, glancing from Kit over my shoulder, then back to me. "I actually was wondering if you had plans tomorrow night."

"Nope. Are we going on another hike?"

His smile is a bit lazy and boyish. "Not exactly. I thought we could keep it simple this week."

"Okay." I smile back. "What are we doing?"

"It's still a surprise, even if it's a small one."

"Alright." My cheeks are sore from my plastered grin. "Well, I'm free tomorrow night."

"Good," he replies, putting his hand on the door frame next to him. "Then it's a date."

It's not. Not in the way his deep voice insinuates. But I'm beginning to wish it was.

"Good God, is this what flirting looks like when you're old?" Kit laughs before losing his balance and falling off the ball.

"Walker's coming tonight, right?" The remote in my hand flings up high enough to hit the ceiling fan and scatter along the floor with the back and the batteries when Dot casually strolls into the living room.

"When did you get here?" I gasp, my free hand spread across my chest, trying to steady my heart rate.

"I've been here since three a.m."

I take note of her lack of scrubs today. Denim shorts and a T-shirt that says, "The Hell I Won't."

Dot passes by me for the kitchen. "Your head is really in the clouds today. It wouldn't have anything to do with that boy next door?"

My fingers busy themselves with the remote. "No. No, it's not that."

"Okay…" The disbelief in her voice is so potent it might as well be a neon sign in the living room that says BS. "Seemed worth asking."

"What are your plans tonight?" I move past the topic of Walker.

"Ah, a little bit of this. A little bit of that." She comes back to the living room with a pink floral mug, steam billowing over the top. "Why? Did you want to do something? I can cancel."

I shake my head. "No, you're fine—"

"Is this"—Dot gestures to all of her—"a problem?"

"This?"

"The whole me not really being home much thing? At first I thought you might like being here alone, but I worry I've given you too much space. Your mom probably wants me around, I just felt like maybe—"

"No." I wave a hand in front of me. "No, I like it. A lot, actually. It kind of feels like living alone, except occasionally a dish is moved or the door is opening at three a.m., but I think that's part of what I like too. I would love to hang out with you, but it's been nice this summer too."

"Well, good." She takes a sip. "Maybe we could do something this weekend? We could find a drive-through safari. Oh, or maybe a—"

My giggle bubbles up from my chest. "No, really, it's fine. I kind of have plans anyway. Tonight and this weekend."

Dot grins over her mug at me. "Oh, do you, now?"

I fear there is a flame spreading across my cheeks and she can see it clear as day.

"Go on, then." She flutters her hand. "Tell me everything."

So I do.

I knew Walker was going to come to Dot's side of the house tonight to mark something else off my (or maybe *our*?) list. He asked if I had a preference of which one to do, and I said as long as we can stay at home, I was good. I've been more tired than usual, and although I am not telling Walker about that, I don't want to be stupid and sign up for another hike or go on some wild scavenger hunt when my body craves rest.

Staying home left not many options, but still, the very last thing I was expecting was to open my door to see him on my front porch in gray sweatpants and a black compression top, forearms flexing as he holds up two handfuls of grocery bags from the corner store a couple miles down the road.

His arms look like someone wrapped him in plastic wrap and took a heat gun to it, the material shrinking into a second skin.

I make eye contact with his right pec as it twitches when he lifts the bags in his right hand.

"Hi, Trouble."

I lift my gaze to see Walker smiling at me, completely innocent.

"Hi, Walker." I shake my hair out a little. "You look… comfortable."

"We're doing cooking lessons tonight," he says, as if that's the reason he is looking fresh out of bed, messy strands of hair strewn about and the little scar above his brow relaxed as he smiles at me. "Number two, I believe."

Truthfully, I forgot about that one.

Learn to cook an actual meal.

It felt silly writing it down, but it was probably the most useful on the list.

I can cook. But nothing I've prepared can compare to a fresh, homemade, *not from a box* meal.

My whole body is warm at the thought of being tucked in my small kitchen alone with him. There is no reason for this… this…commotion in my head. Walker is a friend now. One that I desperately plan to cling to while he is still here. So, if this is my only time left with the one person who still sees me as a capable, strong woman, then I can't ruin it by drooling over a simple compression shirt and sweatpants combo on my front porch.

Walker clears his throat and my eyes lift to see him glancing from my living room behind me to my face. "We could do it at my place too…if that is better?"

Right, yes, this is the part where you are supposed to invite him in.

"Oh, sorry. Come in." I take a few steps back and swing the door inward so he can squeeze through the doorframe.

Walker surveys our living room, and I silently thank myself for picking up the stray socks and underwear.

I try to look at this side of the sister house through his eyes, wondering what a fresh perspective would feel like when you haven't already loved it for years.

The warm light filters in from the windows through the sheer white curtains while he takes it all in: the oversized blue-and-white striped couch, the vintage wooden coffee table, the stacks and stacks of books, and checkered pillows, and a clear vase full of blue and purple hydrangeas.

If Walker notices his tattered cowboy hat still resting on my coffee table, he doesn't say a word about it. He passes the gallery wall by me and flicks me a grin. Framed goose artwork from Dot's needlepoint phase, sporadic pictures of Knox and I through the ages. A picture of her skydiving for the first time, and another of her and my mom both on horses smiling into the sun. At the bottom, in the smallest golden frame, is a cutout picture of my parents' wedding.

I was so obsessed with it when I was little that Dot put a copy over here just for me.

It was the way they smiled at each other, the light in their eyes. It was back when I thought something like this could happen for me too. Watching them dance late at night in the kitchen when they thought no one was watching. Listening to their giggles down the hall. Cringing at their poor attempts to hide making out in the car pickup line at school.

Every single thing about that picture was easy and simple and perfect.

Walker's fingers lift to barely graze the summer quilts laying across my couch. "This looks like you."

"Nana must've thought so too; she left them for me and Dot both."

A whole closet full of homemade quilts in the hall.

Pink and yellow for spring.

Blue and white with little boats for summer.

Burnt orange and navy gingham for fall.

Lastly, a lavender-and-lilac snowflake pattern for winter.

He smiles and leans down to pick his groceries up. "So, it's the exact same layout as my place, just swapped."

I nod. "Yup, so the kitchen's this way." I guide him to the small kitchen, where he sets his bags on the empty countertops.

Once he pulls out all the ingredients—bowtie pasta, white wine, chicken broth, whipping cream, sun-dried tomatoes, dried oregano, chicken breasts, and a pile of different baking supplies beside it all. I try to piece together how brown sugar and baking powder work with white wine and sun-dried tomatoes and completely fall short.

"You have wine?" My hands reach for the bottle and he scoots it just out of reach.

"For cooking, yes. I got it from an old coworker before I moved here, and I'm not giving Dot a reason to let me not come back over if she catches us drinking."

If anything, Dot would join, but okay…

"So, we're making…?"

"Marry me chicken."

I choke up, coughing deep in the back of my throat.

Walker's eyes widen, a slow flush creeping up his neck. He clears his throat, rubbing the back of his head, but it only makes him look more boyish.

"Oh—that's just what it's called. Marry me chicken."

"Because it makes you want to ask a chicken to marry you?"

"Well, I think it's more so in hopes that whoever you make it for will marry you one day."

I am sweating bullets right now.

"But I wasn't… I mean, I didn't. It's just a recipe." He chuckles as his fingers busy themselves wrapping the plastic bags together.

"Right, obviously."

"Right."

Our eyes keep flicking toward each other, neither of us quite sure what to say. Then Walker claps his hands together, breaking the tension. "Alright, let's get started."

CHAPTER SIXTEEN
Walker

This seemed like a good idea in hindsight. Showing Lottie a simple, somewhat healthy comfort meal that she could learn to make on her own. Then again, I didn't take being alone with her in the kitchen into consideration.

"Okay." Lottie shoots straight up with a stainless-steel pan in her hand. "Got it."

"Perfect, set it on the biggest burner and turn the heat up to medium-high heat."

She follows my instructions and reaches for the butter beside me, her eyes glancing over the recipe I have propped up on my phone for her to reference if she wants to remake it when I'm not here. "Then butter?"

"Hold off on it for a sec." I lift a glass of water and dip my other hand in it, spraying water into the pan. "If the water steams or sizzles, it's not ready yet. The food will stick. The water should turn into beads and dance."

"Dance?"

"Mm-hmm. Like a grapevine."

"Well, aren't you an expert?"

A short puff of air leaves my nose, and when I breathe back in, I get a hint of strawberries and vanilla.

"I wouldn't call myself an expert by any means, but I have spent enough nights in a quiet kitchen with nothing but time on my hands."

She flicks water in the pan and watches it sizzle. "You mean like when your parents would leave you?"

I shrug. "Kind of."

"So, you've made *this*"—Lottie points to the recipe propped up—"a lot, then?"

"A few times." Just not with someone else. I keep my eyes focused on the pan. "My grandmother taught me. A while back."

Lottie gives me a careful glance, and I know she's wondering how much she can ask. "I am sorry, by the way. About your grandmother. She was a sweetheart."

Lottie met my Nonna once—she picked me up at the end of one summer when I was thirteen. I tried to just hop in the car, but she insisted on meeting my friend. When her eyes landed on Lottie, she whispered something about my excellent taste, then took three steps to her and squished her cheeks together like you would a baby chipmunk.

Later in the car, Nonna eyed me in the rearview mirror. "Lovely, girl, Walker. Just lovely." She'd like her even more if she saw her now. All that fire and smoke in her eyes.

"I get it all now."

I lift my head. "You…get it all?"

Lottie dips her pink nails in the cup and flicks the water again. This time it forms little balls and circles around the pan. "Oh my gosh, they really are dancing. This is so cute." She claps her hands and bounces on her heels, golden blond hair bobbing with her. "Who knew cooking would be this adorable?"

My pretty neighbor beams at the pan in front of her like she just discovered fire, clueless to the realization that she is far cuter than any dancing water beads.

"You can do the butter now, or I can?"

It's hard to read how much I should do or if she wants to take over, so I take a couple steps back. This entire thing, the entire list, is about her finding this new-old version of herself and finding her independence. If I take the entire thing over, it's nothing for her.

"Nope." She takes a couple steps my way and pops up on her toes, reaching directly across me, her forearm scraping along my abdomen. "I've got it."

Warmth from her bare touch spreads through my belly up my chest, tiny synapses crackling along my skin. My throat clears as Lottie tosses the butter and watches it melt, browning on the edges.

I give her the next couple directions from the recipe, and she follows each one happily. A small question here and there, but for the most part, Lottie hums quiet tunes under her breath. She eventually gets sick of her own humming and goes to turn on a local radio station.

We watch the chicken she heavily seasoned turn white in the pan, and I pull back a bit. I dip my legs enough so we're at the same height and lean so her counter presses into my lower back.

"You, um." I cough. "You said you get it all. What does that mean?"

She looks up at me, a smidge of sympathy resting in her eyes. "Why you didn't come back."

My chin jerks. She thinks Nonna is the only reason I

didn't come back? She thinks something as trivial as a family emergency would be enough to cut me away from her? Of course she does, because what else would you assume when someone you were so close with leaves without so much as a goodbye? I would have assumed the same, had our roles been reversed.

"No, no. That's not… That wasn't the only thing."

"Seriously, it's okay now." Her smile, all wobbly and broken, nearly breaks me right back. "I forgive you, for all of it. Really, I'm glad we're friends now."

"Lottie, I really don't think you get it. I didn't leave because of my grandmother passing." My fingers lift and I tug at my hair. "There was so much more going on, but I just couldn't…"

I *still* can't. I still feel like I'm pushing myself into things that aren't my business. That I'm inserting myself into a life I don't belong in. Making a family of these people that *aren't* my own.

Lottie's head dips down a little, the shorter pieces of the hair by her ears covering most of her face. Her fingers pull at the ends of her oversized shirt, and sage-green eyes stick to the chicken in the pan, watching the oil pop on the edges.

"It was the kiss too. I figured."

My voice gives a firm "no."

I stand straight up, like there is a metal rod keeping me there, my large feet stumbling a little after.

The *kiss*. Such a trite term for what she and I had that night before I left. If that was just a kiss, then the Grand Canyon is merely a crack in the sidewalk. And to think, she had assumed that I left over the one thing that has kept me grounded for years.

My head is shaking violently, like the more I swing it side

to side, the more she'll understand how wrong she is. "Lottie, it was *never* that."

"So, what was it, then?"

It's barely a question—more like a quiet dare. But underneath, I hear it. The doubt. The hesitation. She thinks I left because of her. She has possibly clung to our past in the same way that I have this whole time. Waiting. Wondering. Wishing for more.

"That morning after…everything."

The hay bale, the way we fumbled, and then—God, the way our lips *fit*. Strawberry-flavored kisses, her fingers buried in my hair, tugging, keeping me there with her until the sunrise bled across the horizon. Spread on a checkered blanket, whispered secrets and promises gathering into the late-night and early-morning wind.

"I had to leave, and you were still sleeping, so I was packing all of my bags but couldn't find my spare keys to the locker in the guest area." My tongue feels dry recalling the morning. "I went out to find it in the fields in case I dropped it."

"Oh, so a couple weeks ago wasn't the first time you've had to search for keys in our fields?"

"Right." I smile. "Well, I walked to the bakehouse and saw the lady that used to sneak us extra cookies all the time, the one you didn't like, um…"

"Dahlia?"

The name alone makes my skin crawl. All fried, bleached hair and big puckered lips. "Yeah, her. It was still early; dark enough, so I could see straight through the windows, but they couldn't spot me."

"*They.*" She doesn't phrase it as a question, and despite knowing she's already aware at this point, the confirmation of it in her raspy, emotionless voice still feels like a knife to my gut.

"She and your dad…they weren't doing anything that went too far. But I was old enough to know it was wrong. And I knew it would kill you if you knew."

"Why didn't you tell me?"

My eyes finally reach hers. The hurt lying in them, knowing it's been in them for years, knowing *I'm* the cause…

"Your family was perfect. I didn't want to be the one to shatter it."

Lottie tears her eyes from me to set the spatula on the spoon rest on her oven. I'm almost certain the chicken is done, but I can't put my full attention on anything other than her walking closer. Close enough that she lands a foot away from me, those full lips and tiny chin pointed right up at me.

"Walker, that wouldn't have made you the reason." Her hair shakes as she moves her head. "It would've made *him* the reason."

"I know that now, but at the time, you had that rodeo the next week. You'd practiced all summer; I figured I would tell you after that. Then my mom pulled up earlier than she was supposed to, and I found out about my grandmother, and everything kind of fell apart." I clear my throat. "I should've called. Or at least replied to your emails and texts. Then you stopped reaching out. I thought maybe the whole kiss freaked *you* out, and then me splitting was the final straw for you and our friendship, so I stopped trying to remember it too."

Lottie shakes her head back and forth, replying in only a whisper, "I wouldn't have blamed you for what you saw."

"Yeah, I know."

Her arms cross over her chest, and a row of chill bumps raise on her forearms. "Well, I…I don't know where to go from here."

I glance down at the pan below her, the chicken in it now turning black and smoke rising in the kitchen air.

"Maybe we could just order takeout?" I reach a hand into the extra grocery bag beside us and pull out an old deck of cards. "I've got entertainment while we wait."

CHAPTER SEVENTEEN
Lottie

In some ways, a weight is lifted. In others, it's like more has been added on.

Walker carried that weight of a secret for years without knowing he didn't have to. He ghosted me in some pathetic attempt to save me, and it's equally stupid and wonderful all at once.

With local Chinese takeout ordered and on the way, Walker and I set up a cozy space on my living room floor. Two throw pillows are placed on opposite sides of the coffee table for us to sit, my centerpiece of his hat pushed to the side and a deck of cards splayed out between us as we play another round of seven-card stud.

We've been pretty quiet. Maybe it's the sounds of the night coming from my open screened windows. The chirp of crickets and owls in the near distance. A periodic whirring of someone driving down the gravel road to their other homes on the property, mixed with the pulsing cadence of cicadas. Maybe it's the waiting for food. Maybe we're both just soaking in this moment of two people who had their past reality warped into something new. Regardless, I take my time sitting in this space of the unknown around me.

"You okay? About all of it? You've been quiet."

"I never talk much when dealing a hand with the enemy," I say, smiling as I pick up my hand. I'm going to lose this one, but I don't mind too much. "Besides, I thought maybe the kiss"—my voice croaks—"freaked you out. I feel like I'm in *The Matrix* and I just took the red pill and everything became real."

It takes him a while to respond. I lay down a card. He picks it up.

When he does answer, he speaks in a low voice, making my cheeks go all hot again. "I thought it freaked *you* out."

"Oh, no, it never did."

He nods. "Good."

I nod back. "Mm-hmm."

"Me neither."

"Raise." I set down an added bonus of our currency of Goldfish and Sweet Tarts.

Walker matches with the same amount in our little pile right beside his hat—which neither of us has brought up. "Call."

My nails tap against the cards in my hand. "You…neither what?"

"Hm?"

"You said 'me neither.'"

"Oh." He adjusts the pillow below him. "The kiss didn't freak me out either."

"Oh. Good. Good, good, good."

"Yup." Our eyes stay on the cards like they're possibly going to tell us where to go from here. "*All* good."

We sit in the same comfortable silence as we play one round after the other, taking turns winning back and forth—me a bit more than him. Though I think it's less luck and more him hardly trying.

"So, after your grandmother and everything...what happened then?"

"Well." Walker takes a sip of his drink out of my vintage Pinocchio glasses—I told him they were the only clean ones, but that was a stretch. I just think he looks cute holding tiny things. "First, I focused on graduating and studying for school, but I picked up a job on a ranch too. I started working for Gerald as a butcher's assistant and slowly worked my way up. He let me work for him even though I had plans of going to aerospace school."

"That's where you got the whole drone thing from?"

Walker nods, taking another sip from his Pinocchio glass, and it takes an exuberant amount of effort for me not to giggle. He brought a case of Diet Coke over, and I sliced up some lime and fresh-picked cherries to put on top of the drink poured into my vintage Disney glasses—I feel like my happiness is all built up in my chest and bubbling out of me.

"Kind of. He kept having issues with different diseases in the soil, and it felt like the quickest solution. Took way longer than I thought. I kept waiting for him to give up on me, but with each failed design, he would just pat me on the back and say, 'One more shot tomorrow.'"

My dimples appear. "Sounds like a good boss."

"The best. And an even better friend. He stuck by me till the end, and I swore to do the same for him."

"This is *the* best friend, right?" I reach over and set the hat on my head. Possibly backward. "This one?"

Walker's smile is tilted and beautiful. "The very one."

"Shame I didn't get to meet him. You could've brought him over here."

"He knew you, just not in person."

My back straightens. "He did?"

"I mentioned you. A story here and there." Walker lays down a card, but I don't think he even knows which one. I can't quite say what it is either.

"Really?"

"Mm-hmm."

"Walker, I—" I lean in until my chest is pressed fully into the coffee table.

His eyes are glued to me, golden flecks dancing in the warm light of the lamp shining behind us. His hands hold too many cards, a pile of snacks and candy toppling over next to him, but still, he just holds my gaze. I bounce back and forth between the two pupils. If I stare into them enough, can I pull the memories out myself? Can he see mine? See how empty I am? Can he tell he's looking back at a shell of the human he once knew?

If his eyes stay locked on mine, the truth in mine will match his and he will see every vulnerable cavity in them. Every brokenhearted day of hospital visits, strapped to dozens of wires, so starved and yet no appetite for sterilized tasting food. I fear he'll find the part of me that knows the best version of myself is still back where we left it. He'll see that I peaked when he was last here, and that every version since has only been a downgrade.

If there is a hint of it there, he doesn't show it.

Walker doesn't have the appearance of a man showing pity or disgust. He looks at me like I am a light. Like instead of the lamp behind me, *I* am the one lighting him up.

"Lottie," he whispers from his soft lips.

There is an entire table between us, covered in junk food and old decks of cards, but the way he looks at me tells me the space means absolutely nothing. Like a mile of space wouldn't stop him from leaning closer. My thighs and butt feel numb from sitting on the floor for almost an hour, but I don't have a single care beyond wondering if Walker is leaning closer to me for…

His mouth opens again, but before he can speak, my doorbell rings, loud and obnoxious and overwhelming.

"Who is that?" Walker is still whispering.

"The food." I don't know why I whisper back.

Once the food is paid for, Walker leaves the delivery guy a hefty tip and sets the food on the table beside our cards.

Slow music is playing over my radio, the room softly lit and golden. I have the most delicious meal inches away from my mouth, but all I can taste is the way he's looking at me.

CHAPTER EIGHTEEN
Lottie

I realize it's a blessing to have so many people you love living so close to you.

The only downside to that is you can't make up some stupid reason to pull out of mandatory family dinners to just stay home. All they have to do is walk half a mile and they can see the shining of your TV through the blinds to know you are indeed not "down with something" and "going to bed early."

Tonight's inability to cancel is due to a monthly book club hosted at Flick's. *Book club* being a bit of a stretch, considering there are only four of us total and at the very most two actually read the books. So it's less of a club and more of a bi-monthly gathering where Flick rants about the MMC's muscles and communication skills while the rest of us listen and binge on barbecue salads and locally made cream sodas.

Flick's hands move in exaggerated poses as she plays out the scene.

"Okay, so, then he lifts up Bennett and tosses her over his shoulder, and she's like, 'Oh my gosh, you big strong man, let me go,' and she's slapping his back, but then Ashley—"

"Wait, I thought Ashley was the FMC?"

"No, *Bennett* is the FMC. Ashley is the MMC."

Ada tosses back a dried apricot and talks with her mouth full. "I'm lost. Why is she on his shoulder?"

"HELP!" a loud shout comes from the dining room. Ada and Odelia scan the house for the culprit of the screaming, but I am more than accustomed to this yelling. Nigel shakes his tail feathers in his cage in protest for…who knows, really.

"Nigel!" Flick gasps, hand clutching her imaginary pearls. "You gave me a fright."

"Gave you a fright? Is that what we're calling it now?" Ada squints from my best friend to her bird in his overwhelmingly large cage taking up the majority of the dining space—hence why we're eating on the sectional.

Odie lifts a hand to her chest, catching her breath. "Great heavens."

"Nigel, love, lower your voice," Flick commands.

"Nigel needs to lower the insanity, more like it," I murmur.

"He's been doing better, guys, seriously. Watch this." Flick goes to her bird, or maybe tiny alien taking host in a bird, and lets him out of the cage to rest on her shoulder. "Nigel, say 'pretty bird.' Who's a pretty bird? Pretty Nigel." Flick coos to him like any loving mother would, and after a moment of our conjoined silence, he leans forward, opens his mouth, and shouts "EAT SHIT" back at her.

Flick sighs. "How am I ever going to get this little guy a family?"

"Does Knox like him?" Odie asks, her hands sorting the food on her plate by colors.

"I think Knox is going behind my back and cursing to him so he can stay here when he visits."

Nigel inches his way down Flick's body and waddles over to the couch, climbing up the side arm to sit right next to me.

"Hello, Nigel," I mutter under my breath.

He squawks back at me.

"Maybe Walker could take care of him?" Flick asks.

She says *Walker* like it's the title of a cheesy adult movie, with a raspy voice and fluttering lashes. Odelia and Ada stare at me as if I have been keeping a giant secret. Maybe I have. I haven't told any of them about the list, or the fact that Walker and I have seen each other almost every day for over the past week.

Sometimes it's just in passing, a quick good morning on the front porch or a good night as he knocks on the wall shared between our two bedrooms. Sometimes it's waving from afar and a quick text with a hello after. But it's always something.

Today it was him doing an oil change on his truck in our shared driveway…shirtless. Golden, tan skin leaned over the engine of a truck doing whatever people do when changing their oil. His jeans hung low on his hips, a sliver of his black boxers poking out from the top.

There was a point where I drooled on the back of my couch as I pretended that I was cleaning my windows with a dry paper towel.

The worst part of it all: I couldn't just stay inside. I *had* to leave the house. As in, pass by him in all his shirtlessness to walk my way over here.

Walker rolled out from under the car and his face lit up in a smile. "Hi, Trouble."

My ears burned. "Hi, Walker."

His eyes dropped to my pajamas, a simple matching cotton shorts and tank top set that all of the other girls have on too. It's tradition, and if I don't show up in the matching attire, I will be sent right back home to change, with an escort.

His brows kick up a bit. "Fun night planned?"

"Book club. At Flick's... *Pirates*." Why did I whisper the last part?

"Very nice." He nodded and leaned back to the rolling thing, and I swear his navel was staring directly at me with no shame.

My cheeks are bright red now, and I can feel the heat of my entire body rushing to my face thinking about the whole encounter. "Don't say his name like that."

"*Walk-errr*." Odelia tries to say his name in the same sexual tone as the other two, but it comes out with a hiccup halfway through, and her cheeks flush bright red.

The other three of us are snorting, pirate books and charcuterie boards long forgotten with everyone's minds stuck on my neighbor.

"So strange." Nigel is now less than an inch from my shoulder. His little claws keep reaching out like he's going to climb up to me but can't decide if it's worth it.

Ada raises her glass, eyes twinkling with mischief. "I think what's *strange* here is there is an extremely cute cowboy one wall away from you, and you haven't told us anything about it."

"Not to mention he was her first kiss."

"Flick!"

Odelia scooches her tush across the couch until she is inches away from me. "We need details on this Walker guy."

I don't know what there is to say except...

"He is great."

"*Great*," Ada mocks. "I need details, lady."

I catch them up on what I can but leave the lists out of it. Something about that part feels like it's our thing, just mine and Walker's. And I don't like the idea of sharing it with everyone else. I do, however, accidentally slip up about seeing him outside the practice arena a couple days ago, and well…

"Sonja told me she saw you and Kit practicing riding." Ada wiggles her brows up and down.

"*CHARLOTTE TURNER*!" Flick turns around with the fierceness of a mother yelling at her teenager for sneaking in the liquor cabinet.

"You can't ride!" Odie joins in, but then hears her own volume and tucks her voice back down to its normal whisper. "I mean…maybe you *can,* but it just really seems unsafe, and I love you."

Flick nods. "Agreed. We need you safe and sound."

Safe and sound. If I had a nickel for every time I heard those words, I'd have a lot of nickels.

"It's not like that. I'm not the one riding. Plus." I sigh and smile. "It's the most fun I've had in years."

Ada claps her hands together. "Well, I think it's *great.*" She mocks my use of the word earlier, and I toss a pillow at her face. "Just no one tell Knox, and we will be all good."

Everyone turns to Flick with wide eyes.

"What?" she asks on the defensive, mouth full of cheese.

"I love you. But you and my brother literally have no secrets between each other," I accuse.

"It's called friendship."

Ada mumbles under her breath, "It's called denial."

"Hey!"

"It's true." Odie joins in her quiet tone. "You can't tell Knox."

"Okay, okay. Fine. But let the record state, I will never lie to him, so if he directly asks, then I'm going to say yes."

"Fair."

CHAPTER NINETEEN
Walker

The morning air is thick with sawdust and damp earth, the kind that clings to my skin and settles in my lungs. The back of my arms burn from hauling lumber back and forth from the drop site to the back shop where all of the equipment rests. Despite the growing ache in my lower back, I don't stop. Won't stop.

I was supposed to work on this shop with Knox. That's what he texted me at four a.m., at least. But when I showed up, it was just Lottie's dad under the awning here with the small explanation that Knox had "other matters to handle." A simple nod was all he got back from me.

It's been half an hour of us moving lumber, and I have yet to acknowledge him.

I don't think he remembers me, or if he does, he's specifically ignoring the fact.

If he notices my sour mood at being near him, he doesn't say anything about that either.

Technically, I think he's my boss. If you're looking at it in that kind of way. But I'd rather get fired and just pay rent on the sister house than try to suck up to the man that tore his entire family apart.

"Hand me that beam if you can." Jason dips his chin to the beam beside me. His voice is perfectly nice, and if it were anyone else, I'd respond.

Instead, I don't answer or argue. Just grip my gloved fingers around the plank and shove it toward him, watching as he takes it like the weight means nothing. He's still strong for his age, built solid from years of work. Figures. A man like him, strong enough to hold a family together, and he *chose* not to. He chose to break his perfect life and let his daughter fall with him.

At least with my family being broken, my parents still loved each other. They were shitty parents. But they were never unfaithful to each other or their marriage. Wouldn't have found the time, even if they wanted to.

We both work in silence, hammering beams into place, reinforcing the back wall of the shop that's slowly getting dry rot. Taking out all the bad, replacing it with all the good. It's the kind of work I know—the kind that makes sense.

"You've been working on farms long?" Jason asks after a while.

I exhale through my nose. He wants small talk? Not gonna happen.

A nod, like that tells him enough.

"Figured. You know what you're doing."

No response. Just work. That's all this is. Work. *Just keep your head down and don't explode.* He's Lottie's dad. He's still someone she respects, regardless of what we've both seen.

Still, in my mind, he'll always be the man that caused her to leave everything she ever wanted behind. If he hadn't been in that house with the door locked—probably cheating on his wife—then she wouldn't have climbed that tree and we wouldn't be here. Accident or not, it's still his fault.

But the words press up against my ribs, clawing to get out. *Why'd you do it? Why'd you break your own family like that? Why'd you break her like that?*

The hammer under my strength slams down harder than it needs to.

Jason sighs. "You got somethin' you wanna say, son?"

The word *son* lands wrong. Too familiar, too easy, like he hasn't spent years being a man I wanted nothing to do with.

"You don't gotta like me," he continues, and even in his own upfront way, he keeps his tone light. "But if you got a problem, let's put it on the table."

I straighten, gripping the hammer tight. He wants it all on the table?

"Alright," I say, turning to face him. "What was it? Just needed some younger woman? Or just got tired of bein' a husband and father?"

He stills. Just for a second. Then a slow exhale, like he's already too tired for this conversation.

"You think you know the whole story, huh?"

My jaw locks. "I know Knox heard Lottie cry herself to sleep over you more nights than she'll ever admit. I know you're at least part of the reason for her having epilepsy, if not the whole reason. For her never being able to ride again. I know your wife and kids deserved better than—" My teeth grind together, shoving down the words *a cheating bastard.* I take a deep breath and readjust my grip. "You tell me what part I got wrong."

He looks at me for a long time, something unreadable in his face. No anger. No defensiveness. Just quiet.

"I've made mistakes," he finally lands on. "Plenty. But not the ones you think."

"Yeah? Then why'd you let everything fall apart? Why do you go along pretending you and your wife and your family are all perfectly fine?"

His gaze flickers toward the house, where Lottie disappeared a while ago.

"Sometimes," he says, voice low, "people believe what they need to get by with their day."

I don't know what the hell that's supposed to mean. But before I can snap back, he picks up another beam and keeps working, like nothing happened.

I know one thing for sure—as long as I'm here, I'm making sure no one breaks Lottie's heart like he did.

CHAPTER TWENTY
Lottie

It's nine o'clock when I get a text from Walker. It would be a lie to say I haven't been checking my phone obsessively since we spoke this afternoon about a potential plan to work on the list tonight. It's like my head has been playing this trick on me all day long. Singing this persistent song in my head like an earworm I just can't kick.

Walker. Walker. Walker. Walker.

Walker: You up?

Me: Sleep texting.

Three sharp knocks then two slow ones sound on the other side of my wall, the vibrations bouncing through my headboard. I reach a hand up and knock back three more times in confirmation that I am indeed up.

Walker: Are you up enough for an adventure?

Me: What kind?

I smile at the attached picture of his countertop covered in toilet paper with Kit standing right next to it in plaid pajamas with a shy smile.

Me: You were serious about toilet papering someone's house?

Walker: Initially, no. But the kid talked me into it at work today when I mentioned it. Said he's never gone, and I feel like it's a senior year tradition, so you kind of have to do it.

Walker: We're not going far, I promise.

Walker: I'll keep you safe.

I really need to sleep. I haven't had a good rest in the last few nights and I know I'm already pushing my body out of routine more than I should. But then again…

I slip over to Walker's front door, where he slings it open before I can even knock.

The sight in front of me is, as best as I can describe it, that of a high school, pajamaed-up version of *Call of Duty*. Walker takes up the majority of the door frame, navy long-sleeved shirt covering what I know lies underneath and plaid pajama pants similar to Kit's, but his are filled out where our small friend is drowning in his, the strings tied as tight as possible.

Their outfits alone wouldn't be suspicious, but the ski masks stand out.

I point between their covered faces. "Is that necessary?"

"It adds to the excitement." Walker reaches to the nearby side table, holding up a bright pink ski mask that is a bit smaller than theirs, a big smile across his face. "We got you one too."

Five minutes and a whole lot of arguing about this mask later, we are loaded up. Arms full of cheap toilet paper rolls, ski masks pulled down over our faces, whispering our plans for covering as much ground as possible. We round the corner, walking slowly down the gravel road and through the trees to Riley's cabin down by the creek.

More specifically, the cabin which happens to be hosting Flick since last January. Flick has always jumped from home to home, thanks to her mother that is labeled in my phone as Cruella de Vil, but Riley's is by far the most stable she has landed on.

Kit, in the worst whisper I have ever heard, says, "My blood is pumping. This is insane." He is glancing in every single direction like a seagull on the beach searching for half-eaten fries.

"Do me a favor and never try recreational drugs," I say.

"I won't need to after tonight. I'm high on life."

When we get close enough to see all the lights off in the house, Walker turns toward me, walking backward, and glances from my pink face to the toilet paper in my arms. He lets out a little snort.

"You look cute."

My cheeks burn brighter than my mask. "Shut up."

"Seriously, you're like a law-breaking Teletubby or something."

"That is *not* the compliment you think it is."

Kit, at a completely normal volume, says, "You guys suck at whispering."

"Guys," I hiss, "we are all way too loud to be doing this at nine p.m."

"Is it that late already?" Kit hisses back. "Can we hurry up?"

"Got big plans tonight?" Walker whispers, but it is still way louder than it should be.

"Yeah, big plans with your mom. Biggest plans she's ever had," Kit retorts.

We approach Riley and Flick's house, the new baby ducks on the front porch starting to pop their little heads up from their heat-lamped pen. Thankfully, momma duck is fast asleep to their right. If there's anything to fear in this juvenile mission, it's her.

"Alright, who's going first?" Walker asks, but it's too late. My hand has already reached back and is mid-throw with one of the fifteen-something rolls I am holding. Apparently, I am far better at chucking keys into a field when I'm pissed off, because the roll goes straight up into the air and lands two feet away from me. Not a single hit of damage done.

Walker rolls his eyes, picks up one of the many rolls, and tosses it. White paper flies through the wind like an Olympic javelin before landing on the roof and rolling down.

I follow his movements, and we take turns seeing how far we can throw and racing to get as much coverage as possible; it's absurd and juvenile and so odd, but I don't know the last time I've had this much fun.

After a moment, I realize we're the only ones throwing. I turn around, and Kit is behind us shredding up little squares and scattering them all over the lawn like sprinkles on a confetti cake.

"Kit," Walker and I hiss in unison.

"What is that?" I point to the toilet paper shreds.

"Little damage adds up to big damage," Kit explains.

And because maybe we are a little high on life, too, Walker and I both bend over laughing at that, and like always, I let out a snort similar to that of a pig. This makes Walker all but fall over with spurts of chortles, too, and then Kit can't stop choking on his laughter at the two of us turning red in the face, our masks slipping and rolls dropping into the grass.

The ducklings on the porch have a perfect view of all three of us bent over in the lawn laughing, not one of us throwing the toilet paper.

Suddenly, a porch light comes on and the birds start chirping like a warning sign. The mother duck gets up and ruffles her back feathers. Walker starts frantically grabbing rolls and I whisper, "Just leave them."

I turn to tell Kit it's time to go, but he is already halfway up the gravel road in a full sprint. Maybe it's the previous spurts of laughter or just the fact that I am a bit delirious from lack of sleep, but I can't quite force myself to run. I mean, I try. But it's like running underwater or trying to win a marathon in your dream. My limbs are sluggish and heavy. I'm kind of moving, but not really.

Knox comes running out in his boxers with a paintball gun in hand, because of course he's at Flick's house at nine thirty on a Tuesday.

"I'm not doing this again, Patricia!"

That has even Walker laughing in front of me. He turns to look over his shoulder and apparently doesn't like my proximity to my brother, because he takes a few steps back and lifts me over his shoulder in an instant.

"Who's Patricia?" he asks.

"Our mail lady. It's a *very* long story."

I can't stop laughing even as I bounce up and down on

my friend's shoulder. I can't see much in the dark, but I can hear Knox running faster behind us, and I watch as he aims the paintball gun.

"Take this, Richard."

My brother puts his finger on the trigger and pulls it, and I watch the entire scene play out in front of me in slow motion.

With Walker running mid-laugh, my head tucked into the crease between his collar and his jaw, a smidge of bright green hurls toward us before landing straight on Walker's back. The paint splatters across his back, and because I am bent halfway over him, all over my hair. My bright blond strands are now a vivid lime green, the ends stuck to Walker's shirt.

Walker hisses out a loud "Shit!" which, with his accent, sounds more like "shi-at." His entire body tenses and he picks up the pace, getting us around the corner of the trees, my brother stopping in his tracks at the end of the gravel driveway.

When we're sure Knox isn't close behind us, we meet Kit on Walker's front porch and slip inside. All three of us are in his living room, crouching with no lights on, dying with laughter as we hear Knox calling out our precious mail lady's name.

I'll have to call her tomorrow and prepare her for the storm coming her way. She's quite used to it by now, I imagine.

When he passes our houses to turn toward the main entrance, I slip off the couch and walk to the kitchen, turning a light on to check out the damage.

Walker looks completely normal in the front, save for the tight, red outlines on his face from the ski mask previously being there. Kit, however, is covered in bright green paint from his right side up.

"I didn't think he got you." I wince at the paint covering his hair. It's even in his ear. When did his hair fall out of the mask?

"He got me." He cusses under his breath and holds his ribs. "That hurt more than I thought it would." Kit lifts his shirt, revealing his skinny frame to show a bruise forming on his side. "I gotta use your shower."

Walker shrugs. "Down the hall, first bedroom on the right. Should be towels in there."

Kit slips out of the room, hobbling and whispering promises of never hanging out with us again.

"I don't feel bad," I say once the bathroom door shuts behind him.

"He could've said no."

"Well, he definitely will from now on."

Walker smiles and lifts his hand to pick up a piece of my hair. He raises it up enough to show me the green. "I hope this doesn't stain, or we'll be outed pretty fast."

"Maybe we can wash it out?" My nostrils flare as my own fingers pull at the green paint. "Did it get in yours?"

It's sticky and somewhat crunchy all at once, and I am slightly frightful of what my ends will look like tomorrow.

Walker turns to show me the damage on his back, and there's not much paint in his hair, but it is all over his neck where the mask snagged on my wrists when he was running. I suck in a breath. "Did it hurt?"

He turns and gives me a puppylike pout. "So bad."

"Really?"

"You might have to help."

"Help with what?" I laugh.

"Getting all the paint off. Believe it or not, I actually can't see the back of my head."

My throat tightens. "You have two showers?"

My place just has one shower and a half bath in the hall. And the shower is extremely cozy—which basically means it barely fits one normal-sized person at most. Well, not without touching, and by that, I mean…*touching*.

He makes an odd choking noise in the back of his throat. His cheeks darken in color and his eyes look over my shoulder. "I was more so thinking the sink…"

I follow his gaze and see the large porcelain farmhouse sink behind me. And common sense feels like a smack to the face.

Obviously he didn't mean for us to shower together. Because why would he? Was I honestly expecting the two of us to squish behind those small glass doors and wash each other's hair and shoulders and who knows what else? We have kissed *once*. We have flirted, in my mind, a multitude of times. Big deal. I've flirted around before, and I am sure Walker won't be the last one I flirt with.

I force myself to meet his gaze. Shoot, with that reassuring smile and the blush he's sporting on his cheekbones, he just might be the last one.

CHAPTER TWENTY-ONE
Walker

Hot water burns the tips of my fingers, so I turn the knob to the right so it won't scald Lottie's skin.

When I manage to speak again, it's scattered. "Grab a chair, yeah? It'll be easier on your neck that way."

Lottie nods, and a few moments later, we have a makeshift hair-washing station in my kitchen. My wooden chair is pushed against the front of it and a towel rolled up and placed right where our necks should rest, with two extra towels folded and placed to the side. Lottie snuck over to her place to grab shampoo since Kit was still in the shower.

"You want to go first, or me?" Lottie clasps her hands and twists her body side to side.

"I can go first, mine will probably be the quickest since it's just the back of my hair and yours is..."

"Everywhere?"

"Pretty much."

She laughs and taps the back of the chair. "Saddle up, space cowboy."

I smile and take the seat, leaning my head back for her to wash.

Lottie pauses and I lift my head up a little. This is the oddest position I never imagined myself in with my pretty neighbor.

"Your shirt." She tugs on the edge of my sleeve. "You probably should take it off."

"Yes, ma'am." I sit up and pull the fabric over my head with one hand. It slides down my arms, and I toss it to the side so it's not in the way.

When my head is in the right position, shirt gone, and dignity checked at the door, Lottie finally gets started.

If I thought about it before now, I maybe would've just suggested we wash our own hair in our own showers later. Or maybe I would've gone right along with her thought of taking this to the shower.

What I didn't think of ten minutes ago was how I would have to tamp down every raw, primal male instinct that rushes through my blood when Charlotte Jane Turner has her hands in my hair, leaning over me, the smell of her perfume mixing with the shampoo.

My eyelids feel heavy as her fingernails dig into every perfect spot, like she knows exactly what I need and where I need it. I can't tell if I'm falling asleep or floating into heaven. How am I supposed to ever get my hair cut by someone else? The old guy that always nicks the back of my neck and expects a hefty tip has nothing on her.

She leans in closer, her fingers running rhythmic circles on the top of my head, which we both know paint isn't on. I don't move an inch in fear that she'll eventually stop. I hold back a groan, my mind screaming for more. The urge to pull her in my arms—to cross that line with her—grows unbearable.

And when she does a slow pull, thumbs massaging from the base of my neck up to behind my ears, all the way to the top of my head, teasing and pulling, I let out a low, deep, guttural noise.

The groans coming out of me are quiet, and they threaten to build. The way Lottie's fingers fit just right where my hair meets my neck, thumbs pressing deliciously, there is no holding back the noises escaping me.

"You're way too good at this." I try to keep my voice straight, but it deepens into something lower when she switches her pointed pressure into something light and gentle through my hair.

Lottie chuckles. "Flick made me take a massage class with her last winter to get me out of the house."

"It shows." I sound like I've taken half a bottle of NyQuil and won't resurface from my bed for approximately two business days.

Lottie scoffs above me and her own green-tipped hair slides in front of me, tickling my exposed neck. "You're just saying that."

"Mmm. Serious, you should do this for a living."

"What? Washing men's hair?"

"No, washing my hair."

She laughs, and it feels like tiny bubbles popping in my chest. I feel like I drank the fizzy lifting drink from *Charlie and the Chocolate Factory* and will never come back down; I'm just floating off somewhere in the distance with my head in the clouds. I can't get enough of that laugh. In every way it comes.

Small puffs of air when she's slightly amused.

Chuckles building up when she can't hide a smile.

Bubbling laughter when she knows it's too funny not to laugh.

Full-on snorts when she can't hold herself back; that's my favorite. That's the goal every time I make a stupid joke or toss her over my shoulder.

"Sounds boring. I'd only get to work for like ten minutes once a day," she says.

This is the furthest thing from boring I have ever experienced. I could stay in this position, neck cramping and feet going numb, for days. Weeks.

"No. You'd be surprised how long I could do this. I'm about to fall asleep."

"You better not, it's almost my turn, and mine is way worse than yours."

When Lottie is content with whatever lack of paint I have left, she turns off the water and uses a spare towel to dry off my hair just enough so it's not dripping. She pats the back of the chair, two quick vibrations sliding down my bare back.

"Alrighty, mister. It's my turn. Hop up."

I reluctantly stand, a little dizzy and out of it. Lottie happily plops herself down on my chair and gathers her thick blond hair over her shoulders to let it delicately drape over my sink, green ends mixing with the water already there. She was right: Hers is way worse than mine was.

I turn the knob where she had it previously, the water coming out steaming.

Lifting up the pink bottle she has laid on the counter that says *Shampoo* in a fancy script font, I ask, "This one?"

"Mm-hmm." She closes her eyes and leans into the hot water.

My hands are hesitant, but I push through and go for it, my hands tangling in her hair and the floral smell of her shampoo filling my nose. Like the magnolia tree we used to lay under after stealing strawberries. Or like the fresh air on midsummer days when we walked down the streets of Oak Ridge, her pointing out every landmark and every stranger that never stayed a stranger for long. It mixes with the smell of watermelon ChapStick and stolen kisses.

When I glance down from the lather I have building up on her ends, I see Lottie staring up at me with those big green doe eyes. Her lashes flutter and she looks like she knows every inch of my brain and yet is entirely innocent. I know that look. It's the same one she gives during her many card tricks.

It's the same one a great deal of guys must've fallen for.

"Stop that." I don't look away while I keep washing her hair. I keep my eyes locked right on hers, and when her pink mouth falls open in feigned surprise, I am not buying a second of it.

"What?" Her lashes flicker again and I think I groan deeper than when her thumbs massaged my scalp.

"That."

"I'm literally just sitting here."

"Oh no, you know what you're doing."

"What am I doing?" Lottie laughs and my head is above the clouds, floating among stars and comets and other forces of the universe that could never hold a candle to her at this moment.

"Looking at me like that."

"Walker!" She gasps through her smile and even as my cheeks are turning red, I keep my gaze on hers. "I'm not doing anything."

"You are, flirt."

"Who says I'm flirting?"

"You didn't have to say it. I know what flirting looks like."

"Oh, you do? Explain what it looks like to me, then."

"It looks like me going to my least favorite grocery store

just because I saw you slide in there in those denim shorts with the flowers on them."

It's been four days since we circled the aisles together, laughing at the commotion of Miss Anita Harris waddling down the aisle, watching us and sending out live updates through the phone tree—which she forgot we were both on.

There's a shy smile on Lottie's face, just below her button nose. "You…you were looking at me?"

"Yes, but it would be a lie to say it wasn't the shorts that did me in."

"Every other girl in this town has the same shorts."

"None of them are you, though."

"Walker." She laughs and closes her eyes, breaking our contact. "You are not talking about this out loud."

"Am I not supposed to?"

"No, this is the kind of thing you keep to yourself."

"I've always had a hard time keeping things from you." I shrug. "You know that."

"I know." She smiles up at me. "Keep washing. I better get the same treatment I gave you."

"If you really wanted the same treatment, then your shirt would be off like mine was."

"Oh my gosh." Her laughter bounces through the room, and I feel all my holding back just melt away. "You are letting it all out tonight. Is this like your flirty alter ego?"

"Yes, this is my stand-in when I'm too embarrassed to say what I'm thinking. Runner."

"Runner?"

"Yes. Walker takes things slow, he thinks about it all before he says it. Runner just goes for it."

"Oh, I see. I like this Runner."

"He's one of a kind, I hear."

Her teeth bite down on her lower lip with that same smile, her eyes shut, and I take every moment of this as one I get to keep.

I get to a particular piece of hair where the paint is in one thick knot and try to stay all gentle and tender, but it won't come loose. Lottie lets out a yelp when I try to lace my fingers through it, and I wince.

"Sorry, baby." I let the word slip out in a whisper before I can catch it.

It could be because we've reached that time of night where secrets don't feel so secret and whispered names feel like promises. Or maybe because I have my pretty neighbor's hair in my hands and I can't stop smelling this fruity, floral mixture that has my head in a loop. Or maybe I blame that on "Runner" too.

I should probably take it back, make up some apology for not meaning to call her that. But she hums beneath me with a sly grin and closed, satisfied eyes, and I wonder if she didn't mind it much either.

When I finish washing all the paint out, Lottie insists on me doing the rest of her routine, resulting in a full conditioning mask and a "gloss"—whatever that is—that apparently has to sit for five minutes minimum before being washed out.

"So this is how you get perfect hair," I tease.

"Well, it didn't come naturally. Just look at Knox."

I snort and lean against the counter. "I should probably check on Kit. He's been in there for a while."

"Wait," Lottie whines. "You can't leave me stuck like this."

"You're not stuck." I point to the rolled-up towel behind her. "You have a pillow. And I'll be right back, I just want to make sure he's—"

"He's fine. I, however, am starting to feel my ears go numb."

"Can you ever feel your ears?"

"Mmm. Sometimes. I think."

The water shuts off from my bathroom, the pipes making a clear thud that tells me Kit is fine in there. Lottie raises her right brow at me as if to say, *See?*

I settle back into a chair beside her. "You do this five-minute thing every time you shower?"

"I try to. Sometimes I don't if I'm in a rush."

"Seems exhausting. I usually just use a two-in-one."

Lottie gags, literally gags, beneath me.

"What?"

"Two-in-ones should be illegal."

"They're productive."

"Walker," she deadpans. "Do you like your ketchup and mayonnaise mixed together?"

"Let's have some decency."

"Do you prefer your food all just dumped into a blender and tossed up so you can drink it like a smoothie?"

I sigh her name.

"Do you think we should just stop using spoons and forks separately? Let's just make every utensil a spork. Why even bother having both?"

"You know"—I take a step back to check the time before leaning against the counter—"one time I bought a four-in-one."

She gasps like it's blasphemy. "What were the other two?"

"Body wash and shaving cream."

"I take my flirting back, this is, *by far*, the least sexy conversation I have ever had."

After the five minutes are up and I've got everything rinsed out of Lottie's hair, she is sitting up and stretching with a yawn. She smiles, tosses her hair up into one of my T-shirts, and takes a few steps toward my front door, checking through the glass until she is confident that Knox is nowhere to be found.

"Guess it's safe for me to go."

"If you'd like."

She's quiet for a moment, and I wonder briefly if she'll ask me to come back to her place. Or to just…stay here. If we stand here any longer, I'll blurt out for her to stay. To just keep letting me hear her voice and watch that smile over and over again.

I almost say it, but she reaches one hand over to my arm, fingers curling around my bicep, soft and gentle. My eyes are stuck on them when she whispers a low, "Night, Walker."

"Night, Miss Lottie," I whisper back, a smile in my voice.

"No." She removes her hand to point toward my room. "Only he can call me that."

"And only I can call you Trouble?"

This slow creep of a smirk forms on her pink lips and she looks down my chest and back up to my eyes. "Baby sounds pretty good too."

An amused puff of air leaves my nose and I am smiling at the ground. "Good to know."

I take a step closer. She follows. She leans forward an inch. I follow. Her irises bounce all over my face, meanwhile mine are locked on hers. Waiting for whatever she needs next. Whatever I can give her next.

She pushes her chest closer to me. We're inches apart and I think she might just—

There's a scratching noise and a book falls off the shelf behind me, scaring us both.

We turn to see that actually, it's three books this time. I guess Henry really doesn't like to third wheel.

CHAPTER TWENTY-TWO
Walker

Growing up, everyone told me how lucky I was.

I should've felt lucky. Anything I wanted to do, I could get away with. If I came home at sixteen completely hammered on a school night, not one person would blink an eye in my house.

But it was those moments that felt the loneliest. When friends went back to their strict but warm homes and the late hours of night led into the early cracks of dawn, that was when I thought of my one happy place. A place that was bright and sunny and never made me feel like I was lucky, but merely like I was a normal kid. Where a pretty green-eyed blond smiled up at me, grabbed my hand in hers, and asked if I wanted to try something new.

If I ever knew what luck was, I knew it then. I've never felt luckier than I did propped against a bale with Charlotte Turner sitting beside me.

Everything about this whole situation has me between a rock and a hard place—if I take the internship, I'll lose her. If

I don't take the job and stay here, she knows exactly why. Oak Ridge is a great town, and Willow Creek is the best part of that town. Groundhogs, ghosts, and all—it's incredible, really. All of that is still not enough to keep me here.

She is, though.

If I refuse this job and extend this season into fall, through winter, back to spring, and another summer, Lottie will have no doubt I said no to the internship merely because of her. The woman is like a bloodhound sniffing out commitment.

I can't even find it in me to ask her out on a single date; the closest thing I can do is try to find ridiculous ways to turn this list into ways I can be alone with her. If she had the slightest hint about my lack of enthusiasm toward the NASA job being related to her, we would be back at square one. Friends to strangers to friends, and then strangers again. An endless time loop neither of us can leave.

I am tiptoeing through a minefield, praying each stride is the right one.

I got another voicemail tonight. This one from my mom. The sound of her voice almost made me a bit nostalgic. She was always the quieter of the two. Dad mostly yelled if he wasn't ignoring me, but she was like a ghost.

Something about her leaving the voicemail this time, the sturdy sound of her voice, proper as always, left me shaky.

"Walker…your father knows what is best for you. He has many people watching his decisions. You'd be doing him a noble service by taking this job. For goodness' sake, it is everything you should need. I doubt anything else in that dirt town can impress you. Call him. Goodbye."

That *dirt town*. She knows where I am. She has to.

My shoulders shiver at the thought of one of them being here. In my own happy place where nothing from them should even touch the air. I slipped away after I listened to the message, leaving my phone behind me, and walked to the one place I could think best at.

Though, admittedly, even against this old magnolia tree, I can't shake the feeling of this pit growing bigger in my stomach. This dread that every second I have here may be closer and closer to the last I get. The last I could get of Lottie too. I can't give her up yet. I'm growing more addicted to her with every item we complete on the list. Every night, she knocks a poorly rhythmed tune against her wall, and I knock it right back. Every day, we have a passing interaction on the front porch when I get off work filthy and exhausted and she is sitting pretty and perfectly clean, shuffling a deck of cards with a dare in her eyes.

It's like time never passed between us.

I bite into one of the strawberries I snuck up here, and memories flood back like a movie playing in my head. Five summers of getting to play house with the perfect family.

But no matter how much I don't want it to, fall always comes just around the corner.

Footsteps sound in the near distance, and I don't have to tear my head from the sunset in front of me to know who it is. I recognize those soft treads.

"You stole my spot." Lottie's voice feels like warm honey against my skin, and I shut my eyes, head tilted back.

"Guilty." I take my time looking back at her. She's less than three feet away in denim overall shorts, a small excuse for a white tank top underneath. She's got on those red boots again, worn at the tips, and she twists them around the dry dirt. I smile. "Though, are we sure it's not my spot?"

She squints. "Feels like it's my spot, you know... *my* land and all."

"Feels like it's actually my spot…*my* first kiss and all."

"Unfair, it was also my first kiss." She waves a hand to point at my side. "Scoot over."

I do as I'm told, settling on my side of the tree. I lift up the basket of strawberries and set them in my lap before patting the open seat beside me.

Lottie smiles and plops herself next to me, the smell of her shampoo coming off her in waves. I wonder if there's a way I can get paint in her hair again just to let my hands get tangled in it. She lifts a single strawberry to her mouth and takes a deep breath through her nose.

"Thought you didn't like strawberries anymore?" she asks.

"I…have had a recent hankering for them." *They're the closest thing I can get to tasting you.*

She bites into the large one between her fingers, red juice dripping down her pink lips to her chin. "Really?"

"I may have also been hoping that your bloodhound nose would sniff them out and join me."

"Well, you hoped right. Here I am."

"Here you are."

I watch, entranced, as Lottie continuously takes sweet, sucking bites of the strawberries. She lets out soft, drawn-out moans like she hasn't tasted these a million times. The freckles on her cheeks stretch, and I find myself counting them one by one.

Lottie knows she's pretty. That much is clear. But what I don't think she understands is, in moments like these—freckle-faced and dressed down, strawberry juice trailing down her tan neck into her white tank top—she's the most incredible thing I've ever seen.

She hums around a strawberry before asking, "How's your back?"

"Hmm?"

"Where my brother shot you."

"You make it sound more violent than it was."

"I think he had dangerous intentions to be fair."

"It's fine. Got a bruise the size of a fist." I lift my hand to show an example, and she purses her lips, my attention falling back to them again.

"The size of *your* fist or my fist?"

"Does it matter?"

"Of course." She lifts her dainty fingers up to my hand. I shiver a bit when her cool hand wraps around my warm one—she always said I was so warm. A personal heater. But that was back when we could hug, wrap our arms around each other and not wonder where to go from there. Now every touch feels like a question of just how far I can go.

I open my hand for her, and she pulls it closer to her with a smile, as if it's the most casual thing. As if the warmth of our skin pressed firm to each other doesn't have her on a rollercoaster ride.

"See?" She lays her palm flat against mine, the size difference made perfectly clear. "If it's the size of my fist, you're a big baby. The size of your fist, you're like a war hero."

"Then I'm going to go with the size of my fist."

"Solid choice."

I take a leap and let my fingers fit in the spaces between hers, sliding them down to where our hands are clasped and there's nothing between them. The pad of her thumb toys with the broad expanse of my hand, pressing and running smooth circles over it. I have grease stains that are so deeply set in that no amount of scrubbing will take them off. Her nails are pink with white flowers on them, and I have an intense urge to let them trail wherever she wants to.

She reaches for the strawberry basket and sets it on her lap, our thighs pressing against each other. It shouldn't have my adrenaline pumping, endorphins firing off like rockets. But still, as we eat our strawberries in mostly silence beyond the quiet discussions of our day, my heart is racing.

Hers was "slow." It's how she describes most of her days if she's not either working on the list or working with Kit on riding. She did more research on techniques to fit Kit's body type, telling me how she thinks this week he can ride a bull fully on his own. And how obnoxious the kid will be once he does.

I tell her of my day—how it was my turn this morning for feeding time. The cows bellowing impatiently in the far left field, looking at me like I was late, despite the sun not even rising yet. Horses stomping their hooves, eager for their morning meal before I had to head into the back field with Knox, Miller, and Lottie's dad.

Knox has been anxious about the fields he's learning to take over one day—which turned out to be over 70 percent of the property. The man was stressed to the max today. His fingers dug into the dirt, pulling up crops by their roots, trying to find a way to fix the overwatering. It's not enough that most would notice. Kit looked at me like he couldn't see a hint of what Knox was talking about, but I knew by now. If he didn't get this irrigation system fixed by the end of summer, they're out hundreds of thousands of dollars in profit.

We worked until Miller sent us off, and I went straight home for a shower.

All in all, it was a great day until the voicemail came in.

Stars are slowly beginning to pop up as the day turns to night, the deep oranges and pinks settling into a dark navy over the hills.

Lottie breaks our silence, her right hand squeezing my left. "So, space cowboy: tell me. What are we looking at?"

"Well." I ignore the space cowboy comment and lift our joint hands, still clinging tight, and point to a cluster of stars just over the top of the mountain. A line of them, slightly bent on the end, settles right over the edge, like you could hike up there and reach out to touch them. "See that little handle right there?"

She leans in a little closer to see it from my view, heat burrowing where our shoulders meet. "Mm-hmm."

"It's the Little Dipper."

"What? No way, really?"

"Nah."

She snorts and pushes my side, hands still together. "You're the worst."

"Sorry, I had to."

"How are you going to intern for NASA if you can't name at least a few stars?"

"You know, surprisingly, that's not a requirement."

"It should be."

"Maybe."

When we meet halfway, there is no knot in my back or root in my thigh, nothing but the soft skin of Lottie's body pressed into mine. My arm tingles, begging to be thrown around her shoulders, pulling her as tightly in as possible.

I clear my throat when her fingernails press into the back of my hand. "Nah, space isn't what they need me for. They just like the thought of someone on the agricultural side helping out. AgAir. They want someone to have a plan for developing technologies to apply insecticides, herbicides, fertilizer, and seeds in a new way. They assume I have good ideas in a folder to pass on to them so they can have the engineers fully create models and pass it as their own."

"And do you? Have a plan or a folder or anything like that?"

"I...do not."

"But you *could*."

"I guess. If I spent every waking moment on it, yeah."

"And you don't want to?"

"No. I want—" I pause, searching for the right way to explain. How can you put into words that you're sick of routines? That they leave you empty. A hole that can never be filled. "I want freedom more than anything. And a job where the creative side of me is forced to pump out new ideas constantly feels like the opposite of that."

"That makes sense. So, if you say no, then..."

"Then?"

"Where does that leave you?"

We're pushing our boundaries, and we both know it.

"I'm not sure. I don't have anything concrete. I could take time off, like a gap year. I've got the savings to travel."

"Oh." She turns back to the sunset, the pinks of her cheeks matching the distant glow of the sinking sun. When she finally answers, it's quiet and just for me. "I've heard Vermont is beautiful in the fall."

"It is?"

"Mm-hmm. You could do a road trip, go to Aspen in the winter. I know a guy that teaches ski lessons there. Or maybe New York for the New Year."

I wince. Crowds and cold weather? "Sounds awful."

She chuckles. "I probably wouldn't like it either. I'm too much of a homebody."

She looks up at me in questioning. *Are you a homebody too?* her eyes say.

And, with as much capability as I can muster without

moving my mouth, I answer back. I've never been a homebody because home never meant a house.

I'm a homebody as long as home always trails back to you.

"Walker—" Lottie whispers it and there's a thousand ways I can interpret the word from her, but I take it as a question.

"Lottie," I do my best to answer.

There is so much…space. So much gray, unknown territory in the silence. In wondering where we go from here. But this? Her hand in mine and our bodies pressed together, lips inches away? I know this well.

She dips her head in the slightest nod. So quick I almost miss it. I lift my free hand, more aware of its weight than ever, and wrap it around her jaw. The ends of my fingers tangle in her hair, and when they snag, she gasps, her chest lifted and chin tipping up to me.

Every restraint snaps at once. I dip my head, our lips inching closer. Her eyes stay on mine, and I know it's stupid. I'm as well aware now as I was thirty minutes ago that this is a horrible idea. Really, very bad.

But she's got strawberry-stained lips and is looking at me like I hold all of the answers that she needs. My lips press to the corner of her mouth, and a loud ringer buzzes between us, invisible space pushed between the distance of our lips. Her phone, bright and loud, sits between our hips. Lottie curses under her breath and unlinks our fingers to grab the device.

"Oh sorry. That's mine."

The screen is covered by Knox's contact picture—a blurry shot of him maybe around seven years old with a goofy grin and a large cowboy hat. It's cropped on the edge where a bundle of black curls is beside him—I assume it's Flick.

"It's, uh, Knox. Probably just asking me to duck sit again."

She locks her phone, ignoring the vibration immediately

coming right back. My chest is still heaving, lips and heart heavy. Everything in me screams to not let her go.

Keep her here. Keep her before it's too late.

She stands, pocketing her phone in the back of her overalls. "I—I'm gonna go to sleep." Her voice tilts at the end, eyes sticking just below my neck. It's a question. One I don't have an answer to. Her eyes don't meet mine, and disappointment seems to blanket us both.

Neither of us feel like we can take the next step in this minefield. So we stay stagnant. And in some way, it's much worse.

I manage a dip of my head. It's late; we've been out here a while. I remember her mentioning what causes her seizures—she said lack of sleep is a big deal. If she is going to sleep, I need to leave her to it. Come back tomorrow morning, try again. Try to do this properly.

"Night, Lottie." I grin up at her and put on my own poker face—the best I can muster considering my whole body is thrumming.

"Night, Walker."

I watch her walk away into the night, the distant shining of her flashlight on her phone disappearing slowly. A heavy weight sits in the bottom of my stomach. Regret. And starvation.

Down the field and between trees, she slips inside her back door without looking back. Good. Go to sleep. And for God's sake, barricade the damn door.

I stand up myself, wiping the dirt off the back of my jeans and grabbing the basket full of leftover strawberry stems. My feet move to the gravel road, split between going toward the main house and going to mine and Lottie's house, when a glimmer in the distance catches my eye. The back porch of my pretty neighbor has a light on just above the door. It turns on, then back off, then on again. There is a pause…light off, then back on again.

The curtains in her half window above her sink are open. It's pitch-black up here; there is no way she can see me. Yet, Lottie's eyes land directly on me. I feel it like a graze down my abdomen, hot skin closer and closer.

She lifts her lips in a grin and wistfully turns around to walk out of my view.

I shake my head to myself. "She's not going to sleep."

CHAPTER TWENTY-THREE
Lottie

How is a girl supposed to casually fall asleep after *that?*

It's going to take a gorilla tranquilizer to knock me off the high I'm on.

"I should get some sleep."

Stupid. I'm not going to sleep for the next week. Nothing but haunted daydreams of Walker's perfect lips so close to mine. And a little plotting of my brother's death for ruining what would have been the crème de la crème of second-chance kisses.

That tree is familiar territory for both of us. I know for a fact it's got some kind of romance-inducing hormone pushing through the surrounding red dirt. If that phone call hadn't come through, it's likely that tree would've had a second showing of the kiss we first shared. If you could even call it that. More like two zoo animals who broke free from their cages and cracked out on freedom, destroying everything in their paths.

Maybe it's a good thing. For the best, you know? After all, he is the first friend I've had in years who hasn't been overprotective or overbearing, constantly checking the clarity in my eyes. Waiting for me to stare off into space and slowly lose myself in the darkness.

I've done my best to put it out of my mind—Walker leaving. I think he has too. But the fact of the matter is, he *will* be leaving. Whether he pursues this career path for his own enjoyment—and truly, I hope that's why—or if it's to appease his parents.

He deserves happiness. And I hope this job can give him that. God knows I can't.

My future is this: a slow life with an old dog. Friends and family who will marry and have beautiful babies, and their Auntie Lot—they'll call me Lot 'cause it's easier and it sticks—will always give them hard candy from my pajama pockets and sex advice at the appropriate ages.

Walker's future is…I don't know. Rockets? Agricultural space engineering and high-salary jobs that will lead him to meeting some third grade English teacher that giggles at how he jokingly says "Well, I'll be" pronounced "L-I-B." They'll get married in a stupid fancy garden and have perfect vows, and at their gender reveal party they'll send rockets into the air with blue or pink smoke coming out of them to announce if it's a boy or a girl.

And I will have my geriatric dog named Ferguson. He'll be blind in both eyes and use his one working nostril to find the leftover casserole I poured in his bowl. He'll sit by my feet and dutifully listen when I tell him that Rachel is completely wrong for Bradley—contestants on whatever will be my favorite island dating show—and my fingers will be busy embroidering foul language on fluffy holiday pillows. At night I'll dream of a kiss that almost was and my last summer with the only man who saw me as a whole person.

The end. Happy ever afters all around.

Sporadic knocks sound on my back door and my daydream of smothering Walker's future wife with a self-embroidered pillow suddenly comes to a halt.

It's him. It has to be. He does that funny knock that I am horrible at reciprocating on our joint bedroom walls. Three fast knocks and then two slow ones.

I fluff my hair and throw the door open, wishing I took off my dirty overalls and put on some sexy housewife robe or maybe a vintage shift...whatever that looks like. The pirates certainly love them. And the guy in front of me unequivocally looks like a pirate, here for his treasure.

He crosses the threshold of my door. We both know how this ends. His boots thud on my dining room floor, dry dirt and dust flying off them. I have to lift my chin to meet his eyes now.

When Walker finally speaks, it's husky and rough, like sandpaper in the back of his throat. "You're not going to sleep."

My head is shaking violently before he can finish. "I'm not going to sleep."

I say it with a quirk of a smile, though it doesn't last long. I lift onto my toes and put all of my balance into him. We meet in the middle, both of my hands gripping his shirt while his rough fingers tangle in my hair just like the other night, trying to be tender and gentle but demanding more.

If I pictured our second kiss before now—which I totally have—it wouldn't have been like this. In my mind it was slow. Two lips molded perfectly together, like a potter with his favorite clay, cautiously forming and sculpting. Soft, sweet pecks that build up more and more. Sensible.

Though I should have known better. When have Walker and I ever been sensible? The man jumps off waterfalls and builds rockets, and I con idiotic men out of their money for entertainment.

No, the way Walker kisses me is nothing short of feral. Warmth envelops me when our bodies press against each other, even with the breeze of the June night air coming in through the back door. A row of chill bumps rise on my arms, and I mentally force them down. I can't be cold when my insides are this burning hot.

Walker notices, though. Because he's Walker. He takes a step forward, our lips never parting, as his right hand grips the back of my head while the other tests the weight of my jaw. A swift jerky movement and I hear a loud slam. The breeze on my arms is cut short, and I realize he kicked my door shut behind us.

His teeth skate over my lower lip, and I gasp a moan. He tastes like summer. The rough pricks of his facial hair meet the smooth skin above my lips, around my cheeks. A man so rough shouldn't have lips this soft. Firm, but somehow pillowy against my own.

Want drips through me, a tap that's been slowly being added to over time and is now flooded, pushing waves of heat and desire through every inch of my mind and body.

Stay in the moment. Soak it in. Keep enough mental notes to publish a full dissertation on this kiss one day.

But I can't manage that. I'm lost in him. Caught in a rushing tide of his smell: leather, dirt, and hay, with a hint of something spicy behind it—sandalwood, or maybe amber, a distant pinch of aged whiskey. Lost in the feel of his hands gripping me close like he's afraid *I'll* be the one to pull back. A foolish concept that makes me almost snicker.

Walker must sense it too, because he smiles into our kiss. I chase down that feeling of pure joy when he drops one hand down to my waist and backs me up against the counter. A soft barrier of skin between me and the hard edge. His hips dig into mine, and I can hardly fathom what I'm bringing to the table when his lips pull back just long enough to land on my jaw.

All cards laid down, I fold.

He pulls tight at my waist with a loud "umph." And I realize my hands are gripping his biceps, nails digging in. "I love that you keep my hat on your coffee table."

My head tilts back with a laugh. Walker takes full advantage of the exposed skin stretched out before him, planting hot open-mouthed kisses along my neck.

"It's not intentional," I huff out.

"It's a statement piece, and you know it." He kisses gently where my tank top strap lines my shoulder and smiles against my skin when I keep laughing.

This whole world around us is orange and bright from the lamplight. Distant crickets chirp in the night air and owls sing their own song. A wood wick candle pops and crackles on my stove, but I can't care to pay attention to any of it as Walker's lips press to mine.

It's decadent. Everything I've needed and nothing I've allowed myself to believe I deserve.

Walker mumbles softly against me, a long tender kiss to my cheek. "'Sin from my lips? O trespass sweetly urged. Give me sin again.'"

I'm not certain if I heard him correctly or if my dreams and reality are colliding. My cheek was on his lips for the second half of his speech. I pull back enough to search his eyes, dark and *so* amused.

"Did you just quote—"

"Is it pathetic if I said yes?"

Of course he did. Because he notices everything. He always has.

I smile. "Only because you said it wrong. It's 'give me *my* sin again.'"

"That's what I said."

"You forgot the *my*. It's imperative."

Walker's hands are chasing up and down my lower back, reaching down to pull me close enough that I have to lean back to see him properly. The soft glow of a single lamp in the corner of the counter illuminates his wicked smile.

"Teach it to me, then." He kisses my temple along my hairline, like he can't force himself to stop.

"He's attempting to purify himself in the kiss. She is a shrine to him. That tiny *my* tells us about his passion for her. His barely contained excitement. He needs her to be *wholly* his."

"Something I know all too well." Walker lifts his head from the care he's been giving along my face and grabs both sides of my jaw, forcing my attention to him. As if he hasn't had it this entire time. As if I'm not floating into another dimension solely named Walker's Touch.

"You are unreal. Does Shakespeare have anything to say about that?"

"Maybe in *Hamlet*. Or *King Lear*. But I only know the one."

"Of course you do. My romantic." He smiles, and it's only now that I can understand the weight of the two-letter word: *my*. I like being his *my* anything. Even if it's a horrible idea, I like it.

"I know I'm not good for you," I mumble in the hope that he hears the silent plea. He *is* leaving. And he's taking his stupid hat with him, and I'll be left with nothing but the burned memory of him pressing me into this countertop. But just not yet.

He pulls my waist closer with a low rumble in his throat, like an emphasis. "You're *perfect* for me."

I shake my head and our lips brush side to side. "My life is insane."

He's only seen the surface. He'll change his mind when he uncovers the rest.

"I love it," he counters.

"I'm a handful."

"It's a good thing I have capable hands."

Said hands are showing me just how capable they are, gentle and sweet but still firm.

I want to be so engulfed in this man that I forget I even exist. I want to go to a place where injuries, lies, and family disputes, even casinos, fail to exist and there is nothing but just the two of us.

A chime plays somewhere in the distance. I think it might be a doorbell. Or an alarm ringing to tell me it's time to wake up from this dream.

"Ignore it," he whispers against me, and honestly, who am I to argue?

At my front door, someone knocks. It's forceful and rushed, and I can't muster even a hint of concern.

"It's probably the wrong house." Walker nods and when he mutters "up, sweetheart," I do as I am told. Rough hands pull at my waist, lifting me into his arms and—

"CHARLOTTE JANE TURNER, I KNOW YOU'RE IN THERE."

Okay, so definitely not the wrong house.

CHAPTER TWENTY-FOUR
Walker

"One second!" Lottie calls back to the door, her shaky breath warm against mine.

Right. The door. The door that is being knocked on by what sounded like her brother. Meanwhile my grease-stained hands are gripping her waist, and I am standing here with my mouth gaping like a singing fish mounted on the wall.

I take a step back to adjust my jeans while Lottie jumps down from the counter I don't remember her climbing on and attempts to fix her hair. There is a huge knot where my hands had dug into the back of her head and a pink outline left on her lips that says, "Walker Lane was here." Not to mention her neck is bright red, either from my stubble or from the sheer embarrassment of what is to come.

"Do I look okay?" she asks.

"You look like I swallowed you whole and spit you back out."

"Excellent."

Taking a deep breath, Lottie strides to the door, while I keep myself tucked away behind the corner of the kitchen. Standing at the open door is in fact her brother and best friend with wide-open grins and seven…no, eight ducklings in their arms.

Flick sticks a hand out, two ducks sitting on the end. "Hi, love! Quick question—wait, why do you look like—" She glances over Lottie's shoulders, and our eyes meet. I lift my hand and give it a little shake in what has to be the top five worst waves ever. My mouth opens to say…I don't know, some form of greeting or acknowledgment, but then shuts right back down.

So little blood in my brain right now.

Lottie and Flick are having a full conversation with just their eyes. If I glance back at Knox, it seems like he's trying to have the same with me, so I keep my gaze stuck on the gallery wall. I particularly zero in on one framed photo of Lottie with short pigtails riding a horse, Knox standing beside her with a snaggletooth grin.

"Anyway." Knox clears his throat to interrupt Lottie and Flick's silent discussion. "We need you to babysit the kids."

I think that's the first time Lottie's eyes divert to their hands full of tiny ducklings swaddled in warmth. One sticks its head up and lets out a tiny chirp in Knox's shirt pocket. It's so cute that even I, in my most absurd state, can't stop staring at it.

I cough and say, "The…ducks?"

"Yes. Every time we leave them alone, they fight, and then half of them won't eat for some reason," Knox explains.

Flick steps in. "The vet thinks they have anxiety."

"You're asking me to duck sit…now?"

Knox takes a single baby bird that's curled into the crook of his elbow and lifts it out, glaring at me while I try my best to seem like I could belong here in any normal way. My leaning stance and elbow propped on the wall doesn't seem to help.

"Well, Hulk Hogan is here with you, seems like you have plenty of help to me."

"I don't know if we—"

"Please, Lot." Knox's voice is desperate and his wide eyes are flashing back and forth between his sister and Flick, who is overly fidgety.

I have no idea what is happening, but it's clearly something I don't need the details on. Duck sitting is not where I saw this night going, but if that's what keeps me here with her longer, I'll take it.

"How long?" I ask.

"Forty min—"

"AN HOUR," Knox says over Flick. "An hour would be great."

"Oh, yes, an hour!" She nods feverishly.

Lottie takes one in her hand, and the duck circles in her palm before snuggling in.

"We can do it." I take a few steps, now that I know Knox won't try to deck me, and lift one duck out of Flick's offering hand.

"Great." Knox sets them all on the floor a few feet away, but they immediately run back to him. "Okay. We've got Duck Norris, Alfonzo, Duckleberry Finn, Harry, Hubert, Howard, and Bubbles."

Five minutes later, Lottie and I are on the floor, leaning against her couch with eight ducks surrounding us. We had initially made an attempt at corralling them into halves—Hubert and Howard kept fighting to make their way back to each other, though, so we decided to let them roam in the open space.

The one in my hand—Alfonzo, I think—keeps shivering like he's cold. When I try to cover him up, though, he wiggles his way out of it.

Duck Norris is easy to pick out; the only one with mostly brown feathers and a little pale yellow chest that looks like he has a perfectly shaved triangle right below his neck. He also is the one actively attacking his brothers and sister.

"Come on, stinker." I pick him up and set him on my shoulder where he shakes out his feathers a bit in protest.

"This is the cutest thing I've ever seen," Lottie coos at them. "I am not a bird person, but this is so much better than Nigel."

"Who's Nigel?"

"I wish I had the privilege of asking that question."

I start to ask more when Bubbles snuggles into where my legs are crossed and settles herself into the crook of my knee. "Hi, pretty girl." I lift the only female duck and gently pet the top of her yellow head.

"You could really do some damage like this."

My lips curve into a smirk. "Yeah?"

"For sure. The only thing that would make it better is if you were shirtless, and maybe if I had a Diet Coke and some lime."

Duckleberry Finn—who I've been calling Finn—keeps falling on his side every three feet. I set him straight again just for him to slip onto his right wing again. I snort. "They really are like little toddlers."

Lottie has two in her scooped hands, watching them waddle around her palms. "Are they? I don't know if I've ever met a toddler."

"The family I worked for had a ton of kids and grandkids and even great-grandkids, so I got used to being around them pretty often."

It was a little hard. Leaving them after Gerald's funeral. I didn't tell half the kids I was leaving; I just let his wife tell them for me. Occasionally I think about them, wondering where they are. How they're doing and how summer is going. I mostly wonder if that family feels as betrayed as mine did when I left them too.

"Do...*you* want a family?" Lottie asks and lifts a duck like an emphasis. "I mean toddlers, babies, all that."

It feels like a tricky question. Her eyes are lighter. Kind. Like the answer wouldn't matter to her either way because she's betting on me not being around to see a family grow. She smiles when Duck Norris drops his head to the bare skin of my neck and falls asleep.

I answer with caution. "Not necessarily babies. But, yeah, a family would be great."

"Right." She nods.

"Do *you* want a family?" I dip my head to her lap where the ducks all seem to gather around her. "Like, kids and all."

"Maybe. I don't really see it happening for me, though."

"Because...?"

"A lot of people with epilepsy have babies. I've been on forums and looked online, and it's not impossible at all. They say you just have to have the right systems in place for emergencies. I know a lot of people do it. But I just... I think *I'm* not one of them. I want kids, maybe. Or maybe I just want to be a super-fun aunt. But I think mostly I want to be surrounded with people that love me and that I'm not constantly a burden to. And having kids would mean me putting this burden back on them."

My brows furrow. "I don't think so."

"You don't?"

"No." I go to explain more, but Lottie opens her mouth. Considering I rarely get this kind of depth from her, I soak in every word she has to say.

"There's also the safety issue of it all. I tried babysitting once last winter and I had two absence seizures in a row with the kids watching me. They were older, three and seven, and they assumed I was spacing out or something. Their mom was home thirty minutes later, and I couldn't fully recall what happened until they told her about it. I got fired the next day. They were sweet about it, but I was still disappointed. Thinking back now, I get it. What if it was a baby? A newborn and I had..." She doesn't say the words. Just shivers a little.

"You said other people do it, right?"

"Yeah, other people." Lottie laughs, and it's not the one I know and love. "Not me."

"Why not you?"

"You know, it really doesn't matter."

"Because you're so young?" I ask. Because she's still got so much time, so much life to live.

"Because it won't happen. I won't get any of that: marriage, babies, not even one more ride. I lost the chance at all of that, and I can't get it back."

I'm silent for a moment. I wonder how much Lottie pulls herself back from because she assumes she's undeserving or incapable. Or maybe it trails back to the whole burden thing. I can't fully relate to that. I have never had a disability that caused me to rely on others. But I have been a known load on my own family. And I know how frustrating it is to carry that alone.

As far as the baby side...I've got nothing. I am not a medical expert, and no amount of googling statistics would make me one. So, I only say the one thing in the back of my mind. And I say it with every fiber of my being.

"I think you would be a great mom."

Lottie glances up at me with a big smile. She doesn't ask

why or argue back. But she smiles at me with the kind of gratitude a man can only dream of.

And I soak in every bit of it.

When Knox and Felicity pick the ducks up—an hour and *thirty* minutes later—they explain they were just "setting stuff up" for some adoption event at an animal shelter this weekend. I have reason to believe otherwise, judging by their dubious expressions, but I have had enough duck sitting for a lifetime, and I am dying to get Lottie alone again. So I pretend that they're not lying to us both.

Lottie does the same. That or she doesn't notice her brother and best friend sneaking around.

When the door shuts behind them, Lottie comes around the coffee table to stand closer to me with her arms crossed. "So…"

"So." I smile.

"Wild night, huh?"

"Certainly not where I saw it going."

"You and me both."

I wonder if we can find a way to pick up where we left off. But then she yawns, and I recognize that faraway, dreamy look in her eyes as exhaustion and I remind myself there's a way to do this. And throwing it all into one night isn't how I make it permanent.

"Hey, Lottie?"

"Hmm?"

"Go on a date with me."

"Are you asking or telling?"

"Both? I'm asking because I want to be a gentleman, but I'm telling because I know sometimes you need a push."

"Hmm." Her eyes squint into two low lines and she sighs. "Okay."

"Saturday night? We can check off an item or two. Or I can give the list a break and we can just have fun without an ulterior motive."

"That sounds really nice."

"I'll pick you up?" I offer.

She rolls her eyes and pushes me out the door, her hand on my chest. "Right, because it is *such* a far walk."

CHAPTER TWENTY-FIVE
Walker

In all of the chaos at Willow Creek—and my chasing the head farmer's pretty daughter—I've had very little time to see the rest of Oak Ridge since I set foot in it.

Therefore, showing up to the town farmers market with a Willow Creek shirt on as a relatively new local with expectations of not catching attention was a foolish thought.

Though, it wasn't exactly my choice to come here today.

I shift the crate full of produce in my hands. Mine is mostly packaged strawberries and blueberries, while Kit has squash and cucumbers. He warned me that farmers markets were a big deal here. But how big can something really be when it's a town this small?

I underestimated it.

There are rows and rows of tables, each one with something different. Crocheted animals, carved wooden toy cars by an old man in a rocking chair whittling a stick, custom pet portraits, baked goods, homemade honey, locally raised meats. There's even a table with a lady in a very long wig that says for ten dollars, she will serenade anyone you like. I consider sending her over to Knox's house.

A booth is all set up for Lottie's mom to handle the selling and money—the talking, mostly. Kit and I set our final crates on the table and take a seat behind it, giving polite nods to the many, many rounds of people waiting on Mrs. Turner to get here. Neither of us misses the stares we get from locals trying to figure out who I am and where I'm from.

"Hi, Kit." One girl comes around the corner of the table beside us. She's around his age, I think. They both have that fresh, naive look in their eyes, like they have barely even experienced life yet.

"Oh." Kit coughs and his voice goes down a notch. "Hey, Claire."

"I didn't know you were coming today."

"Knox talked me into it."

"Sounds about right."

"You…you come with your dad?" He is staring at her so intently that I think a vein just popped out of his temple.

"Yeah, he would love to see you." She points down the aisle of tables packed in this parking lot. "I've got some honey with your name on it if you pop by my table on the way out?" She smiles, all young and innocent.

"Uh, yeah, for sure." He nods.

She smiles from him to me and back to him, before giving Kit a quick wave. "Bye, Kit."

"Bye, Claire."

When the girl walks far enough away to be out of earshot, I turn to Kit. "Is honey like a euphemism young kids use now?"

"What?" he chokes out. "No. She is a beekeeper."

"Ahh. *Nice*."

"Shut up."

"You're sunburnt." I point out his neck and cheeks. "Or are you blushing?"

"You're one to talk. I hear you talking to Miss Lottie. You're not as smooth as you think."

I smile. I imagine I'm probably not too smooth around her. The girl makes my head go haywire.

Lottie's mom shows up a few minutes early, and I walk with Kit to find his (as he insists) not-girlfriend's table. On the way down the aisles, we pass by a booth that sells freshly cut flowers.

A sign labeled "Hey, Bud" sits at the top of the booth and an older woman sits underneath it, surrounded by vases and wildflowers. I pause, seeking the wallet in my back pocket.

"Which do you think Lottie would want?"

Kit squints and scrunches his nose. "I don't know if she's a flower girl."

"All girls like flowers. It's not about the flowers themselves. It's knowing you thought about her."

"Well, I don't know anything other than roses, and I don't see any."

I lean down to the table. There's a few that *feel* like her, but I'd rather get something I know she'll like for sure.

"Just call her if you're so worried." The kid rolls his eyes and pulls out his phone, typing away in a search engine. "This isn't rocket science, space boy."

God help me.

When I finally call, Lottie answers after two rings, the sound of her voice like a song I want on repeat in my truck with the windows rolled down. "Let me guess, you need me to carry those big strong crates for you?"

I smile. "If I said yes, would you come help me?"

"Mmm. Probably not."

"Ahh. Then no."

She giggles into the phone, and I imagine her propped up on her front porch with a mug of coffee and a blanket draped across her long legs. "What can I do for you this early morning, *Walker*?"

"I was wondering what your favorite flowers are."

"Are you going all out tonight?" I can hear the squint in her eyes and the smile in her voice. "Because I should warn you that I had no plans of getting *you* flowers."

"Lottie."

"Hm?"

"Please answer the question."

She chuckles and gives me a quick and blurry answer that I *know* I am hearing wrong.

"Walker? Did you lose signal?"

"No, no. I'm still here." *Just replaying what I thought you said to make sure I am not an idiot.* "I, uh, can't hear well though. Say it again—your favorite flower?"

Lottie repeats her answer, and I still keep hearing the same thing.

"Sorry, it's hard to hear with a bunch of people around." I plug my other ear and try to listen better.

She laughs, and whereas I normally would delight in the sound, I am nothing but lost as she repeats her answer. I know what I'm taking in. My ears do the work, that's not the problem. The problem is I am almost positive what I'm taking in is *not* what she's saying.

Unless this is another one of those things like the light outside her house. My hat on her coffee table after weeks. Her own way of telling me what she expects from me next. But I can't just go grab those on a first date and pretend it's *not* the weirdest move ever.

"One more time?" I just need some kind of confirmation.

Lottie's voice is still full of humor, but there is a twitch of confusion behind it, too, when she confirms exactly what I thought.

No, no, she definitely just said *that*.

"Okay. Got it." I cough into my fist and avoid the eye contact Kit is trying to make with me.

"Why?" She giggles.

"I… No reason. I'll see you later."

"Okay, I'll be waiting for you."

Good Lord, my throat is so tight I can't even answer that. I just hang up and stare at my phone, wondering what just happened.

Kit asks, "So, what'd she say?"

"Huh?" I turn, and he's staring at me expectantly.

"Geez. You say I'm sunburned, but you should see your whole face right now."

"I…" I stay quiet and try to piece together how in the world I'm going to make that happen.

"So? What's her favorite flower?"

"I…don't want to tell you."

Kit looks as confused as I feel, and I am certainly not about to tell him what I am going to make a poor attempt to do on a first date.

I look up at the woman waiting patiently for me to buy something, and I feel guilty that I'm about to leave here empty-handed. "Sorry, ma'am. She's not a flower girl."

Kit scoffs and crosses his arms. "You said all girls like flowers. What about all of that effort stuff you just said?"

"Apparently, I'm putting in the wrong kind of effort. Here." I pull out a twenty and offer it to him. "If you were smart, you'd grab some for that girl."

Kit groans something before taking the twenty out of my hand and shoving it to the woman across the table. "Do you have any sunflowers or snapdragons?"

"Snapdragons?" I ask.

"Google says they're good for bees," he mumbles under his breath.

The older woman giggles. "I've got something I'll put together."

She packages up a bouquet that is small enough to not seem over-the-top, but big enough where they don't look cheap in an array of pink and yellow.

We head out, stopping by a table that is covered in animated bee signs that Kit's girl is standing behind. She smiles bright when he approaches, and the smile only grows when he practically throws the flowers at her head. Literally. He tosses them at her like they are embarrassing. He's shrugging, hands in his pockets, and even though I can't hear what he's saying, I already know the gist.

"I got these flowers for you. They're so stupid, right? Women don't like flowers, and neither does my preteen angst."

He opens his mouth and points a thumb over his shoulder to where I am a few feet behind him. She sends a polite wave my way, which I return, before she turns back to my young friend.

When he inevitably leaves her table, flushed cheeks and a huge jar of honey in tow, we make our way to my truck.

Kit opens the jar, takes the sample spoon that Claire (or was it Blair?) gave him, and eats at least ten spoonfuls. He tosses his head back and groans. "You want to grab some food on the way back?"

I shake my head, still trying to sort out how I'm going to get what Lottie said. "Sorry, kid, I wish I could."

I'm a man on a very, *very* confusing mission.

CHAPTER TWENTY-SIX
Lottie

I can't remember if I've ever had a date.

A real one. Not a meaningless kiss done for a dare at a bonfire. Not flirting with a man over a card table in hopes it drops his attention. But a real date, one with someone I genuinely enjoy spending every second of my time with. Maybe never? Not unless you counted mine and Walker's old outings. Which means I am entirely out of practice.

Walker's dated. I don't know who or how many, but it's a scientific fact. A man *that* good looking doesn't just not have a line of girls from his past. He has no condition or disability that would make dating a chore for him, not like it is for me. He's going to know what to do tonight. The moves to make. The places to go. And I will be…there. Just a floating speck wondering what to expect next.

General rule of thumb, I assume, about dating is I would much rather be prepared for a nicer night than underdress. Plus, he asked me what flowers I liked—*multiple times*—which means he's going all out. So I plan to do the same for him.

I take every bit of hot water I can from my shower until I am scrubbed raw and there isn't an inch of hair or dead skin on my body. If I were an Olympic swimmer, I would cut through water like a hot knife through butter.

If nothing else, it's nice to feel pretty. And I really, really do.

I'm wearing a white, skinny-strapped dress with a completely open back that flares out and settles mid-thigh. The dress is straight from Dot's closet; she called it a "classic," and it's cute, sure, but the icing on the cake—cherry on top, the crème de la crème—are my boots.

I've been saving them for something special, but I was never sure what exactly. I think even months ago I knew I would find a perfect excuse for these boots. And I finally have.

They're white leather, which is typically a no-go for me, but these are the only exceptions. Because on both sides of them is the outline of the queen of hearts. Her silhouette is outlined in red thread, and she is winking at me in the mirror from her card.

They're *perfect*.

I have full expectations of letting Walker soak in this getup for at least three minutes straight when he first sees me. But when the time comes for me to open the door for him, I pause in my place and take a moment to just *look*.

I've never met someone so effortlessly good looking as he is. His tall frame is complemented by the way his dark jeans sit just right over his well-worn cowboy boots, every bit the picture of the rugged guy I've known him to be. The sleeves of his button-down are casually rolled just enough to hint at his arms. The soft glow of my porch lights against the warmth of all that tan skin he got from working in the fields is beautiful.

But it's his smile that truly catches me—bright, genuine, and sweet enough to make a girl's heart stutter. There's something about it that makes me feel at ease, like this night is exactly where I'm meant to be. And I'm going to soak that in as long as I can.

The look on Walker's face as he stares down at my dress tells me he's going to soak it in as well.

His throat clears. "You look… Yeah."

"Yeah?" There's a gooey smile in my voice I can't get rid of.

"Yeah."

"You look very *yeah*, yourself." I reach a hand up to pet his jaw. "I like the stubble on you."

"I had plans to shave it, but you said you liked it the other day when we…" He pauses, and I notice his neck turning a bit red under my hand. "Yeah."

"Yeah." I laugh. "And your hair is styled." I want to run my hands through it, but I imagine it took some time to settle the wild strands down, so I decide to save that idea for later.

"Well, *someone* still has my hat. I didn't have much of a choice."

"Wow, that someone sounds very selfish."

"I think she's more selfless than she lets on."

My cheeks are sore from all this constant smiling. If I think back to last month when Walker was the last person I wanted to see, to now as I'm hanging on his every word, I could laugh.

"So, are you ready?"

"Let me grab my purse really quick." I grab the strap off the hook to my right, and when I turn back, Walker is holding an enormous bouquet my way. His cheeks are flushed, and I want nothing more than to take a mental screenshot of this look on him.

"Oh." I smile and take it in my hands. "You didn't have to—"

My words drop off as I try to figure out *what* kind of bouquet I am looking at. I glance from my hands to Walker's face, which over a thirty-second period has transitioned from a light pink to bright red.

My fingers brush against one of the flowers which is shaped like a rose, but to the touch… Is that *fabric*?

"Wha—" I chuckle a little, and he gives me a nervous smile like this is an inside joke that neither of us understand. "What is this?"

"You said they were your"—he coughs—"favorites."

Is it like some kind of reusable flower thing? Because if so, I have to say it was not what I was expecting. I mean, sure, the effort is great, but I am feeling a little lost on the whole thing.

My fingers tug one "flower" out and my eyes land on white cotton and lace that unrolls to reveal a single pair of women's cheeky underwear. I look from the—admittedly *very cute*—panties up to my date.

Walker is fidgeting with his watch, leaning away from me with his eyes stuck directly on the underwear in my hand. His Adam's apple bobs up and down furiously. And I'm still trying to piece this whole thing together.

"Oh. Well." I try to fix my scratchy voice, but it still comes out all high-pitched. "Thank you."

Walker nods way more than normal. "I didn't know what kind you liked. You, uh, just said *panties* so…"

I have heard many, many wild things in my life. But when the word *panties* leaves Walker's mouth, I have no choice but to rethink if I am hallucinating or if I am really witnessing this entire scene play out in front of me.

"Wait. What?"

"When I asked you for your favorite flowers, you said panties. Three times in a row. Maybe four."

"Walker. When you asked me what my favorite flower was…"

He nods with wide eyes as if to say, *I am so glad you can see how weird this is.*

"Yes, you said panties. It felt *super* wrong, but you said it multiple times. I made sure. I thought maybe you were flirting or something, I don't know."

"PEONIES!" I correct and it truly takes every bit of my strength to hold my laughter back. Oh this man; this wonderful, and partially clueless, genius of a man.

"Yes, that's what I said."

"Peonies."

"Precisely."

"Pee-ah-nees."

He shakes his head like, *come on, lady, get with the program.*

"You're saying the same thing, baby."

Baby is hitting the nail on the head, and I can't hold in my howling any longer.

"No, Walker. The flower? Peonies. They're my favorite." I look to my left where there is a framed watercolor that Odie made me years ago—a blue vase with light pink peonies. I take a couple backward steps into my house and gesture for Walker to follow. Once he does, I turn him to the watercolor and point to the petals. "Peonies," I clarify, though, now that I say it out loud, it does sound awfully similar to panties.

Walker is quiet for so long that I start to wonder if I need to find a reset button on him. Finally, he groans, head bowed. "Can we please not talk about this ever?"

Any hint of anxiety I had over this night has instantly vanished, and I could just kiss him for it. "No, this is my favorite thing."

"Give me those, I'm taking it back." He reaches for my

hand, but I jerk it back. It would take an act of God to rip this from my hands.

"We don't even have a Victoria's Secret near us. How did you get this?"

"I don't want to talk about this anymore."

"Come on, tell me you didn't drive an hour there and back for these today."

"Alright, you're staying here." Walker turns to the door, and I wrap a hand around his large wrist.

"To what? Admire all my new fancy underwear? There's *lace* in here. I didn't think you had this side in you."

"That's it, you're letting this go to your head." With a lightning-fast motion, he reaches behind me, takes the bouquet back, and tosses it in the bushes between our two porches.

"Those are mine!"

"Not anymore."

"Walker," I hiss and take a few steps around him to retrieve my favorite gift in the world. When the bouquet is secured in my loving arms, I carefully take it inside and set it on the coffee table beside his hat. "Okay, I'll drop it if you let me keep them."

Walker eventually agrees, and we leave it all at the door. Though as soon as the two of us are confined in the space of his old truck with nothing between us on the long seat, my lips start to curve up again. He really did go all out for this.

I can't remember a time I've been this excited.

When Walker pulls into the familiar parking lot of my favorite restaurant, Effie's, I breathe a sigh of relief. It's not that I was expecting anything specific, but I wasn't sure where we were headed. It's nice to go somewhere familiar.

"Your mom mentioned you liked this place." He says it

like an open-ended question. Like if I turned to him right now and said, "Actually, let's go home and pick weeds and make out on my couch," then he would immediately veer out of this parking lot.

"You talked to my mom about our date?"

"More like Kit mentioned I would see you later tonight, and she heavily suggested this restaurant would be the best if I had a ring with me—which I do not, by the way—and that it was your favorite."

"Oh no." I duck my face into my hands and laugh. "She's got baby names picked out for sure."

Walker huffs in amusement. "What do you think she would call them?"

"Hmm. She's picturing two boys and a girl. The girl would be named Lily after her."

"Obviously."

"And the two boys need *L* names like..." I think for a moment. "Lance and Luke."

Walker guffaws. "*Lance*?"

"Short for Lancelot."

"Poor kid."

"I know." I wince. "Although he is head of the debate team and gets a good bit of action from the girls at statewide competitions."

"I am so proud."

"As you should be."

The hostess leads us to a table. We sit in a corner that is dimly lit by candlelight and the warm glow of the yellow sconces beside us. Walker asks me what I recommend, and I pretend I don't order the same thing every time. I tell him the steak frites is delicious—because it always is—whereas I order my usual of a club sandwich with mixed vegetables. It's much fancier than it sounds. Or maybe it's not, because Walker stares at me like, *You made me order steak when you're just going to eat grilled broccoli and a sandwich?*

While we wait on our food, I take a moment to look at the man across from me.

He's gotten tanner since he first moved here. I never thought the white line where his work shirt rides up, exposing his skin from the blaring sun each day, would be sexy, but here we are. The scruff around his chin and jaw has grown out too. Not a ton—I wouldn't call it a full-blown beard—but still, it's there. My eyes lazily trail his every feature. His brown eyes and that single fleck of golden honey in them. The almost unnoticeable scar above his right brow. His smile. His teeth. His neck.

Him, him, *him*.

"*You*"—he squints across the table—"are staring."

"So are you," I accuse, busy counting the freckles across his nose and cheeks to know for sure.

"Hmm. Should we stop?"

"I'd rather not."

"Okay."

He smiles and I tilt my chin. "Is this where I get to ask you all the questions I have circling in my head?" I ask.

"Should I be scared?"

"Only a little."

He narrows his eyes playfully, and I have the oddest urge to giggle like we're in middle school and this date isn't even a real one. Our parents are a few tables away talking, while we pretend we drove here and order Sprite in martini glasses and virgin rum and Coke—which is just Coke.

Yet here we are.

"Shoot away."

"How many dates have you been on?" I start.

Walker coughs mid-drink and I wince.

"That bad?" I ask.

"Nah, it's just... Don't ask that."

"Why? I won't like the answer?"

Please say no. I know you weren't mine, but it feels like you always have been and even if I've flirted with other men, I need to know that your heart isn't caught up with hundreds of girls across the south.

"No." His smile is a mix of humor and a grimace. "'Cause I won't like the answer back when I ask you the same thing."

I wave a hand. "Oh, there's a whole armada of them, really. They are waiting on my sign to rise against the patriarchy."

"I'm sure they are."

I lean back in my chair. Walker pulls forward to the table, like we're connected by a string and wherever I go, he will follow. It makes me lean closer so he's not the only one. If he's following me, I'll meet him halfway. "Really, though. I want to know about it all. School, work, girls, all of it. I want to not feel like there's this huge thing I'm missing out on."

He shakes his head in a small, quick motion. "You're not missing anything. I promise. Those days were fine, I guess. But here is better."

Here. Here as in Willow Creek, or here as in this date with me? I'm unsure. But I take it as mine all the same.

I pout and he relents. "I'll share it all if you will."

"Well, you're not missing out on anything on my side," I admit.

"Oh, I'm not?" He smiles into his glass. "Including the fact that I still have no idea how you got to be a card wizard."

"Well, funny story—"

We trade our pasts like kids swapping baseball cards.

He tells me of the details of the last two years of high school; graduation, skipping prom, spending his nights researching ways to get out of town. He wraps up his dating past with a neat bow—he's dated two girls since our last summer together. Both somewhat long-term. Or long-term to me, anyway.

A ceramicist who went by Poppy that he met through Gerald's son. They stayed together for about three months. She was in love with the son, it turns out.

And Rebecca, who sourced out Gerald's grains for two months, but she lived too far away, and he said it wasn't worth it.

"I don't do long-distance," he declares, and we stay silent for a moment, the air thick between us and our half-eaten plates. *If he didn't do it then, he won't now either.* "I was too busy for anything substantial." He tries to cover his last sentence.

But as quickly as the reminder of our impending doom circles in, it leaves the moment I tell him of my card lessons with different men at Riley's. How an older nurse at the hospital named Mike taught me everything I know about cards. How he distracted me from slow IV drips with quick sleight of hand and card tricks that, to this day, I have no idea how he pulled off.

I tell him the memory of that first trick, the first moment I fell in love with a deck of cards.

"You can get a terrible hand." Mike hands over a set of five cards. I flip them over and wince, a draw of a couple twos, a king, a four, and a seven. Very little to work with.

But the weirdest part is Mike knows it is a bad hand before looking at it. "How did you—"

"And play it to your strengths." He rearranges the hand, and in an instant, it's a royal flush, like pure magic.

"What—"

"Or"—he shuffles and pulls out five more, laying them flat and flipping them over—"you can get a perfect hand." He grabs my royal flush and flips it, suddenly back to the random spur of numbers it was before. "And completely ruin it."

How did he manage a perfect royal flush just like that? I still couldn't say. But I can tell you I have never stopped trying.

While I tell him, Walker is an excellent listener. He has it down to a science. He smiles at the right parts, gasps at others. He leans in close, like he's hanging on to my every word, and even as I trail on about my "boring" years, he is entirely enraptured.

I tell him more about my diagnosis—what helps, what doesn't. He keeps quiet beyond asking a question here and there. Just constant listening. I don't touch on the subject of my exes, or my lack thereof, near as much as he did. But I do lean into my early days of the epilepsy diagnosis. The darker ones that still loom over me at night.

I tell him how a town this small, something as big as a fifteen-year-old getting diagnosed with epilepsy, no matter the scale of it, spreads like wildfire. How sometimes I can still smell the hint of sterile hospitals in my parents' house. How the first few months, it seemed like life was a never-ending revolving door of pity glances in stores and cautious eyes. How school was relentless stares and judging scowls. How I went from riding steers on a Tuesday to being forbidden to even sit in the driver's seat of a car in a flash.

Once, I climbed into my old Bronco just to *feel* something. I didn't dare put it in drive. Even before the diagnosis, I was a horrible driver when I was attempting to learn. I did it to wrap my fingers around the thin steering wheel. To lean into the worn leather of my grandfather's seat and picture driving over Alabama's rolling hills, nothing but the sunset in front of me and the promise of something good to come. I did nothing but dream of that moment and naively assume that maybe one day it would become real.

I tell Walker how when my dad found me in it, he initially thought it was a stranger on the land with intentions to steal it. I watched with clarity as his eyes flickered from anger to fear like a lightning strike. Like he'd caught me about to stick my hand in a blender or something. He nearly cried when I stepped out, and with shaky hands, he forced me to go back to my room.

That night I heard him and Mom sobbing downstairs. About the affair or my attempt to get in a car, I'm not sure. But the sounds of their joint sobs still haunt me.

While I spill everything to Walker, he sits there, quiet and nodding.

When nearly an hour of me dropping my own lore has passed, our waiter asks us if we need to-go boxes. Walker slips a hand over our table and tangles his fingers with mine. He's saying everything with his eyes but only one sentence with his lips.

"I'm so glad I'm here with you."

Overall, it's the best date ever, and it's not even over yet.

My phone buzzes in my lap and I whisper an apology until I see it's Flick. I hang up and she dials back immediately, so I shoot off a quick text.

Lottie: Hey! Sorry, I can't answer right now.

Lottie: Walker asked me on a date, and oh my gosh you won't BELIEVE what he showed up to my house with. I'll call you as soon as I am alone!!

Flick starts typing, and then it goes away. She starts again, and again, but never replies.

“Do you need to go?” Walker cuts into my staring at the device. I decide I will call Flick the second I am alone, but right now, my time is his.

“Nope.” I smile at him across the table. “I’m all yours.” *Tonight,* I mean to add, but it feels better leaving it off.

CHAPTER TWENTY-SEVEN
Walker

Lottie stares in amazement at the sight in front of us. Blue, purple, and red lights dance around her face, lighting her up as she watches the entire city walking around this place.

"How did you even know this was going on tonight?"

"Kit, actually. He had a flyer, and I thought maybe you'd like it. You said lights didn't affect you, but if there's anything that makes you nervous, we can—"

"It's perfect." She reaches over and our fingers slip together. "I love it."

I squeeze her hand in mine. "Where do you want to go first?"

She hums and glances at our surroundings. The sun is low, casting long shadows across the boot-stamped concrete. A canvas of warm orange and pinks, the colors in the sky deepen by the minute as the sun sinks lower behind the Ferris wheel. Questionable metal rides cling around us, mixed with the faint hum of the carnival games where people are laughing and shouting. Lottie visibly winces at a teenager vomiting beside the Tilt-A-Whirl.

I see her eyes land on it as she smiles. "That." She points to the Ferris wheel that looks to be held together by duct tape and WD-40. "We need to do that."

My Adam's apple bobs in a swallow. "Solid choice."

We make our way over to the long line but get distracted halfway by the large flashing sign saying Hand-Scooped Ice Cream. Lottie widens her eyes at me in this "are you thinking what I'm thinking" gesture and I pull her to the very front. There's little she could ask me for that I would say no to right now.

Lottie and I stand in line for the Ferris wheel, each of us holding an overloaded cone of ice cream. Her laughter covers the sounds of the fair as she watches two large men in leather vests cling to the metal of their seat, crying out with every round the wheel does.

"Lottie? Lottie Jane?" a voice all but shouts at the front of the line, and a tall, skinny blond man steps out, waving his unnaturally long arms our way. She smiles at him, and he lights up brighter than the Ferris wheel behind him.

I hate him. In his stupid neon vest and neck tattoo of a… Is that a groundhog?

"Buck." Her laughter is a mix of nerves and apprehension. "What are you doing here?"

"I handle a couple rides before the big show. You know, when I'm not doing pyrotechnics, I volunteer at a few different fairs in the spring."

"Pyrotechnics?" I try to not say it with a snarl.

Lottie gives me a quirked smile, like there's an inside joke between us, one that's just ours. "Buck has a firework review YouTube channel. It blew up a couple years ago." She laughs a loud "ha" to herself. "*Blew up.*"

Buck shrugs and leans closer to her to add, "Seven hundred thousand subscribers, but no big deal."

He sounds like he would like it to be a very big deal.

"What...does that include?" I ask, and it's not like I force the ability to not care into my tone. There's just so much of it naturally sitting in the air that it's impossible not to come off this way.

"I review every firework that is legally allowed in the U.S."

"Ah."

With his boss yelling at him, Buck groans and points at my pretty date. "When you get to the front, I'll do something special just for you." He winks, and a heat simmers in my spine. Am I not obvious enough? Am I even here?

Lottie thanks him, and he slips out of line to operate the ride.

"*Buck*?" I groan.

"Short for Bucky."

"Which is short for...?"

"Buckifer? Buckaman? Buckalot? Richard? I'm not sure."

My lips twitch at that, and she takes her thumb and pokes it right in my dimple like she just can't help herself. "How do you know him?"

"He graduated from my school this spring. He *bucked* around quite a bit." Lottie wags her brows and I groan again.

"Did you two...*buck*?"

I will throw up right here, right now.

She laughs. "Absolutely not. Though we kissed once in a bet."

"You made out with a pyrotechnic expert?"

"My junior year was not very kind to me."

When we reach the front of the line, we slide into the small yellow cart. My nose scrunches when Buck gives Lottie a finger gun gesture.

I feel my chest rumble. "He's about to Buck around and find out."

"Cute." She leans into my chest, and I wrap my free hand around her waist, my fingers curling into her belt loop.

The ride lifts us up one slot to let the next couple on, and then another, until we've done a full circle for the ride to fill up. And whereas my ice cream was entirely gone in two seconds flat, Lottie's is barely dented at the top.

I tap on her waist. "You're eating that way too slow. It's going to melt while we're in here."

"Nah." She takes a slow, long lick with her tongue to torture me. "This is like a three-minute ride."

It was, in fact, not three minutes.

Thanks to our *friend*, Buck, after going around and around in circles, both of our stomachs dropping with each push forward, we end up pausing at the very top of the ride.

"Sorry, folks." His voice sounds like a pilot over speakers two stories below us. "Having technical difficulties."

I can't complain.

Because Lottie and I are together. In a very tight space. At the top of a Ferris wheel. With nothing but ice cream and the distant sounds of laughter and music around us. The smell of popcorn and fried food drifts through the air, mixing with the hint of fresh-cut grass.

I've never really been a huge fair guy, but being here with her makes me wonder why we didn't do this when we were younger.

"I think Buck is doing you a favor." She snickers and lands a finger high on my chest, trailing it down.

I glance from her to where the small ride management station is, and he is now shooting finger guns at me while an older couple at the bottom begs him to get off. "I think you might be right." I keep staring until Buck turns his hands from finger guns to two fingers pointing at his eyes and then up to me in the universal *I'm watching you* stare.

My shoulders shiver. "Actually, no. You're wrong."

She sighs and leans into my arm, taking another slow lick of her half-melted ice cream. "Well, I love it."

We sit there for a while, just taking in the view with the thin lap bar being the only thing between us and our death. Lottie is tucked against my shoulder, so every time I turn to my left, my face connects softly with her hair. Strawberries and honey and everything sweet in life. I have kissed her temple so many times that she looks up at me and kisses mine right back.

This is just *one* date. I know that. But it feels like so much more than that. It feels like everything before this was just… an appetizer. A first act in your favorite play.

"How do you want this to go?" I ask.

"What do you mean?"

"After tonight, if all goes well—Pantygate and all—" She snorts. "Where do we go from here? Your birthday is in less than a month and school is coming back…"

She freezes under my touch at the mention of it. "Oh. I was thinking we could maybe add a couple new things to the list."

"Mm?"

She looks up, our eyes locked together with a mix of stormy emotions between us both. Then she barrels past all the confusion. "Maybe add something…different."

"Yeah? Like what?"

"Like the two of us just seeing where this goes? Until you know for sure what you're doing." She sucks in a breath. "Maybe pretend like everything doesn't exist for a bit. I know you're leaving—I mean you *are* leaving, right?"

No. Not if you're here. And not if you still want me here.

I can't shackle her. I can't throw her in a cage like everyone else who has ever loved her. If I admit to staying here, to loving her, then I am forcing her to live next door to a man she's barely even dated. I won't make her go along with something that's not even her own choice.

"Depends."

Lottie tilts her head as she takes a slow lick of her ice cream. "On?"

Just as I am about to answer, a freezing-cold drip of water hits my wrist, and I startle. I glance up, expecting rain or maybe the person behind us to be throwing water in the air, but they're busy watching a geriatric woman competing in a Hula-Hoop competition below us. I turn back to my wrist and see a dot, then two, of bright green and white landing on my hot skin again. It's Lottie's mint chocolate ice cream. And in just a small moment of time, it's everywhere.

I don't mean just a little. The flavor of the week is, without her even realizing, melting down her forearms onto her pretty summer dress and puddling by our feet on the metal floor.

"You're melting, Trouble."

"Shoot." She licks the side of the cone that is melting fastest before she sees the carnage around us. It doesn't help that the opposite side's scoop is inches away from dripping onto the floor. "Give me your shirt."

"My shirt?"

"Well, *I* don't have one."

I shake my head. "I don't want your ex-boyfriend blowing up my house when we get off and he sees me shirtless and you all flustered."

"Ex-boyfriend is *quite* the stretch. Plus, our houses are connected. Buck would never allow that to happen to me."

My eyes shut. There is ice cream pooling in my lap, and I have every intention of throwing it off this ride and right onto the man who got us here in the first place. "That is not the affirmation you think it is."

I look around us, like this metal box that is destined to break any moment could possibly have a convenient napkin holder, but I come up short.

"Ugh, it's everywhere," she whines, and she tries to hold the ice cream out but it's still dripping on her dress. Her boots. "Why didn't you tell me to eat this faster?"

"You know what." I reach a hand out for her ice cream and do what I can only describe as pure instinct. I pull her wrist to my mouth and suck the dripping mint chocolate off her warm skin. Blood runs straight down my spine as my tongue cleans the melted ice cream and I get a taste of her with it.

Lottie gasps and my eyes shoot up to hers, mouth still on her wrist. Her eyes are half shut and her chest is heaving harder than mine is. I begin to drop her wrist, but she's pushing it gently back to me, despite the lack of ice cream, and I want to do it again. To just get my mouth on her again. I lean in—ice cream the least of my concerns now—with the intention of putting my lips on hers, right when we are jolted downward. Lottie shrieks as we push forward in our seats and Buck's voice comes back over the intercom, a little more frustrated than before. "Issue fixed. You can get off now."

He stops with us at the bottom first and Lottie quickly apologizes to another worker for the whole ice cream fiasco and offers to clean it up. They shrug it off and go to wipe up the mess themselves. She wraps her fingers around my wrist and tugs me away from the ride.

We are both covered in ice cream—all except for Lottie's

wrist, which I just licked like *that's* something you do on a first date.

We take a few steps away from the line waiting to get on the Ferris wheel and stand around like I didn't just lick her.

"Do you want to"—I swallow, the taste of her skin still dancing on my tongue—"do anything else while we're here?"

Her head shakes alongside mine. I didn't even realize my head was already shaking until she started mirroring me.

"Me neither," she says.

"So, maybe we could go to my place?" I offer.

"Or mine?"

I smile and parrot her previous words. "Right, because they're *so* far apart."

We make it halfway up the driveway before Lottie grabs my tie and lifts up to kiss me.

We fly into her house and I stare at the lock. "Did you not lock the door?"

"I never lock the door."

I pull back enough to stare her in the eyes. "Lottie, that's really, really bad—"

"You can get on me for it later."

As much as I want to push for her safety, I don't want to waste any more time of us being apart. Her lips mold against mine, the fullness resting in each dip and curve. I sigh into her when she rests both hands on my chest and around my neck. Her fingers slip under the collar of my shirt, where the cool touch of her skin feels like the ice cream she had dripping on us earlier.

She tastes like mint and chocolate and something spicy behind it.

I kiss her until there is nothing between us but lips and teeth and so much left unsaid. I kiss her with every word I can't say out loud. I kiss her with the intent of showing that I'm not leaving here—not leaving her.

She takes the opportunity when I open my mouth more to bite down on my lip, and I toss my head back further.

"You feel—" I snarl in the back of my throat. No word is appropriate enough to tell her. She feels like *silk*. Like sand falling through my fingers that I am so desperate to keep together. She's all messy hair, lowered straps, and mile-long legs wrapping around me. "Like mine. Are you?" I pull back enough to look into her eyes. "Mine?"

She gives me a curt nod, and one corner of my mouth lifts as I press a soft kiss to her cheek. "Yeah. Yeah, you are."

I feel her cheeks tighten in a smile against me. "I think you might be an angel, Walker."

My head tosses back with a laugh. "You're the only person who would ever say that."

"Good." She pulls me up for a long, slow kiss on my lips. "I hope I am. I think you're the best thing to happen to me, Walker Lane."

"I *know* you're the best thing to happen to me, Lottie Turner."

And of course, like he had to prove he has the worst timing, Henry thumps against the frame by the door.

"Ugh," Lot whines, "not now, Henry."

She lifts a middle finger to the door, and I laugh, nuzzling into the warmest part of her skin, placing a kiss just above where her heart rests. Where I want to stay forever.

The thud comes again, but this time it's louder and followed by a loud, "Open the door!"

I lift up. "Is that your dad?"

Lottie brushes her fingers in my hair. "I don't think I care."

Eyes trailing back to the girl in front of me, my smile goes all wobbly. What a privilege to just sit right here with her.

"Lot, baby—"

"Open the damn door!" That's enough to knock us both out of it. I move my feet off the couch and stand up, taking her with me, her feet dangling above the floor. I force myself to lift up the two straps of her dress and adjust her hair before glaring at the door behind her. "Get over here *now*."

And that's about all I can take of that.

CHAPTER TWENTY-EIGHT
Lottie

"Who the hell is talking to you that way?"

Walker pulls back, and the sudden loss of his lips on mine leaves me breathless. He strides to the front door, a man on a mission, but just before he can reach it, Knox comes storming in like a bull in a China shop, slinging my spare key onto the couch.

I attempt to correct my hair. "Knox, what are you do—"

His nostrils flare, fire burning in my brother's eyes. "I am so pissed at you I can't see straight."

He *knows*. He knows about the riding lessons. And the waterfall. And rolling Riley's house. He very clearly has somehow found my list—or maybe Flick let it slip on accident—but that has to be the only plausible explanation for the amount of anger he is putting off.

"I didn't think you would—"

"What's the date, Lot?" His face is so red I expect steam to flare out of his ears at any moment. "Huh?"

I look to Walker for some kind of clue, but he is busy

staring at Knox with anger burning in his eyes. "Uh…I don't know?" My voice is shaky as I try to piece together the day. "The 30th?"

He nods, and my confusion is only ramping up. "And the day?"

"Saturday?"

"*Yup.*" Knox is staring at me like this date is supposed to mean anything special, and I am trying to mentally consider when his birthday is. "And what was going on tonight that wasn't important enough for you to show up to at all and stick around with this guy looking like every woman's wet dream?" He tosses a thumb over his shoulder to Walker.

"Flick. Flick's charity event was tonight."

My stomach twists—I should know this. I should have been there. I've had it in my head for weeks. I promised her over and over and over I was going to make it. It's at least nine o'clock. The event started at six thirty. An hour after she had called me. She tried over and over, and I wasn't there.

"Uh-huh. And you know who didn't come?" Knox has his fists clenched at his sides.

"Me," I whisper.

"*NOBODY.*"

"What?" This empty, dark feeling in my stomach grows and grows. In the chaos of everything around me, I just… forgot. It's been over a week since we spoke about it, and it somehow slipped. I know I screwed up. I know this is a huge, colossal, *ginormous* screwup on my end, but no one at all showing up? Odie? Ada? Even Lawson and Ledger?

Nausea rises in my stomach. My precious best friend. The girl I always claimed was my number one soul mate forever has spent over a month prepping this, and no one, including me, showed up for her.

"That's right. Not one single person in town tonight besides me. Instead, everyone seemed to go to some last-minute county fair that's held together by duct tape."

He blows out a breath, and I swear he is so angry that a tear forms in the corner of his eye. Knox isn't a sad crier; he's an angry crier. "I spent the entire day setting up tables and banners and watching her get all excited for these guys to get adopted. Not one person in this town showed up for her. I've called *everyone,* and no one is answering. Not even her own mother came. And the one person, *the one person* she needed there tonight, was in her house doing God knows what with a random guy in her living room."

"Knox, I'm so—"

"Don't. Don't you dare say it to me. You call the love of my life and apologize right now, or I swear, Lottie." Knox is practically foaming at the mouth he is so angry. I've never seen him like this. So angry that I take a step back, and my eyes shift to Walker for some kind of help that could make us go back and change the past. To fix this. If Knox is this mad at me that he's finally letting it all out, then this is *bad.* Knox and I haven't argued since my diagnosis. Closest we've come to it is playfully fighting over the last of Mom's cheesecake, but even then, it was never real. Never this.

"Alright, watch it." Walker stalks across my living room and his jaw flexes, eyeing my brother.

Knox doesn't acknowledge Walker's threat. No, his eyes stay locked on me. The anger he held in them, rimmed with tears, melts into disappointment. It's that look that breaks me the most. He is so disappointed in me, possibly more than I am in myself.

"I've tried so hard to stand up for you all the time. I carry so much with me—" He sucks in a shaky breath and doesn't elaborate. "I'm not making excuses for you this time, Lot. You screwed up. Big time."

"I'm not—" I sniff and realize I'm crying too. I was never an angry crier. Only a sad one. "I'm not trying to get you to make excuses."

"Good. Because I'm *done*."

Knox turns on his heel, ignoring Walker's death glare, and slams the door shut behind him. He left the spare key on my couch. Does he know? Is he giving up on me?

A weight falls on my back, and I realize Walker has his arms wrapped around me. His voice, husky and somehow soft, lands in my ear. "Shh, it's okay. We'll make it up to her, alright?" His large hand rubs up and down my back, and if I wasn't so caught up in wondering how I am possibly going to fix this, I would appreciate the sentiment. "I'm so sorry. I'm… so, so sorry. You told me about the event, and I still… I didn't even think about the date and… I am so sorry, sweetheart."

I lift a hand, wrestling between hugging him back and wiping my own tears. My fingers reach for my cheek first, and I guess that's my body's own answer.

He holds me for a moment, a few. Maybe two minutes. Maybe twenty. When I eventually do pull back, the tears on my cheeks are still wet, but my breath is a little less shaky.

"You should go," I muster.

Walker pulls back and searches my tearful eyes. I can't bear to meet his. "If that's what you want."

I nod. "Yeah."

Walker slips out of the house, and when I hear his door shut, I blow out a breath and frantically search for my phone.

I have loads of notifications, but I am solely looking for Flick's contact.

It takes five calls. Five voicemails of my long-winded

apologies and begging for her to call me back, only for the answering machine to cut me off mid-sentence each time. But on the sixth one, after the sixth ring, she answers.

"Hello." Her voice is shattered, and I can imagine her crying. I feel like I am right there to witness tears stream down her brown face. I hear the heartbreak in one word, and the nausea in my gut only rises higher.

"Flick," I gasp, pressing a shaking hand to my chest. My throat is so tight it hurts to speak. "You answered."

"Knox told me not to. You know I don't follow his instructions well."

She tries to toss humor in, but it falls flat.

"I-I'm so sorry." My voice wobbles, and I swipe at the tears burning down my cheeks. "You called. You called and called, and I was in that stupid restaurant with Walker doing the list. I was so focused on what's absent in my life that I didn't even think to wonder what I am missing out on in yours. It's horrible. It's so wrong. I should have been there. We were going to get all of those babies adopted, and I was going to clean cat litter and hang signs and take cash, and I wasn't there for any of it. I am so, *so* sorry."

It's silent on the other end, and I almost keep rambling about my mistakes just to fill the space, but she's just so quiet.

When she responds, it's so small I almost miss it. "It's fine, Lot."

"It's not."

She laughs again, and it's fake and hits like a punch to the gut. "It's no big deal. We both know no one was going to adopt any, and I would have had to beg Knox to put at least a dozen more animals on the land. Which reminds me—"

"Why won't you just yell at me?" My voice cracks, raw with frustration.

We've done this before. The same cycle. The same silent forgiveness that only makes me feel worse. And it always ends the same. I do something wrong. I screw up. I hurt her. She pretends I didn't. Because she assumes if she comes to me in anger or disappointment, it will be enough to send me into a seizure.

I break the dance, stop the game. I am so over pretending.

"I screwed up. Colossally. I don't know if I can even forgive myself. Why can't you yell at me? Or get pissed off?"

"Lottie, it was an accident. I know you didn't mean to..."

"That doesn't make it okay. Just...stop pretending I'm so fragile and yell at me."

"I would never yell at you."

"Really? Cause you yell at Knox. You fight with Ada sometimes. Even Odie. It's not that you hate conflict, it's that you think conflict with me will make me go into an episode."

"That's not true. I'm just not mad..." There's another big sniff, and my heart cracks.

"You *are*. You absolutely are. I know you are because I'm pissed at myself. Flick, this was *huge* for you, and I dropped the ball in so many ways. So, please, just yell and scream so we can figure this out."

"I've got to go." Flick sniffles, and the silence between us stretches unbearably long.

My stomach clenches. She's crying—I know she is. I can feel the weight of it even through the phone. She's crying and I can't even threaten to beat up the one who made her cry because it's entirely my fault.

"Flick, please..." My voice is barely a whisper.

"We'll talk later," she says, and then the line goes dead. I stare at the phone, heart pounding, knowing that no matter how many times I call, I can't undo tonight.

CHAPTER TWENTY-NINE
Walker

This is either the best idea I've had all summer, or the worst. The jury's still out. Unfortunately, I won't have my answer until tonight. Still, I press on.

Standing beneath the neon glow of the Happy Tails Haven sign, I watch the neon golden retriever's tail flick back and forth as the light pulses on and off. Through the glass door, Knox is leaning against the counter, one elbow propped up, the other hand absently tugging at his short blond hair. His dark eyes droop lower than they did Saturday night, purple bags beneath them, and his cheekbones are prominent. He looks sick.

A handful of kittens sitting on the counter beside him climb his arms and chest, vying for his attention, but he barely glances at them.

I haven't seen or heard from him in days. Neither has Lottie, I assume. Not that we've discussed it. Since that night, we've danced around certain topics—the missed event, the inevitable end of summer. Our conversations remain light, skimming the surface of something deeper we both refuse to acknowledge.

Each morning, we pass each other on our porches. She sits on the swing outside her door, a quilt draped over her lap, an old paperback propped on her knees. The kind with yellowed pages and a shirtless man holding a swooning woman on the cover.

I leaned down to eye the title.

Surrender to the Duke's Desire.

"Does she surrender?" I asked.

Lottie straightened, eyes meeting mine. "She does."

"Good for her."

A small smile tugged at her lips. It was the first one I had really pulled out of her since that night.

"Good for him too."

Beyond that, our communication has been sporadic at best. I texted her last night about Henry's return—three books knocked off the shelf in one evening. She replied, "Funny, none of my books have fallen today. I think Henry is a historical romance lover."

I made a passing comment about Knox's absence from the farm yesterday. Her response was a simple "I wouldn't know."

That told me enough. She and Felicity still hadn't talked. If they had, I think Lottie would have called me. Or maybe we're not at that point and it's just wishful thinking.

I know I should probably leave it alone. Let things simmer. It's technically none of my business. But the shadows under Lottie's eyes and the way stress coils tighter in her expression each time I pass by makes my stomach twist to the point where I can hardly sleep.

So here I am.

The bell chimes as I push the door inward and take a step

inside. An eruption of barking follows from behind the yellow flowered curtain hiding whatever is behind the counter.

"Welcome to—oh." Felicity looks up from the desk, surprise flickering across her face.

Knox barely acknowledges me, as if he's too exhausted to summon irritation or anger. His shoulders slump as he mutters to the parrot perched on the counter, "I'm gonna wash some blankets. Come on, Nigel."

The green-and-red parrot flaps onto his shoulder as Knox turns away, two kittens jumping from the counter to the chair and down to the floor, trailing after him.

It's…cleaner than I expected an animal shelter to be. The walls beside me are a mix of different pastel tones all pulling together—mint greens, buttery yellows, and sky blues. There are a couple murals of animals playing in meadows or napping under trees. The one of a pug eating a deli sandwich on a checkered blanket with sunglasses on is really hard to look away from.

I take a step closer to the counter, and my boots squeak loudly against a rubber mat. My eyes stare down at it, questioning.

Before I can ask, Felicity is answering. "It's nonslip. For older dogs. They like to look out the windows when the sun sets."

"Ahh, very nice."

Then, as if she realizes she never actually said anything when I walked in, she whispers a small "Hello" before crossing her arms and looking like she wants to follow Knox into the back so she doesn't have to have this conversation. But, to her credit, she stays still, only tilting her head. "What are you doing here?"

"I'm here to apologize."

She blinks. "There's really no need for you to—"

"*And* to adopt a dog."

Her posture shifts, eyes narrowing and back straightening. "Really?" Felicity squints at me across the counter, and the move is so much like Lottie that I almost laugh. "Because if this is short-term and that dog ends up right back here, it'll break their heart. Animals are very emotionally sensitive, and we're talking a ten-plus year commitment—"

"I know. It's not for me."

Her brow furrows. "Oh?"

"It's for Lottie."

It's a last-minute idea. Though, really, it's been in place longer than I've been here. I think Lottie would be the first to jump on this change, this commitment, and I do think it's one she would lovingly stick to.

At the idea, Felicity's entire demeanor changes in an instant—a broad smile breaks out across her face and she bounces around on her toes, wild curly hair bouncing in the air around us. "Oh my God. Even better!" Dogs, and whatever else is back there, all erupt in their own noises at the squeals coming from this lady. I can hear Knox trying to settle them back down, but it seems to be a useless effort.

Felicity flings open the swinging door to the counter and gestures for me to follow her to the chaos behind her.

"I've tried a hundred times to get her to take one of these babies home, but she always says no to me." She boops a French bulldog on the nose in passing. "But I have a feeling she'll say yes to *you*."

I follow along as Felicity is bouncing on her feet and weaving between kennels. Every dog, cat, and…I think that was a ferret, make themselves known. Out of the corner of my eye, Knox is glaring at me, but it lightens a little when Felicity looks his way. There's a wiener dog who looks approximately sixty years old and a cat with one ear missing, even a hamster in a small cage that is running in circles. None of them feel exactly right. I think a big dog would be good. A protector. Someone, something, to watch over her and comfort her and—

"Hey, buddy." Felicity stops in front of a small crate in the corner of the room.

She falls down to her knees and fumbles with the lock. "I've got a friend I want you to meet."

Felicity reaches a gentle hand in and pulls out the smallest golden puppy with big brown eyes and oversized paws that stares up at me like I'm his savior. I swear his eyes are taking up 90 percent of his face. And his head is so big and his body so small that it's like he can barely hold it up.

"We've had this little guy with her in mind for a week now, but I haven't had the chance to mention it since, you know…" Her voice drags off and I just nod, staring at him.

He's so cute and somehow—I'm just going to say it—*so* ugly all at once. Like this adorable trainwreck you just can't take your eyes off. "Poor guy was abandoned in the parking lot," she murmurs and rubs behind his floppy ears.

"I think he was the runt of the litter. Maybe they didn't think he was good enough for breeding? Ridiculous." She readjusts the pup, cradling him across her forearms and stretching the little guy out to me. "He deserves better." She looks up from him to me with this almost menacing look. "He deserves Lottie."

He's not big. He's not ferocious and protective and certainly not going to ward off strangers, as he runs up and immediately starts licking my shoelaces. But…

I reach down and rub behind his floppy ears. He nuzzles

into my hand before I cradle him to my chest. "Hey, little man."

The fluff of gold and brown sniffs all around my shirt, probably picking up on the smell of cattle and horses from today's work.

I know it makes no sense, and I know this is the exact opposite kind of dog I came in here for, but Felicity's right. He is perfect for Lottie.

"We're gonna be good friends, huh?"

The little guy looks up at me with those massive eyes, and I know in my gut I am not going a single day without this dog in my life. Not as long as I can help it.

The adoption process is quicker than I expected. The thing that took the longest was pulling Felicity back to the front as she tried to talk me into leaving with Nigel and a ferret, and I think that last one might have been a bunny? It was so fluffy I couldn't tell what it was. But by the time we're done, Felicity is still buzzing with excitement.

Before I leave, I glance at her—it hits me like a ton of bricks that I haven't said the second thing I came here to say. I blame it on this big head and big paws and tiny body sleeping in my hand. "You should talk to Lottie." I say it firmly enough that she has no choice but to take it in. "She really misses you."

Felicity's smile falters. "I was just—"

"I know." I know it's my fault more than anyone else's, and I know in the same way Lottie is at home saddled up with guilt, Felicity is saddled up with her own emotions too. "She knows too. Just…talk to her."

She exhales a long sigh, looking from this nameless pup in my hands back to me with a small grin. "Yeah. I will."

As I step into the parking lot, I hear my name being called

out behind the glass. Knox runs out after me, the bell of the door chiming behind us. I turn back to the wagging tail sign that he's below, and he's got his hands in his pockets, balancing back and forth on the balls of his feet.

"I can get hotheaded," he admits. "Felicity says it all the time."

"She might be right."

He huffs a quiet laugh. "Yeah. She usually is." A pause settles between us, mostly silent beyond my new friend snoring. "How's Lot?"

I look up to meet his gaze and answer honestly. "Rough."

His jaw flexes. "I kind of figured. She and Felicity...they don't ever *not* talk. Getting them to shut up is usually the issue." He lets out this shaky laugh, and when I don't follow, he settles on "I know I should reach out."

"You should." I am about to head to my truck but hesitate. "She's not mad at you or Flick. She's more disappointed in herself than anything. A call from either of you would mean a lot."

He nods but doesn't promise anything.

I adjust the squirming puppy in my arms and turn toward my truck. "I guess I'll see you later."

I have an entire list of things I need to do before I pop onto my pretty neighbor's front porch with a dog between us like a formal peace offering for my mistake.

Before I hit the truck though, Knox calls out, "Hey, Walker."

I glance back.

"Take care of my sister," he says with authority. "You're good for her."

"She's good for me too."

He nods. "I'm starting to realize that. Just...don't break

her heart if you leave again." A smirk tugs at his mouth. "I'll come to space camp and kick your ass."

I snort. *Space camp.*

"I don't plan on it."

Not now and not ever again.

CHAPTER THIRTY
Lottie

"I have something for you." Walker's voice immediately calls out through the walls before I can even croak a "hello."

Three days. It's been *three* entire days of silence from Flick and Knox. The only thing that assures me the two are even alive is the sound of Knox driving off to the shelter like clockwork at 6:48 every morning and the updates from Mom that Dad and Knox are working on a few projects and he seems fine. Other than that…just radio silence.

Walker, as sweet as he is, has tried everything he can to lift my spirits, but without my own ray of sunshine, how am I supposed to? How am I supposed to move past this when the first person I call about this stuff is the one avoiding me?

"I hope it's as funny as the last surprise." My mouth feels dry when I try to force humor into it. Though glancing over at the bouquet of underwear in a vase on my dining table does have my lips tilting up slightly.

"I thought we came to an agreement to never discuss it again."

Following his response, a knock sounds at my door. Walker's knock. Three fast ones and two slow ones following.

"Is that you at my door?"

"Open it and see."

I slip off the couch and force myself to stand up and trudge my way to the door.

There are a limited number of things that Walker could logically have as a surprise for me at my door.

However, the very, very, I mean *bottom of the list into the core of the earth* last thing I expected to see is what is standing in front of me right now.

Maybe I should have zeroed in on the fact that Walker is wearing an old T-shirt with the sleeves cut off low enough that I can see chest and armpit hair. And whereas that should not be as hot as it is to me, I can't exactly find a single thing about Walker that *isn't* hot.

However, it's the small item in his hands that grabs my full attention. A wiggly item.

A wiggly puppy.

A squirming, golden yellow puppy with floppy ears and oversized paws in Walker's hand, snuggling right into his chest. My favorite place to be.

"I brought a friend with me this time. Hope you don't mind."

My mouth opens and shuts repeatedly before I land on "Your shirt is ripped. I can see a small corner of your nipple."

Walker's entire face is beet red as he adjusts his shirt—if you can even call it that.

"Is that what we're really focusing on right now?"

"You should know it's a bit distracting."

"Can we come in?"

We. My eyes are stuck on the "we" in question. This

six-foot man in my doorway is holding this yapping, yawning puppy that is staring at me with the sweetest big brown eyes.

"You have a dog in your hands." I open the door far enough to let Walker in and point to his chest. "What's he doing there?"

He settles in on my couch like he's always lived here. Back slouched against the right cushion—he always favors that one—and his boots propped up on my coffee table beside his hat.

"I thought he'd be a good friend to you. And I felt bad about the whole"—he clears his throat—"Pantygate. And the end of the date, and just, you know, kind of all of it?"

Friend to *me*?

"So…you…" I look down at my lap and realize I am now sitting on my living room floor, staring into Walker's thighs that are holding the sleepy guy.

"Dogs are a lot of work, I know." He nods and keeps his gaze firm on me, but I can't bear to lift my eyes off his lap. "I just thought, you know, in your list you were looking for a pet, and I don't know, you wanted something new and exciting. Something that could be *fully* yours and I saw him and… Well, look at him. You guys are basically twins." He lifts the puppy beside me so we're cheek to cheek. It yawns centimeters from my face, and it smells like puppy breath with a hint of Cheerios. "I mean, identical."

I stare from the cutest dog in the entire world up to the cutest, kindest, most generous boy in the entire world, and I shake my head. He's got it wrong.

He's the one that's identical to the little guy. All big hands and a bigger heart.

"You…got me a dog?"

He trusts me with a dog. With something so small and so precious and perfect and…

"Well, I thought he would be a great service dog," Walker amends.

Honestly, I hadn't even considered that. A few of the members in forums I'm in have service dogs and they all have good things to say. They share stories of their dogs nudging them a certain way when they can tell a seizure is coming. Or if they pass out, the dogs will lift their heads to be safe.

"I looked it up, and statistics show an average 31 percent fewer seizures after months of having a service-trained animal to help people with epilepsy."

"He's trained?" He's so tiny, I don't think there's a way he could possibly lift my head. Actually, I don't think he can do anything besides eat, sleep, and poop at this stage.

"No." Walker chuckles when the dog readjusts and curls back into him. "But there's this place in Birmingham that said they could start him as soon as ten weeks old. I thought maybe I could drive him back and forth for you? It wouldn't be super far. Two hours or so. I could make the drive with him on the weekends. Or maybe you could go with us? We could drop him off to train and make a day out of it. Go out to eat, visit that botanical garden, and there's that bundt cake place that you like—"

This boy. This beautiful, wonderful, strange, and perfect boy.

I love him.

I tried. I really, really did try to avoid this. I've known for weeks what I was getting into, and still, all I can feel for the boy in front of me is love.

I attempt to imagine a life of not loving him, where he takes the internship and I stay here, and I can't. I don't think there is a universe out there in which I *don't* love Walker. I'm just lucky enough to live in the one where I get to fall in love with him twice.

"Walker." I look up to him and he frowns. When his thumb gently drapes across my cheek, I realize I'm crying.

"I love him."

You. You. You. *You. I love you and him, and I love you even more for getting me him.*

"You do?" Relief floods his face, lips curving up and eyebrows lifting.

"So much." I sniff into the puppy's fur. It smells like Puppy Chow and a hint of Walker. I want to keep it like this forever. "Gosh, look at him."

"He's perfect, isn't he?"

I lift the little guy up where we can both see him and pout. "So, so, perfect. Where did you get him?"

"I, uh, paid a visit to Knox."

I raise a brow. "Did you guys duke it out and this was the prize?"

"Not even close, actually." He snorts a laugh as I nuzzle my nose into the puppy's cheek. He is so tired that he just allows it. "I went to the shelter to apologize to Felicity and he was there."

"You saw Flick?"

He nods.

"And?"

"And I think you guys will be good soon."

"Yeah." I scoff. "Because you adopted a dog from her."

"Because she knows *you*. And she recognizes that you have a really, really good heart that would never mean to hurt anyone."

I grumble. "Some heart. I can't even set aside my own desires for a single night to be there for a friend that's been dragged around to every single party with me. Did you know she didn't even yell at me, Walker?" My voice is shaky. "I mean, what happened was awful. When we finally spoke,

I could hear the tears in her voice. I knew she was torn up. And still, through it all, she was so focused on my health that she couldn't even work up the courage to be mad. She was so nervous about my anxiety sending me into an episode that she just pretended like it never happened. You know how much that hurts to hear? That even when the lowest, worst part of yourself comes out, your friends still have so much pity for you that they can't even be angry to your face?"

Walker is silent for a moment. He lets my tears fall and doesn't wipe them away. He soaks them in and lets me feel it right there with him.

"I know you see it as pity. I get it. Or I get it as much as I *can.* But, I think..." He sucks in a deep breath and pulls back enough that I have to look at him. "I think she loves you so much that sometimes fear and pity can be disguised as each other."

I sniff. "You do?"

"Yeah. I mean, she was there for it all, right? The beginning of everything?"

My head dips. "Yeah. She was in the ambulance. Dad was in shock at all the blood and couldn't respond to any of the EMTs. Mom was at the farmers market with her phone off. It wasn't until she saw the ambulance turn out of our driveway that she even realized. Flick was the only one that could answer it all." I finally wipe at my cheeks. "She knew my blood type. *I* didn't even know my blood type. While I was in and out, having multiple seizures back-to-back. Grand mal and absent. She sat there the entire time until they rolled me back to the ICU."

"That must've been hard." His hands brush up and down my arms.

I shrug. "I assume. She's never told me everything she saw that night. I know she's seen countless of my seizures. A lot of the time I don't realize it happens until it's over and she's checking my pulse."

Walker hums and I take it as a sign to keep going. "I think…I think she forgot who I was before all of that. Who I am way down inside. I think everyone else has too."

I glance up at him. His gaze bounces between me and the sleeping puppy by my neck. "I think the only person who sees me as that version of myself is you."

He stares into my eyes, those dark-brown orbs with that little pour of honey zeroed in on me.

"I think you're the only person that actually knows me, Walker."

He smiles. It's pretty and big, and I want to hold it tight to the hollow in my chest. "I'm honored."

He lifts both hands to cradle my head, wipes the tears off my cheeks, and plants a small kiss to my temple. "Now." He grins into my skin. "On to the real important stuff. What are you going to name the little guy?"

"Waylon?"

"I feel like everyone's got a Waylon."

"Shiloh?"

"Meh."

"Russell."

"I don't know. I mean, look at him," he says. I lift up the golden retriever, and his ears flop to one side. "He's kind of… distinguished."

"Oh. He is *definitely* distinguished."

Walker nods. "Like a gentleman."

"A scholar."

"He's the kind of dog that could give out bank loans."

My laughter builds up like tiny bubbles in my stomach. “Or cut ribbons at art ceremonies.”

“He *would* cut ribbons at art ceremonies. And new car washes.”

“I bet he’d take a fancy internship at NASA.” I don’t know why I say it, but when I do, it comes out with a small sniff.

Is he leaving me with this dog as some kind of consolation for his departure next month?

“Ah.” Walker shrugs one shoulder. “It’s easy for him. He hasn’t clung on to anyone yet.”

I smile. I hope he does cling to me. Long-distance or neighbors. Friends or more. I hope he clings to me as much as I do to him.

“Hm. What about Apollo?”

“Apollo?”

“Yeah. Like the space thingy. That way—” I suck in a shaky breath. “If you do go, I’ll have a piece of space down here with me.”

Walker nods with a smile. He leans close and whispers low in my ear, “You do know there is literally no way I am going to space. At all. Not even a tiny bit close.”

“I think it’s a requirement to work there. You have to visit one of the planets and bring back a souvenir as a prize. Bonus points if it’s an alien.”

“So that’s what they’ve been doing at Area 51.”

“I would know. I am a very clever girl.”

“That you are, Trouble.” He smiles and I bask in the glow of it. “Apollo, huh?” He outright steals my puppy and cradles him like a baby. I dare say it’s even cuter than his baby voice with the ducklings. “Is that your name? *Apollo*.” He pouts and the pup yaps beside him. "Oh, is that a yes? Your mommy *is* so clever, isn't she, bud?"

I haven't always felt it, but I think I might be. At least clever enough to fall in love with a man like him.

CHAPTER THIRTY-ONE
Lottie

Apollo and I quickly become best buds.

Turns out, after a quick appointment at Magnolia Animal Care on Main, he's only six weeks old. The vet, Maria Kari—who absolutely despises being compared to *the* Mariah Carey—also believes he's not just a golden. She thinks maybe there's a mix of something else in him as well, which might explain why he was left at the shelter. Unwanted.

Walker and I left clinging to the baby, fighting over who got to hold him on the ride home. Although, the joke's on him, Apollo is a mommy's boy. On the ride back, Walker told me he believes our friend to be the runt of the litter. I smiled down at Apollo when he said it. "Me too, buddy."

We cling together like Velcro for the next two days. No matter where I am, even at work, he's there with me. I brought him to yesterday's afternoon shift at Riley's with zero apology. I'm a working mother; they have to understand that. Though I didn't even have to work up to my reasoning before he was being passed around by the staff up front. Ada carried him around in her overalls like they were a baby sling.

Even for today's riding lessons with Kit, Apollo stayed in my T-shirt, his tiny legs tucked into my sports bra and his head popped out like a baby kangaroo. It effectively took away from my *very* serious coaching voice, but I didn't mind too much. I had Kit working on a practice bull. Kind of like a mechanical bull, except we pull a rope with each jerk. A *manual* bull, if you will. He fell off twice as many times as usual, his eyes constantly going back to Apollo's squirming, and I quickly decided this was probably not the best tactic.

When Walker comes over to see me now, I think it's an excuse to see the pup. Apollo follows me everywhere. Walker's tried giving him new treats or toys, even going as far as buying him a nice, fancy bed—which he never uses, instead sleeping on a rolled-up blanket at the end of my bed. And still, Apollo prefers me. Something I enjoy rubbing in Walker's face quite a bit. It's about time I get a one-up on the guy.

Maybe it's ridiculous to let something so tiny and squirmy enter my life for two days and feel like my whole world is rocked, but I can't help it. I look at the little guy and it's like we're attached. Like he was always made to be mine. Two runts of their pack that are better off together than alone. We give each other a bigger purpose.

The riding lessons, the almost-completed list, Walker, Apollo… In the span of two months, my life has slowly worked itself out in a way that feels like cracks in a driveway being filled up one by one. None of these things are life-changing. They're just these small, daily habits that make me look around and suddenly realize that I am happy.

Apollo is in my lap, chewing on the frayed edges of my shorts.

"You're lucky I love you." I scratch behind his ears, his favorite spot. "Huh? You know I love you?"

He glances up at me, head tilting side to side, and I know. It's a yes. He is as infatuated with me as I am with him.

I lift him up to my chest. "What are we doing today, huh?"

He bobs his chin as he tries to find a piece of my hair to chew on. I've been wearing it up nonstop because it's Apollo's strange little addiction to chew on it, and whereas my shorts are easily replaceable, I've spent years of hard work and far too much money on my hair.

"Maybe take Kit to get his gloves back? Yeah? You love Kit, don't you?" His tail starts to wag, but I think it has less to do with the words themselves and more to do with my low-pitched, pouting baby talk.

He yawns, big and stretched out. This puppy breath is transitioning into, I don't know, toddler dog breath? Either way, it's the one thing that's getting slightly less cute about him. I am just about to tell my newest friend the importance of hygiene and ask if dogs have to brush their teeth, when my doorbell rings.

"Or maybe Kit is gonna come to us." I grunt, pulling me and Apollo to a full standing position to answer our friend at the door.

He's forgotten his gloves the last two times we've met, and each time I tell him to grab them, it's instantly in one ear and out the other. I swing the door open with his gloves waving in my hand.

"Hey, you forgot your… Oh."

On my front porch stands my best friend of the last ten years.

Flick looks at my door like a total stranger would. She's sheepish and blushing and *so* wonderful to see that I could just squeeze her. When her eyes land on mine, it feels like a true punch to the gut.

Apollo yaps at her, and she, without breaking eye contact, leans in to grab him from me and settles him into her arms.

"Hey, little guy." Flick pets his ears, looks down as she checks something with his hips, and then looks warily back at me.

"Hi." I answer for him. Or maybe for me too?

I've never so much as had a single awkward encounter with Flick. From day one, ever since Knox yanked her into our living room and said she unexplainedly needed a pair of shoes, we've been tied at the hip. I gave her a pair of high-top Converse that didn't fit me anymore. She looked at them like they were a rare artifact.

"If you like those, come see what I've got in my closet." It was a pair of extremely pointy brown leather booties that were the closest thing I could find to what Cameron Diaz wore to the *Charlie's Angels* premiere. I worked all winter cleaning windows and scrubbing baseboards to earn up enough to buy them. I hadn't even worn them yet. They sat in their box in my closet with handwritten No Touching signs, like a shrine built around them.

She instantly followed me up to my room. Taking the stairs two at a time, we threw ourselves into my room on our bellies and stared at the beauty in front of us. Everyone else, friends and family, thought it was an absurd thing to save up money for to spend all at once.

But Flick…she gasped and smiled and stared at them in awe the same way I had months and months before, my face pressed into the boutique's windows and fogging up the glass.

In that moment, a bond like no other connected us. She was my girl and I was hers.

She respected my love for all things beauty and fashion, and I respected her love for constantly begging for us to go to the creek to collect tadpoles.

Still, from the very beginning, we've never had a mix-up. A dry patch. A moment of passive-aggressive built-up anger and disappointment and everything exploding in front of us in a way where neither of us had a clue where to go from there.

Silence falls between us, and even in the discomfort, I am *so* excited to have her near me that I could cry.

My lips quiver. Watching this, she allows hers to as well. And before either of us can so much as take a breath, we're in each other's arms, rambling back and forth. She smells like piña colada shampoo, and I am so relieved at the scent that it makes me cry more.

"I'm sorry I've been weird, Lot," she says.

"I'm sorry I've been weird too. And I'm really, *really* sorry I missed your event."

"I know you are. And I'm sorry I didn't yell at you about it."

"Please yell at me," I beg.

"I still don't want to."

"I kind of need you to?"

"I'm not a very good yeller."

I pull back to wipe my tears on the back of my hand. "I have a distinct memory of you on the phone with that pet insurance company that says otherwise."

She laughs a little, and we both step back, trying to collect ourselves. "Do you want to come inside?"

There's silence in her hesitation, and I am mentally begging her to come in. To be normal and leave everything else around us on this porch. Except Apollo. He's scratching at the door to go inside. He's a bit of a couch potato.

"Something *happened* with Knox." She blurts it out so fast that I have to do a double take.

"*What*?" I choke, and Apollo scratches at my ankle. "When?"

"On Friday night."

"And I'm just now finding out?" My voice is at a level-ten volume. Birds scurry out of nearby trees in a frenzy. Apollo looks taken aback. He's still innocent and doesn't know Mommy is crazy yet.

"Well, it's been weird. I brought Diet Coke and limes?"

I look behind her for the first time and see two brown paper sacks set on the stairs behind her. I grab her wrist frantically. "Get in here and tell me everything."

We sit by the couch, actively shaving the cushions with our automatic lint rollers as Apollo gnaws on my fingers, teething like a menace. Two iced Diet Cokes with sliced limes floating around in our drinks, we talk faster than we ever have. It's like we're on a game show, and the game is to see how many topics you can jump around to as fast as you can without breaking a sweat.

I have to say, we are winning. By a lot.

"So, what happened?" I ask first, because no matter how much I am dying to share details of my first date with Walker, Knox and Flick have been skirting around this kiss for twenty some odd years. So it takes the cake.

"I thought he was going to kiss me."

I gasp, "Flick!"

"But now I think it was an accident?"

I narrow my eyes. "No, it wasn't."

"No." She sighs in resolve. "It wasn't. It was more like...

well, more like an experiment, I think. We were just about to, I mean I could practically taste his gum, and then Richie barked and everything stopped."

"Dang it, Richie. Well, before that, how was it?"

Flick sighs wistfully, playing with the end of her hair and staring at my living room ceiling like it's full of the sky's prettiest stars. "If you have half the talent in your mouth as your brother has in his just leading up to a kiss... Walker is a *very* lucky man."

I let out a fake gag but can't stop myself from laughing. "Ugh, gross."

"It's the truth. I think he's made of magic."

Knox is made up solely of hard work and too many Red Bulls. No magic involved there. "I think you're delusional." I take a sip of my drink and lean back against my coffee table. "So, what does this mean?"

She shrugs, and there goes that sheepish look again. "Well. We haven't talked about it since. Or talked hardly at all since Saturday night beyond both of us volunteering, so..."

"Oh, Flick." I sit up in a flash. "You haven't talked to me or Knox since Saturday?"

"Yeah. Now things are weird with him, and he keeps avoiding me." Guilt seeps in further than before. I had people on my side, and her favorite people were both radio silent.

"Have you tried calling?"

"Ten times today," she groans. "He's always 'busy.'"

"Hmm." I think back to the way my brother came running in my house like a crazed man. I know him. I know him enough to be certain that whatever this is between them, it's *not* casual. And Knox doesn't quite handle anything other than casual in his life well. The way his voice shook at me...

You call the love of my life and apologize right now or I swear, Lottie.

"I think..." I lean in so she will meet my eyes. "He cares a little too much. And wants to give you time."

Strands of dark curled hair fall in her face. "I didn't need *time.*"

"I know, but maybe he does?"

"Maybe."

"I think his mind is busy. And maybe when it slows, then all the rest will just...stop with it. You know?"

Flick nods and goes back to the couch. "Yeah. Yeah, I can see that."

We're sitting there. Her successfully pilling my couch and me just staring at her with the biggest smile.

"What?"

I coo, "I *missed* you."

"I missed you more."

Apollo lets out a small whimper, struggling to climb the couch. Flick snorts and picks him up, cradling him to her chest.

I move closer to scratch his ears. "Walker says he could maybe be a service dog. For my epilepsy."

"He mentioned that."

We share a glance, her eyes clearly accusatory. *He's perfect for you*, they say.

"I know, I know," I groan, unable to take it.

I've been dancing around it so long, but it's living proof. Walker *is* perfect. Even in his imperfect ways, he is perfect. I learned the other day that he rolls his socks together when he washes them—instead of washing them, drying them, and *then* rolling them in a ball—and it was kind of an ick. And the whole time, I just kept thinking, *Oh thank God there is something wrong with this boy, because I am slowly becoming convinced he's not even human.*

"This guy is special."

"I *know*."

"I mean, has he decided anything yet? About leaving?"

"We don't talk about it." I watch my puppy wiggle in her arms. "It's a double-edged sword. If he leaves…well, he's gone. And if he stays, it means he's only staying for me, and that's…not fair."

"To you?"

"To him."

"Lot," Flick sighs. "You know he is clearly obsessed with you."

He did get me a puppy. And multiple dinners. And has almost completed the most absurd bucket list ever with me.

"Him staying doesn't mean pity. And it doesn't mean you are a burden in his life. It means he lo—*likes* you enough to leave a distant dream."

I stand up and start pacing around my living room, in my kitchen, and back. One big loop over and over. Like I'm Princess Peach on her third lap of Rainbow Road tied in second place.

"That's the thing. I gave up my distant dreams. I know how that feels, and thinking of Walker going through that? Just to, what, be a ranch-hand cowboy forever in this small town when he has so much more potential? He could be a freaking astronaut."

"I really, *really* don't think that's what he's going to do."

"He could. He could go off and do anything. Him staying for this ranch-hand thing is just…silly."

It feels silly to say *silly*, but that's the only word I can come up with to suffice.

"He wouldn't just be getting the farm job if he stayed. He'd get *you*." Flick puts emphasis on *you*. Like I am some grand prize. Like yeah, maybe you have to use all your tokens on this last carnival game, but look at the giant stuffed giraffe you can take home if you win. "And I think that's a pretty incredible trade-off."

I snort. I am no giant giraffe. I am the lowest on the shelf, the tiny consolation prizes they give toddlers to avoid meltdowns. A knockoff, cross-eyed, missing-stitches Minnie Mouse that falls apart the second it gets home.

I want to be enough for him. I want to be the grand prize on the top shelf. But reality is, this is just one summer. One summer of pretending like I don't have this massive unknown thing dangling in front of my future. One summer of pure bliss before my senior year comes crashing down on me.

Flick stares me down enough to stop my pacing. "Seriously, Lot. Try to imagine it. A life with him here."

I don't need to be told to. I already do—every morning, every night, and every moment in between. And even if it's only a distant dream, it tastes so sweet. Too sweet for me to keep.

CHAPTER THIRTY-TWO
Lottie

I lean against the railing, watching Kit tighten the rope around his glove. His jaw is set, brows furrowed in focus. He's nervous, but he's trying really hard not to let it show. The sun hangs low in the sky's distance, casting long shadows over the makeshift practice pen. It smells just like it did years ago. Like the scent of dust and leather and blood and sweat have been encapsulated in this place, never to leave.

I smile over at my little protégé, standing there with one boot hooked over the bottom rail, hat pulled low. He looks the part. Almost.

"Alright, kid, get in there." Ledger stands on the other side, nodding toward the chute. I might have had to also sweet-talk him to be more hands-on than I can be. I don't know, technically, what I can and can't do in here for my health. I don't know where the line draws from safe to unsafe. Everything until now has been less physically exhausting than my morning jogs. Trying to handle a bull, being a barrel man or a pickup man, seems highly out of my wheelhouse of safety.

I am willing to push the limits, but not *that* much. After all, I have two very sweet boys to come home to now. Safe and sound.

Kit hesitates for just a second before pulling himself up, swinging his leg over and settling down onto the bull's back. The bull is on the smaller side, leaning closer to a steer. Still, it's nothing like the practice barrels or Goliath at Riley's he's hopped on a hundred times. This one is real.

I watch as he finds his grip, adjusting his seat just like we talked about. My heart beats faster—not just for him, but because I remember this. The anticipation, the charge of energy in the air before the gate swings open.

It's probably for the best that when I asked Kit's mom if she wanted to come watch, she said she was unable to get off work, but that she would do her best to see the next one.

Even I'm a little nervous just watching him get ready.

"You good?" I call out.

Kit nods, sucking in a sharp breath. He looks so tiny up there, and I am genuinely worried he's going to snap in two. But I know how it feels to be on the receiving end of that look. So I turn my head and give Ledger a thumbs-up. "Alright, then."

Ledger gives him a final once-over before signaling to Gus to let the bull loose. The gate flies open, and everything happens all at once, like I'm watching it in slow motion.

The bull surges forward, its muscles rippling under Kit's weight. He holds on tight, free hand flying up for balance. The first jump rocks him back, but he recovers. The second one is sharper, twisting hard to the left. I grip the railing so tight my knuckles turn white.

"Stay with it, Kit!" I shout, but I don't know if he hears me. Actually, I know he doesn't. He is locked in, entirely set on his balance.

Brows furrowed and face scrunched, he's hanging on, riding it out. Four, five seconds—much longer than I thought he'd last. He's got the grit, the stubbornness. But then the bull jerks to the side, and Kit doesn't recover in time. He goes flying, hitting the red dirt hard with a thud that makes my stomach drop.

I'm moving before I even think about it, swinging myself over the fence and running to him. Lawson and Gus both distract the bull to get him back in the pen, but I can hardly care about that. My shins ache from the drop over the fence, but I don't care about that either.

Kit groans when I reach him, rolling onto his back, dust clinging to his clothes and sweat-soaked hair.

"You feeling okay?" I ask, breathless.

He blinks up at me, a dazed grin spreading across his face. "That was amazing."

I let out a sharp laugh and shake my head. "You did way better than I thought."

"I thought I would've lasted longer."

We share a glance at the clock on the far left wall.

"Six seconds. That's great."

Ledger takes a few steps toward us once the bull's contained. "Good for your first real ride." He nods those dark curls to me. "You've got a great teacher."

I shrug nonchalantly, and Kit slowly tries to stand but groans and flops right back down. "Thanks, man."

Ledger nods with a laugh. "Anytime you need riding lessons and Lottie can't do it, I'm glad to help out."

As soon as Ledger, and his very impressive muscles, walk off, Kit turns straight to me to whisper, "Did I at least look cool?"

"Yeah, you looked really cool, right up until you ate dirt."

He laughs, taking my offered hand and letting me pull him up. The guys, mostly Gus and his few helpers, are at the fence clapping, shouting their approval. Kit dusts himself off, still grinning like a fool, and I can't help but smile too. Because I remember. I remember how this felt. The rush, the challenge, the way time stretched and slowed in those few breathless seconds. I miss it. God, I miss it.

But truthfully, I don't know if those times compare even a little bit to what I have going right now.

I mean, yes, I'm still the girl who lost her dreams. And I'm still the woman that everyone in her family keeps on a tether. I'll probably always be a little sheltered because of that. But watching Kit ride a bull—something that couldn't be done without my help—it hits me like a ton of bricks.

I made a difference in this kid's life by taking a few hours a week to teach him how to balance on a ball. By taking some of my completely useless time and actually pushing it toward something *useful.*

We climb back up to the top rail of the fence, settling in to watch Ledger work with one of the younger bulls in the pen. He moves like it's second nature, every shift of his body perfectly in sync. Kit watches him closely, his expression more serious now.

"Do you ever miss it? Riding?"

The question pulls me out of my thoughts. I glance at him, then back at the arena. "Hm? Oh, yeah. All the time."

The adrenaline, the push to go further, to be better. The way every second felt like an eternity, and every ride was a battle. The thrill of winning, but more than that—the thrill of surviving. No, *living*. What I've been doing the last two years is just surviving. I haven't really lived since then, not until Walker came into my life.

Kit's quiet for a moment, then asks, "Would you do it all over again? If you had to. The riding, the awards, missing it all. If you knew you were going to lose it one day…would you still do it?"

I consider it for a long moment. I already know the answer, but the weight of it sits heavy in my chest anyway.

"Yeah." I nod. "I'd do it again."

Kit watches me for a second, like he's trying to figure something out. The moment stretches, comfortable and quiet, until I can't take it any longer.

"I would do it still if I could," I admit.

"You'd be great, Miss Lottie. I'm sure."

A snicker pulls from me. "Thanks, kid."

"Kit."

"Hm?"

"It's Kit. You always say my name wrong. So does Walker."

"No, I'm not… That's—" I sigh. "Never mind. Thanks, Kit."

He smiles up at me, teeth a little crooked and nose all scrunched. "I'll have to tell Walker now. He put my name wrong on the time sheet the other day too."

"Well, you won't have to worry about it much longer. He's just seasonal."

The words taste like vinegar coming out of my mouth.

Kit gives me a knowing look. "You don't actually think that, do you?"

"What do you mean?"

"Walker isn't going to leave."

My heart drops. Did he… Has he officially denied the job? Did he tell Kit before me? Why does that kind of sting? Still, hope builds and builds in my chest.

"He told you that?"

"Well, no. Not outright. But it's obvious."

I shake my head, the inflating hope in my chest falling like a sad balloon. "I don't know. I think he wants to stay, but he's been chasing this dream for years."

For as far as I can think back, to our many summers together, Walker's talked on and on about his dad's connections at NASA and how one day he was going to be a big-shot engineer. He used to drone on and on about schools he could go to for it and programs he could squish into. My little space cowboy.

We take time to give Ledger and Gus and the rest of the guys another thank-you and a goodbye. Ledger says he will do it anytime as long as I give him Ada's number. I shrug and say, "Maybe get it yourself," to which he replies with, "You think I haven't tried that?"

Before we know it, Kit and I are back on Willow Creek property, walking along the gravel road together. When we're close to the main house for dinner, Walker's on the porch steps, smiling and waving Apollo's paw at us. I can practically hear the baby talk from here.

"For the record"—Kit shakes his head—"I don't think he's going anywhere."

"I sure hope not."

CHAPTER THIRTY-THREE
Lottie

There are only a handful of traditions that my family has stayed loyal to over the last almost eighteen years of my life.

Every spring there's a Turner-wide cleanout, in which the whole family pitches in for an entire weekend dedicated to cleaning out old drawers and closet corners in the main house filled to the brim with dusty vintage Coca-Cola signs and candy wrappers from the ghosts of Easter Bunny past. The end results are usually a slightly cleaner home for us and a much fuller home for Ada, as anything that gives off a whisper of vintage she sneaks away with like a bat in the night.

In the fall there's always the weekly pumpkin patches—mostly a ranch event and less of a family tradition, but I will count it as such for the sake of a clean list—where we have giant hay mazes and costume contests and potato sack relay races and chili cook-offs and, of course, pumpkins.

During the Christmas season, we all go down the road to a local tree farm that shares a tree with us in exchange for quality stocked beef for their freezers, and we pull out old ornaments to decorate while Aunt Dot makes her famous Red Hots apple cider (questionable if there's alcohol in it or not.)

But even with all these seasonal traditions, Fourth of July trumps them all.

Maybe it's because summer is by far the best season around here—a strong argument between Flick and I versus Knox—or maybe it's because up until the last two years, I have associated the holiday with Walker visiting. Regardless of the reason, Willow Creek's annual Fourth of July fest has always been top of the list in my heart.

Cherry pie–eating contests and fields of picnic tables under tents and live music with an actual banjo. Red, white, and blue bounce houses for the kids (and Knox). A long row lined up with different food trucks for barbecue or tacos or funnel cake. The smell of fresh-cut grass and sunscreen and citronella candles mixed with the Bake House's booth covered in peach crisp, zucchini bread, and strawberry shortcake. Sounds of laughter and firecrackers and music dancing in the air.

It's impossible not to have it at the top of your list of Willow Creek to-dos.

And it's even more impossible for me to tone down my excitement knowing Walker is going to be back this year.

The last time we went together, we snuck off halfway through to find a good fireworks-viewing spot over by our tree, watching the rest of the town facing opposite from us so I could sneak in tiny cheek pecks and hand-holding without feeling like the story would end up in the *Oak Ridge Gazette*.

I wasn't sure what today would look like, but when I woke up first thing this morning, Aunt Dot handed me a white waist apron with splotches of dried pastel paint on the pockets and said, "You and lover boy are stuck with me today."

So face painting it is.

By the time Walker was done with his morning shift of helping Knox, Dad, and Uncle Miller load up tables, chairs, and tents, the place is covered in vendors and volunteers in high-vis vests and a petting zoo full of our sweetest and most tame animals. Mom, with the energy of a very enthusiastic cruise director, assigned us to table twenty-three between the rubber duck races and the flower-picking booths.

"Sorry." Walker pushes a shaky hand through his already sweaty hair, and I find myself jealous, wanting to replace his fingers with mine. "That took way longer than it should have. Turns out Betsy really is a stubborn gal."

"I tried to warn you." I smile up at him, and the warm look he gives me back makes me wonder if maybe we should sneak off again this time.

"I like your boots." He smirks and from the curve of his lip, it feels like my boots are the last thing on his mind. I wiggle the red Hunter boots.

"Thank you. I like your…" My eyes dance over his getup—a simple heather gray T-shirt with a Willow Creek logo and denim jeans with those same old cowboy boots he's always wearing. "All of it."

"All of it?"

The tiny dance of pink in his cheeks grows red and stretches down to his Adam's apple, which bobs once, then twice.

"All of it." I nod.

"Yeah?" His laugh is sheepish and sweet. "Well—"

"Alright, alright." Dot steps in the middle of us, all five foot nothing, her hands stretched out with two plastic cups filled with brushes. "You're here to work, save the rest for later."

Walker catches my eye and winks. *For later*, he mouths, and I keep it tucked away like a child promised ice cream for good behavior.

We each grab our brushes and turn to the face-painting station. It's a U-shaped booth with six wooden folding chairs and red-and-white checkered tablecloths holding a multitude of washable paints and palettes, as well as handheld mirrors and paper towels.

"How exactly should we be doing this?" I ask. "I'm not much of an artist."

Dot shrugs. "They can pick from a star, a heart, or a groundhog. That's all I can do."

I start to question the last part, but Walker lifts a hand. "I would personally love a groundhog on my cheek."

Soon enough, kids begin to line up at the booths, most getting stuck on the knock-down-pins game to win stuffed teddy bears wearing tiny Oak Ridge T-shirts and holding an apple pie slice. So far no one has won, but Walker has made a promise that he will be bringing me my own bear in the near future when we get a break.

Then, our first victims arrive. Our librarian's twin girls: Abigail and Amelia.

Dot smiles at their Americana outfits of red, white, and blue with bows so large that they would be considered oversize on a gorilla. "Stars, hearts, or groundhogs?" she offers, and both girls concur with stars.

Abigail runs up to Dot's chair, eagerly pushing her left cheek out, ready to be painted, and I start to volunteer for the other star, but I catch Amelia smiling at Walker like he lights up this entire event, and I know my offer will fall flat straight on the grass. I can't even blame the girl; I'd want a star from him too.

By the time they're done, both girls are squealing over their matching cheeks and Walker is grinning at his paint job, which is more of a rounded yellow starfish against the girls' dark skin rather than a pointy star like Dot's, but very cute nonetheless.

"I want one." I lean his way when the girls run off to get frozen strawberry lemonade from my mom.

"A kid? Sorry, darling, we'll have to wait a few years."

The snort out of my nose is awfully Wilbur-like, and the pink in my cheeks probably matches his too. "A face painting from you."

Though a future with Walker, kids down the road or not, sounds more appealing by the day.

"Now, *that* I can do."

Walker grabs the bottom of my chair and yanks me so my knees are positioned between his spread thighs. His fingers drop to the bottom of my shin as he straightens my seat.

"I don't think I can paint a groundhog; hearts and stars are more my style."

I hum and ignore the pulsing in my veins at how close we are. "Surprise me."

"Good choice."

I close my eyes and lean in close, my right cheek facing his while the few kids walking up are occupied by Dot's painting one corner over. When we're close like this, it's so easy to forget the entire town is right here. Friends and family and local legends are all strolling past us, but my eyes are shut to the whole world.

It's so easy to pretend like this with him. To pretend there's no last year of school coming up or pretend I'm not dreading being in this town without him. It's just me and Walker and his strong fingers brushing gentle, cool strokes of paint on my cheek. There's definitely a curve in there somewhere, so I'm leaning toward it being a heart, but truthfully, it could be a poorly drawn chicken wearing coveralls and I would be just as thrilled. I may even ask him to do the other side just so I can stay exactly like this.

Walker uses one hand to hold my jaw in place and the other to make his tiny masterpiece. He smells like paint and spice and the color green. I bet he would taste like it this morning too.

The distant sounds of acoustic covers of nineties country and cotton candy machines whirring float nearby, but I am much more interested in the grunting hums of satisfaction every time Walker pulls back to take a look at my side profile.

"Alright," he says two or maybe twenty minutes later. "All done, ma'am."

I turn to the mirror and cackle at the view.

In bold red paint is indeed a heart. But the inside holds our initials: LT + WL, with a squiggly underline as if to emphasize the statement.

"I love it!" I immediately reach for my own paint and take advantage of the slow line of people to say, "Scoot over, it's my turn."

It takes longer than I'm willing to admit, but I am more than satisfied with my own artwork when I hand the mirror back to Walker and watch his smile light up brighter than any firework.

In royal blue on his left cheek is a small arrow pointing to his lips that says "Lottie Was Here." He grins my way. "I suddenly wish I could change yours."

I grab a lipstick from Dot's purse nearby, which always holds a bright 1920s red for a touch-up.

"One final touch." I grab Walker's chin and pull him close, planting a kiss on his cheek to match the red on mine.

He takes another look in the mirror, and that sweet smile only stretches farther. "Much better."

Walker turns out to be surprisingly good at painting, but he's even better with the kids. Always smiling and nodding, asking how their summer has been and listening to every summary of Disney cruises or summer school or the details of Timmy Lockett's recent IBS issues. You would think he could be acting, but I believe he's genuinely loving every minute of this.

Dot plops down on the seat across from me, a cone of pink cotton candy the size of her head in hand. She tears off a piece and holds it out for me. The moment it dissipates on my tongue, my tastebuds dance with sugary pink air, tasting like summer and a golden sunrise.

Walker is finishing up his current customer, a little boy named Elijah who desperately begged for a football instead of stars or hearts.

"He's pretty good; he should've been here when I did it by myself last year. It was like the whole town was told they should come here just for the face paint. Even the adults were in a massive line down the aisle."

A smidge of guilt at my previous years' absence at any family event makes my stomach churn. I don't think I was expected to be here the last two years, but there's still this silent exhortation that no one will say out loud. It feels sticky, like I'm a bug stuck between two glue traps—if I'm too involved, they're concerned for my health, and if I'm not here at all, my lack of presence leaves a mark.

A burden no matter which way I go.

Dot must catch the drop of my lips, because she quickly

hands me another piece and talks with her mouth full, pink dripping from the corner of her lips.

"Not that it was that bad without you, I just like that you two are both here this year. It's nice. It's…"

"I know what you mean." I smile, and it feels a little too tight to be real. "I'm glad we're both here too."

"Done!" Walker calls out and taps the top of the little blond-headed boy with the end of his paintbrush, handing him a mirror. "Not bad, right?"

"It's perfect!" The kid wraps his arms around Walker with endless thanks while almost smudging his wet cheek. He runs off to his mom standing by the pinball game as she watches my uncle Miller in a tight shirt lift all the heavy prizes for the kids.

After our tables are left empty, there's enough of a lull in the line, mostly due to the fact that Ray's barbecue food truck just opened, that Dot turns to Walker and me.

"Why don't you two go get something to eat? I think we've painted half the population already."

I turn to Walker, and he's already smirking down at me, glancing from my seat over to the knock-down-pins game.

"I *do* have a promise to fulfill."

Dot nods next to me with a wink. "Go on, I'll catch you later if I need you."

With that, Walker and I sprint from our chairs and head straight to the pin games where only two stuffed bears have been pulled from the twenty hanging up. On our way there, Flick calls out from her and Knox's table. "Lot!"

I turn my head and catch the two of them under a petting zoo sign covered in muddy paw prints and dalmatian dots and little horseshoes. Behind their ticketed table is a set of pens holding the ducklings and their little tub of water in one and another with a few Angora rabbits that are so fluffy, it really is a mystery how they can see from under all that fur.

The owner of the shelter that Flick works at, Rowen, sits between the two crates, frowning at something behind us. Or maybe just frowning in general, who could say.

Flick smiles at us as she wordlessly hands off the bunny in her hand to Knox. "Are you guys going to get food? Can we join? I heard there's a vegan option at Ray's."

I start to wonder if Walker minds—not that this was a date by any means, but maybe he just wanted it to be the two of us? I glance up and he's already nodding at them both.

"For sure." He sticks his hands in his pockets and frowns at the ducks by themselves. "You guys are leaving the ducks?"

"They like Rosie more than us." Knox shrugs and pulls my best friend by the hand to join us on the other side of the table. "Plus, Rowen needs to work on his social skills."

The shelter's owner scowls in his seat behind Knox, and I smile at him.

"Hi, Rowen."

"Hello, Charlotte."

He's one of the only two people I allow to call me by my full name; after everything he has done for Flick over the years, it's the least I can do.

"We'll be back in thirty," Flick tells him, but Rowen's already shaking his head.

"Everyone is about to get ready for the fireworks by now. It's hard to have a petting zoo in the dark without bit fingers and potential lawsuits. Go ahead and do what you need, I'm fine here."

"But the—"

"The kids are fine."

Knox and Flick glance from each other to the ducks and

back in some unsaid song and dance, but they eventually nod and blow their ducks kisses in tandem.

"Alright, I heard we're winning some bears?"

I have to give it to Miller…he really put some heavy weights in these pins. Or maybe he hot-glued them to the table?

Either way, this is clearly not my uncle's first rodeo. Literally.

Walker has spent at least double the cost of the bear prizes and has yet to even get a pin to budge.

"Are you sure you're using your right hand?" Miller crosses his arms and leans against a post to his right.

Walker grumbles to himself, "I'm sure."

Knox snorts. "Five dollars says I get it in the first go."

"Oh, I'll take those odds!" Flick bounces on her toes. "I like the pink one."

"Pink it is, hon."

"I didn't know we could preorder." I take a step closer to the man huffing like a bull. "Walker, can I get the one in the blue sweater?"

"You're getting a damn bear if it takes every dollar in my account."

Miller's grin grows even further. "There's a ten-try limit."

"Since when?"

"Who's in charge here?"

As cute as this is, it is clearly not going anywhere. "Come on, Walker." I tug the crook of his elbow, and he leans into my side, hip to hip. "We could probably just find one tomorrow in the community center, and it's about to get dark."

"I have a flashlight."

"That's not what I—"

“Last chance,” Miller singsongs.

“You said we had ten,” Walker argues.

“I changed my mind. Ten more bucks, kid. All or nothing.”

I narrow my eyes. “Really?”

“Business is business.”

Unfazed, Walker slams down the ten-dollar bill, smooths his hair back, and holds the heavy ball, rubbing its rough surface against his skin. We all stay still and silent as he rears back, reaches behind him, and slings the ball directly into the pins.

Flick gasps. My breath hitches. Knox hisses through his teeth.

The bottom-left pin tips and collapses after the pins wobble, resulting in the remaining pins falling, as the sound of the pins clanking echoes before the soft thud of them hitting the grass.

With a squeal, I watch as Walker raises both of his hands in a victory pose, then pivots toward me, using both of his arms to scoop under my denim shorts before throwing me up into the air. My laughter bubbles out as he spins faster, the world blurring into a kaleidoscope of delight.

Bear, no bear, I’m the winner here.

That being said, I’m extremely grateful when Miller reluctantly tosses the cutest stuffed bear my way. Tiny, stitched grin, soft eyes, light-blue sweatshirt, and apple pie in his paws. I hold it to my chest, tucked between my shirt and Walker’s stretched cheeks.

Knox rolls up his sleeves and cracks his knuckles. “Alright, pink it is.” He slams down a handful of crumpled-up ones from his pockets and points to the hanging bear that Flick has been eyeing. “You’re coming home with me.”

“Go, Knoxy!” Flick claps her hands.

I don't know what it is about these pins, but Knox is regrettably as bad as Walker—or they're that heavy. Maybe Miller has a button he uses to let them fall down?

Either way, it takes another twenty dollars before a fuming Knox takes his fists and pushes down the pins manually before pointing at our uncle.

"Not one word, or I'll tell your wife about the side-by-side you've been keeping in the far back shop."

Miller's lips seal so fast I'm not sure he'll ever open them again, even as Knox reaches up and grabs the pink-wearing bear.

"Here you go, honey." He hands Flick the bear, and she completely bypasses it by squeezing her arms around Knox's neck instead.

"Are you sure they're just friends?" Walker asks as we watch the two of them in their own world.

"They say they are." I shrug, not wanting to reveal Flick's secret almost-kiss with Knox. "I think they're just that close."

"Huh, okay."

"Fireworks will begin in about twenty minutes, please find your seating." There's static followed by a monotone, "Buck promised not to go overboard, but proceed with caution as we may need to run. Thanks."

"Wow. Buck wasn't kidding about the pyrotechnics," Walker notes.

I shake my head. "He was not."

While Flick and Knox grab food, Walker and I dance around the busy crowd, rows and rows of stretched-out lawn chairs and blankets spread out with laughing kids wearing light-up bracelets and necklaces. Half of the crowd has painted faces, and there's something so satisfying about seeing our jobs laid out like this. Even Kit, who is sitting beside his parents with a bored expression, has a little sunshine on the apple of his cheek, provided by yours truly.

"It's packed out here." Walker scratches at his jaw. "Any ideas?"

I squint at the sea of a crowd. There are waves of tin beer cans and frosted lemonades and banana puddings in a cup, but very little space between.

"Hm."

Then, just between two green lawn chairs, I see a dark opening beyond all the people of Oak Ridge, past just a few trees.

A long dock extends halfway out into the pond, connected to the running creek. Two wooden rocking chairs sit side by side on the dock and there is a reflection of fireflies dancing in the distance.

"I think I know a place."

By the time Walker and I sneak off, I've already texted Flick to meet us there when they're ready, and Walker has happily picked a seat, his lap serving as a table for our overflowing plate of barbecue.

"You're in Knox and Flick's chair."

"What?" he snorts, rocking back. "Like assigned seating?"

"Mm-hmm. And this one is mine."

"How would they even know? They're identical."

"Check under the leg." I point to the bottom right chair leg, and Walker bends down to squint at the old scratch.

"Wow." He eyes the carved letters that read "Knox and Felicity's chair." "You weren't kidding."

"Nope."

Walker stands from the chair and scoots closer my way, crossing his legs before sitting on the wooden deck.

I rock my chair forward and prop my boots by him. Walker

takes the opportunity to caress the back of my exposed calf with a soft thumb stroke. It tickles, but I will never willingly move from this spot, except…

"You could sit in my lap." I pat my thigh, a welcome invitation.

"I would crush you."

"I'm a hardy girl. Sturdy. Give it a try."

He mouths the word *sturdy* with a barely contained smile. "Sorry, can't. Your legs are too nice to be snapped just for the sake of a seat."

I expect that to be that, with Walker rubbing my calf and smiling up at me. Nope. He flies up from the chair, and before I can process it, he has me up and back down in his lap in one swift motion.

He places me across his wide thighs, my hips backed up to his waist. His touch, firm and gentle all at once, has shifted from my calf to my waist.

"Much better." The smile he gives me dares to be innocent despite the heat dripping down the base of my spine.

His hand stays there, curled around my hip sweetly. Never pushing for more. He said before he had old Southern manners, and I'm starting to think he's right. Because even as badly as I want to curl deeper into his lap and plant soft kisses along his painted cheek, he never acts like he needs more than this right here.

Just him and me on a dock under the dark night's blanket, punched with tiny holes of light poking through.

My phone lights up in my lap with a text from Flick saying they're on their way and the fireworks are starting in five.

Walker unashamedly reads the text with me, and I feel his stomach muscles tighten behind me.

"Lot?" His voice is a low rumble, like he's nervous to let even the one syllable out.

"Walker," I hum back.

"I don't mean to be insensitive, but I feel like I have to ask—"

"Exactly what every girl wants to hear while sitting in a boy's lap."

He huffs a laugh. "The fireworks, they won't… I mean." A cleared throat. A tiny cough. "I know you said lights don't… I just want to make sure you'll be alright."

I shake my head. "I'll be fine."

"You're certain? Because I don't really feel the need to stay if—"

"In my experience, anxiety or lack of sleep has caused it. Sometimes my electrolytes are off; my sodium can be too low, and that will trigger it. Sometimes it seems like it's nothing at all…it's just one minute I'm fine and the next…"

My shoulders shudder, and Walker runs his thumb up and down the one closest to him, like maybe it will stop the shakiness creeping in.

"How long has it been now? Since your last one?"

I count the months backward on my hand and… "Huh. Four months, I think."

"Is that a lot?"

"For me it is. Even if it's a small one, it's enough to count."

"What's the longest you've gone?"

My throat bobs, and a ball of anxiety forms its way there. "Since the initial accident? Five months."

"How long do you have to go to be cleared to drive?"

"A year for me. Some people are different and can get clearance after six months depending on the severity of it. But my doctors say they want a whole year since it's been persistent enough that there's no real guarantee I can keep myself or other drivers safe. Plus even if I go a whole year, my parents both demand such strict rules around it that it would hardly make a difference."

He blows out a breath. "Is there anything I can—"

"There you are!" I turn to see Flick carrying two heaping plates of food with my brother trailing behind her, his hands full of various stuffed bears, bunnies, and I think a frowning frog wearing cowboy boots.

Flick runs up to the table between our two rocking chairs and sets down their plates. She grabs some of the stuffed animals and lines them up in a row so they can see the fireworks coming too.

"Sorry, we made a few pit stops on the way."

"A few?" Knox huffs out a breath as he finally takes a seat in their chair. "I don't think there's a single stuffed animal left in the city."

"Knox is very good at throwing and fixing things." Flick smiles and plops down in his lap like they do every other time they're here.

The pride on my brother's face is unmatched by anything else I've seen all day.

"What time is it?" Walker asks roughly by my ear. "Shouldn't it have started by no—"

POW.

A pop in my ear, a deep, chest-thumping *boom* like the sharp crack of thunder. And then, appearing without warning, it was there. High above the main house, the sky is nearly empty, save for red streaks dissolving into golden fizzles, like bursting star shells.

With each single bright streak shattering into vibrant colors like crimson, sapphire, gold, and emerald, a high-pitched *whizz* follows or a rushing *whoosh.* I hear collective oohs and ahhs in the distance where everyone else is sitting.

Flick hums at the waterfall effects, telling Knox that those are her favorites.

Walker and I stay wrapped up together. Quiet with unsaid words impossibly loud.

I've seen these exact fireworks year after year—sometimes from my bedroom window, sometimes from the back of the property, sometimes in this very chair—but the sight feels like something entirely new sitting with this grown version of Walker.

I think he must feel it too, because he curls his back to hunch over me before pressing a simple kiss to my forehead.

"Thank you," he whispers, just loud enough that I can hear him over the fizzle of fireworks.

I don't know what for, but I whisper the words right back to him.

Unexplainable gratitude for this moment right here.

CHAPTER THIRTY-FOUR
Lottie

Walker and I have completed all but four of the items on our summer Eighteen Before Eighteen bucket list, and we still have three weeks before my birthday.

Last week alone we knocked four off the list. On Monday, we took a yoga class at the community center hosted by Miller's girlfriend, Emma, where Walker sweat and cussed profusely every time he couldn't stay in downward dog. At the end of the class, he reached past me and grabbed the water bottle I had been drinking from on and off. Those deep brown eyes locked on mine, and he took a sip exactly where my lips had been only moments prior.

We had to leave earlier than everyone else.

On Wednesday night, we made plans to tick off the bonfire portion. It was going to be a small one, something intimate and not enough to cause potential problems for the ranch. We ran to the general store for marshmallows, chocolate, and graham crackers. We packed blankets, pillows, and chairs in the back of his truck. Unfortunately, the one thing we didn't plan for was the sudden downpouring of rain the second we got outside. So our bonfire with s'mores ended up being us going to his place next door where he put a fireplace ambience on his TV and used the oven's broiler to make inside s'mores. They didn't taste nearly as good as a bonfire s'more, but the company more than made up for it.

On Thursday morning, I fully expected to wake up to a text from Walker detailing our plans for the day, but instead, I woke up to Dot standing above my bed with streamers, clapping her hands with "No Scrubs" playing on a speaker in the living room.

"It's girls' day, up, up!"

She wasn't kidding about it being a whole day either. We stopped in Glazed and Confused for glazed croissants before bouncing all over the town. We started with a haircut for us both: only a couple inches for me because the commitment of any shorter made me nauseous, whereas Dot went from chest length hair to a short bob with curtain bangs. It suited her surprisingly well. We had lunch at the diner—which was more so brunch considering we just ate chocolate chip waffles and hash browns—followed by her wonderful idea to go roller-skating.

Dusting off old helmets, pads, and skates, we meandered poorly up and down the only paved part of the property in front of the main house. To my shock, she is horrible at roller-skating, whereas I can surprisingly manage a steady pace as long as I keep my eyes on the horizon. It was more fun than I expected it to be. Well, until Mom found out by our loud laughter and came to supervise, which basically sucked all the fun out it.

We ended up leaving, going back inside our house and ending the day with a movie marathon. All 2000s romance gold: *27 Dresses*, *How to Lose a Guy in 10 Days*, and *13 Going on 30*.

A girls' day it was indeed.

Then, that Saturday, Walker informed me we were going to a pottery painting class one town over—Just Kil'n Time. We saddled up in his truck while Dot babysat Apollo, and listened to the playlists we had made for each other. Burned CDs with Dolly Parton and Garth Brooks played the whole ride. He manually cranks our windows down, the summer wind flinging my blond hair all over the place. Walker laughed every time we stopped long enough for him to get a good look at the hair stuck in my lip gloss. It made me laugh too, and before I knew it, I was scooting closer to the middle of the bench seat, leaning my head across his sturdy shoulder. Every time we laughed the rest of the ride, it was side by side, vibrating the seat together.

Walker's painting skills went beyond faces, apparently. The mug he painted—with a tiny black outline of a man riding a horse—looked far cuter than my deck of cards on the salad plate I was attempting to finish.

But by the time we were done and laid our projects with the older woman up front to finish in the kiln, I'd like to think we were experts.

All of this being said, the list was down to only four little empty boxes.

I should be excited.

Should be thrilled at the summer we've shared and the thought of an upcoming birthday. A legally adult birthday. A birthday where I could drink in Mexico… I mean, if I ever got to go.

But even with all of these wonderful moments, there's this sense of dread. Like the closer we get to my birthday, the closer we get to the recognition of my return to school and of Walker's potential to take the opportunity of a lifetime.

Thankfully, I'm not given much of a chance to sulk on the

impending doom because my phone vibrates next to me on the couch with Walker's name.

"Hellooo?" I sing.

"Good morning."

"A very good morning."

A morning made better already by his voice.

"Do you have plans today?"

"Nope." I pop the *p*. "Why?"

"Feel like crossing something off the list?" I can hear the smile in his voice.

"I thought you'd never ask."

Truthfully, I was expecting today's list item to be one of the easy ones left: have a picnic by the old tree or take a long walk through the hiking trails. But Walker sent me off to do this one on my own.

He drove us to Common Ground and said he would be right back, but to order him a white mocha hot chocolate with a pinch of cinnamon. I turned to tell him that sounded awful, but when I did, he was gone.

And I found out why right after I gave Walker's order to the young girl working the register, and she handed me a folded slip of paper with his handwriting on it.

CLUE ONE: "Even a broken clock works twice a day."

My brow scrunches as I look up to see the girl is gone too.

Huh… Is this…?

I run through the items left unchecked on the list, and only one can come to mind right now. Number twelve: Do a scavenger hunt with no help.

That sneaky little…

I read the note over and over again. Maybe the whole

"without help" thing was a mistake to tack on. I used to love doing the scavenger hunt that my mom and Dot would plant around the ranch every summer when we were kids, but I was horrible at following each clue. If it weren't for Flick or Walker being there, we never would've gotten to the end of it.

But this *is* part of the goal of this summer, right? To figure out exactly what I can or can't do at this point.

Even a broken clock works twice a day.

I turn to the door and step out to scan the early-morning street for any more clues. Agnes Whitmore walking her dog in a baby stroller. Theodore Wilson setting up an Open sign outside his hardware store. Birds chirp, the bell above the café's door dings, someone starts a lawn mower nearby. But no hints anywhere that I can see.

Except…

The town's old clock tower just across the town square—or the town oval if we're being technical—sits high, shining down on me. It hasn't worked for as long as I can remember, but the last town meeting where someone dared to mention getting it replaced sent the entire city into an uproar.

There has to be something there, right?

I cross the street with ease, only a couple cars driving by. Sitting under the clock tower's plaque is a tiny bench that's usually empty. Only this morning, there is a little box with a bow around it.

Inside there's another note in Walker's scratchy handwriting.

CLUE TWO: Downstairs. Crooked book. Under someone's very curious eye.

While I have no clue who this curious-eyed person is, I do know there are only two options for this one, and considering the library is always closed on Mondays, it has to be the town's only bookstore, the Page Turner.

Fortunately, the layout of Main Street allows me to easily visit different places. So, I walk two doors down to find Maria at the Page Turner sitting behind the front desk.

I push open the creaky wooden door, and the tiny bell above it jingles—a delicate, old sound. To my right, a box fan hums lazily in the corner, pushing around warm air that smells like aged paper and worn leather with a hint of vanilla, like Nana's attic if it were full of fairy tales instead of forgotten boxes.

"Morning, green stickers are 20 percent off, and if you see any signs of a—Lottie, look at you out and about this morning." Maria gasps as though me coming off my parents' property is worthy of applause.

"Hi, Maria." I read the note Walker left me one more time. "Super weird, but um, what's downstairs?" Any kind of reading I've done here in the past has been strictly for Flick, and that was usually near the romance section by the bathroom.

She pushes up her glasses with her thumb, and there's a secret smile somewhere in there.

"Oh, that's our nonfiction section. Not as popular as you might think. Though, last week Tommy had a meeting on the existence of dragons and if they were misclassified as dinosaurs. It got a bit rowdy."

Well, that's...

"Right. So"—I point to the staircase I've never taken—"just down here?"

"Yes, ma'am. Best of luck to you."

Okay...

I push open the heavy door and eye the concrete steps. They're shallow and look more like something out of a horror book than a bookstore, but I wanted adventure, and here adventure is.

There's a string dangling at the bottom that says, "Pull Me." I follow its orders, and two small bulbs turn on enough for me to see the basement's rows of shelves. It's about half the stock upstairs, which isn't much, but at least up there it's easy to follow the signs in order of author's last name.

Down here, the books are stacked two, three deep, with no real order to them, unless Maria understands the secret system. Titles in faded fonts, cracked spines, cloth covers bleached by sun and time.

I pass by the desk with a dusty handwritten sign taped to the counter: "Back in 10 (or so)." Underneath it, a mug of cold coffee rests next to a thick, half-read Faulkner novel.

Ten years, maybe.

Up and down the aisles I wander deeper, fingertips trailing along the shelves. No sign of a crooked book anywhere in the chaos that is the basement, but I do find one other friend down here.

A stuffed monkey sits on the far back shelf, half in the shadow and half in the light. Not just any stuffed monkey, but a Curious George.

"Well, he *did* say curious. But where is the note?"

Scanning the nearby shelves, it doesn't seem like there's anything standing out. No crooked books. No notes poking out of the margins. No suspicious titles.

I open the note again and reread it.

Downstairs. Crooked book. Under someone's very curious eye.

Under his eye? Curious George is sitting on a shelf, but I haven't found anything remotely poking out. I lift my gaze up to the stuffed animal and recognize he's not facing toward the other shelves, he's sideways. Pointing to the back of the room.

Repositioning myself so my eyes line up where his do, I see it. A large yellow-spined, crooked book facing the far wall by the old HVAC ducts. I pull it off the shelf to inspect.

Horseback Riding for Dummies.

I snort and open the first page, only for a cream note to slide out. Reading the third clue aloud to myself, I can't force the smile off my cheeks.

CLUE THREE: It's never where you think it is, but always where you find it.

Now where in the hell…

Six, *SIX*, clues later, and I have truly gone through every single piece of this town square before landing right next door to the clock tower at the Bake House.

"Please let this be the last one," I mumble as I open the door to the familiar bakery, but the words fall short as soon as I see what's waiting for me.

Cleared-out empty tables, lights off. It's like the place is completely closed.

The last clue literally said, "It rhymes with Shmake-mouse," so if I'm lost on this one, then I give up.

"Hello?" I call out.

No response. Nothing but…I think I hear the soft hum of music somewhere?

I follow the sound through the tables to the back hallway and out to a view of the back courtyard to see my final clue.

Less of a clue and more of the prize itself.

I step out through the back door, and the heat wraps around me—humid, golden, and buzzing faintly with the sound of cicadas. The sun is high, casting sharp shadows across the bricks under my boots.

In the center of the hidden area is a red checkered blanket spread across the grass, wrinkled at the corners from the breeze that stirs the hanging ferns above. There's a wooden tray on the blanket holding two sweating glasses of sweet tea and a small bowl of chilled peach slices glistening in the sun. There's a basket behind it, a secondhand radio humming low in the back, lyrics of Southern nights and first kisses sweeping through the air.

And in the middle of it all is a very proud, smiling-bright Walker Lane.

"I knew you would do it super fast."

I huff a laugh. *Super fast* seems to be a lifetime to me, because it feels like half the day is gone already.

"I… How long have you been here?"

Walker shrugs. "Not long."

Which is Walker for he's been here waiting on me this whole time but is too polite to ever say so.

"Not long?" I smile and squint up at the midday sun.

"Anyway." He claps and points to the setup behind him. "You want to…?"

"Yes." I very much want to do whatever he has set up here.

Following Walker's move, I take my seat on the checkered blanket. I stretch my legs out, lean back on one hand, and reach for a peach slice with the other.

It's cool against my fingers, slick with juice, the skin flushed and tender. I bring it to my mouth and bite.

Bursts of sweet and sour, a little sting against my tongue. An edible ray of sunshine.

"I know you rarely eat a big lunch—"

When had I told him that?

"So, I just packed a few things. But I thought if you're hungry after, we could stop at the diner, or maybe I could make something at the house?"

I love how he says the house as if we live together and don't have walls separating our rooms.

"After?" I ask.

He nods with no other explanation.

We eat our peaches and a variety of cheese, and for a moment, everything else slips away—the heat, the noise, the short stretch of only a few weeks ahead of us—and it's just this: the burst of flavor, the whir of cicadas, and the quiet comfort of Walker humming low to the music around us.

When we're done eating, he hands me a napkin. I wipe away at the sticky juices on my fingers to clean them up. Walker huffs a small laugh.

"What?"

He takes an extra napkin and lifts it to my chin where peach juice still rests, rubbing his covered thumb over my skin. "I've got you."

Don't I know it…

"How's Kit's training going?" he asks.

Yes, a distraction, *please*.

I hum around my bite of another peach that I would like to write a love letter to. "Good. He's finally getting the hang of things, and I think he might actually be ready for the junior competition in September."

"That's great. Have you thought about what you're going to do with him after that?"

"I… No. Not really."

Why had *after* never really crossed my mind this whole time?

"You'll figure it out." Walker pokes his elbow into my upper arm. "Find a new student or project and do it again. You're good at that."

I snort. "At what? Finding desperate people?"

"At helping people find their path. I think you're like a compass always pointing north. Maybe not everyone stays on the same route as you, but you seem to always be the reason they find their own route, you know?"

Hm. "Maybe."

Silence pulls between us for a long moment before I ask, "Is that what I am for you this summer? Your compass?"

"Trouble, you're the destination."

"I think we've lost hold of this analogy," I comment with flushed cheeks.

"Speak for yourself. I know exactly where I'm going."

I'm glad one of us does. If I'm a compass, he's the unknown laying before me.

CHAPTER THIRTY-FIVE
Walker

Three grown men are sitting in a circle staring down a six-week-old puppy attempting to chase his own tail. And I happen to be one of them.

Knox and Miller are laughing, and I can't help but stare, too, as Apollo flops onto his side with all the grace of a milk-drunk calf. His paws are still too big for his little body, and his legs don't seem to know how to work together yet, so he just kind of staggers into the ground when he tries to run.

"Why is he so clumsy?" Kit snorts when Apollo does a little barrel roll on his back.

"'Cause Walker got him," Knox answers with a snort. "He couldn't get any of the normal dogs in there."

I bend down, scooping my baby up before giving the guys a glare. "Shut up."

We're supposed to be pouring cement for a new concrete pad Knox's uncle Miller had plans for, but the moment Lottie and Flick started getting ready for their book club afternoon, I volunteered—maybe forced—my way into bringing the pup along. I thought it'd be easy. Turns out, handling wet concrete and a clumsy puppy at the same time are about as smart as tossing a lit match into a hay barn.

Needless to say, we've gotten very little done today.

"You aren't clumsy, bud. You just gotta grow into yourself, huh?" I scratch behind his ears, and he practically melts in my hands, eyes closing in complete trust. "You're a good boy, aren't you?"

Kit snorts. "Is this how you got Miss Lottie to go out with you?"

"It took a *whole* lot more than this." My brows raise.

"Okay, can we not?" Knox grimaces. "I need to know less about you two in general."

I huff a laugh, pushing my hat back to wipe the bead of sweat running down my forehead. It's hotter than usual today, the kind of thick heat that sticks to your skin like plastic wrap. Apollo lets out a high-pitched yap, and without thinking, I take my hat off and plop it onto his head before setting him down.

The moment his paws hit the dirt, he takes two steps forward before his oversized head pulls him off balance. He flips forward, does a full barrel roll, and lands sprawled in the dirt. Knox and Kit double over in laughter, and even I can't hold back a chuckle as I crouch down to pick him up.

"He's still learning," I mumble, setting him back on his feet. "Come on, bud. Show 'em how your momma taught you to sit."

I raise my hand, mimicking Lottie's training technique, and repeat "sit" in different tones, hoping something will click. Apollo stares at me blankly, tail wagging, not sitting.

Kit crosses his arms. "Why's he broken?"

Knox grins. "I knew Felicity gave it to him for a reason. My girl knows what she's doing."

I ignore them both, resetting my hat on Apollo's head, where it tilts slightly to the side. The sight of him, tiny body, big head, tongue hanging out in contentment, makes me grin. I pull my phone out and snap a quick picture.

Me: Hi, Mom.

Her response comes back immediately.

Lottie: He taught you to take selfies and text already, Apollo? They really do grow up quick, don't they? Such a smart boy.

Me: He said he gets it from me.

Lottie: I'm sure he got something from you, but I don't think that's it.

Me: Keep that mouth in check, Trouble.

I shake my head, smiling like a fool at my screen. Behind me, Kit tries his own luck at getting Apollo to sit, followed by Knox, who swears he's an expert because his method "worked perfectly on Nigel."

After a few minutes, Knox wanders off to Miller's truck, and I take the chance to lean down to Kit. "How's the riding going?"

I already know the answer. Lottie has sent me every update possible—videos, notes, even a whole meal plan she's put together for him—but still. It's nice hearing it from him.

"Good. Great." He laughs, scratching the back of his neck. "She's got me on some bulking meal plan and working me on this manual bull simulator during the day. But at night, sometimes we sneak into Riley's, and she fires up Goliath."

I grimace, thinking back to how my back was sore for two

days after riding that old beast. "If you can handle him, you're in good shape."

Kit shakes his head. "Not quite yet. When she cranks up the settings, I don't last long. But she says I'm close."

I slap his shoulder and take my dog back. Lottie's dog. Maybe partially my dog. In my head, he calls me Dad, so I take that for what it's worth. Only once I set him down, he goes right back to Kit's boots.

"That's great, man. Glad you asked her to help. She's the best teacher you'll find."

"Yeah, she's the best." He hesitates, then adjusts his stance. "Actually, Miss Lottie thinks I can sign up for the first fall rodeo."

I raise an eyebrow. "Really?"

He nods. "It's a local one that's just for fun. Nothing major, but still. She's gonna talk to one of the guys who oversees the cattle and see if he can get us in."

"That's great. I think it—"

Knox's boots scuff against the ground as he walks back over, cutting the conversation short. Kit and I exchange a quick glance—one that says we'll finish this later.

Knox jerks his head toward his uncle's truck. "Dad called Miller. He needs help with the back field."

I frown. "Irrigation giving you trouble still?"

We spent almost the entire last week trying to gear water away from the crops. Between the ditches we've dug out and the lining we've laid down, I don't see how any more revisions would help.

"It's…a lot. Don't worry about it." He waves a hand. "You guys head out. This'll need time to set, anyway."

Kit straightens. "I'll help."

Knox shakes his head. "You're good, man. Got it covered."

"If you're good, I'm good," I say, shrugging.

Truthfully, I know Lottie is almost done with her shift, and I'm desperate to see her. We don't have plans to check anything off the list today—I'm putting those off until next week—but I just want…her.

Everyone splits up, and I start my truck's engine, pulling up Lottie's contact.

"Hi, Walker," Lottie answers on the second ring, voice like warm honey.

I lean back in my seat, letting the sound of her settle over me like a blanket. "Hi, baby." There's a smile in my voice that I'm thankful Knox and Kit aren't around to hear. "What are you up to?"

"Almost done now, clocking out. And you?"

"Just waiting until you say I can come grab you."

"I am free to grab."

There have never been sweeter words.

Ten minutes later, I've got her in my passenger seat; she's wearing cutoff shorts and an oversized Riley's T-shirt, hair pulled up, eyes sparkling with curiosity. I adjust my rearview mirror where her shoulder accidentally bumped it coming in. There's a perfect lipstick stain on my cheek where she kissed me in Riley's parking lot. I make no attempts to rub it off.

"Are we doing list things today?" She leans closer to me, and my legs spread enough so our thighs are touching. Heat burrows in my stomach. I don't know if I'll ever get used to it—the way she stirs me up. How she always has me chasing after more and more.

"In a way." I toss my right arm over her shoulders and trail my fingers on the bare skin of her arm.

At times like this, I am incredibly thankful that Gerald gave me this truck. There's no storage, and you'll slide around if you take sharp turns, but it allows me to keep this girl as close to me as possible. A very, very fair trade in my opinion.

"In what way?"

"You know that one bet we've been pushing off?"

"*The* one?"

"The one and only."

"Tonight?" she squeals, and it's like a bell in my chest is rattling through my body.

"Tonight."

I've been planning this for weeks. Every little detail—from packing the truck, to researching and checking out the very best routes and ways to not get caught.

It's our very last item, and coincidentally, it's only two nights away from Lottie's birthday. When our list is supposed to be over and done with.

See, there's this apparent legend about a ghost in the deep forest mountains behind Willow Creek. The old man who works the hardware store down the road swears he saw three women in a circle holding hands and chanting. And with Lottie's own ghost in the sister house, she made a bet—more with herself than anyone else—that she will go up there and camp overnight.

The only problem is the camping I've done in my life has been purely accidental and definitely wasn't done with a tent or a fire or sleeping bags. A few times in high school, I drank too much to drive home, so I set up a portable hammock in the woods outside a friend's house and slept it off there until the sun rose.

But real camping? No. Not even close, actually. Which is why I pulled out all the stops for tonight. I ordered everything we could possibly need, including emergency supplies if something were to happen, like Lottie having a seizure. Pillows, blankets, a list of her medications and extras if she forgets (thanks to Dot), a first-aid kit, and a list of emergency numbers just in case.

I have no plans of telling her that, though.

As soon as I wrapped up work with Kit, I picked her up, and we ran to her house for a change of clothes and anything else she might need. I overheard her shout to Dot about spending the night at Flick's house and promise that she'd be safe. My stomach twisted a little at that; I'm a horrible liar. But this was on her list. And who am I if not a guy that can do this simple thing for her?

We grabbed dinner to-go, and I followed the directions that Kit got from Knox, telling him that his "buddies" were going on a ghost hiking trip, just leaving out the minor detail of *who* exactly was going.

Once I got us on the road there, we landed on a dirt path surrounded by trees. It was narrow and straight enough that I felt fully confident turning to Lottie and pointing to ask, "You want to take it for a spin?"

She squealed so loud that Apollo literally jumped in the air and hid behind the seat. Her reaction alone was worth the questionable situation I was about to put us both in. The thing is, I know in the deepest parts of myself that I want to give her a chance to drive again in a place where no one else would be hurt in the worst-case scenario.

I think she must know that, too, otherwise she never would have accepted the offer.

If it were a main road and I had any, and I mean *any*, inkling of doubt in my mind of her safety, I would've never asked. But there was a point to be made on this single-night camping trip. A point to be made from this whole list, really.

I am not going to hide her in a bubble and tell her to sit and be good and expect that she'll never stray where her heart wants to take her. I'm not her brother, or her dad, or any of her friends. I'm not going to just watch while she loses herself in a diagnosis that is very dangerous but also can't be fully prevented. If I'm there to catch her—and I'll always be there to catch her—then there is nothing to fear. So why not let her fully be herself while also being safe next to me?

Lottie jumped from her seat, crawling over my lap with her ass in my face before I can even shift the gear to park. I keep a calm breath and hand, but a steady eye, as I watch her relearn the gears in my truck. At first, she scans everything around her, like something in the trees might jump out and attack. But then after a few dips and curves in the road, her shoulders drop back down, and the focused frown on her lips turns to that easy smile I love. And she takes *off*.

She's not extremely fast, no faster than I would go in an old truck down a dirt path, but she is steady and confident. She keeps glancing back at me with this unbelievable smile that somehow says, *"Can you believe this? Wild!"*

I let her drive as long as she can take it, and as long as I can, too, until the road starts to rut out and the small curves in it turn into giant potholes every ten feet. She happily slides from the driver's seat over to her side, and I swear she lights up the rest of the way there, bouncing around in her seat and telling Apollo just how good she did. "And to think, I didn't hit a single parking meter."

I settled us exactly where Knox suggested. In the midst of the trees, off the dirt path, is a small enough clearing that no one else would know about it, but big enough that I can fit my truck in between the spaces. I slip us in, and my eyes instantly catch on the spot Knox told Kit about. A soft bed of pine needles, nestled between two sturdy trees. A perfect, flat spot to set up a tent, and a black circle on the ground a few feet away where someone else had a fire going not long ago. Towering pines and ancient oaks stretch out toward the sky, their branches whispering in the warm late-summer breeze. There is a sound of rushing water from the creek in the distance.

Lottie and I both hop out, glance around, and immediately get settled in.

Immediately is a *bit* of a stretch. It took me a while to get the tent set up, which was more embarrassing than I thought it would be. I had plans of just googling how-to videos when we got here but forgot to take note of the lack of signal, so I had to mostly freestyle it. But eventually, it stood there, tall and proud and just enough for the two of us to squeeze our things into. My face flames at the thought of spending the entire night next to Lottie. Lying beside her. Her hair on my pillow. Her wrists near my blanket. Her scent filling up a small space for just us.

I forced myself to focus on what mattered and got to work on the fire, which took way faster than I thought to make, as there was wood already stacked to the side and I had a flint that I've used a hundred times before.

Lottie pulled out the chairs from the back of the truck, unfolded them, and set Apollo in one and our food in the other, while she and I both sank down by the fire.

And now, with the tent up and a fire crackling low before us, the sky melting from shades of pink and orange to dark blue, it feels like nothing in the world could ruin this. Like not a single thing of the outside world can touch us here. Like it's me and Lottie and our dog, and this sliver of a view could be our future. Like a life in this small town with us being together is a true possibility.

"You know..." Lottie chews on the last of her fries, which are actually *my* fries that she stole after eating all of hers. She's leaning back by the tent while I keep pacing around the fire to watch how big the burn is going to grow. "You really are a hunk, Walker Lane."

I don't think she realizes it, but when she gets extra excited, or nervous, or mad, or really over-the-top with any emotion, she has this accent come out that makes her I's sound like ah's, and it's so cute. I keep a mental tally of every time she does it. "Ice" sounds like "ass" or "fire" sounds like "far." It's so rare that I get to hear it, but tonight she is letting that accent out left and right.

She hums, and I poke at the fire with the rod again. "Quit messing with it and come sit by me," she orders.

I look over my shoulder to see Apollo nestled at Lottie's feet, tail thumping lazily against the dirt. She's already changed into her pajamas, which are actually not pajamas but her demanding I give her my shirt. My entire body feels like a furnace, and I know it's not the fire's fault.

My eyes trail up her bare shins, glowing from the orange light in front of her, up to where her thighs cross. My teeth bite heavily on my lower lip, and she must feel my gaze, because she clicks her tongue and I shoot my eyes up to her smirking face.

She lifts a hand and curls a finger toward me. "Seriously. Come in here." She jerks her head back, and while I am so tempted to say screw this fire and take her inside, I know I can't comfortably be distracted if I think she's in danger.

I glance from the fire back to her. "Two minutes?"

She smiles. "Two minutes. I'm counting."

God, let it go by fast. I poke at the fire, debating whether I should throw on another log to keep it going through the night. Lottie shivers in her sleep, even if it's a warm seventy-three degrees, so I doubt it will be any different up here. I brought her extra blankets, but she usually kicks them off in her sleep.

"I forgot to tell you what happened at the pen yesterday." Lottie giggles behind me, and I grin.

"What happened?" I ask and keep my eyes on the logs. The quicker I get this sorted, the quicker I get in that tent with the woman I'm in love with.

"So you know how I told you I've been trying to teach Kit how to lasso on the side? So he can help Knox with cattle and stuff?" I nod. "Well, Kit grabs the rope, and he's got the knot right. He didn't think about his palms, though, so when he threw it out..." She trails off mid-sentence, like she's questioning if I am even hearing her.

I realize my attention is split in half and that it probably seems like everything she says is going in one ear and out the other. "Go on, baby, I'm listening," I say, still trying to settle this fire just right.

One more minute. I'm so close to being done and taking her in that tent and laying down with her and tugging her close to me and breathing in her shampoo and giving her the softest kiss... One more minute. That's all.

Lottie stays quiet for another second but picks right back up. "He threw it out and the lasso was so close and... and..." Her voice just...cuts off. It's there one moment and completely gone the next.

A slow, creeping unease coils in my stomach. I turn around, hoping to see her laughing or searching for the right words. Hoping to see Apollo distracting her with her shoelaces again. But none of that's happening. She's behind me, just... staring. Her gaze is locked on the fire, like she's looking straight through it. Like she's not even here with me.

"Lot?" I wave a hand in front of her face. Nothing. Not even a blink.

Panic spikes in my chest.

"Sweetheart?" My voice sharpens as I snap my fingers near her face. No reaction. No recognition.

Her right hand starts jerking into the air, over and over again, like some kind of muscle twitch she can't control. It's not a big motion. She's not waving it around, but it is the same small jerk repeating wildly. My brain is scrambling, trying to process what's happening while my body moves on instinct.

"Shit, shit, shit," I whisper to myself, forcing a deep breath as I go through the steps I half-remember from a medical video Knox sent me to watch two days after moving in. "Uh, check for danger."

I clear away anything she could hit her head on, shifting the firewood and pulling the sleeping bag behind her in case she goes down hard.

"Symptoms," I mutter under my breath, trying to keep myself grounded. No drooling. No rolling eyes. Just that empty stare into the fire, unblinking and unwavering. That one hand, moving over and over like a broken record that can't be stopped, and her jaw grinding as if she's still chewing.

Shit, is she still chewing? Is she *choking*?

Fear climbs up my throat. I can't check her to see if she's chewing or choking or anything, or I'm at risk of making it worse. Do I lay her down on her side just in case? The videos, all of them, said not to touch her, but she's right there and I am right here, and how can I not touch her and fix this? She's having a seizure and I can't help her. I can't do anything.

Apollo whines and nudges at her leg, like he's also sensing something's wrong. I gently pull him back just enough to be out of the way.

We're useless, both of us whining and desperate to get her eyes to fall back in line and her arm to slip back down. I watch as I pace around like something here will save us both from this moment, and still, nothing changes. She's still having a seizure, and I'm still fumbling around like a terrified fool with nothing to do.

I am at the mercy of time. Time…

"Time it. Time it. Shit, what time is it?" I fumble for my phone on the nearby seat, my hands shaking as I unlock it.

6:52 p.m.

I need Knox. But there's no signal in the mountains besides my phone being in SOS mode. So do I call an ambulance? He said they usually don't have to, but what if this is the time she needs one?

I've researched and researched everything to do at this moment. I've taken an online course, read forums, joined groups of friends and spouses of those with epilepsy. I have done every single thing I could to understand what exactly I needed to do in this moment, and yet I am sitting here useless.

How long has it been? Two minutes? Ten? It feels like an eternity. Feels like time has stopped for me, while everything else moves around us. I check the time again.

6:52 p.m.

Crickets still chirp, water still rushes down the creek, the fire still crackles, but I'm left motionless as I watch the worst thing I have ever seen unfold in front of me.

Every medical training video I watched did *not* show it like this. They never describe the fear you get. How all of your instincts fly out the window when the time comes. They say it's like the person is daydreaming, but daydreaming implies that there is something for them to even dream of and Lottie…

Lottie looks like she's not even here on Earth with me. Like she is a ghost of herself, and I am left with no idea how to get her back.

I keep checking the time on my phone.

6:52 p.m.

Impossible.

This is taking so long. I need Knox, or Flick, or her mom, or even her shitty dad. I don't care, I need *someone*.

Then, just as suddenly as it started, she blinks, like nothing ever happened. Her arm slips down, her jaw drops its grin. She shivers a bit. Then there is a confused recognition as she sees how close I'm standing to her.

"Sorry, sorry," she says, rubbing her temple in slow circles, her brows drawn together. "I lost my train of thought. What was I saying?"

All I can do is stare at her, my heart still racing against my ribs.

"Walker?" Her brows knit together. "You okay?"

Am *I* okay?

She just had a seizure. I mean blanked out—completely *gone*—for God knows how long, maybe only a minute according to the laws of time, but forever to me. And she's acting like it was a mere lapse in conversation. Like my entire world, every moment that I shared with her these past few months wasn't just completely flipped on its end.

I understand, logically, I have to stay calm here. For a person like Lottie, this situation means everything. My reaction means everything. If I freak out and do what her brother or friends would, she'll see that I'm no different from them. That I am just as terrified to leave her alone.

Maybe I am now. Maybe I'm just as bad, if not worse. At least they know how to handle this.

"Are you..." My voice is dry and hoarse, so I clear it. "Are *you* okay?"

She waves a hand, dismissing my concern with a small smile that doesn't meet her eyes. Her head is shaking side to side, like this whole thing is just so silly of her. "Yeah, I didn't even realize I did it. It's fine. I'm fine."

Fine? I feel like my whole world just tilted sideways.

The waterfall. The running around at night. The riding lessons. The driving up here. I don't regret any of it. Not even a little. But I am terrified of what *could* have been. My mind is on repeat, playing all of those scenarios out but with a different ending. Taking her to the waterfall—what if she had a seizure from the fall and hit her head on a rock while we were running? What if that happened just an hour before, when I willingly let her behind the wheel with trees and obstacles all around us? I had so much faith in my ability to take care of her that I never realized I was never going to be strong enough to do it in the moment.

It keeps coming back to that—what could have happened. And what comes next.

Lottie is fine. I try to process it, but nothing comes up. She's *fine.* She told me herself. She's right there, inches away, living and breathing and existing.

"It's just the altitude," she explains, that easy, reassuring smile still spread across her lips.

"The *altitude*?" I echo, my mind still playing catch-up.

"Yeah, sometimes the change messes with my blood pressure, makes it drop or rise too fast. It didn't bother me with our last hike, and sometimes it just happens randomly. I'm fine."

But her eyes are somewhere else, somewhere distant. The look she gives me weighs heavier than any calf I have ever had to lift. It's this pleading, almost sympathetic stare. As though she feels bad for *me* that I had to witness her seizure, and all I can think about is if there is any way I can strap her to my back and carry her with me everywhere. And even that thought isn't comforting, since in the darkest hour, I was a useless, stuttering man just staring in shock.

Lottie wipes the look off as much as possible, smiling and pretending to laugh at Apollo licking her cheek. She knows. She can tell *exactly* how much this shook me and is trying to diminish this whole thing. Using everything in her power to squash my memory of the last...however many minutes.

I glance down at my phone.

6:54 p.m.

Two minutes? Is that really all it takes to shift my entire life?

"Look at me," she says softly, reaching for my hands. I didn't realize they were shaking. I turn my eyes back to her. "I'm alright."

Instant heat fills my body at the reassurance. I let her pull me back in, let the moment settle. I slowly crouch to sit next to her and keep my shaky hands to myself.

She's alright.

Time goes on. I pretend to nod along and listen while she goes about finishing her story of Kit and pretending that nothing is different. That nothing has changed.

Smoke from the fire billows and follows her wherever she sits.

She smiles at one point. "My mom used to say fire smoke always goes to the prettiest one in the room."

I let out this unconvincing puff of air that could technically be considered a laugh. "It picked the right one, then."

We joke about Apollo chasing fireflies in the night air,

huffing in defeat when he can't fully catch them due to constantly tripping on his big paws. She asks me to name some stars, and I make up some fake lineage of the ones we can see just to make her laugh. She tells me stories of the groundhogs taking over the town—apparently there is an ongoing phone tree about peoples' garages being broken into and wires getting chewed up in crawl spaces. Our laughter, tense and wobbly, fills the air so that we never have to linger in the silence long.

None of it is enough to erase the past.

We finish the night like this is our new normal. She's said before about how tired she gets after an episode, so I make a few casual comments about how tired I am and lay back in the rolled-out sleeping bags where there is enough room for both of us.

She follows my lead and slips under my arm with her head on my chest, tucked between my collarbone and my jaw. It's everything I should want. Everything I've craved this summer. And yet my mind isn't here—I'm still standing by the fire; not a moment has gone by.

I take slow, deep breaths into her hair, reminding myself over and over that everything is okay.

Lottie is *here*. In my arms. She is warm and safe, and I am capable of watching over her for the night. She is here. In my arms. Warm and safe. I am *capable*.

The words fall in an endless pattern until my racing heart starts to eventually slow back down.

"Are you sure you're not cold?" I lift a hand to the back of her neck. "I can put another log on."

"It's like eighty degrees out, and I'm lying next to you under a blanket. If anything, I'm about to start sweating."

"Shit." I pull back a little. "I can get the other sleeping bag?"

I'm already moving frantically to open her own bag for her own space. Am I smothering her? Does she feel it? Does she know all I can think about is keeping her safe?

"Walker." She lays a hand firmly on my chest, and all the blurring motions around me slow to a stop. "I am perfect, okay? I'm camping under a pretty night sky. And Apollo's sleeping at my feet. I'm stuffed to the brim with french fries and chocolate bars. I'm in my favorite pajamas." She makes a point of gesturing to my shirt on her. "And I'm with my favorite person. So stop fretting, okay? It's just us. Nothing"—her hands keep patting my chest in this steady rhythm, like she's trying to calm herself down too—"*nothing* is different. I'm still me, you're still you."

I suck in a breath and nod, not trusting my own words.

Either she doesn't want to talk about it either or my nod is sufficient enough, because as soon as I put my head back on the inflatable camping pillow, she follows suit, blond hair splaying across my chest. My fingers reach for the ends, curling them around my fingers as I listen to her breath fall steady.

"Hey, Walker?" Lottie whispers and looks up at me. The fire is dim enough so she can't see the tears that threaten to leave my eyes.

"Yeah?" I swallow everything down.

"Don't be weird after all of this, okay?" She reaches over for my hand, and our fingers link together. She gives them a gentle squeeze. "I meant it earlier. It's still me."

Of course it's still her, and that's what makes it so hard. Because I *love* her. More than I have ever loved anything in my life.

"I won't. It's still you." I give her a gentle squeeze back and listen to each breath she takes, counting them like sheep, until she is passed out in my arms.

I feel like I'm holding glass in my hands. Bound to slip and shatter any moment. Like if I make one wrong move, it will happen again, and I'll watch that lifeless look slip into her eyes and lose my girl again.

And for the first time since I came to this town, I finally understand everything. I understand Knox pulling me aside. I understand her best friend's careful eye. Her parents, even her dad, constantly circling around her.

Each of them has had to sit through what we just did, possibly even worse. This entire summer I have had this third-party, outward view on her life. How dare they put her in a box? How dare they force her to be anything other than who she is?

I never thought I would become them.

If I gave it the power, this night could ruin everything for us. The good news from this is that I *do* have a choice. I can't pretend nothing happened. But I can be her realistic escape from the things she can't outrun in life. I can stay here, make her lists of safe and exciting things to check off. Take her wherever her heart desires, and do my very best to stay the solid rock that she can lean on.

If I can't, then I need to leave sooner rather than later.

And with that thought passing through my mind, I realize there actually *is* no choice.

I'm not sure there ever was. The moment I stepped onto Willow Creek's dirt roads, I knew the chances of me leaving them behind were slim to none.

The next morning, the second we get back to civilization and I have a single bar of service, I open my email to send the one thing I should have weeks ago.

CHAPTER THIRTY-SIX
Lottie

Something I learned at a young age: Birthdays are always, *always* disappointing.

Maybe it's because I build them up in my head. Even before the accident, I always had these pictures in my mind of what my day would be like. Dips in the creek, tanning in the August sun. Eating pink cupcakes, dancing with boys, laughing with friends.

And never once did they add up to be what I wanted. Something always disappointed me on the day, and without a doubt, I would have at least one good birthday cry.

However, the tradition is going to break today. Because this birthday was not going to be like the others. And if tears are shed, it will only be due to happiness, and maybe because I am slowly getting older.

I know it's going to be an amazing day because Walker has made every day since he got here a practically perfect day.

The way he reacted after my seizure the other night was nothing short of terrifying. I watched this beautiful light in his eyes die out, knowing I was the one who snuffed it. Fear laced me all night, even in my dreams. Fear that we would wake up, pack our things, come home, and he would either a) realize I am too much to take care of and this whole summer was a mistake, Or b) freak out completely and buckle down on the safety measures just like everyone else around me.

However, any assumption I had was squashed the moment we woke up that next morning. Walker packed us up, drove us into town, stopped for a baker's dozen that contained our newest obsession—glazed croissants from Glazed and Confused—and ended up eating them in our field before making out on a checkered blanket.

Not my worst morning to say the least.

Walker didn't fade away or tuck me under his wing. If anything, he doubled down on our time together. We run errands together (there is something so intimate about knowing what brand of toilet paper we both prefer), and when he has to go to work, he calls me and leaves me in his pocket, headphones in so we can talk all day. Even if neither of us have anything to say, the silence we sit in while he works the fields and I read on my porch swing is more comfortable than anything my passed-down quilt can provide.

Walker even lets me drive his truck now. Only on the flat, clear pieces of the property, and only with him in the passenger seat, of course. But still, it's a freedom I didn't know I needed. A small, simple gesture that makes me feel trusted. Safe and capable all at once.

Just as I am up enough to change clothes and make a cup of tea, a steady buzzing comes from the living room. I slip through the doorway and find Walker's phone on the coffee table. No wonder I didn't wake up to any texts from him. It's flipped face down, and curiosity pulls at me to see who is calling. But we're not there, right? I mean, I certainly would give him my phone and let him scroll through whatever he wanted to. My texts with Flick about his chest might be awkward, but he would be amused if nothing else. But something about answering his phone for him feels off, so I ignore it, heading straight to the coffee machine.

It stops vibrating. A couple seconds go by. It starts again.

The process repeats at least four times, and it hits me. What if he's looking for his phone and it's Kit or Knox calling to help him find it?

I rush over before the ringing can stop, not bothering to see the contact.

"Hello?" I sing.

"Walker?"

The voice is a man for sure, but an unfamiliar one. One that definitely doesn't work here.

"He's not available at the moment. Can I take a message?" I would kill it in a receptionist role in another life.

"I'm looking for Walker Lane," the man says, his voice cold and impersonal.

Not even a hello? How are you? Yes, is this the proper number I am looking for?

It takes me a second to respond. When I do, I stutter my way through it. "Um, he's probably in the fields somewhere? He got called out early."

I reach for my phone and open our text thread, unsure what to even say.

"I could maybe get him to call you?"

Then I realize, duh, he can't, because I'm holding his phone.

The man exhales a short, humorless chuckle like maybe he knows how ridiculous I am too. "Yeah, I've been calling him for weeks, so I don't think that'll work, sweetheart."

My fingers tighten around the edge of the phone. *Sweetheart.* The way he says it isn't kind or familiar like how Walker says it, just dismissive. Condescending. Like I am a mere speck of dirt on the bottom of his custom leather loafers and he is attempting to scrape me off on the heated concrete of his driveway. In a flash of a moment, he coughs. Familiar…

And then, like puzzle pieces clicking into place, it hits me. I pull back the phone and read the contact.

"Are you… Is this Walker's *dad*?"

A sharp "yes" comes back.

I stare at the phone. This man. The one who dropped young Walker off like he was nothing but a pet to be taken care of for a month and picked back up simply because he had to be. The one who made him feel like he had to fight, had to prove himself, had to be *more* just to be worth anything. My stomach twists into knots so tight it's hard to breathe.

My phone in my other hand flings itself across the room and lands on the couch before flopping onto the floor. Or maybe I threw it. I can't be sure what I am doing when my anger is building this high this fast. I flex my fingers, popping my knuckles as my pulse picks up.

"You know, I've been waiting years to have a talk with you." My voice is steady but laced with heat. "Do *you* even realize what you did to him? What you and your wife put him through? You treated him like garbage. For years."

There's a condescending scoff that seems to only rile up my anger. "He had a very nice childhood. I have the private school degree and mortgage to show for it."

"I don't give a shit about school or houses or bank statements or your…Bitcoin. Or whatever other fancy, degrading thing you have to throw at me or my Walker. Money means *nothing* if your parents are never around you. You can't throw cash at a kid and expect it to be taken as love. Did you know Walker broke his wrist here one summer?"

"No." The man on the line clears his throat. "I am certain he has had no broken bones under my watch. Or my wife would have handled the operations and referrals."

Okay, no, he didn't. But that's not the point. The point is if he *had* broken his wrist, this asshole would've never known or cared.

My words stammer as I try to piece together ten years' worth of anger in one quick front-porch conversation. "Did you know he dreaded the end of each summer? All because he never wanted to see you two again? And how he was so desperate for any form of love or attention that he now spends his time nonstop trying to make everyone around him happy. Because you never bothered to be a father; you were just a bank. A credit card can't replace love for a child." My throat tightens, but I push forward. "And now, after all this time, you just show up asking for him? No. You don't get to talk or see my Walker. Not now. Not until he says otherwise."

It's quiet for a moment. And then, with a small laugh, he says, "Oh, I get it. You're it."

"I'm what?"

"You're the reason he turned the internship down. There had to have been something. Though, he could have found any perfectly fine girl up there as well. Still, he lets it all go for a young girl in a dirt town—"

The words keep coming, and they each hit like a slap. The job. Turned down. My mind stutters. "Turned… Walker said no?"

I can practically hear his greasy smile, and I hate that I've unknowingly handed him the upper hand.

"Didn't tell you? He's good at that, not answering."

My pulse pounds in my ears. Like water just flooded all my systems and everything is just…rebooting. He's staying here? Officially? I mean really, actually staying right here with me. Walker living on this land right beside me for…however long I can keep him. It's like every emotional state I can muster is hitting buttons, unsure of which one to land on.

Walker didn't tell me. Why didn't he tell me?

"When did he decline it?"

"Day before yesterday. It's why I have been calling him nonstop." There's some garbled mess still spouting from him, but I'm stuck in place. "Tell him to call me. Now."

The last two sentences don't even register. In fact, nothing registers except that Walker declined the NASA internship. Not only did he decline, but he also did it the *day* after my seizure. He promised not to be weird or to change, and yet, that next day he was declining a job he has been on and off about for months?

"Did you hear me? Tell Walker—"

"I hope you choke on something." I nod, mind made up. I hate this man. I hate, hate, *hate* him for everything he's done to my favorite person in the world. For ruining my morning. And for having his stupid fancy shoes and his even fancier car and his probably fancy housewife who knows nothing about a mother's love. "I hope you stop at a fancy, over-the-top Italian place on your way home and order the carbonara pasta and shovel it so far down in your gullet that it lodges there. And you'll have to call 911, but they won't hear you because you are too busy choking on your forty-dollar pasta bowl that didn't even come with a salad. And I *really* hope to God I never have to see your face. You better hope it too, if you know what's good for you."

Before I can stop myself, I hang up the phone and toss it

in the spare bedroom before closing the door like it's a grenade about to pop off any second.

My hands are shaking as I turn to my living room. My chest feels tight, my thoughts racing. Why didn't Walker tell me? Why would he keep this from me? He wouldn't do it on purpose… not unless he thought I couldn't handle it. The thought makes something sharp and ugly coil inside me that I force down.

No, no. It's a giant misunderstanding. Walker doesn't just do things without thinking. Maybe he was going to tell me tonight at dinner.

I wasn't supposed to find out like this. The fact that he declined the job right after the seizure…it's a coincidence. It has to be a coincidence.

I just need to find him. I need Walker. He'll explain, and everything will be back to our normal routine.

My hands reach to grab my phone off the floor and ring number after number. Going from Kit, to Flick, to Knox, to Miller, to even my dad. Not a single person on this property is answering their phone. All I need is a general idea where Walker is at, and I can take it from there.

At the very least, *someone* has to be at the main house.

I fling my door open and rush down the porch stairs.

The calm, reassuring part of me keeps saying there's a reason. That Walker isn't going to hold back from me on purpose. That he has a plan. But the other side is full of doubt. And fear. And a jumbled mess of questions.

The day after my seizure. What if that's not a coincidence? That it's not by mistake?

What if his outward promise of us still being us and that no changes would happen was a compromise to an inward promise he made to treat me like everyone else but just make it less obvious?

My jaw clenches down as I head toward the main house. I creak the front door open. But the moment I step inside, I hear voices. Some whispering, some louder. Following them to the dining room, I pause just out of view.

The entire family is gathered around the big wooden table—Knox, my mom, my dad, Uncle Miller, Aunt Wyn, even my mom's distant brother I haven't seen since the accident—Eli, and his wife, Rory. Almost all of the employees, including freelance movers, and…is that *Flick*? Knox sits beside her, tall and broad, his blond hair slightly mussed like he's been running a hand through it too much. Flick sits beside him with her arms crossed, her tight, curly hair framing her face, eyes narrowed in concentration. Everyone except Dot, Walker, and Kit sit there. And me.

I hesitate in the doorway where I'm out of view. They're deep in discussion, their voices low and serious, but it's so scattered I can't pick anything up until my mom waves her hand around for everyone to be quiet.

I hear my dad's clear voice first. "Look. I know it's expensive, but can we not…"

"It's not just expensive. It's detrimental." That's Uncle Eli. "You can't honestly say that any of this is alright. We don't have enough income pulling from the other sources to recover from this."

Knox clears his throat, his dark eyes worse than they were last week. He's lost weight recently too. His cheeks look a little sunken in. "I tried everything, okay? I've spent weeks working on irrigation—"

"This isn't an irrigation problem. It's a management problem. You're expecting a child to understand this," Eli grumbles, and Rory nods along beside him.

"Can we please settle down?" My mom's smooth voice. I

see the back of her head, watch as her hand strokes my dad's arm in comfort. "Everyone is family here."

Except not everyone is family here, because they are missing one piece of the actual family in there and have substituted her with seasonal employees and my best friend?

"Surely we can find a way to fix this?" Mom turns to him for answers, but Dad is silent.

Flick clears her throat. "Knox has really been trying. He's worked harder than anyone else, and between that and taking watch over Lottie..." I freeze in place. I need more than anything to have none of them see me here. Taking *watch* over me? What am I? A pet that needs to be properly fed and watered and shoved back in her cage? The way she says it so casually has my stomach so tight, a wave of nausea crashes over me. "It's been a lot on him."

Knox shakes his head. "I don't..." He sighs. "Figure out what you all want. Vote or whatever the hell we're all doing, and tell me what I need to know moving forward."

I keep listening, keep waiting to find some kind of context to what is going on in here that is serious enough to warrant literally *everyone* on the property but me. My eyes scan the table. Apparently Kit and Walker weren't invited either. That minimizes the sting by a bit, but still, it sits there.

"*Lottie*?" A voice calls out, shaky and watery. It's Flick. Our eyes lock from opposite ends of the room. Heads turn, necks crane. Everyone else is staring my way. But I am busy bouncing between my brother and my best friend.

Knox's head falls down with a massive sigh. Mom shudders a breath, and Dad, as always, won't look me directly in the eyes. I take the time to look at every face at the table, but no one even hints at what is going on right now.

"What is this?" I gesture a hand to the whole room. "What

are… Taking *watch* over me?" I whisper the last part to Flick, and her watery eyes are now dripping tears down her cheek. I'm pushing questions left and right with my stares and I'm only met with blank sympathy.

"Oh, Lot," Mom whispers. "I'm so—"

My head is shaking. "What are… What is this?"

Uncle Eli clears his throat. "Charlotte, good to see you. We just had a meeting."

"A meeting?"

Miller groans and pulls at his hair. "Can you shut your mouth for ten seconds, Eli?"

He's yelling at him, but I'm still stuck on whatever this is. I can understand if it was just the workers on the farm, but everyone, literally everyone, is at this table. Flick doesn't even handle a single thing with the land. She's far less connected to it than I am. And yet, she's right beside my brother, rubbing slow circles on his back like *he's* the one about to lose it. Even an ex-employee who hasn't worked here in two years is seated next to my mom. They're all discussing the future of this land, and no one dared to invite me?

Is that why they didn't invite Walker? Or Kit? Because they knew they would tell me?

"Without me?" My voice is a whisper. "How often do you guys do this?"

"Lottie…" Flick starts like she has some explanation, but she shuts it down just as fast.

"What?" I snap. "What is happening here?"

"It's nothing, Lot." Dad turns enough in his chair so he can give me the same smile he has ever since that day. It's not his real one. It's not even close. It's not the smile he gives my mom, or the other workers, or even Knox. It's a flinch. There is a wince behind it.

"It's clearly not nothing, I heard you all arguing over something." They're going to vote on something, something big enough that Flick and ex-employees are there, and yet, I'm not. "Does my opinion not matter?"

No one responds to my question though. So maybe I *am* useless. At least enough not to be considered.

My uncle Eli, the only one seeming to be unattached enough to give me the truth, speaks up while everyone else at the table stutters along. "Knox discovered issues in the back three fields concerning insufficient watering stunting plant growth, leading to smaller and lower-quality agriculture yields. Whenever surface water is insufficient, we have no option but to use groundwater, but this has…exacerbated the problems for the entire field, as groundwater levels have been declining over time."

He takes a deep breath before continuing. "That being said, all of the time and energy that was put into those fields this last season was possibly pointless. It's tens of thousands of dollars wasted in manual labor and the loss of potential income for our outsources. He's tried to fix it himself instead of telling any of us, and now"—Flick reaches over to grab Knox's hands while my uncle's words hit everyone around us—"we are making further business decisions collectively to decide if we have time to pull and start over or if we should see the crops through. We're voting on if we think it's still a good idea for Knox to take over the ranch when he's older."

I turn to Knox. His cheeks are bright red, eyes lowered and brows furrowed. He won't even look at me. A handful of people nod their heads or murmur a yes. But Knox doesn't even spare a passing glance. Anger burns hotter in my stomach. "So all of those times you were so stressed out and I asked you what was wrong and you brushed me off?"

"She doesn't need to know all of this," Knox mutters under his breath at Eli before looking at me. No. Looking *through* me. This isn't the Knox I know. This isn't my brother. It's a ghost I've found that has replaced the old version of him. "The stress…it's not good for you."

"You know what's not good for me? Knowing that my entire family, and my best friend, are all meeting up behind my back once a week to discuss issues on the property I'm living on." I take a deep enough breath so I can shout the next part. "And on my *birthday*?"

In the grand scheme of things, all of this happening on my birthday isn't a huge deal. I think it's more that it's the cherry on top.

"We were going to tell you tonight. I have cake for you at my house." Flick sits up high enough where I have no choice but to look at her. "We were all going to vote and then tell you the results tonight at our place."

Does that really make it better, though? No. Not in my mind. And maybe I'm stubborn or dramatic or just *wrong* to get upset in this scenario. Maybe I am sensitive, but that doesn't mean my feelings aren't valid.

If they wanted to not cause me stress, maybe they should have thought about it before casually conducting a life-changing decision for this entire farm without me.

"I'm not…" I shake my head, searching for the words. Fat, angry tears build under my waterline, and I blink them away. They can't have them. These tears are mine and mine alone. "I am a part of this family too."

Multiple streams of "of course you are" and "we know" and "we love you so much" hit me all at once, but it doesn't matter. Because I am already halfway out the door.

The exhaustion from the seizure the other day, the lack

of sleep, the stress of it all. It overflows from my brain, unable to hold the load, and runs down to my chest, settling there like a stone. My breathing is uneven and ragged as I rush the whole way home. Someone calls my name. Knox, I think.

Once I'm inside, I run to my nightstand, fling the drawer open, and grab the set of emergency keys for the Bronco. They're foreign in my hands, and the metal keys dangling fill me with conviction, but I shove it down and keep pushing.

I fly out of the house with the keys in hand at the same time Kit steps up to the front porch beside mine with a confused smile. "Slamming doors on your birthday, Miss Lottie? Did Walker piss you off? You know I'll kick his—"

I *adore* Kit. He's a really great kid. But he is not enough to keep me standing around for chitchat.

I don't bother answering his question. My legs barrel forward straight to the Bronco. Shaking hands and thumping heart, I can't take it anymore. Everything is muffled and fuzzy and like I'm swimming underwater, but there's nothing in me that cares for what the world outside is offering me. I need away. I need to be anywhere but this property, and I'm not asking a single person here to take me away.

The engine stutters as I try to bring it to life, the keys rattling in my hand.

"Come on, come on, come on," I whisper to myself like a silent prayer for one thing to go right.

It takes longer than needed, but the motor roars to life, the SUV shaking beneath my body like the steady heaving breath of a young bull.

My fingers stutter as I try to piece it all back together. It's been so long since I've driven stick, and even if I've been driving since I was twelve—taking loops in the field with my dad for fun—I pause just long enough to wonder if this is a bad idea.

The question doesn't last long, though, it's in and out as I fly out of the driveway faster than I mean to. Maybe this isn't *quite* like riding a bike, but it doesn't matter. I am moving. I am leaving this property, and I don't care if it's selfish or overdramatic or whatever else I'm bound to hear from my family in an hour's time. I just don't want to be here right now.

The last thing I see when I pull out of the driveway is Kit chasing me down with his phone to his ear. I'm sure he's calling Walker. Or Knox. Or my dad or Miller. I see the worry on his face, and I know that what I'm doing is ridiculous.

It's a petty thing to do. To worry everyone by going out on the road with no doctor's clearance in a car that hasn't moved in years. And I don't care. Maybe I am petty. At least enough for this.

My phone buzzes nonstop against the leather seat beside me, and I don't even check the names.

I reach over, manually roll my window down, and toss the device into the wind, watching behind me as the screen smacks the asphalt with a satisfying crack.

Just like that, a single tear forms at the corner of my eye and slips down my cheek.

And the tradition continues.

CHAPTER THIRTY-SEVEN
Walker

The second I find my phone, on the floor of the spare room of all places, I call Kit back. He's hollering in my ear. I've never heard the kid scream this loud as he shouts over and over to me "Lottie's gone!" I instantly jump back in the truck, bringing the engine to life. "Gone, *where*?"

"I don't know." He's panting, and possibly crying? "Something happened, okay? Knox and I have been looking everywhere. He won't say exactly what's going on, but it's not right, she's not…"

She wouldn't… I mean, she couldn't possibly know I turned everything down for her?

"Where is she now?"

"I'm serious, Walker, I don't know. She got in the Bronco. I couldn't stop her."

My heart feels like it slows to a stop. Everything around me does too. Nothing but the empty sound of my blood roaring in my ears and the never-ending loop of imagining worst-case scenarios.

"She's driving? *Alone*?"

Shit, shit, shit. I take the corner faster, dirt kicking up behind my tires and dust flying. Even if she went to the empty fields where we've been practicing, things could still go wrong. What if there was another repeat of what happened the other night? What if she blanks out for even a minute and goes straight for a tree without knowing?

"Which way did she go? Behind the house?"

I already have my steering wheel pointing to the back of the property when his next words lock me into place.

"No, Walker. I mean she *left* Willow Creek. She's not on the property anywhere."

Fear wrangles my stomach. "I'll find her. Stay there in case she comes back, and call me if you hear anything."

I hang up before Kit can answer and immediately call Knox next.

He answers after a single ring. "What?" he hisses out.

"What happened?" I turn down the dirt road onto the main street. "Where did she go?"

He groans. "It's a long story. We had a meeting about the ranch, and I said she didn't need to be there because of her stress. She came in, heard us talking, freaked out, and ran. I wasn't… I didn't mean it to sound like—"

"She's *driving*, Knox." I don't really care to hear whatever excuses he's about to come up with. If he thought he was angry when we accidentally stood up Flick, he has no idea what he's about to face if he's the reason Lottie gets hurt.

"I know. I know."

"No, you apparently don't. She had a seizure forty-eight hours ago, and she's driving. Alone."

"I know, Walker. You think I don't know? You think I don't recognize this entire thing is my fault?" I hear the fear in his voice that matches mine. "I'm going as fast as I can. I already called the phone tree, so everyone in town is on the lookout now. Flick called a second ago and found Lottie's phone on the road. She must have thrown it."

"If she gets in a wreck"—my throat tightens just saying that—"I will—"

"Believe me, if she gets in a wreck, whatever you're thinking about doing to me, I will already be doing to myself. I'd throw myself down that waterfall if I find out she's hurt."

The…the waterfall. I make a sharp U-turn and ignore the sound of honking from the stickered minivan behind me. "Have you checked the waterfall? The place where you park before you hike?"

"No, but she won't be—"

I hang up. Yes. She *will* be there. I know because I know her better than anyone. And I know right now she feels like she has to prove herself. And driving across town, halfway up a mountain, would be enough to set that in place.

For the sake of all our anxieties, I'll let you know something. She's exactly where I thought she was.

Leaning up against the white Bronco, arms crossed and eyes glued to the distant view of rushing water, refusing to acknowledge my truck pulling up right beside her. She's *fine*. She's right here. She's mere feet away from me, and yet I can't find it in me to be calm. Anger and relief and leftover fear all wrestle for prime position in my head.

I slam my truck door loud enough that she jumps and has no choice but to look at me.

"You scared the shit out of me." I cross from my truck to her.

"Good. I'm not sorry," she replies.

My throat feels tight. She's safe and right here. I know that. But still, I can't stop thinking *what if.* If I close my eyes, I see this made-up image of her car on the side of the road. Blood everywhere and everyone around us silent. It's not real, but it might as well be by the way it lingers in my mind.

"I know you're not sorry, and it's pissing me off."

"Good." She leans back, eyes glaring. "I'm pissed off too."

"Fine. Tell me, then. Don't you dare get back in that car without another person in there. What were you thinking, Lottie?"

She starts to laugh, this big sarcastic one that almost reminds me of my dad's. "Oh my gosh, you're just like everyone else."

"Don't say it. Don't you even think about it. You *know* I'm not like everyone else. I don't cage you in—"

"Then why didn't you tell me you declined the internship? Because you assumed I would freak out and stress about our future?"

"Well, did you?"

She's silent, opening and closing her mouth, and then growling low in the back of her throat. "Not the point. You declined it the DAY after I had the seizure. Don't tell me it wasn't why you made the decision."

"The seizure didn't make the decision final..." She opens her mouth to argue, but I cut her off. "But it did push me to finally email them back. I've been decided on it for weeks now. Maybe longer. I didn't tell you when I did it simply because I didn't want you to freak out and assume you're the only reason why or that you're the only thing in this town for me."

"Of course I'm the only reason why. Why else would you give up this dream job that you never in a million years would've declined for any other reason?" A bird goes flying by us when she yells the last part. Her chest heaves in deep breaths, and she closes her eyes with her next sentence. "I don't want to be some pity girlfriend. I don't want you to quit your dream, have us get married, pretend that you're happy, and then have a kid that will find you miserable and unfaithful seventeen years down the road."

My response is a croak. "You think I'm like your *dad*?"

"I think my dad is a good man, like you are. But I think quitting your dreams and forcing yourself to be tied down to a woman you feel obligated to be with can make you a different person."

"Really?" My laugh is a scoff. A quiet, rough thing. "You know what your problem is?"

"What? I would *love* to know what you think—"

"Your problem is that you cannot differentiate between sympathy and love. I worry about you because I *love you*, Lottie. And I don't love you because I feel *bad* for you. I love you because I have no choice but to. Because ever since I stepped foot on this property, all I can think about is you and that big brain of yours and that smile and your attitude that drives me insane."

I pull at my hair and just throw it all out at her. "Lottie. You could have died that day. I could have never seen you again after you fell out of that tree. The realization of that didn't hit me until we went camping and I saw a small version of it myself. It *did* freak me out, alright?"

She opens her mouth to protest and points a hand at me as if to say, *See!* But I keep going.

"I know I've judged Knox and Felicity and your parents this whole time for their overprotection, but really, I just didn't understand the extent of your disability—"

"You *still* don't understand, Walker."

I nod. "And that's on me. I wouldn't have changed a thing about the last three months, but I would have at least tried to understand what this is going to look like for us more in the future." I take a few steps closer to the SUV. To *her*. "I would have figured out the details of everything so I could properly take care of you."

"That's just it." She sighs and sinks against the Bronco's tailgate. "You 'figuring out details' without talking to me and researching all of this stuff without learning directly from me on how to take care of something I know best feels just like everyone else. There's no difference in you or Knox or my dad—"

"Don't say that."

"It's true. I don't want to be someone that everyone has to research how to take care of. I don't want to be that person. I don't want to have to be fully taken care of or watched over all the time. I'm so *tired*, Walker." Her voice makes a shift from angry to disappointed, and I can't not touch her.

My fingers reach out to graze her cheek, and the contact makes her tears fall. "You have no idea. No one does. It's so hard, every day. To feel like you're this…cargo for your family. And that everyone has to take turns carrying the mental and physical load of watching over me. I'm so, so tired of feeling like the runt. Like my body is betraying me." She reaches up to wipe at another tear, but I grab it first with my thumb. "Isn't that enough? To have your body fully against your own healing? But on top of that, I have to be this overbearing burden on everyone I love the most? And now that includes you, too, and I just—"

"What about Kit?" I cut in.

She squints up at me. "What about him?"

"Is he a burden to you? Because you're helping him learn. Because you're trying to watch over him and make sure he doesn't get hurt?"

Lottie's blond hair scatters wildly as she shakes her head. "You can't compare the two."

"Why not?"

"Because he's…different. Kit could never be a burden even if he tried."

"Why?"

"Because he's *Kit*. And because we both care about him. And because he actually carries his weight around the place when all I am is a prop in my family's lives."

"Lottie," I say, my voice softening as I take a few steps closer, "no one, not one single person on this property thinks that you don't carry your weight."

She coughs out a laugh and wipes an angry tear off her cheek. "How do I add anything to this family?"

Doesn't she know?

"Anyone that meets you is instantly changed. You carry this light with you everywhere you go, and I don't think you even realize it. It's like…it's like…" I suck in a breath and try again. "You know how every fifty years or so a random artist discovers a new color? Like a whole new blue we've somehow never seen? That's what it's like. Like…you've shown me all these new colors I didn't even know existed. My life was all grays and neutrals, and then I moved here and reconnected with you, and all of a sudden, these pops of colors came into play, and I can't look at anything else the same. And I know I'm not the only one."

"Yeah, because—"

"Because we *love* you. And loving you isn't a sacrifice. It's a privilege. One I'm glad to take for myself."

Lottie sniffles a little and leans closer to me. "You said you love me."

I nod. "I did."

"Did you mean it?"

If only she knew the half of it. I laugh a little. "What do you think?"

She shrugs. "I don't think I've felt it before. I don't…I don't know."

"Yeah, you have." I tuck a stray hair behind her ear. "You just forgot what it feels like. Don't worry." I lean in to press a single kiss to her forehead. "I'll show it to you. Again and again."

I wait for her to bring up another point. To argue with me more about it all. Instead, two small arms pull around my waist and yank me closer.

She sobs in my chest for an unknown amount of time. And everything around us just slows to a stop. I know her mom and Knox are probably on their way now. I know everyone is going to freak out when they hear what she's done and where she is. But for now, I just keep her right here with me. Tucked into my chest where she belongs.

"I haven't forgotten what you've done." I rub a hand down her back. "Driving by yourself—what were you thinking?"

"I didn't go far." She shrugs. "Just across town. And I feel pretty okay."

"You went too far from me."

Headlights beam in the distance, and I recognize her mom's SUV pulling onto the dirt path, parking directly behind my truck. Her dad hops out of the passenger seat and is instantly hugging her mom as she sobs, shoulders shaking and knees buckling.

"Oh boy." Lottie winces. "She's worse than I thought."

"You really did a number on all of us."

"It was deserved," she huffs.

"You might be right."

She smiles a little at that and turns to me. "I cussed your dad out."

"It's only fair; I cussed yours out months ago."

She gives me a small, patient smile and meets her parents halfway.

CHAPTER THIRTY-EIGHT
Lottie

Walker drops his hand from me when my mom curves around his truck toward me. She stretches her arms out wide and yanks me into the tightest hug, pulling me close to her chest and practically wrestling me into hugging her back.

"I was so scared—"

"Mom."

"Charlotte Jane Turner, I have never, *ever* felt so—"

"Mom."

"I mean, really, half the town is—"

"I'm fine." I lift a hand to push her back enough so she can see me eye to eye. Black tears from her mascara slip down her cheeks and a smidge of guilt rises in me. "It's not a big deal, really. I'm fine."

"But you could've not been."

I nod. "I could have not been fine. But I am." I look up at Walker staring down at us with a soft smile. "Walker found me, and I'm fine."

"You're fine." She brushes hair from my face. "I'm so angry

but so glad, and I think I need a whole bottle of wine after this."

I chuckle a little. "You deserve it."

"I really do."

Behind her, my dad's boots thud into the dirt, and I have no choice but to look up at him. I wait for it—the flinch. The wincing that happens every time we're face-to-face. But it never comes.

For the first time since the accident, my father meets my eyes, and he doesn't flinch. He stares directly into them. Like he's admitting to it all. The affair, the accident, the years of pretending. Like it's too much and he just can't carry it all.

I think that's why the question slips out before I can stop it. Why I don't even acknowledge him before it comes out.

"Why did you do it?"

His eyebrows dip and he glances from me to Walker like he isn't sure what should be said around him. "Do what?"

"Cheat on her."

My mom gasps beside him, and I don't acknowledge it either. I am so tired of pretending. For myself and for them. I am over leaving everything I need to hear unsaid.

Dad glances at my mom, and there's hesitation from both of them. He looks at the truck, not me, when he answers. And I know it's not the full truth. "I think we were both having a hard time with money. Finances drove a wedge between us, and we became so dry toward each other…"

"So, you got with another woman?" Walker adds in behind me.

They both turn toward him in a flash, and Walker raises two hands. "I'm gonna"—he points to where his truck is—head over here. Lottie." He gives me that same wink I love and a sly smirk that says he has my back. "Get me if you need me, alright?" Walker heads toward the back of his vehicle to give us space, sitting down and leaning back where I know he can still hear.

"I didn't mean that like an excuse," Dad mutters, finding his next sentence. "I just mean that's where it started. And if I'd known what it would turn into…" He shudders at the thought. At the memory of watching me fall. Of the blood. "We haven't been fully honest with you. For years. And that was wrong of us."

"Jason…" Mom places a hand on my dad's back and nods. "It's okay, really. You can tell her."

Dad shakes his head, and apparently she doesn't care, because she turns to me and blurts it out anyway. "The truth is, we planned on getting divorced years ago."

I squint. "Right. After the accident…"

"Before."

"Before?" I feel like I'm trapped inside my twelve-year-old self, catching my parents dancing around the living room together and watching as the image dissipates into thin air.

"*Years* before." Mom nods. "We'd had the papers drawn up. Everything was ready. We were prepared to split the land and keep you kids in the middle when you were old enough."

That doesn't make sense. They were *always* together; they never even fought, not once, around us.

Dad steps closer to me and stares me dead in the eyes. "We were going through a rough time. When you were maybe twelve? Thirteen? Money was bad; some days we were inches away from losing the property. Each morning I would check the papers just to make sure no one saw our names on the upcoming foreclosure lists. We had this wedge between us, and we weren't doing well for years, and eventually—"

My mom steps a little closer too. "I decided we needed to divorce."

"*You* decided?"

She nods. "I felt like I was already losing my whole family, and I wanted to…get it over with. My dad used to say, 'If you're going to cut a dog's tail, just do it once. Don't do it in pieces.'"

My whole body cringes. "I hate that analogy."

She sniffles and wipes the back of her hand across her cheek. "Me too. But you know what? I made the decision anyway. I served the papers, and we made the plans. We would live together and act entirely normal around you two, but once you both graduated from high school and were ready to move out…we would have the sister house ready for you."

The realization of it all is too much. My head spins, and my whole body feels tight, like I will throw up right here. "The house…wasn't for me and Flick?"

All of the visions of my teenage dreams of living next door to my best friend come crashing down.

"No, it never was. It was put exactly halfway on the property so you and Knox would have a place where you could each be halfway to us one day."

"I…I can't believe this. You were apart for *years*?"

Mom confirms it. "Four, technically. A long time. And your father tried his best, he did. But I'd made up my mind—"

"You get your stubbornness from her," my dad cuts in.

"From you as well, love." She places a hand on his arm and squeezes.

"A double dose, I would say."

"Eventually, I all but forced him away." She looks from me to Walker, who is facing away, on the phone with probably Knox or Flick or whoever is before him on the phone tree.

"You know how that can be. Anyway, it took him years to accept it, and when he did, we had hired Dahlia. And I saw how she was with him. How she looked at him. The same way I used to. And how he didn't want to be the same way back, but…I knew there was something there. And I knew if I pushed them to be together, then it would make things official. And I could stop torturing myself by thinking there was even a chance."

I move from her to my dad. "So, you dated Dahlia? I mean, actually?"

"For less than a month." He looks over at my mom. No, he looks to his *wife*, with tears in his eyes. "The worst month of my life."

I mumble, "Didn't seem so bad from my point of view."

I'm still haunted by the thought of him hugging a random woman, placing a kiss on the top of her head.

"Your point of view was skewed. What you saw was me breaking up with her. It was a final hug goodbye. Knowing I would never love someone the way I love your mom." He squeezes her hand.

I nod. "Okay, so you were getting a divorce, and then maybe not, and then I catch you cheating and the fall and the hospital, the diagnosis…my accident just made it all so much worse for you guys."

"Honey, no." Dad says, "You're not getting this. Your accident wasn't the driving point between our marriage. It was the *saving* point. It was the rope cast out to save us. Not a lasso to tie us down."

"But"—I turn to my mom—"I heard you in the hospital. When I was pretending to be asleep. You said you were done."

"Yes, I was done. Done with our break. Watching you be in pain, witnessing what we did. It showed us how precious every day we have together really is. And I was done pretending I didn't love the man I pushed away. We worked hard, and it wasn't easy, but with your grandparents' and then my brothers' help, we were able to save the farm from foreclosure, and somehow, I think we realized all at once just how easy this all could be as long as we put our heads together."

Dad stares me dead in the eyes. "You know I love your mom. I love our family. What we did... What we caused you..." He sniffs, and oh God, I think we're both crying now. "It eats at me every day. Every time I used to look you in the eyes, I saw my little girl on the ground foaming at the mouth with blood pouring all over your bright hair. And every time, it stings just like it did that day. It took me so much longer than it should have to realize that by only seeing you as that one event in your life, I was taking away from who you are."

My mom aggressively nods and wipes at her pouring tears beside him while he goes on. "You thought for years I didn't care about what I did? What I caused? It haunts me, Lottie. For so long, I died a little more from it every day. And yet, somehow, something so awful turned my marriage around. Turned my wife back to me.

"And I sometimes wished we'd just been fully honest with you from the beginning. But then I don't know if I would be standing here with you both. I don't know where I would be without the two of you. When we should have fully given up, your mom held my hand and lifted me up, showing me what we could be and not what we were. She's the most amazing person in the world, and believe it or not, you are just like her."

All three of us are sobbing now—four, I think, if you include Walker pretending that he's not listening behind the truck.

I sniffle and do what I should have done years ago. I wrap

my arms around my dad's shoulders and *squeeze*. "You're pretty great too."

"I haven't been. Not to you, and certainly not to your brother, but that changes now. We can start over now. All of us."

"Including me?" We all turn around, and Knox is there beside Walker with his arms crossed. He's parked his truck at the bottom of the hill and his shoulders are shaking, like he ran up here and is trying to catch his breath.

"How much did you hear?" I ask.

"Enough." He shrugs with each heavy breath. "I'm glad you're okay, kid."

I nod. "Me too."

Knox steps up, gives each of us a hug, and that's that. In a single moment, with a single conversation, our family has looked each other in the eyes and recognized no more lies between us. We're all the same: flawed and hurt and *completely* filled with love.

After my parents peeled out of the restricted area with the Bronco, Knox gave me that look that he used to when we were little and he wanted to race me to the creek.

You thinking what I'm thinking?

And just like back then, I could never back away from a challenge my brother put in front of me. So when he voiced it out loud "Let's go for a hike, Lot."—I had no choice but to say yes.

So, with Walker happily waiting back by our cars, Knox and I took off on my favorite path. We wove through kudzu vines and large bushes, their overgrown branches leaning over the unkept beaten path.

"I'm sorry, Lot."

"For what, exactly?"

Knox blew out a slow breath with his hands in his pockets. "A lot of stuff. But first for not telling you about the land." He gave me these big apologetic eyes.

"I want you happy, Knox. And if taking over the land makes you happy, then I want that. God knows I could never take it over myself."

"I still should have told you. But honestly, I didn't want to say it out loud to you. Because I knew if I did, then it would be real."

"And you don't want it to be?"

"I don't know what I want anymore, Lottie. I do know I am really, really sorry. Yes, for the land and the meeting, but also, I've been watching you a little too closely for a long time." He picks a weed with a white flower blooming at the end out of the dry and cracked dirt road and hands it to me. I twirl it between my fingers. "When you got out of the hospital that first time, I took an oath to myself."

I snorted. "You're such a Boy Scout."

Knox's elbow shoved me, and my feet stumbled. "I'm serious. I wasn't going to let anything happen to you ever again. I didn't realize at the time that if nothing happened to you then...nothing would happen to you." He closes his eyes. "I didn't realize I was the one stunting your growth. That I was holding you back from the right life you wanted. I won't apologize for keeping an eye out for you. That's built in me. I don't think I can help it, but..."

I shut him up by wrapping my arms around his skinny frame and squeezing him tight. I couldn't even tell you the last time I hugged my brother and let him hug me back.

We hugged it out as long as he would allow, before he raced me back to his and Walker's trucks.

Now, as Walker pulls into our shared driveway, I realize that talking to Knox and my parents and clearing everything up with Walker was probably the easy part. Because standing on the front porch are all of my favorite people in this town.

And smiling right at my door with an apologetic *so glad you're home* kind of smile is Flick.

We take a moment to just…stare at each other. Thinking about who we were then and who we are now. Who we've come to be. Sometimes you're so busy growing up that you don't realize you're already there. Like having your eyes closed for an eight-hour road trip, then opening them to see the beach right in front of you.

Then, in a flash, she has her toned arms wrapped around my frame, yanking me down to her height, dark curly tendrils in my nose and poking my eyes, but still, I hug her right back.

"I missed you," she whispers in my ear.

"It's only been about thirty minutes," I whisper back.

"Longest thirty minutes of my life."

She gives my arms the reset. Squeezing once on my shoulder, once above my elbow, and lastly on my wrist. Grounding me.

"I'm so, so sorry, Lot. I know you and Knox talked already, but I need you to be aware that we did have plans to tell you everything, and I… I'm not great at this. Let me try again." She pulls my fingers into her tiny palm. "I love you. You are the best friend I have had for"—she looks off in space and scrunches her nose up like a bunny—"ten years?"

"Feels like an eternity." I smile.

"It really does. But in all of that time, it seems I still haven't quite figured out how to be the best friend I can be to you."

"Flick."

"No. Lottie, it's really not okay. I've made it seem like epilepsy is your only trait, and I can't even begin to say how wrong that is." She lifts our joined hands to wipe her own tears. "You and Walker watched the ducks for us so we could try to find some way to work this out on our own for an hour without distractions. When we realized we weren't getting anywhere with just the two of us talking it through...I said we should call a meeting with everyone. I went to that meeting, *only* that meeting, because I felt like Knox needed me there. He was so stressed, and the weight he's been dropping and—" She takes a deep breath and shakes her head. "Doesn't matter. Doesn't matter. I lost sight of my first ever best friend, and whereas I could have been there for both of you, I was swapping sides back and forth, thinking that I could somehow manage to make it all perfect. And I can't. Because you both have your own things, your own problems. And that's a good thing. I'm sorry for always trying to keep your life simple and quiet and low. We're hitting the reset button right now."

I nod. "That would be nice."

"I think so too." She yanks me back into her arms and holds me there for a little longer.

She pulls back from our hug, and over her shoulder stands my entire future.

Walker is a couple feet away, smiling timidly with Apollo in one hand, the other stroking the back of his neck. Kit is next to him, still frowning at me. I have a feeling I'll have a good bit to make up for in training.

Behind them is...well, everyone.

It's taken me a while, but I think I am beginning to see that this new beat-up and rebuilt version of myself is just as, if not more, impressive than the shiny one that had no dents and sat on the highest shelf. That girl still lives in me somewhere, the wild and free one. The one that was so naive to what the future could bring. But up front, before her, is the woman I am now. Still wild and free, but now with security too. Now with comfort and safety nets.

Looking at everyone around me, possibly for the first time ever, I feel the tint over my eyes being lifted. And I see all the people taking their time in front of me as more than some sympathetic motion. I see real, true, genuine *love*. And it's orange and lamplit and warm. And it's like nothing I've ever felt.

It's my parents sticking together for us, despite all they'd been through. It's them building a house for me. It's Knox installing security cameras so he knows I'm safe. It's Odie and Ada always trying to cheer me up. It's Flick driving me to parties for the past couple of years. It's Walker pushing me further and further, his hands waiting to catch me if I fall. It's Dot letting me stay for the summer and making sure I know I'm loved, even in her absence.

It's *home*. And I have really, really missed it.

CHAPTER THIRTY-NINE
Walker

A few weeks later, Lottie and I stand around a small wooden table in the "backstage" area of the local rodeo arena, the air thick with the scent of coffee and fresh biscuits. Kit picks at his food, barely eating; his nerves have made him all antsy.

We initially came here with hopes of actually getting Kit into the show. After all, it's a local match with mostly grown men who have been here for years. It's less of a match and more of a trial run. Not a huge turnout, but Lottie and I both have come to the same conclusion that we are not leaving until we get this kid on a bull.

A man clears his throat behind our table, and we both turn to look over our shoulders. It's the guy Lottie warned me about, the one in charge of local matches and practice trials here. Clive something. He's older, grizzled. She told us on the way here that he would be the one setback. That he's stuck in his old ways and refuses to allow inexperienced riders on his bulls during his matches. We've watched from the sidelines as he's gone from table to table, rider to rider, and eyed them up and down, giving a stamp of approval or a wave out the door.

Kit sits there, drowning in his button-up, my hat resting on his head, barely hanging on. His teeth pick at his lips, fingernails tapping against the edge of the table.

Even though it's just a local practice trial with a handful of small bull riders, Clive still eyes Kit with skepticism. "You're young," he muses, looking Kit up and down, "and *tiny*."

Kit chokes on his biscuit and hacks it up by punching his own chest.

Before I can step in to answer for him, Lottie rests a hand on my arm, stands up, and silently excuses herself with a wink over her shoulder at me.

She steps toward the man with a smile, and I watch as his face softens immediately. Recognition flickers in his eyes.

"I… Miss Turner?"

"Hi, Clive." There's that voice—the same she uses when she's playing cards. The one that no man, woman, or child can say no to. I would know, I've tried my best. "Causing trouble?"

He grunts, his bottom jaw poking out like a bulldog. "The usual amount."

She nods and eyes Kit before tossing her head to the side. "Can we talk real quick? In private?"

Clive glances from her to Kit and I, and gives in. "I've got thirty seconds for you, and not one more."

They head off a few tables over, and while Lottie's back is turned toward me, I can sense the charm she's working. She's doing what she's always been best at, which is getting people to fold.

Kit chews on his nail, glancing across the table at me. "You think I'll get in?"

I glance back at Lottie. She's said something that has them

both laughing, their heads tilted back as she shares some story between them, her hands gesturing animatedly.

"Yeah," I say, watching the way even Clive falls completely under her spell. It's impossible *not* to love her. "She's got you."

A few moments later, the man nods, claps Kit on the back, and gestures for him to follow the others inside. As Kit straightens up and follows, he turns an excited thumbs-up toward us, and I laugh while Lottie squeals.

I slip an arm around Lottie's waist, pulling her chair just a bit closer to mine.

"What'd you say to get him in?"

She grins, leaning into me. "Just told him about my fancy space cowboy boyfriend, and he happily agreed."

I laugh. "You could not be more wrong. Except maybe the boyfriend part?"

"Well, you are. Right?"

"I am." I nod. "If you're mine."

She hums, considering. "I *can* be your boyfriend if you'd like, but girlfriend sounds much nicer."

"Hmm, guess it does."

After half an hour, the announcer calls family and friends to take their seats, and Lottie and I plop our chairs down in the very front row. There's hardly anyone here—mostly just people close enough to the main riders and some locals who Lottie says comes to every trail, rodeo, or practice.

Each rider comes up one by one in order of bull size, smallest to largest. Four riders have come and gone. If Kit is next, then I know he's got a pretty good-sized one. Only he isn't next. He is the very last one in the line. I see the tip of his hat just outside the fence, standing next to Lawson, who's giving him advice on something that's got Kit chewing on his fingernails.

"God, Clive is going to kill him." Lottie bites down on her thumb. "I don't know if I can watch."

I grab her hand and pull it down into my lap, our fingers intertwining. I squeeze it tight. "He'll be fine." I plant a kiss to her temple. "He's had a great coach."

The announcer calls Kit's name over the loudspeakers, and Lottie and I both cup our hands around our mouths and make as much noise as we can. The rest of the stadium is quiet, except for a small, high-pitched holler from the top row. Lottie and I glance back to see that honey girl from the farmers market waving her arms at Kit.

Either he doesn't hear us or he makes a point to not glance our way, because his eyes lock straight onto hers and he waves right back, any anxiety in his face dissipated.

After routine checks, Kit mounts the bull, his body coiled tight with focus. They really did go from smallest to largest bull. Kit is like nothing but a flea on his back.

The massive animal shifts beneath him, muscles rippling, nostrils flaring as it senses what's coming. Kit wraps the rope tight around his gloved hand, his grip firm and steady. The gate man, Gus, gives him a nod, and Kit returns it, his jaw set, his chest rising and falling in deep, measured breaths.

Then, the chute bursts open.

The bull launches forward in an explosion of raw power, kicking up dirt as it bucks violently. Kit moves with it, his body fluid, instinctive, gripping tightly but not in a stiff way, letting the motion carry him rather than fighting against it. The bull twists in midair, jerking hard to the left, but Kit holds, his free arm cutting through the air to counterbalance the wild movement.

"Come on, Kit!" Lottie shouts beside me, and I'm counting under my breath.

One second. Two. The small crowd behind holds its breath.

The bull kicks again, a fierce lurch that would send any lesser-balanced rider flying, but Kit sticks with it. His expression is tight with concentration, his muscles straining. The animal spins, nearly throwing him sideways, but he pulls himself upright just in time. I feel like I'm watching Prince record "Purple Rain."

And finally, the buzzer sounds, eight long seconds that feel like an eternity, and Kit releases the rope, flinging himself off just as the bull bucks one last time.

He hits the ground and rolls to his feet in one smooth motion, raising both fists in victory as the crowd, but mostly Lottie and I, erupt in cheers.

"I'm so proud of him," Lottie cries out, and before I know it, I'm turning to lift her off the ground, spinning her in excitement. When I set her down, our eyes meet, both of us breathless, smiling. I lean down and plant a kiss on her sweet lips. "You did it, baby." I kiss her again. And again. And once more on her forehead. "You got him there."

Her expression shifts, something warm settling in her gaze. "I love you."

I smile, letting her words settle deep in my chest. "I know."

She scoffs, pushing me lightly. "That's not what you're supposed to say."

"It's not?"

"No," she insists, playful but firm. "You have to say it back."

I brush a strand of hair behind her ear. "I know you love me, just the same way you know I love you."

She exhales, a soft, knowing smile on her lips. "I do."

We turn back to watch Kit, still riding high on his win as he talks with the other riders.

I chuckle, shaking my head. Kid's got a *long* journey ahead of him. If he's good enough to hold on now, I can't imagine where he's going to be at my age. The difference in the boy I was back then to the man I am now is unfathomable…

"What do you think he's thinking about?" Lottie hums as she watches Kit saddle up next to Lawson, who seems to be giving him tips about a specific move as they both gesture wildly with their hands.

"I honestly couldn't say. Though, if it were me at that age, I would just be thinking about you."

"Me?"

"Oh yeah." I smile and wrap an arm around her waist. "Now, if I could talk to my fifteen-year-old self…"

"Oh?" Lottie tilts her head. "And what would you tell him?"

"There's this blond-haired, green-eyed troublemaker of a girl that's going to take you for a spin. And you better practice a good grip, because she's going to be the *wildest* ride you'll ever have." She laughs and I pull her tighter against me. "And she's gonna feel like the closest thing to home you've ever known."

Her fingers tighten around my free hand, and I hum. "And you?" I ask. "What would you tell yourself?"

"That there's this messy-haired, brown-eyed *space cowboy* of a man who's going to love you in a better way than anyone else in this universe ever could. That he brings fun and freedom and love and laughter everywhere he goes. And that you never have to fear the future when he's with you, because he's all there is to it."

"You know we've got the kid to take home before we can

be alone, right?" My voice rattles low. "So, maybe let's save all this for when I can take my time with you." I lean in to kiss her, but I barely have a moment of her lips on mine before someone clears their throat behind us. We turn to find Clive behind us, staring daggers at me but lighting up at my girlfriend.

"I have to say, it is very nice seeing you back near the ring, Miss Turner."

Lottie smiles politely. "Ah, I'm just here for my friend today." She gestures toward Kit. "You had to stick him on the biggest bull tonight?"

He shrugs. "Seemed to have managed it just fine to me. That's actually what I wanted to talk to you about."

Clive tilts his chin, stepping to the side. "Let's go for a walk."

Lottie looks from him to me, hesitating. I wave a hand. We have time. All of it in the world. She's in her element here. And I'm glad to take a step back and watch it from afar.

I watch as they stroll a few paces away, their voices hushed but casual. The man gestures as he talks, occasionally glancing back at Kit. It takes a while, but when they shake hands, Lottie turns back to me with wide eyes and a stunned smile. She shimmies over with shaking shoulders and laughter in her voice.

"He wants me to be an agent. For some of the local riders."

I straighten up. "You're serious."

She nods, mouth dropped like she still can't believe it either. "I don't… I told him I can't work a consistent schedule. I mean, with my health and my last year of high school and all." Her smile is contagious; my jaw is sore from grinning as she all but bounces around me. "But this would be purely freelance, working when I want. If I can't make it, I can have one of his 'people' fill the gaps."

"Lottie." I grin. "You have a *job*."

"I...have a job."

"For a rodeo."

"Mm-hmm." She exhales, shaking her head in disbelief. "And you love me."

I laugh, pulling her close to my chest. "And I love you."

With all my cards laid down, I fold everything I have to her.

EPILOGUE
Lottie

Overall, the start of my senior year *is* actually pretty incredible.

I wish I could say that I randomly one day slay the big dragon and kick epilepsy's ass and that I have *no* more seizures. Or that I can drive myself anywhere. But not every happy ending has every perfect answer filled in. I think if it did, it wouldn't be nearly as exciting. Because once you get that happy ending, it's like, *Okay...now what?*

I will say that my epilepsy is...controlled. It's not as much of a burden as it is just an accepted part of my reality. Of what makes me, me. And I think I'm beginning to love that part of myself as well.

It's taken a bit of time, but the last six months have worked out to be the best for everyone so far.

Flick has had an excellent start to fall. After a rerun of the animal shelter event, she managed to find half of the animals somewhere to stay. I should mention Nigel did not get adopted. Unless you count Knox taking him home early for himself.

Kit has been practicing like a beast for the last six months since his first trial. Lawson has taken him under his wing. He's got three sponsorships—one being Flick's boss, Rowen. He is absolutely killing it.

Knox has been officially appointed as the newest manager in training for the ranch. Despite my uncle Eli's desperate attempt to get him pushed down the line, everyone, myself included, voted in my brother's favor. He seems to be sleeping better now. Seems to be chasing Flick around a whole lot more too.

Even Henry the ghost got his happily ever after. Though, turns out, he was much less of a ghost and much more of a *very* large groundhog that's been getting into Knox's crops and bringing them to the crawlspace of the sister house.

And Walker? Well, he still insists on adding to our original list. Even for our date tonight, he is *swearing* we are crossing off three things we've added—what they are, I have no clue. He never tells me. But I always love them the same.

I climb over to my side of the bed to open the drawer of my nightstand to get my phone charger, but my eyes don't land on a charger. Instead, I find my list from early summer.

Take a yoga class
Learn to cook an actual meal
Go line dancing
Fall in love with something new
Have a picnic
Go to an estate sale with Ada
Get a pet (??)
~~Find a new hobby~~ Go camping for one night—in a real tent!

Try pottery painting
Go to the Fourth of July fest this year (don't be a chicken)
Have a girls' night
Get Kit into a junior competition this fall
Finish a book for the book club
Take on one of the long trails
Collect more physical media (CDs, DVDs, VHS, other three lettered words)
Go night swimming
Have a bonfire (s'mores are mandatory)
TP someone's house (apologies in advance, Flick)

I glance at each item with a smile but pause at the last line on the list.

Walker, at some point in time, has scratched through half of one word and written a new one next to it.

Fall in love with some~~thing~~one new.

I actually did them both. I fell in love with something and some*one* new.

Her name is Lottie Jane Turner.

She is a retired bull rider that now is training to be an agent for young up-and-comers (those who can't do…agent, I believe). She still steals strawberries from her family's ranch. And occasionally hikes behind waterfalls. She's relearned herself, and her diagnosis, and has a whole new view on it. She has a professionally trained dog that is probably her best friend (sorry, Flick) and a newfound love for the last year of her schooling.

And she is in love with the most incredible boy from her past named Walker Lane that coincidentally happens to be her future. And she can't wait to fall for him over and over again.

In fact, he is the best spur-of-the-moment bet she's ever made.

ACKNOWLEDGMENTS

It's probably silly, but acknowledgments are one of my favorite parts of writing. It feels like tying everything up in the prettiest, most thankful bow and sending it off to my closest people. I always want to thank basically the entire world for this opportunity, but since that would cost my publisher a ton to print, I'll keep this as simple as I can.

First off, as always, my husband: Something to know about Justin Smith is that he is a touch of a pessimist (love you, honey!). That being said, I am the exact opposite and shoot for the stars with everything I touch, whereas he tries to keep my expectations grounded so I don't get my feelings hurt. I basically like to think of myself as Phil Dunphy and him as Claire Dunphy. And yet, with my writing journey, my husband is the most supportive, over the top, "YOU ARE WORTH MILLIONS OF DOLLARS DO NOT SETTLE" man I have ever met. He brags to so many people and never stops reminding me that I am talented, loved, and worthy. So maybe he's a pessimist about other things, but he has never once been that way about my work, and for that I am so, so grateful.

A very close second, my Saylor: You were at SUCH a fun age as I worked on this book!! Always laughing and playing and so obsessed with Minnie Mouse that I caught myself writing out quotes from Camp Minnie and having to erase them over and over. You're sweet, fun, and your always silly personality is the biggest reason I keep going. I pray when you read this one day, you'll know you're so, so dearly loved, and not just by me, (though I like to think I am number one) but by so many others as well!

Next, my editor, Kylie: Kylie is SUCH a joy to work with! Going from indie to traditional publishing was so daunting, and yet she made me comfortable every step of the way. I will forever be grateful for the chance that she, and everyone else at Bloom Books, took on me and my little YA cowboy series! I am so excited to work with Kylie and the whole team at Bloom, (marketing, audio, social media, sales, SO many excellent people) and I can't wait to see what else we can pull off together!

Of course, it wouldn't be my acknowledgments if I didn't thank the obvious: Madison and Kelsey, my two best author friends who keep me sane and listen to my never-ending (minimum of five minutes) voice messages. I'll never understand how three girls across multiple states connected and became basically platonic soulmates, and yet here we are. Love you both forever!

Last, and never ever least: a big, massive, overwhelming, wet-sloppy-kisses thank-you to my readers! What a joy it is to have you here, new and old. You are so cherished, and just know that with every page read and book sold, you are on my mind. I have been so blessed to be able to do what I do for a living, and for that I will never lose my gratitude. Thank you for reading my stories and thank you for sticking by me through thick and thin.

All my love and more,

Juliana Smith

ABOUT THE AUTHOR

Juliana Smith grew up in an Alabama small town and still calls it home—along with her husband, daughter, two dogs, and an ever-growing collection of unfinished stories to come. She writes sweet, feel-good romance full of charm, laughter, and just the right amount of yearning. When she's not falling in love with her fictional characters, she's probably in the Chick-fil-A drive-through or deep-diving into *Star Wars* theory podcasts. Juliana believes in happily-ever-afters, second chances, and that life is better when you're laughing (preferably with a Diet Dr Pepper in hand).